SHIPS
IN THE SKY

Compiled from Uggi Greipsson's notes

BY
GUNNAR GUNNARSSON

.

THE BOBBS-MERRILL COMPANY
PUBLISHERS
INDIANAPOLIS   NEW YORK

Printed in the United States of America

TRANSLATOR'S NOTE

IT HAS been an honor and a pleasure to translate these first two books of Gunnar Gunnarsson's cycle, *The Church on the Hill.*

I think it may be useful to explain that an Icelandic farmstead usually consisted of a group of gabled houses, each house being one room. These were generally built side by side in rows and were connected by passages which reached from one end of the row to the other. Timber was used only for the framework of the houses, as it is scarce in Iceland; the roofs are of turf and the walls built of sod and pieces of rock.

The word *badstue,* used so often in the original, I have, in consultation with Professor Nordal of Reykjavik, translated "living room." The *badstue* or *badstofa* is a combined sitting and sleeping room, the beds being fixed to the walls and used as seats during the day time.

I have introduced as few footnotes as possible, and have anglicized proper names, place names and titles wherever possible with a view to making the whole easily readable in English; but it has not been possible to do this in every case. The Icelandic "ð" I have turned into "d" throughout.

In conclusion, I would sincerely thank Mr. Humphrey Gilbert-Carter, of the University Botanic Gardens, Cambridge, for his kind help in connection with the names of flowers mentioned throughout the book; Mr. Herweg, of the University of London, and Professor Nordval of Reykjavik for the kindly interest they have taken in the translation.

E. R.

SHIPS IN THE SKY

PART ONE

1

GONE are the years when I was young and still innocent except for original sin . . . the years when adventures brought me experience without bitterness . . . the years when my sympathy with all things living was uncritical and intense . . . when God seemed to me a generous, friendly grandfather, the Devil a rather dangerous and moody but, on the whole, essentially stupid and harmless godfather . . . the years when light was triumphant indeed, and all evil, all fear, could be turned aside by an *Our Father* or the sign of the cross . . . the years when in the morning I could but dimly foresee the evening, and sat safely in the shelter of a wall of sods playing with straw . . . these indeed are the years that will never return.

And it is not only the years that have passed. Many of those then living are now dead, others scattered to the winds; even their memory only peeps out intermittently, like stars between the breaks in a cloud-covered sky.

One day in May when the meadows must already have been thickly sprinkled with bright little dandelion clocks, my mother, Cecilia Ketilbjörnsdottir, gave me birth in my parents' little cottage near Ofeigsstadur Parsonage. My father, Greipur Uggason, was at that time acting as bailiff to his brother Sigbergur Uggason, fifteen years his senior, who was the parson at Ofeigsstadur.

As Bergljot Sigurdardottir, the oldest servant on the farm— Old Begga, we called her—had prudently hidden the herb known as "rose root" among my mother's pillows, my birth took place without difficulties.

I began my career, as so many others have before me, by instantly causing my parents anxiety. Scarcely had I caught a vigorous hold of life before I threatened to let go of it again.

My good parents therefore let my uncle, the priest, pour water over me a couple of days after my birth, giving me, as their first-born, my grandfather's name, Uggi. Perhaps they did not wish me to depart as empty-handed as I came—or was it merely that they wished to insure my salvation?

The honor which had so undeservedly been accorded me at my christening did not seem to mollify me to any great extent. From a poem which a rhymester uncle of mine dedicated to me on my first birthday, and which has been preserved, I learn that for the whole of my first year I continued to show great reluctance to settle down this side the grave.

I well remember this uncle. His name was Arni, he was the youngest son of Uggi-from-Fjall and he died insane when I was in my ninth year. He was a most well-meaning—aye, lovable—creature, and his virtues as a human being were rivaled only by his failings as a poet.

In this poem he describes the tears, by no means few, shed during my first year as "precious dew," and expresses the hope that they may be of use to me in future years—a thought good enough in itself, but hardly practicable. Time after time he describes me as a flower—in one place as a flower planted in a spot "especially sheltered by God." And that is not all: at the end of the poem he insists that he has seen nothing less than "Fortune's holy sun" shining about me—and after that it seems hardly worth mentioning that in each stanza he wishes me a special "blessing from Heaven." Dear Uncle Arni! No one else has spoken of me so beautifully, before or since, in verse or in prose. And I would beg you to remember that the poem was written several years before illness shadowed his merry heart.

Time and again I have taken this poem out and read it through with pleasure, in spite of its halting meter and other literary shortcomings. The truth is, I always enjoy the impression that I was an exceptionally delightful baby, for the poem makes it quite clear that Uncle Arni considered me something decidedly out of the common. Indeed, I can remember that he frequently told me so. When I rode on his knee, as I often did, and he now and then interrupted the ride to tickle my face and neck with that brave mustache which was his pride and joy, it is difficult to say which of us was the happier.

I have another proof of what an attractive baby I was, in a remark of my Cousin Sigga's. Once when we met, not having seen each other for twenty years, she looked at me and exclaimed, "My goodness—and you were such a pretty baby!"

I shall not repeat my answer, but of course I let her know that the frivolous way in which she was talking, as well as the subject matter of her remarks, showed that she had been in England too long, and that she had had both her taste and her language corrupted there.

I should lay myself open to a well-founded suspicion regarding my truthfulness if I left this subject without mentioning that my mother, when she first saw me, felt a little disappointed. The reason for this was the reddish tinge of my hair. As this was the one thing above all others that she had feared while she bore me under her heart, her disappointment can easily be imagined. But it is difficult to understand why she had such a fear before my birth, since the oldest person living could not remember red hair in either of the families—of this she had herself made certain. But everything has some explanation. And that three of her five children were red-headed was considered by my mother as a just punishment from Heaven because in her youth she had, from dislike of this color of hair, teased a redheaded man on her father's farm in "an unchristian manner," as I have heard her confess. Needless to say, her disappointment did not last very long. Anyone who has ever seen a mother develop—and who has not?—knows that no sooner has maternal love taken possession of her than, womanlike and independent of all human and psychological rules, and amid tears and with joy, she undergoes a complete change. As the old proverb puts it, "Every bird finds her own nestling lovely."

It must be said to my credit that the pleasure my mother found in my appearance was repaid in the same coin by me. Of all creatures she was in my eyes the loveliest; she was not merely beautiful, but far more than beautiful. When I now call her to mind (there is no picture of her except in the hearts of those few who still remember her), I see that her lips were thick, her nose not particularly well-formed and her cheekbones too prominent. But I realize all the more the wonder of her smile with its mixture of patience and love—the vitality in her gray eyes, which shone with goodness and joy—her expressive mouth, which seldom uttered words that were not gentle. So far it has never been my lot to find a face more delightful to me than my mother's.

One of my earliest recollections, as a matter of fact, is a remark of hers about her own appearance, which at the time surprised—in fact, frightened—me. . . . Let me say here, by the way, that I cannot, of course, answer for the chronological order of these, my earliest experiences, but I can very accurately remember which of them occurred before my fifth birthday, for just about that date we moved away from Ofeigsstadur for the first time. Each separate event in this group of memories is very vivid and as a result stands by itself without any particular connection with any other event, reminding me of those little glimpses of life we see when walking past a row of lighted windows on a dark night, before the blinds have been drawn.

The first part of this (as far as I can judge) my first memory-picture is rather hazy—for instance, I cannot see how many of us there were in the room. But in any case I was sitting on my mother's lap, eating cake crumbs from a gold-rimmed saucer. On the table, which was covered with a white cloth, lay an open album, the leaves of which my mother was turning. I know that on the front of the book, which was bound in red velvet, there was a shield from which the yellow had been partially worn off, and that it had a sort of metal clasp which kept it shut.

My mother opened the book at a photograph of my father which occupied an entire page, the opposite page being empty. Directly I set eyes on this photograph I grabbed the book and began loudly comparing the photograph with the original—who, I recall, was sitting on the other side of the table. What excited me most was that I could not find anything about my father that had not been included in the picture—the brown waving beard, the dark parted hair, the nose, lips, eyes, both the ears, the forehead, collar, necktie, buttons, the shining ring on the right hand—all were there.

Above my shouts of delight I heard another voice saying:

"When am I going to have that picture of you, Cecilia?"

However I search my memory, I cannot find Madame Anna, Uncle Sigbergur's domineering wife, anywhere in the room—but the voice was hers, and hers was also the album.

"I've often told you, the day after Doomsday," answered my mother, with a little laugh. This remark set me wondering, for I had always heard Uncle Sigbergur speak of Doomsday as the "Last Day."

However, I had scarcely begun to consider this tiresome problem when I heard my mother add, in the teasing voice which I had learned not to take too seriously:

"With a face like mine, it's best to keep away from the photographer."

Neither the Last Day nor any other day could fill my mind with such anxious bewilderment as did this statement of my mother's. That she, whom I had never seen frightened, dared not go to the photographer with such a face as hers (for this was what I understood by her remark) seemed to me incredible. Was the photographer, then, a bad man with an ugly wife, and did he lie in wait to steal a pretty face for his ugly wife? And if my mother were to go to him, would he take her face and put it on his wife and send my mother home with his wife's ugly face (which I could clearly see before me)? The thought was terrifying. The photographer must be a very powerful man, for if he could take people's faces and put them on paper there must be very few things he could not do.

I was just about to implore my mother to keep to her resolution when she took the album from me and, pointing to one picture after another, said:

"Look at this—and this—and this! Is there anything funnier than pictures of ugly people?"

Such a solution to my mother's puzzling words was the last I should have expected, and I was completely taken aback.

As unobtrusively as possible I slid down from her knee and went over to the other side of the table to have a full view of her. With my chin resting on the edge of the table I stood looking at her for a long time—but I could not see that there was anything wrong with her face. I had of course seen people who frightened me and whom I thought ugly, but they did not look in the least like her.

With heavy heart and a strange dread in my soul, I finally slipped out of the room and went off to look for Old Begga—the only person to whom I should dream of going for advice in such a difficult matter.

I looked first in the kitchen; she was not there. Then I went to search the bedroom.

A broad flight of stairs with low steps led up to this room, and I was strictly forbidden to go up or down them alone, but I did not always take this restriction seriously. On this day I noticed at once that the steps were exceedingly clean and well scrubbed, and that the bedroom, a long narrow room with beds fixed all along the walls, was also clean and scrubbed white. Above every bed on the south side there was a little four-paned window set in the sloping roof, and through these windows the sunlight was pouring that afternoon like a row of slanting golden beams. Many a happy hour I have spent pretending that these rays were solid but that I could walk through them as I imagined elves—the Little People—walked through their rocks and stones. One of the beds on the window side was Old Begga's and there she was seated now, reading a book (so it must have been Sunday), and luckily she was alone in the room.

I knew that the book she was reading had an odd name—it was called *A Book of Homilies*—and that it contained sermons something like those my uncle preached in church on Sunday and through which I always slept so pleasantly. I knew, too, that these sermons had not been preached in our church, but in quite a different one—and that they were by a man whom Old

Begga always called "my Jon Vidalin" or sometimes simply "my Jon." According to Old Begga they were the best and most powerful pronouncements ever made by any sinful creature on our sinful earth; and this was not to be wondered at, since "God put the words into my Jon's mouth." Oddly enough, in spite of Old Begga's praise of these sermons and of Jon Vidalin, I never felt any great desire to know more of them. As for "the Word of God," I had already formed my own opinion about it, based on experience. Stories and adventures from the Bible were all right. But sermons and psalm-singing in the middle of the day only made one sleepy. Why grownups bothered about such things was a mystery to me. I once asked Old Begga if this Jon Vidalin was her late husband, and if that was why her son was called Jon—I had not bargained for her answer!

Old Begga's bed was the cleanest and tidiest bed in the room, and the many-colored woven blanket that covered it was by far the prettiest. I could quite understand why Pussy had chosen just that bed to lie on and sun herself. She lay there most of the day, and at night she wandered noiselessly around, her eyes shining green in the dark. It did not please me, though, that Pussy should be there today with Old Begga, as Puss and I had never been friends. The enmity was not of my making. Fascinated by her white-and-yellow coat and her whole appearance, I had at one time made certain advances, such as pulling her tail in a friendly way or playing with her whiskers. But it seemed that Puss did not know how to play. On the other hand, she knew only too well how to hiss and scratch.

As usual, Puss looked beautiful and enticing. But it was, as always on a Holy Day, Old Begga who claimed my attention.

On weekdays I saw Old Begga only in the kitchen where, slatternly, tousled and sooty, with running eyes and dripping nose, she looked after her three fireplaces and her many pots, kettles and pans. That it really was Old Begga from the kitchen who sat there so fine and beautiful, looking just as I pictured the good old queens in her fairy tales, seemed to me almost impossible. But on the other hand it was, of course, a tangible and very welcome proof that those transformations she especially loved to tell me about could actually take place. When Week-day-Begga could become Sunday-Begga, it seemed possible for any monster to turn into a princess.

The sight of Old Begga sitting in state was one that always filled me with respect and wonder. Her iron-gray hair with the silver threads in it was brushed smoothly back and plaited in thick firm braids, the ends fastened up under a black cap. From this cap dangled a long black silk tassel, attached to the cap through a broad beautifully-engraved ring of silver gilt. A brightly-colored silk scarf was fastened to the low neck of the tightly-laced black bodice, and spread itself over her bosom in a large bow, the wings being fastened with pins, while in the center it was kept in place by an old silver-gilt brooch. Beneath the scarf there was a glimpse of starched linen, the whiteness of which was accentuated by the broad black velvet edges of the bodice. The most conspicuous thing of all was the richly-pat-terned, carefully-arranged silk apron, below which a pair of ankles in thick brown woolen stockings innocently peeped out. The whole was finished off by a pair of simple Icelandic shoes, made of soft untanned leather, and fitting the feet tightly, low-cut and open, in color blue-green, edged with white and yellow.

It was when I saw this stately Old Begga bending over her book of sermons, her bright steel-rimmed glasses on the tip of her nose (which for once was dripping scarcely at all), that I realized that Sunday was indeed more holy than any other day in the week. On such a day it behoved one to behave properly and be good.

So I approached her reverently and quietly, put my album on her knee as unobtrusively as possible and looked cautiously up into the wrinkled face, where the hair on a wart glistened almost as brightly as Pussy's whiskers.

At first Old Begga took no notice of me and simply went on reading, impressively and silently mouthing the words with her thin sunken lips.

When at length she lifted her head and looked at me over the top of her spectacles, she did not seem to know me at once. "What are you reading, Begga?" I asked in a puzzled voice, although I knew very well—it was her silence and the remoteness in her gaze that made my heart beat and my tongue chatter.

"What should I be reading, little curiosity!" she answered shortly. "It is God's Word I am reading! . . . Did you think that I was sitting here enjoying myself with sinful books on a Lord's Day? But why have you come disturbing me? And why don't you take care where you put your album . . . don't you see that I'm wearing my silk apron? Let me look at you—you are as dirty as if you had come straight from the dunghill. Well . . . well. Here's a piece of candy for you. Now be a good boy and run away. Perhaps I will tell you a story presently."

"The one about Golden Eyes and the Enchanted Princess?" I asked excitedly.

"Good gracious me, no!" exclaimed Old Begga, horrified. "Would you entice me into telling you a profane story on a Holy Day? Surely you are not tired of hearing about God's chosen people and Little Jesus?"

Rather shamefacedly I murmured that of course I was not, but Old Begga looked as if she could see through me.

"For worldly things there are six whole days, for the things of God only one . . . so easily satisfied is the dear Lord!" she instructed me. "The least we can do, therefore, is to devote that one day to Him. It is about time you learned to distinguish between Holy Days and weekdays. . . . Holy Days, you see, have been created by God not just for rest and enjoyment, but so that, when at length we stand in His presence, we shall not be able to excuse ourselves by saying that we have not had time to think of Him or to pray to Him. . . . You are still too young to understand God's Word as blessed Jon Vidalin explains it in the book here, or as your uncle expounds it in church. But you are old enough to enjoy many of the stories in both the New and the Old Testaments and to profit by them. . . . Well, hurry up now and run out into the sunshine, my little sparrow, for the sunshine is God's Word to children."

In spite of the candy I did not want to go away before my doubts had been dispelled. But anxious not to bother Old Begga more than was necessary, I asked her straight whether *she* thought my mother ugly.

This way of approaching the matter proved to be the wrong one. Old Begga pushed her spectacles high up onto her forehead and looked at me with a pair of eyes that seemed just about to jump out of their sockets to punish me.

"What in the world are you chattering about, child?" she asked angrily. "Your mother ugly? What an idea! Who in the world put that into your head? You simpleton! It must have been Björssi or Sigga Mens. You would never have thought of it yourself, you wee mite. Do you really think that your mother is ugly? What do you think God would say if He heard you speak like that?"

When at length Old Begga let me explain, I told her in as few words as possible what my mother had said.

Old Begga listened to me attentively.

"Oh, is that all!" she said in a calmer voice. Then she thought for a minute and went on emphatically: "If you want to know what *I* think, it is that I have never seen anyone half so lovely as my dear Cecilia! Your mother's soul is good and beautiful, my boy, and that is what really matters. . . . What good will it do anyone to appear before God with ever so lovely a face and say, 'Look at my face, God!' God does not care about faces. They are all of His making—and that's my opinion. He would not so much as glance at anyone's face. He would only answer, 'Show Me your soul.' And if the soul has been corrupted, or perhaps altogether lost, how do you think it will be for you then? . . . No, when your mother meets God He will smile and say, 'I never saw a lovelier soul—enter into My glory!' And when at length you die and get to Heaven—as I trust you may— you will be filled with a great wonder, for you will scarcely be able to look at your mother, she will shine so brightly. Perhaps you will not even recognize her. But don't be afraid, poppet. If it is granted me to be near my blessed Cecilia, there as on earth, I will keep an eye open for you, and as soon as I see you I will show her to you. I should recognize you anywhere, you little goldilocks."

Old Begga patted my head, wiped a tear from her eye and continued:

"What a happy day that will be! So far you are too young to know the snares and temptations of the Devil . . . children slip through the meshes of his net like baby trout. But one day you will know that all true joy is in Heaven . . . one day you will realize that this beautiful, deceptive world is a vale of tears, a muddy pool. How many there are whom God will fail to recognize when they return from their life on earth! 'Are you the one I let down to earth as an innocent little child?' will be His sorrowful question to the unclean sinner who has gone astray. 'Go and wash yourself in Purgatory . . . if you can endure its torments you shall remain My child.' But the sinner who returns from Purgatory unpurified (and great fortitude will be needed to endure its cleansing flames), with him God will lose patience and the Devil will get his prey."

I waited until Old Begga had finished and then I asked her why she thought my mother had said she was ugly when she was not. To this Old Begga had an answer ready:

"Even the best of people are sometimes guilty of unnecessary words, my boy," she explained to me. "A word is like thistle-down, so lightly does it rest on the tongue. The slightest puff will blow it away, and once it is in the air no power on earth can recapture it. Still, it would have been worse if your good mother had praised herself. Modesty is no offense against God, but the Devil loves pride as the drunkard loves spirits."

Pondering on all this wisdom, and gnawing my piece of candy, I left the room with a light heart.

I cannot say definitely whether it was on this very Sunday, or on another, that I lounged out of the house with my hands behind my back and found a man's saddle on the mounting-stone in the middle of the yard. (That I had candy in my mouth for the first part of the ride proves nothing, particularly when I tell you that I had a special name for Sunday, and the name was "Candy Day.") I climbed up, sat astride the saddle and started off on a long ride.

My journey was an extraordinarily satisfactory one, with no misfortunes. I visited all the places the names of which I could remember, and a good many more, and I can scarcely believe that a more speedy and less troublesome journey has ever been undertaken in the memory of man. I was, of course, welcomed everywhere, spoke to a number of people, discussed crops, the weather forecast and sanitary conditions with professional ease, and incidentally was offered fantastic prices for my horse, which I did not in the least wish to sell. If I forgot to say "Thank you" and "Goodbye" anywhere, I galloped back and made good the omission.

The journey was as successful as could be and I was already on my homeward way when I had a strange experience. I suddenly found myself in a farmyard that I had never seen before. . . . I had been familiar with all the other places I had visited, but what farm could this be? I sat quite still on my horse and studied it carefully. . . . I wondered why one of the buildings was painted red when the others were not painted at all. And why was this red building standing sideways to the yard when all the others turned their gables squarely toward it? Why hadn't the red building, like all the others, just one line of large windows instead of two, and who could be living behind the top windows, up there in the "loft"? I felt sure that those people must have a milk jug with blue flowers, just like my mother's. I must remember to tell her so when I got home! . . . And why was the gate into the churchyard shut, while the door into the church had been left open? . . . And where was the living room? Could it be there behind the row of buildings? And who was the owner of all those sheep clambering about the steep rocks behind the house and never falling down? The people living here must be rather peculiar, or they would have come out to receive their visitor, I thought. Hadn't they heard me ride into the yard? Ought I to dismount and knock at the door?

I had reached this point in my cogitations when my cousins— Sigga, who was a few years my senior and whom I have already mentioned, and Greta, who was a couple of years older than Sigga—came rushing out of the house. Clearly they were just about to interrupt my journey by dashing up to me and addressing me as if they knew me.

"What are you doing, Uggi?" they cried in one breath. "What saddle have you borrowed? Who lent it to you? Oh! let us get up, Uggi darling—do let us get up!"

I liked my cousins very much when they behaved themselves properly, so much indeed that I had sometimes even envied them for being girls, for having long yellow hair, checked skirts and patterned aprons (an envy, of course, which I very carefully hid). But when they came and tried to drag me off my own special horse and ruin an important journey for me, I felt anything but friendly toward them.

"Can't you see I'm a stranger?" I growled furiously as I clung to my saddle, kicking and breathing hard. "You girls! Let me go, you *girls!*"

Happily they were wearing their Sunday frocks and so dared not risk a hand-to-hand fight, or they would have made short work of me. So circumstances forced them to negotiate.

"Just for a minute, a tiny minute," they both begged coaxingly. "Do let us try the saddle—just try the saddle."

"How do you do?" I said, once I saw the danger was over, assuming the gruff tones of a would-be stranger. "Is this your farm? Do you live here?"

"Uggi darling," they begged together, looking at me with assumed piteousness, "*do* let us! We will never forget it. We'll . . . "

"What is the name of this farm?" I interrupted in my assumed voice—and then I added softly in my own: "You must answer properly, or—!" Then once more adopting the rôle of a visitor: "Well, and what is the name of this farm?"

"Ofeigsstadur," grunted a subdued Greta. "Ofeigsstadur," sighed Sigga, like a faint echo.

"Ofeigsstadur!" repeated the stranger, wrinkling his forehead. "I can't believe it! For that is the name of the farm I come from. Is it, by any chance, called Brattahlid?"

"Yes," murmured Greta. "Yes," added Sigga, both gazing earnestly at the stranger's face—they would not for the world displease him, it seemed.

"Does this farm belong to you both?" he asked again. To this they just nodded, very proud of their ownership.

"Haven't you time to stop a moment and have some coffee?" asked Greta, so mellifluously that the stranger saw through her at once.

"No, thank you," he replied with dignity. "But if you have a drink of whey I will wait while you fetch it. It is thirsty weather."

"Wouldn't you rather rest your horse for a while?" asked Sigga, trying in vain to look sincere. Finally, they went away and came back with a bowl of extremely sour whey.

When the stranger had drunk it, he said a polite "Thank you" and "Goodbye" and rode away.

The two small landowners immediately forgot their rôles and began loudly and tearfully to upbraid him for breaking his word. But the stranger pointed out vehemently that he had made no promises, and added seriously that he did not suppose they expected him to go back to Ofeigsstadur on shank's mare. Then he clicked his tongue, touched his horse briskly with his whip, thumped him with his heels, tugged at the reins—in a word, continued his interrupted journey.

"Will you get home soon?" asked Greta, tonelessly, after

some time had passed; and a minute later Sigga repeated the question even more pitifully.

I, of course, was much too far away to hear what was being said in the yard at Ofeigsstadur! But I willingly let my good horse gallop at top speed, hurrying as best I could, and who should be standing there to receive me on my arrival but my two cousins!

"Why, good day, Greta," I exclaimed with surprise, holding out my hand. I greeted Sigga in the same way, adding, "I have ridden such a long, long way. My horse is dripping with sweat, as you can see. Well, how have you been getting on while I have been away?"

"Quite well," muttered Greta, crossly. "Quite well," whispered Sigga, peevishly. "May we *now?*" they asked, together.

I had already decided to let them have the horse; but I had not yet settled the price.

"After all, it's not really any fun," said Greta, suddenly. "Ride on, you old weathercock. *We* are going to walk, we are. If you had been a really nice boy, but—it doesn't matter."

"What will you give me?" I asked calmly.

"I *should* have let you have a bite of my chocolate," crowed Greta. "Now I shan't."

"Of mine, too," seconded Sigga. "Now I will never give you any more again."

"Pouf!" I said, as if chocolate were my daily food. And, since negotiations were now well under way, we soon agreed that I should give up my "horse" and pledge myself to make no demands on it till after the evening meal. In return I was to have a bite of Greta's chocolate, and one of Sigga's. These bites I was to take while still astride my horse, and they agreed to give me a corner each. Furthermore, I was to be allowed to play with their "farm" for as long as it took me to milk the cows, count the sheep and "go to market," a journey which might take me all around the churchyard.

But even the first condition was only grudgingly fulfilled. Greta stretched out a corner of her piece of chocolate, but that corner was hedged about by a pair of very solid fingertips, and, when I tried to take a larger bite than the one she intended, she yelled: "Only with two teeth, I said, only with *two!*"

"No, you didn't," I replied, deeply hurt.

"Yes, I did," insisted Greta, craftily. "I said it to myself; you didn't hear, that was all."

"Well, then, it doesn't count," I growled querulously. But Greta insisted that it counted and that it was my fault I had not heard. Needless to say, Sigga followed suit and cheated me in exactly the same disgustingly sly way, defending herself in exactly the same words.

In my heart, however, I was quite indifferent about the chocolate; it was their farm that I cared about. I therefore overlooked this breach of contract and, not unwillingly, gave up my horse.

Greta's and Sigga's farm was to the south, right up against the wall of the churchyard. This wall was the "mountain" behind the farm. The farm buildings were very primitive, for they had no roofs and no walls, and were simply marked out by long rows of small, parti-colored stones. They were linked to each other by an involved system of crooked paths defined in the same way. That was what they looked like on the face of it, but to us, of course, they were real houses. It was the same with the cows. They *looked* like a row of sheep's jawbones, colored with soft chalkstone and stuck fast by the "snouts." But to us they were real cows, and I milked them carefully, udder by udder, and if here and there an udder was missing I acted as doctor, spat in the sore and filled it up with earth. As soon as a cow had been milked I immediately turned it out to grass as far as my arm would reach. There was a terrible lot to do on the farm; scarcely were the cows nicely settled before the sheep, which were so round and dumpy, curiously like knucklebones, began to drive me almost mad with their hungry bleating. There could be no question of counting them that day;

why, they would only knock me down if I stood in the doorway as they rushed out. There was nothing for it but to let them skip and leap, and to feel amused at their playfulness. Then I saddled and bridled the horses, which bore a certain remote likeness to shankbones—the reins were not, of course, really bits of string!—chose the one I liked best to be my mount, tethered the others in a long row and was just about ready to set out on a long business journey when my cousins arrived to disturb me.

"What *have* you done, you wretched boy?" they yelled in chorus, and began to shed real tears. "Oh, our cows! Look, Greta! Look, Sigga! Oh, our sheep! We shall never find them again—never! Come here at once and help us, you disgusting brat. I'll give you a slap for every sheep that's missing! Come along, now!"

"Can't you see I haven't time?" I grumbled . . . but added immediately, in a conciliatory tone, "Is there anything I can buy for you?"

Instead of answering properly, Greta snatched the horses from me.

"And *you* think you are going to ride on *our* horses!" she howled. "I could break every bone in your body! And I expect I shall, as soon as I have time!"

"You daren't, because of my father," I exulted. "Just like a girls' farm. Here you leave the animals indoors and starving, even in the middle of the day. Now I am going, and I'll never come back."

"I wish you would," sighed Greta. Then she pulled herself together and threatened me. "You just wait! In a minute I am going in to Mother, to change into my old frock."

"Do you think I'm afraid of you?" I asked with burning ears. Greta in her everyday dress pleased me a great deal less than Greta in her Sunday best.

"I'm not afraid to give you a good whipping," she continued to threaten me. "My father's a clergyman—yours isn't."

"It doesn't take so much to be a clergyman," I answered scornfully. "You wait till I'm one myself. Then I won't even marry you—ha, ha! Then you'll be an old maid, ha, ha!"

Greta looked me up and down. "You a parson!" she snorted scornfully. "No. You may be thankful if I am kind enough to give you work as a cowherd on my farm when I marry and settle down."

"You think I can't intone as well as Sigga's papa?" I asked boastingly. "Come into the church and you shall hear me—ha, ha! You daren't."

"You aren't really going?" asked Greta, terrified. "Are you mad—what do you think Father will say?"

"I don't care!" I answered, and went resolutely away.

I had achieved my desire—I had given them both a regular fright—and now, I thought, I would go in to my mother and beg a well-earned piece of bread. At the corner of the church-yard, however, I looked back, and when I saw the two of them staring after me I could not, for my honor's sake, do other than go toward the gate into the churchyard to see whether they believed my threat and would follow me. Unfortunately, when I had been standing there for a little while, and for the sake of appearances had pulled at the gate, which I knew very well was fastened and which I could not open, they peeped around the corner. I pretended that I did not see them, and apparently it now struck me for the first time that I could cut in as usual through an opening in the fence where a rail had been missing for as long as I could remember. At the door of the church I stopped and surveyed the neighborhood, and was able, by glancing out of the corner of my eye, to see that my cousins had reached the fence. There was, therefore, nothing for it . . . I must go in. And in I went, although my courage was fast diminishing. I cast a fearful glance at the carved and colored apostles who ornamented the sides of the pulpit. I wondered vaguely whether they could stretch their arms backward into the pulpit and do me some harm if I were forced to go up there. I dared not lift my eyes to the crucifix above the pulpit, but I cast a fearful glance at the picture over the altar which represented Our Lord with little children. Happily, it appeared that my cousins had given up watching me; in any case I saw nothing of them, however often I looked furtively toward the door. On the other hand, I saw that all the windows swarmed with small, greenish-blue buzzing "birds."

I soon forgot everything in the world except those "birds." I climbed up onto a bench beside one of the windows, the better to be able to follow their flight. I had not been kneeling on this bench for very long before I began to feel that it was most unsatisfactory having the "birds" at a distance, and that I must look at them closer. At last I managed to catch one of them by the wing, but to my astonishment the wing came off—and there he lay with only one wing, wriggling comically and turning round and round! What if all their wings were put on as loosely as this?

As craftily and quietly as possible I moved the tips of my fingers toward the swarm where it was thickest, and had just caught another "bird" when my hand was seized from behind. I jumped violently, shrieked and, turning round, met the serious face of Sigga's papa looking at me without the vestige of a smile.

"Do you know what you are doing?" he asked in an odd voice, sitting down on the bench beside me.

"I am only seeing if the wings are just as loose on all of them," I answered with the impatience of a doubtful conscience, and suddenly I felt my cheeks burning as if I were sitting on my mother's lap in front of the fire.

"What would you say if someone came and began pulling your arms and legs off?" Sigga's papa continued very gravely.

"There's no one who dares," I answered shortly; but now I could no longer meet his eyes, so I looked attentively out the window, studying the view.

Sigga's papa talked to me for a long time. He told me that a bluebottle is also one of God's creatures, and that it hurts just as

much to have its wings pulled off as it would hurt me to have a
leg or arm amputated. I soon had tears in my eyes, but not for
the world would I give in and cry.

I longed for Sigga's papa to stop. Did he really think I
was so stupid that I had not understood what he was saying,
long ago? Or was he determined to make me cry?

"Look at the mountains on the other side of the valley—
aren't they lovely?" I said, trying to distract attention from the
painful subject. But the interruption only made Sigga's papa
take me on his knee and begin all over again.

I had always considered Sigga's papa a man of intelligence,
not only because he had so many books and filled so many sheets
of paper with writing but also, and perhaps especially, because
he, who had to speak so often and at such great length, had had
the sense to shave off his beard in order to move his jaws more
freely. But today he seemed to me almost stupid, since he
thought it necessary to talk about the same subject for so long.
From this kind of stupidity, which I knew from experience to be
very general among grownups, I had until now thought him
free.

However, not many minutes had passed before I again had
the opportunity of recognizing the rare wisdom and exceptional
superiority of Sigga's papa.

When we had left the church hand in hand and were walking
away between the graves, I asked him, mostly to make sure that
we had now quite finished with the flies: "Don't you think,
Sigga's papa, that sheep are very brave animals?"

"Now what makes you ask that?" he said, and suddenly he
was himself again, answering me politely and seriously as if I
were grown-up, and neither smiling nor making fun of my
questions as so many others did.

"Because they dare climb so high, so high up into the mountains," I answered him eagerly. "Aren't sheep the bravest of all
the animals?"

"No, lions are braver," answered Sigga's papa, informatively.
"The lion is the king of beasts, and the bravest of them all."

"Have you ever seen a lion climb so high?" I asked incredulously. "Do you think a lion would dare to climb so high? And don't you think he would be frightened if he met our old ram?"

"Personally, I have seen a lion only in a cage, behind iron bars," Sigga's papa answered conscientiously. "But I have read a great deal about lions and I can even show you pictures of them. A lion is afraid of nothing. A ram, on the contrary, is far from brave; haven't you seen how a little dog can get a big ram on the run?"

This argument was so illuminating that somewhere within me I felt hurt and ashamed that I had not been able to think of it myself. In a moment I had been brought to a standstill. But at the same time I did not want to let my sheep down. So I asked anxiously:

"But sheep are very good animals, aren't they, Sigga's papa?"

"Sheep!" answered Sigga's papa, amiably. "Yes, certainly they are, much better than lions. Besides, lions are beasts of prey, and one cannot eat them."

"There you are, then!" I said, delighted that I was still holding my own, for these admissions not only strengthened my self-confidence but also increased my respect for Sigga's papa.

Many of my memories of this, perhaps my last summer at Ofeigsstadur, are concerned with small and chance happenings, such as some hasty drops of rain, a glimpse as a window was opened or shut, the shadow of a cloud across the sun, or sunny hours that made me happy and sleepy with their golden warmth.

My farm was in a sheltered corner southwest of our cluster of buildings, and there I spent many solitary hours. This farm of mine was like my cousins' in every respect except that it was smaller and poorer. As soon as I had eaten my breakfast I used to try to slip away without the company of my sister Sigurveig; this, happily, I managed pretty often.

This sister, eighteen months younger than I, was a great trial to me. I certainly thought her pretty, and because she was a dear little thing and, moreover, my sister, I tried in every possible way to make her reasonable and sensible. But I was never very successful and so, quite frankly, I often did not bother about her at all. Among other things she had the annoying habit of snatching my playthings away from me just when it was most inconvenient, and the excuse that my mother put forward on her behalf—that she was only two—never seemed to me adequate. What made it all the more difficult was that her weapons, besides her small sharp teeth, were shrieks and yells; and if I tried to keep my own things her howls were sure to produce a voice from somewhere or other that said: "What are you doing to little Veiga *now?*"

If Veiga wanted to come with me, as she always did, and I had not time to wait for her, because I was too busy and she had practically no legs, I heard behind me: "Are you running away from your poor little sister, you unkind boy?" If I extracted from her refractory little mouth a nail that she was about to swallow, and in return had my fingernails bitten until they bled, someone or other at once exclaimed in a hurt voice: "How can you be so unkind to that poor innocent child?" Yes, if Veiga got herself wet, or fell down and hurt herself, it was always my fault. In the first case I was blamed out of hand for not having helped her, and in the second for not having looked after her well enough.

If I allowed her to come with me to my farm, things almost always went wrong. Not only did she try to eat my animals, hide and hair and all—a danger I had to prevent, as I had been told expressly that gnawing bones was bad for her— but she also destroyed my houses, flung down the "walls," devastated everything, spoiled the little order I had been able to create, and dribbled everywhere.

That farm was generally in a dreadful mess. My animals, for example, were scarcely ever at home. And if half of them were there the other half were sure to be missing. For, besides Veiga, there was a puppy who always wanted to play; and his form of play was to run away with all he could get hold of, hide it or bury it and then come back to me, friendly and unashamed. He was, however, so very engaging that I could never bring myself to punish him, and this the little brute seemed to know and count on. If I spoke harshly, he would just lie down and wag his tail, ingratiating himself with his ears while his eyes shone and his whole attitude expressed an assumed piety and desire to make amends. But he soon fell back into his old ways. Many a horse and cow did he hide so successfully that I never saw them again. And if, at long last, I found an animal that had been hidden away, it was generally so shamefully bitten and mutilated that a respectable farm could hardly be expected to feed it any longer.

However, the puppy, Vigi, and I were very good friends. When I worked on my farm, built up its ruins or swept it with a brush of newly-plucked straw, he lay by my side and sunned himself. If he thought I had ignored him too long, he pushed his nose into my hand or suddenly gave a short, merry little bark. Sometimes I picked dandelions and made chains both for him and for me. Afterward we strutted proudly round, Vigi like a big dog, with his tongue hanging far out of his mouth, I like a big man, with a poker down my back. Proudly we showed ourselves to anyone who cared to look at us and perchance admire us. This game generally ended when Vigi had suddenly had enough and scratched his chain off his neck with his front paws, jumped up onto me and snatched at mine and was not satisfied until all our finery had been torn to shreds. If I threatened him with a thrashing, he rushed impudently away with his tail in the air, glancing backward to see whether I could be tempted to follow him, which, as a matter of fact, I generally did.

Vigi was the son of my father's snappish red-and-white bitch, Gryla, for whom everyone on the farm, with the exception of my father, had a very great respect. But in contrast to his mother Vigi was dark gray, and had not a trace of snappishness. I imagined that he belonged to me, and when one day my father asked Nonni, Old Begga's son, whether he did not think it time to begin training Vigi and teaching him obedience, I lodged an indignant protest which my father set aside with a few merry words. To my great joy, the first attempts to train the pup failed miserably. If Nonni wanted to make him follow when he set out for the haymaking, he had to carry him under his arm. Every morning Vigi was carried off in this way, and every morning he came back victoriously, as happy as if he had escaped from torture and death, and delighted to see me again. As a rule he found me sorrowful and alone in my corner and immediately rushed up to me, knocked me over backward, licked my face with his soft tongue and then lay down beside me with his head on my breast or tummy. For some time it was against the rules for me to move; if I did, he barked at me. He was often wet and dirty from the streams and bogs he had crossed on his way home; but however dirty he made me, and however certain I was of a scolding and other unpleasantness on that account, he was always welcome just the same, and I shouldered his guilt without a murmur. It never occurred to me to tell on him.

The Nonni I have mentioned was Old Begga's only child. He was a gentle youth who always spoke in a soft voice and who very seldom smiled—except at us children. He was so good-natured that he could not refuse me any request it was possible to fulfill, so we were the best of friends. If I could have imagined giving Vigi up to anybody it would have been to Nonni. But I did not entertain the thought for a moment; I would rather have been separated from all my other animals put together than from Vigi. Nonni knew this, and I strongly suspected that it was only for appearances' sake, and to avoid disobeying my father, that he continued to take Vigi with him.

Naturally I abused Nonni's good nature to an incredible degree, claimed a great deal too much of his free time, begged him to make toys for me (which I broke as soon as I got, or threw away when I was in a bad temper), and so on. But apparently it did not disturb him to see the work of his clever fingers thus broken and disdained. Even when I was most discourteous to him he only smiled patiently and promised me another and a better thing as soon as he could get time to make it.

In the end, I *did* give him Vigi as a present. . . . But to this magnanimous action there was, of course, a prelude—which was, unfortunately, extremely painful.

Before telling the story I must mention that, as far back as I could remember, my father had always agreed with me absolutely that I was one of "the men."

This "manly dignity," of which I was exceedingly proud, depended on the tacit assumption that whatever happened to me I was never to pity myself or cry. I must admit that it sometimes seemed to me an honor almost too dearly bought and that it was always one of two things—either wearisome or painful. But no power on earth could have made me acknowledge this. My father's praise, of which he spared as little as he did anything else, sounded so sweet in my ears that I think I would have preferred to fall down dead rather than to give in when he was near. His praise was always peculiarly concise and pithy; and as I was not suspicious it never occurred to me for an instant that the whole thing was an educational trick.

If I went out for a walk with him and got so tired that I could scarcely lift my feet, he would say:

"Men don't know what it is to be tired!"

Then, thanks to these words, I would drag myself on farther and pretend that nothing was the matter.

If I knocked my toes against a stone or a doorsill without falling, he would cry admiringly:

"My word, what supple feet!"

And although my toes burned like fire, or felt as if they were swelling to the size of sacks of corn, I would meet his gaze with something that I imagined to be a smile.

If I actually fell, which happened pretty often, and gave myself a big bump, or a cut which bled or smarted, he quickly turned defeat into victory by saying:

"Yes, that is what a man ought to be, hard as flint!"

And hard as flint I swallowed my howls and tears, thinking to myself that I must at least remember to cry when I was alone.

If a stranger happened to be present when misfortune overtook me, and if this stranger was surprised at my three-year-old courage (as well he might be), my father would observe casually:

"Oh, Uggi, he's hard as a stone—he fears neither fire nor steel."

The gravity with which he said that, but especially the fact that he said it just in passing, as it were, was a triumph such as I have rarely experienced since.

And so dawned the day when I was to make Nonni a present of my puppy. . . .

That summer my father had two horses on the farm: his own, a lively young brood mare, Brunka, whom it was impossible to approach because of her importance and the care with which she was surrounded after just having had her first foal, a thin-legged, broad-backed, red little thing with an almost white nose, legs and tail; and an old black-and-white saddle horse, Skjoni, a relic from my father's young days, superannuated and full of wandering rheumatism and bad habits.

On this particular morning, just as I stepped outside the door with my hand in my father's, and before I had had time to blink off my first meeting with the sun, Nonni came into the farmyard on Skjoni, riding between the group of houses and round the corner of the churchyard.

From the conversation between my father and Nonni I gathered that Nonni had been out since early morning looking for some strayed ewes, and that he had taken Skjoni because he could find none of "Parson's horses." He had, apparently, seen nothing of the sheep. I did not feel inclined to stay and listen to their long-winded guesses as to where the sheep could have hidden themselves, and as I was lucky enough to have an old ball in my hand I began to throw it against the nearest wall to see how far out it would bounce. My father and Nonni stood on either side of Skjoni, both leaning on him. Perhaps that was why Skjoni laid back his ears, half lowered his eyelids and was so sulky that when I offered him a handful of grass he snapped, not at the grass, but at me. This brought him a slap on the jaw from my father, a smack on the flank from Nonni and angry words from all three of us. As my father and Nonni were still far from having exhausted all possibilities regarding the lost sheep, I left the ungrateful Skjoni to look after himself and went on playing with my ball.

Skjoni, however, did not seem to appreciate having a ball roll in and out between his legs and a little boy crawl after it, and to make this quite clear he kicked me in the seat as I bent down to pick up the ball. He kicked so hard that I was sent flying a good way down the yard. Even during my flight through the air my nose was still a nice little nose . . . but after I landed it was no longer recognizable. I cannot be blamed for not trying immediately to find out how much of me was still unhurt, nor for the fact that I simply lay there till my father came and lifted me up—particularly as I did not have to wait long. I did not scream, even when my father quickly and eagerly felt me all over and showed me clearly that it was not my nose only that had gone wrong. The strange look in his eyes arrested my attention fully as much as did my own feelings; so also did the voice, unlike his own, in which he asked me, harshly and breathlessly:

"Where does it hurt?"

"Nowhere," I managed to stammer through chattering teeth . . . a declaration more courageous than truthful, since my head hurt as much as if something inside it had been shaken to pieces, my nose was like a well-stocked pincushion and my bottom felt as if it had been dipped in fire—not to mention the pains I had in my fingers, which made me think of the rusty crooked nails that Bjarni the blacksmith always kept hidden in a pot at the side of the forge.

My father felt me again, this time with a somewhat firmer hand; then he stood me up with a relieved sigh.

"Well, apparently there are no bones broken," he said shortly and looked hard at me, frowning. "But it hurts you very much, doesn't it? Were you frightened?"

"No!" I answered, although my chattering teeth almost betrayed me. If he asked me any more questions I should just have to nod or shake my head, I thought to myself.

The fact that Nonni was standing there looking at me helplessly, with tears in his weak, gray-blue eyes, strengthened in some indescribable way my fortitude . . . for by this time I was finding it exceedingly difficult not to cry.

My father stood there for a moment looking at me; I did not dare meet his eyes. Then he nodded his head at Nonni and said, with a smile that infinitely enhanced the words:

"There's a true soldier for you! Won't give in, whatever happens. He must have inherited that from Ketilbjörn."

Ketilbjörn was my mother's father—Ketilbjörn-from-Knör—and it disappointed me a little that it was from him and not from Uggi-from-Fjall, my father's father, that I had inherited such an obviously valuable characteristic.

But on this occasion my pleasure at my father's praise was weak and short-lived. As I stood there with his handkerchief pressed against my nose I felt, to say the least, very uncomfortable. I scarcely dared stir, for with the slightest movement my breeches rubbed against me and I feared to expose my courage to the pain this gave.

Happily my father seemed too absorbed in his quarrel with Skjoni to think of sending me in to my mother, which would, I knew, be the end of it all. That my father was having a difference of opinion with Skjoni, and that a very serious one, I gathered from the fact that he had fetched his old muzzle-gun, a formidable weapon, the butt of which was only a couple of hand-breadths shorter than its long barrel. He now went over to Skjoni, took off Nonni's saddle, flung it down on the ground and went off with the old animal, who was as heavy to drag as a sledge on bare earth.

Before my father left the yard he remembered me and called over his shoulder to Nonni:

"Take Uggi in to his mother and ask her to undress him and look after him well."

Nonni's "yes" was softer than ever, and he glanced at my father with a curious, almost shy look when he received this order.

I whispered to Nonni how to take hold of me, and he carried me carefully along the passages and up the stairs to the loft, my parents' bedroom. There he laid me gently on my father's bed, which was also mine, and then hastened down to call my mother.

I quite forgot to cry, although there was now a chance, and reason enough. I lay and listened. How long the time seemed! If only my father would change his mind! . . . Poor Skjoni!

My mother came running. She also had a strange look on her face. It surprised me that she did not kiss me as she generally did when anything had happened to me. And what surprised me still more was that she did not say a word, but only undressed me with quick, careful hands, while the tears fell, drop by drop, from her gray eyes and ran down over her unfurrowed cheeks like tiny streams.

Nonni, who had stolen up behind her, stood with bent head and wandering eyes, and something expectant in his bearing. His appearance seemed to me so strange, and suddenly I knew why. He also was listening as I was.

By this time my listening had taken such possession of me that I scarcely noticed what was happening to me, and I gave only a desultory moan, as if on another's behalf, when my mother unwittingly touched one of my tender spots.

When at last I heard the shot I looked quickly at Nonni and met an equally quick glance in return. Nonni reddened a little; I felt my cheeks grow warm too. My mother looked in astonishment from me to Nonni; she seemed only slowly to become conscious that there had been a shot.

"Who is shooting?" she asked casually.

"I think . . . I think it was . . . the master," answered Nonni, almost inaudibly and without lifting his eyes.

My mother's hands stopped suddenly. Her attentive gaze became for a moment remote; a little frown on her forehead came and went. Then she was herself again, and went on with my undressing.

When at last she discovered my tenderest spot, she murmured in swift sympathy:

"But my poor child!"

Then she whispered hastily to Nonni:

"Fetch your mother. . . . Ask her to bring her ointments with her."

When he had gone she began to cry softly; and now that the suspense was relieved I cried with her, both for company and because I could not help myself. It calmed me and was soon over.

My mother patted my cheek and said:

"What a brave little boy!"

The sweetness of her words and her touch passed soothingly through my body.

Before it had quite left me, Old Begga arrived, with a leather bag from which she produced many large and small pots of ointment. It appeared to me that she gave rather too much time to smelling and tasting with a view to finding the right ointment, but on the other hand I was glad of any delay, however slight. Long before Old Begga had found the ointment Madame Anna had come into the room, and I began to appreciate a little the importance and the advantages of what had happened. When she told us briskly that her brother's leg had once been broken in two places by a horse, I felt rather outdone and wished that things had gone equally ill for me. But when I heard that Madame Anna's brother had dragged his leg from that day to this, and that it was so susceptible to the changes in the weather that he complained whenever the wind turned, I began to console myself and envied him no longer. Madame Anna gave me a whole packet of chocolate, my mother fetched some raisins and Old Begga promised me candy. Madame Anna and Old Begga looked at my scratches, and Madame Anna assured me gaily that

I need not worry—"They are sure to heal before you get married." Old Begga, who smelled strongly of smoke, smeared me here and smeared me there, tore long strips from a sheet, wound them round me as if she were trying to make me into a ball of yarn, and was altogether in her element. When she complained that my bottom had "taken half the jar" and that she would be obliged to sit up all night to prepare ointments, it did not sound like a complaint.

My mother was tactless enough to suggest that perhaps it would be just as well to send Nonni for the doctor at once. No sooner were the words out of her mouth than Begga stopped her work, stood up and began to repack her pots. Only after my mother and Madame Anna had begged and prayed her to go on, interspersing their remarks with slighting references to doctors in general and ours in particular, would she agree to finish her task.

One of the things I realized very early was that women cannot bear to see a boy or a young man anywhere near them without immediately sending him on errands. And it was not long before Madame Anna sent Nonni down to order coffee. Was it possible that Skjoni's kick was actually going to bring me my first cup of coffee? Nonni went, Nonni came back, Nonni was sent down again to say that pancakes were to be baked. By degrees there was a great feeling of gaiety around my bed of pain and I lay as still as possible so as to be able to take part in the fun. My head was aching very badly, but I tried to lessen my pain with chocolate, looked forward to the pancakes and the possible coffee and laughed when Madame Anna said anything funny—even if I did not quite see why it was funny. Whenever Nonni appeared the brains of the three women began to race again. Old Begga sent him for her scissors, my mother for her bunch of keys which she knew was somewhere about and eventually found in her pocket; Old Begga sent him for her sack of candy, Madame Anna for a new bag of coffee which was in the drawer next to the top one in the chest of drawers on the right, my mother for a handful of corn for some little birds that were flying about outside the window, and Madame Anna again, when the coffee and pancakes eventually arrived, to fetch Sigga's papa.

I knew from experience what it meant to be sent all over the place, and I was therefore very sorry for Nonni. But there was another reason for my sympathy: I had got it into my head that he would take Skjoni's death very hard and would feel in some way responsible. Then there was a third reason: I had a feeling that he held himself somehow to blame for what had happened to me. These reasons, combined with my own success, which was quite overwhelming (my mother had even promised me "sweet soup"* every day until my wounds were healed), made me tender-hearted. And so it ended by my calling Nonni to my bed and whispering shyly in his ear:

"You mustn't be unhappy about it, dear Nonni. You shall have my Vigi."

Nonni smiled his gentle smile and patted me awkwardly on the cheek. His soft downy chin twitched.

"Thank you, Uggi," he said softly. "If we both live till autumn . . ."

He could not say more, but remained standing there stroking my hand. I knew very well that his words did not imply any real doubt as to the likelihood of our surviving till autumn, but that it was only a way of speaking of the future which his mother had taught him. No doubt his unspoken promise had to do with some toy or other that he would buy for me when he went to town after our sheep had been slaughtered.

I decided in a hurry that it was to be a horse, a real horse with a tail and a mane, and on wheels—such as my cousin Greta had once owned—and I was just about to tell Nonni my desire when the door opened sharply and my father came in.

His sudden appearance produced in the room a strangely insecure and, to me, extremely painful feeling. It seemed to me that everybody, including my mother, looked at him in such

---

* Soup made of fresh fruit, eaten instead of pudding.

an odd way, and I imagined that he avoided meeting their eyes. He came over to my bed, smiled and asked of the air:

"Well, how is he?"

"He's splendid," answered my mother, warmly. "Old Begga has rubbed him and bound him up, and he will soon be all right now, the darling."

Madame Anna, who was standing with folded arms at the foot of the bed and—without losing any of her calm dignity— pulling faces at me every time I looked at her, said in a hearty tone and with a quaintly serious expression on her fat face:

"Uggi, you ought to be satisfied. . . . You can get a great deal of good out of this experience, my boy. When you grow up and someone wants to attack you, you have only to say: 'Leave me alone, will you? . . . There was once a horse that attacked me and he died of it.' And I should like to see anyone who would dare touch you after that."

I thought it all sounded very fine, and determined to remember it. A swift flush of color came into my father's weather-beaten cheeks. Then he bent over me and said, with a gravity which was rather too obvious:

"You need a horse, don't you?"

As he had himself raised the question I quite agreed with him, but I shook my head—a courtesy which my father seemed to understand.

"Well—if you don't think so," he brushed the question aside. My ears grew hot.

"But I have no saddle!" I exclaimed, so as to keep him to the point.

"Oh, if that is all!" answered my father, gaily. "One can ride without a saddle . . . but, on the other hand, scarcely without a horse! Or perhaps it's the other way round with you. As a matter of fact it will be some time before you are fit to sit a horse, or your horse is fit to carry a man! I am thinking you will both be ready for riding about the same time, you and Brunka's little red colt. But perhaps you don't like the idea?"

I threw my arms round my father's neck, and tried to find his lips in his beard. I was far too overwhelmed to be able to thank him in so many words. When he put me down I stretched out my arms to my mother. Then came Nonni's turn, Old Begga's and Madame Anna's . . . they all had to have a kiss.

Sigga's papa came in meanwhile. He had a picture book in his hand, and I gave him a specially good kiss and a specially warm hug.

When he raised himself after having joked a little while with me in his gravely merry way, he said to my father:

"Apparently old age has not yet driven bad temper from Skjoni's old rheumatic joints."

My father's eyes caught and held his brother's.

"As far as I know, Skjoni will never suffer again from either rheumatism or bad temper."

"Why, that's splendid," laughed Sigga's papa. "Perhaps Old Begga can cure not only little boys kicked by horses but also horses that kick little boys! . . . What sort of miraculous mixture did you give him, Brother Greipur?"

"A mixture of lead," replied my father, indifferently. "I thought you must have heard the shot."

They stood for a moment looking straight at each other. Then Sigga's papa shook his head. He did not give the impression of being greatly surprised.

"Could you not have postponed that dose for a few more years?" he asked quietly.

"Perhaps!" answered my father, evasively. "But it is not my custom to consult anyone about what I do with my own animals."

"No, no, Brother Greipur," smiled Sigga's papa, in the tone he always used when he called my father "Brother Greipur." "But in spite of all his bad habits, Skjoni did not, as a rule, bother children, much less actually kick them. . . . That was all I meant to say."

"Skjoni's fault was not that he kicked, but that he was usually gentle and then *suddenly* kicked!" explained my father, shortly and unwillingly. It seemed a very curious explanation to me.

However, the others did not seem to find it unreasonable; at any rate no one argued about it. On the other hand, they all smiled as with one mouth when my father added:

"Besides, we need shoe-leather."

I could not understand what they were all smiling at. Does one generally shoot a horse when his skin is needed? . . . And then I could not understand why all the gaiety around me seemed suddenly to vanish. But so it was. Everybody enjoyed his coffee in silence—and all I got was pancakes.

As soon as the coffee had been drunk, those who did not belong to the loft went away and only my father and mother remained. Madame Anna and Old Begga took the cradle, in which my little sister Beta was lying, away with them.

I was very fond of this little sister who was red-headed like myself. Now and again, though very seldom, she babbled quietly to herself and no doubt thought she was talking; and then her blue eyes shone and she was sweet and charming. But then at other times she roared furiously like a little troll, and contorted her bit of a face, until I almost believed Sigga Mens, who never missed an opportunity to tell me she was a changeling.

When my father and mother were left to themselves they sat silent for a time and did not look at each other. My head hurt me dreadfully. It had been aching all the time, but now I suddenly felt as if I could endure it no longer. I did not know why I felt so unhappy. I asked my mother what I could do about my head and she gave me a powder and turned me carefully over onto my other side, kissed me and told me to go to sleep.

When I had lain there for some time, and wonderful pictures had just begun to flicker before my eyes, I heard my father's voice:

"Do you, too, think I acted wrongly?"

In the short minute while I was waiting for my mother's answer I became wide awake.

"I don't quite know," answered my mother, hesitatingly. "No . . . it does not seem so to me. . . . I only wish you had not done it in anger."

A strange sorrowfulness took possession of me. I opened my mouth so that my parents should not hear me sobbing.

"I am like that," said my father, after a time. "You have seen me in a temper before today."

"To me it makes no difference," answered my mother, quietly. "It is only that I cannot bear that the others should have it to talk about."

As neither of them spoke again, I became more and more anxious. . . . At last I heard the sound of lips meeting. A lovely feeling of peace stole over me. The tears dried on my cheeks and made them stiff. I felt so pleasantly tired and comfortable in spite of my pain. Soon I fell asleep.

2

WHILE I was ill I was tormented with troublesome and disturbing dreams.

Most of these dreams centered in Old Begga and, strange to say, when she showed herself to me at night she appeared as two different persons. The one Begga persecuted me, the other Begga saved me.

It was generally Weekday-Begga who ill-treated me, Sunday-Begga who came to my rescue. But now and again it was just the opposite.

At the beginning of a dream I was never certain which of the two Beggas it was who had caught me, and this, of course, increased the tension. It was not until the Begga with whom I was at the moment engaged tried to put me into a boiling-pot to cook me for supper that I knew she was Bad Begga. Then the Begga who at the last moment snatched me from her, and made me a present of some many-colored kittens, which did not scratch and whose tails could be stretched to infinity, was, clearly enough, Good Begga. In the same way I knew that it was Bad Begga who, after a long race, captured me and put me down among her pots of ointment and legged it over mountains and valleys to bring me to her husband, Jon Vidalin, who I suddenly knew, was the Devil himself before he became a preacher. And it was Good Begga who, light of foot, came running after us, pulled me out of Bad Begga's sack without her noticing it and, in a storm, took me straight up through the clouds to the blue sky, to bring me home to the Lord God at Ofeigsstadur. But how was I to know which was Good Begga and which was Bad Begga when I saw both the Beggas rushing toward me, one from each side? So I used to run, first a little to one side, then a little to the other—and suddenly one of them would grab me and off we would go! For the first few moments I breathed freely because, for some reason or other, I always thought it was Good Begga who had caught me. But no sooner had I calmed down before something showed me that it was, after all, Bad Begga.

If I woke from such a Begga-dream in the middle of the night it was difficult to get to sleep again. On the whole these dreams, in spite of the excitement, were more tiring than actually amusing. The worst of it was that I did not dare tell Begga of them for fear she would be angry with me; nor could I bring myself to tell my mother, because I was afraid she would be angry with Old Begga.

Perhaps it was not so extraordinary that Old Begga just at this time had such a prominent place in my dreams, as she was with me most of the day. Not only did she put on the ointment and change my bandages, but when I fell asleep, either at night or at midday, she was always sitting on a chair at my bedside, her knitting in her hands, telling me stories.

That Old Begga had so much time to spend on me was accounted for by the fact that she had been temporarily set free from her duties in the kitchen. (These had been passed on to Sigga Mens who, highly offended at being taken away from the haymaking to work under my mother's supervision, burned the porridge and let the coffee boil too much.) This arrangement, which had been made in my honor and for my comfort, appealed to me strongly. I enjoyed the porridge, and the over-boiled coffee did not affect me. Old Begga herself seemed pleased too—except for the coffee. But as no one can tell adventure stories from morning till night without wetting her dry tongue with coffee which has *not* been too much boiled, it was arranged that she and my mother should in turn make "just a drop" for themselves and enjoy it together. I soon learned to prize these times for drinking coffee almost as highly as the stories. And yet Old Begga was a real story-teller. She could always rack me with suspense to such an extent that, time after time, I would breathlessly interrupt her to ask:

"It *will* be all right in the end, won't it, Begga?" It was only when Old Begga saw that I would "die" if she did not satisfy me that she would nod almost imperceptibly and very unwillingly. But generally she left my questions unanswered and went on with the story quite unmoved.

As a matter of fact there was never any need for apprehension—Old Begga's stories always ended happily.

One day I suddenly became philosophical and asked Old Begga how that could be.

"Nothing else would do, my little one," she answered without a smile. "Things always end happily for the good; but for bad people, on the contrary, they always go wrong. Don't ask such silly questions."

"Yes, but how can things *always* go well for the good and *always* ill for the wicked?" I urged.

"Because that is how children like it to be," answered Old Begga.

I felt that she was probably right. Naturally, it would not do for things to go ill for good people and well for the bad. But then there was another thing. A few days before this when my mother and Old Begga sat drinking their coffee, I had heard Old Begga expatiate on "God's judgment," "Our Lord's inscrutable dealings with men," and "the poor innocent child, Gudda," to whose sufferings death had at length "put an end"; while the "old sinner, Torgrim, the godless old devil," was now in his ninetieth year and had never been ill, and doubtless one day "he would pass away and scarcely notice it." The countless times Old Begga then had crossed herself, on top of these wrathful outpourings, and her earnest prayers for forgiveness because she had spoken thus "within the hearing of a child," had fixed her words in my mind. I had no doubt that Old Begga was right, that Gudda who had suffered and died was good, while Torgrim who still lived and prospered was a bad man. But how was I to reconcile Gudda's unmerited sufferings and Torgrim's offensively long life with the legitimate demands of a "story"? I had given some thought to the matter; and, as we were now on the subject, I took the opportunity of drawing Old Begga's attention to the delicate question.

No sooner had I mentioned the names of Gudda and Torgrim than Old Begga looked at me in a frightened way and began to have great difficulty with the stocking she was knitting. She stretched it lengthwise and crosswise, then counted the stitches, scratching her head meanwhile with the knitting needle that was free.

"Never think of such things, my little sparrow," she answered when at last she had time, beginning to knit so furiously that the needles rattled. "If things happened in real life as they do in stories, what would be the good of stories? . . . And besides, you must always remember that the whole thing evens itself out in the long run. . . . The good reach Heaven and are happy, the wicked are banished to the eternal fire where they get what they deserve."

"Then Torgrim will go to the eternal fire when at last he dies?" I asked excitedly.

"God help you and me and all of us!" exclaimed Old Begga, and her cheeks became rosy, which happened very seldom. "Don't for goodness' sake talk like that! . . . 'Judgment is Mine, saith the Lord.' "

"I only meant that it would be unkind to wish him to die soon," I explained, and could not understand her emotion.

"You are right, my angel!" said Old Begga, and patted my cheek with her wrinkled hand. "God speaks through the tongues of babes! God forgive me and guard my tongue! . . . Would you like to hear the story of Bukolla?"

Although the story of Bukolla was one I had been looking forward to for a long time, it was hard for me to listen attentively to the beginning. I lay there with the same dissatisfied feeling as when I had "drawn attention to myself" by an awkwardness or by ill-timed curiosity during an interesting conversation between grownups, and in this way had stopped the con-

versation or been sent away. I said to myself that I ought not
to have spoken, and that it would be my own fault if Old Begga
for the next few days guarded her tongue too carefully when
she and my mother drank coffee together.

It was not long, however, before the story of Bukolla made
me forget everything else and just listen. The hero was a boy
called Nonni, who had been very kind to Bukolla, a cow. He
received no reward for his kindness, for Bukolla had no possessions. "But if you get into danger, call my name," Bukolla
had said. Of course, Nonni got into danger, and not just an
everyday sort of danger either. He was pursued by giants.
When they were just about to catch him, he remembered
Bukolla, and shouted "Moo, dear Bukolla, so I may know
where you are!" Immediately Bukolla stood by his side and
said: "Pull out a hair from my tail and light it." Nonni hurried
to do as Bukolla told him, and the hair flamed up and became
a mighty blaze which the giants had to put out before they
could come any farther. In this way Nonni gained the advantage; but boys have short legs and giants long ones, and it was
not long before he was again in danger, and had to shout again:
"Moo, dear Bukolla, so I may know where you are!" This time
Bukolla's tail-hair became a river, which not only took time for
the giants to drink up but also gave them heavy stomachs, so
that again Nonni had the lead. . . . I was too well acquainted
with Old Begga's stories to be surprised when it appeared that
two leads were not enough, and that Bukolla had to offer still
another hair from her tail, which this time became a mountain.
(Possibly the mountain came before the river, but the order does
not matter.) The story ended by Nonni's receiving half a kingdom and a whole princess, and "they lived well and happily
ever after," as, of course, they should.

Most of Old Begga's stories were of the same kind, and I
listened to them with the same excitement over and over again,
with only a few weeks, sometimes only a few days, between
them.

The days of my illness brought other enjoyments besides Old Begga's adventures.

My cousins visited me almost every day. They stood beside the bed and wriggled their legs, and looked at me shyly out of the corners of their eyes. They always ran out again very quickly. Sigga's papa was also a daily visitor, and lent me papers and books with pictures in them; so was Madame Anna, who, together with my mother and Old Begga, kept my store of sweets very well supplied.

It may have been this supply of sweets which induced Bjössi, the shepherd boy, to look me up faithfully every morning before he set out for the distant grass meadows with his sheep—as to that I cannot say. Of course, I was too young to cherish so low a suspicion, and I was only too glad to divide my sweets with him. Even when I had only a few, he received the lion's share.

Bjössi was six years older than I, but in spite of the difference in age we were very good friends. We had various interests in common which could be carried on best by two: for example, the curse and the oath. In this special line of speech, Bjössi was a master whose equal it would be difficult to find, while I was a willing but not too highly gifted pupil. Bjössi gave me lessons in swearing, and went at it very systematically. First of all, he taught me the usual words one by one. Then he went on to teach me the art of "twining an oath." A "twined" oath has the advantage for a pupil that it is short, as it can be composed of two ideas only. Its art consists in finding stupendous comparisons—an art by no means easy. When Bjössi had given me a good supply of these twisters, we went on to the three-part oaths (that is, oaths consisting of three ideas). The importance of a three-part oath lies in its harmonious rhythm. It must glide along smoothly, melt on the tongue, as it were, and yet fall like a lash. The next stage was Bjössi's teaching me to "plait." A "plaited" oath is composed of certain kinds of words and ideas—a composition which must never be broken by anything unimportant, much less by anything so simple as breathing. Neither is one allowed to stop for a single moment to think,

and of course one must not repeat the same word. The greatest
height I reached after a six months' study of plaiting was the
following oath:

"Satan-in-Hell's-sulphur-stinking-pools-lowest-pit's-
cursed-depths."

I myself thought this was a very handsome oath, completely
interminable as it seemed to me, but Björssi shook his head dis-
couragingly. Such a strip seemed to him like a one-syllable
word. When all else failed, he tried to make me take trouble
by showing what an inferior person I really was. In this praise-
worthy effort he unselfishly plaited miles of very strong oaths
out of his broad, curiously wide, pathetically childish mouth.
He always found something new, and always went on until
there was no breath left in his body. Since he had no one else
to race with, he raced with himself. Finally, it seemed as if the
tremendous words took possession of him. His face swelled up,
became red and then blue. His eyes became bloodshot and
nearly jumped out of their sockets, but his mouth worked and
the words bubbled out like water out of a bunghole. Even after
his breath had left him at last he still went on, forming with his
blue lips silent words, the meaning of which I could only half
catch. It generally ended in my becoming frightened and shaking him to make him stop. But my tears and my entreaties only
made bad worse.

One day I shouted, sobbing: "You will die, Björssi! . . . You
will die!" But even that had no effect.

Afterward he said to me, with the brisk indifference with
which he always impressed me: "If I should die with an oath
in my throat, I should go straight to Hell! God Himself could
not help me, however much He wished to! But I don't care—
I'm not afraid of the Devil!"

I would have been more surprised to hear that the Devil was
not afraid of *him!*

We were not always equally good friends. Björssi was very
unkind about teasing me, and when he teased me I forgot the
difference in our ages and could see only how small he was.

I got some very bad scratches in this way, but Bjössi himself did not escape unhurt. Had I not nails and teeth? Did I not know how cats and dogs fight? If I was quick enough in my turnings I might now and again get him on the run by arming myself with a big enough stone. It was never very long, however, before he also had a stone in his hand, and then inevitably both stones left our fists. Happily, the God of fools protected us. Nearly all our battles ended by our helping each other to wipe away all traces of the skirmish. We both of us agreed to keep our differences to ourselves, through thick and thin. If we were unlucky enough to be questioned, we used the system of denying everything. Either we were only "playing" or else we somehow or other "had happened to hurt ourselves." Our feasts of reconciliation we also celebrated in secret. On the whole, we had an inborn distrust of allowing outsiders to interfere in our affairs.

It cannot be denied that the comfort that Bjössi brought to my bed of sickness was a peculiar one.

"Naah, you've got yourself a proper one, both behind and before," were his first words. "You will never be a man again, you can be quite certain! At any rate, you will have a broken snout all your life. But don't worry about that. With a mug like this one you can take your blows without showing them."

It did not occur to me to take Bjössi's honest words amiss. In my heart I thought he was right; it was undoubtedly an advantage to have a face that could stand this or that without giving itself away.

Another day Bjössi said: "Maria Mens has been crying all night, and is still crying. If she goes on much longer, a great deal may happen before evening. . . . If this is the last time we meet, good luck to you."

Maria was one of the farm servants and an older sister of Sigrid Mensadottir—Sigga Mens. But while Sigga Mens had been given her surname to distinguish her from my cousin Sigga, there was no real reason why her sister should have been known as anything but Maria. Nevertheless, she was almost always called Maria Mens.

These two sisters were astonishingly different. Not only was Maria dark, while Sigga had beautiful golden hair, but in temperament, at least from a superficial point of view, they were as different as day and night. It was very seldom that anyone saw Maria other than in tears, whereas it was scarcely possible to meet Sigga without finding her laughing and gay. If there was nothing to laugh at, she laughed all the same—and who knew why Maria cried? What was mysterious, yes, almost uncanny, was the queer feeling one had that it ought to be the opposite. Maria's continual weeping did not always seem justified, nor was one always made happier by Sigga's gaiety. Now and again I was astounded to see an almost cryptic smile on Maria's tear-sodden lips; and it sometimes happened that Sigga's laughter echoed coldly within me, darkening the day and making my heart lonely and sorrowful. When such glimpses of understanding came over me I wondered why people smiled so willingly with Sigga, and were so saddened by Maria's tears. Generally, however, I felt the same.

Björssi could not stand Maria Mens and her tears. There was no end to his scorn and suspicion. One day he was quite certain that she must have "done something." Another day he was sure that someone had "done her wrong"—which he thought was quite as it should be. A third day he told me that Maria only "cried her salt tears from longing for the salt sea" . . . a remark which, in exact opposition to his intention, awakened my sympathy and compassion. This sympathy was rather lessened when he went on to say that Maria Mens had concocted the dreadful plan of "crying the valley full" and drowning us all, which fact Björssi "had just happened" to discover. It was difficult for me to believe this. When Maria Mens managed to look out of her eyes she had not an unkind look, but Björssi reminded me that the surest sign of a witch is that she is crafty and beautiful; and in one thing I had to agree with

Bjössi—that Maria's tears were not the usual sort. So Bjössi managed to persuade me, and I asked him meekly whether he thought we could save ourselves by running up into the mountains when the waters began to rise in the valley.

"Yes, if we only knew the day and the hour beforehand," answered Bjössi, with that peculiarly disdainful superiority which marked his tone toward me. "But why do you think she is always crying? So that she can suddenly surprise us; anyone could tell you that. When it happens, it will happen all in a moment, and not many will escape alive."

"What will you do, dear Bjössi?" I asked with a last glint of hope.

"Drown like the rest of you," he answered indifferently, as became a hero.

"Then I will drown also," I whispered. But this remark only brought me a disdainful smile.

The secret fear I had of Sigga Mens was quite different from that which I had of Maria. My fear of Maria kept me away from her. My fear of Sigga drew me unresistingly toward her. Sigga Mens knew that I feared her, and it seemed as if she liked it. Apparently she also knew that my fear was not an unmixed feeling, but rather the opposite, for with it were blended admiration and curiosity as well as many other indefinable sensations. I do not know why it amused Sigga Mens to feed these feelings (for undoubtedly it did amuse her). This is how she did it. Whenever she saw her chance she filled me up with fantastic, carefully described horrors which now and again were of so gross a nature that I felt my blood run cold in my veins. These horrors she very seldom served up as actual stories. Generally, they appeared as a sort of commentary on the events of the day, my childish questions or her own thoughts. Finally, I went about with the fixed conviction that there was nothing in Heaven or earth or under the earth about which Sigga Mens did not know something that would make the roots of my hair tingle. Sigga Mens could, when she wished, make me feel dizzy. At times I had the sense of hovering, without foothold, in mid-air. It was not really pleasant, but it was exciting and instructive and not to be missed. Unfortunately, I was generally obliged to promise not to repeat what she "confided" to me. Some of it she made me solemnly swear that I would never repeat. Even now I feel that my tongue might wither away if I broke any of these childish oaths.

In spite of her bad temper, Sigga Mens did not fail me in my illness. When she reckoned that I should be alone in the loft she stole up to me. These little excursions from the kitchen probably resulted in still more burned porridge and over-boiled coffee.

Sigga Mens did not come up to bring me sweets. The only thing she brought was the extraordinary wormwood of her mind. Nevertheless, her visits were quite as welcome as anyone's.

The very first time she came she almost surpassed herself.

First I thought she was going to kiss me, for she leaned over and brought her face close up to mine. It was, however, not my mouth but my ear she sought.

"If Skjoni had killed you outright, do you know what I would have done so that you should not lie alone in your black coffin?" she whispered—and her hot, queer breath in my ear tickled me right down to the soles of my feet. "I should have brought a nasty, clammy, hairy spider down to you."

My fear blazed up into a shriek—and her delight into shrill laughter.

"What harm could that have done you?" she asked, and devoured me with her eyes just as I had at times seen Nonni devour Maria. "Is a spider worse than worms? Haven't I shown you the carcass of a bird that was full of worms? That's what death is like, duckie. But do you know what I once saw? . . . I saw an old man who lay in his bed and was *swimming* with worms—I suppose they thought he was dead, the little devils! The sheets, the pillow, the floor by the bed—all were covered with a gray crawling mass. No one dared to come near him. And so he died."

"I expect he was well washed before they laid him in his coffin?" I asked, sick with disgust.

"Who would do that?" laughed Sigga Mens, and began to twirl toward the door. The sun sparkled in her golden hair, her blue eyes had a strange radiance . . . lovely she looked. "Would *you* have done it?" she added. And she twirled out the door as if spun round by a whirlwind.

Another time I told her about my foal.

"A pretty sight that will be!" she shrilled mockingly. "A red-haired boy on a red-haired horse. . . . Oh, I shall die! Why don't you have a red-haired dog, too?"

I told her that I intended to buy a lead comb to part my hair with, for Bjarni the blacksmith had told me that if I did so my hair would become black. Sigga Mens did not listen to me. She had already begun to twirl.

"I should never have believed that your father would make such a fool of you, you poor little devil!" she smiled, and vanished.

When I told her about Madame Anna's brother and possibly was clumsy enough to express the fear that the same thing would happen to me, she got an attack of laughter.

"Why, then you will be able to be a weather prophet!" she groaned, choking. "We shall cut the seat out of your trousers so the air can get in! Then when you get a long beard you will be a sight worth seeing."

The good days in the loft came to an end all too quickly. The sweets and the soups were no longer part of my daily fare. The scabs peeled off my scars and ceased to be profitable. I was not even allowed to keep my prize-fighter's mug. When my mother showed me my face in the looking-glass, I looked practically as before Skjoni did me the service of kicking me from behind—and reaped the world's reward.

On my first days up I wandered homeless around. There was no Old Begga and her stories, Sigga Mens I scarcely saw, my mother was busy, my cousins had not forgiven all the sweets

I had received. Veiga was more impossible than ever and Vigi seemed to have forgotten me—only sniffed at me casually, openly despised me and had ceased to play with children.

During the first few days I hung round my mother wherever she went or stood, stuck my little paw into her warm hand whenever it was free, begged for a piece of sugar or a slice of bannock between meals and was always restless. In spite of her patience and kindness I felt I was neglected.

The end came when one day I threw my arms round her neck, looked into her eyes and said with tears in my voice: "It *was* very bad, wasn't it, Mama?"

"Yes . . . but it is all over now, little Uggi!" she answered smiling, and after giving me a kiss she went on with her work.

It was certainly over. . . . I realized this and began by degrees to grow accustomed to it.

I knew where I could find Old Begga; but as she was generally Weekday-Begga now, stories and foolishness were the last thing she had time for.

"Oh, you little scrap!" she sighed, and was Weekday-Begga through and through (Sunday-Begga scarcely ever sighed except over the sins of mankind and the godlessness of humanity). "You don't know how lucky you are!"

Weekday-Begga was a sooty bundle that went from fireplace to fireplace, raking the glowing coals with long tongs, breaking dried sheep-manure on the hearthstones, pushing it in under the black-bellied pots, lifting kettles off the cranes, putting kettles on, removing a wooden lid, stirring with a pot-stick, sniffing at the steam, fishing a piece of meat up to the edge with a long fork, cutting off a morsel carefully (so as not to burn herself) with a half-blunt knife, putting it into her mouth, sucking in air until the scalding morsel was cool enough to be chewed, munching it dissatisfied . . . and she had no time at all to look after her dripping nose or pay attention to childish chatter.

"Dearie me . . . childhood days!" she sighed when, for the second time, I whispered something about an adventure story. "Those who live long enough pay a heavy price for *that* adventure! . . . If any of us were to suspect in our early years what awaits us of sorrow and trouble and toil and cursed kitchen smoke! . . . But no, none of us foresees his fate, let alone his last day. . . . How wisely it has been planned!"

When Old Begga talked at all, even to herself, it was a good sign and invited patience. (She was often so cross and silent that it was best to keep out of her way; but on her silent days the smoke was generally so thick that it was impossible to see a hand held out in front of one, while from the doorway the glow of the fire could be glimpsed but faintly.) At last my patience would be rewarded, although indifferently; for when the story came it was in bits and pieces, and even, perhaps, had no end. Bjössi, one of my most important and most willing sources of information, had told me once that if an earthworm is cut up and the bits left lying about they will find each other and grow together again. That was not always the case with Old Begga's kitchen stories. Cut them up she certainly did—just as easily as an earthworm is cut into pieces—but very seldom did the pieces find each other. However, it sometimes happened that she produced a short tale without a break.

"Well, so you want a story, goldilocks?" said Old Begga . . . she seemed just now to hear what I had said half an hour ago! "Then my stories are still good enough for you, my little lamb? I thought you complained the other day that they did not tally with reality. . . . That does not matter? . . . Well, then it does not matter. There's time enough for you to experience your adventures . . . time enough!"

Before she began the story she looked at every single fireplace, lifted all the lids, filled up the kettles, blew her nose into the fire with two fingers, and then sat gazing into the fire as if she had forgotten both me and the kettles.

I dared not, as I valued my life, remind her of her promise. Weekday-Begga must be treated carefully. With each minute that passed it grew more and more silent in the kitchen. The light rattling of the kettle-lid became a loud clatter, the fire gabbled nonsense and the pots shouted—the first with a thin exultant sound, the second fat and ill-natured as if suffocated in its own porridge, the third mildly conciliatory: "Steady-there-steady-there."

At last Old Begga began:

"This time you shall have a story in which things happen as they happen in the world. One morning at six o'clock a boy crawled up onto the roof of a farm and sat down to wait for the wishing-moment. I do not know his name, but that does not matter. He held his cap in both hands and was in good spirits, for he hoped that before six o'clock the next morning he would be rich. And in order to do all in his power to attain his object, he sang at the top of his voice, and without the slightest pause between the repetitions: 'My cap full of gold! My cap full of gold!' . . . There is only one wishing-moment in each twenty-four hours, and as it only lasts the blink of an eyelid it is important to pay attention.

"Now the boy thought that if only he could hold out long enough the wishing-moment could not possibly evade him, so there he sat the whole day; he sat there the whole night, and still he sang the same words: 'My cap full of gold! My cap full of gold!' . . . Just before six o'clock the next morning the farmer came out of the house and, as he was tired of hearing this fruit-less and endless repetition, he shouted crossly to the boy: 'Your cap full of horse-dung!' The boy was disconcerted for a moment and stopped—but now there was something in his cap! . . . He looked, and behold! the farmer had found the wishing-moment!"

"Was the boy's cap full of horse-dung then?" I asked doubt-fully.

"Of course!" answered Old Begga, grumpily. "Don't you understand what you are told? . . . Are you such a little fool?"

"I expect he tried again another day?" I asked, hoping that the story was not finished.

"Perhaps he tried again another day!" answered Old Begga, morosely, and heaved the kettle off the fire. "How do I know? Only one thing I know: if there were two wishing-moments in every twenty-four hours it would be useless! You go and find out whether anyone has ever become rich by waiting for the wishing-moment . . . since you believe others more than me. Perhaps then you will feel convinced, you little pillar of wisdom!"

I had been given something to think about. When I left Old Begga I was determined to find the wishing-moment sometime. I could not understand grownups. Why did they not sit on the roofs of the farm, one on each house, instead of working the whole summer day, coming home in the evening tired out? But grownups were so stupid. . . . I had known that for a long time. Probably they did not even believe in the wishing-moment! When I became a farmer and owned a farm I would show them how stupidly they were behaving! I sat in my corner and continued to speculate on how best to utilize the wishing-moment, and what I could do to make sure that no one would shout "horse-dung!" I forgot entirely to build up my farm, which, as usual, lay in ruins. . . .

Red (after much thought I had named my foal "Red" because of that unfortunate color common to us both) refused to have anything whatever to do with me. He would not in any way recognize my undisputed ownership, but set off at top speed and kicked backward whenever I approached him. I made long admonitory speeches to him from a distance, but what was the good of that? Finally I complained to my father, but he only answered unfeelingly:

"You will become friends as you both grow older. It's better not to finger a foal!"

I failed to understand why we could not be friends with each other immediately, or what harm it would do if I "fingered" him a little. It would be so splendid for him to graze in my special corner of land while I played. We could be so cosy together if only he would show a little sense! . . . However, he must not suffer for his folly. He was only an animal and therefore lacking in wisdom. . . . When I, therefore, came on Bjarni the smith just about to light up his furnace, I generously ordered four shoes for Red.

"Well, I never—four shoes!" answered Bjarni the smith, attending to the bellows with one hand and raking the coal and slag together with the other. "Cannot Red really manage with less?"

"No, because he has four legs," I explained.

"Four legs?" Bjarni repeated thoughtfully, and hammered away at the glowing end of his iron bar, so that the sparks filled the little smithy. "Four legs? . . . That's right. That cannot be denied. . . . If he had either one more or one less, what use would it be to him? Perhaps the skin could be used, although I'm blessed if I know! No one would get *me* to put a pair of shoes made from the skin of a deformed animal on *my* honorable feet! . . . Ah, yes, four legs are what an animal must have. That's the rule. I am not speaking now of feathered creatures. I am not speaking of fishes or centipedes. I am not speaking of monsters or miraculous creatures. I am speaking of *animals*. We humans, you see, have two legs, and what should we do with more? Why a cock should have more than one, that you must ask someone wiser than I. But we were speaking of horses. Now, that particular animal has four legs. That's the rule for horses. . . . But then there is another point. If your Red has four legs, does it necessarily follow that he needs four shoes? Now then, can you crack that nut?"

"No," I answered honestly, eager to learn how Bjarni would explain anything so absurd.

"Well, well . . . dull old eyes see farther than sharp young ones . . . put that in your pipe and smoke it!" growled Bjarni, dropping the finished horseshoe into water that closed over it with an angry hiss. He then gripped the iron bar and went back to the anvil and bellows. "What do you know when it comes to the point? Nothing. What do I? Everything. But at your age I also was stupid and believed that a colt needed four shoes! . . . Oh God . . . one becomes wiser with the years! . . . Certainly. . . . But very few ever become so wise and clever that they can make horseshoes. Yet most people, when they reach years of discretion, learn to calculate for themselves how many shoes are needed for a horse, and how many for a colt."

"How many ought there to be then, Bjarni dear?" I asked humbly.

"How many ought there to be?" repeated Bjarni, looking at me thoughtfully out of the corner of his eye. "That depends, now; yes, indeed, that depends."

"I mean, how many must I have?" I asked patiently.

Bjarni the smith opened his eyes wide, pulled his long, bulging face up, pulled it down until it looked like the face of a horse, and then burst forth aghast: "*You* have? But are *you* then a horse? . . . Are *you* going to have horseshoes?"

"You know well enough that it is for *Red* I want them!" I answered in a hurt voice.

"Well, I never—for Red? Well, well," said Bjarni, seriously. "Those discarded by the late lamented Skjoni would hardly fit him, I suppose . . . no, they would hardly fit. For Red, you say? You want to know how many shoes to get for Red?"

"Yes," I sighed despairingly.

"That I will tell you," announced Bjarni, and considered the problem carefully. "For Red you should use . . . now, let me see . . . just as many horseshoes as you have in your possession! That's the rule. That's what it amounts to."

"But I have none, dear Bjarni!" I informed him with forced patience.

"None? So you actually have none? Well, well," answered Bjarni, scratching his head. "But that is just the number you must use, isn't it?"

"What do you mean?" I gasped, not understanding. "*How* many ought I to use? Tell me that, now."

"None," Bjarni snapped out, hammering at random like a madman. "None! Why, it couldn't be cheaper. . . . That's the rule."

I stood there crushed, gaping at Bjarni. I was quite at sea. He had confused me to such an extent that I felt dizzy. I had not even sense enough to shut my eyes against the flying sparks; and the deafening blows of the hammer fell full on my defenseless ears. Not until the glowing iron spluttered again in the water did I turn my head, but my eyes were so blinded with tears that I could scarcely see the bucket. Bjarni's answering me like this, without giving a proper explanation, must mean that he no longer liked me. And yet we had always been good friends. How had I managed to offend Bjarni? Where could I now get shoes for Red?

Suddenly I felt Bjarni's heavy, reassuring hand on my head. "What's the matter now?" he asked, blinking comically and encouragingly at me and clicking his tongue. "Are you going to cry? Is old Bjarni such a bad man that he makes children cry? . . . Shall we hit him on the head with the sledge hammer and see if sparks fly off him? No? . . . Well, then, we shall leave him alone! . . . You said something about shoes for Red? . . . You shall have four, one for each foot. . . . For I don't suppose he needs double-shoeing?"

"Double-shoeing?" I asked. "What is that, dear Bjarni?"

"Well, if you knew *that* . . . you would be wiser than I am!" answered Bjarni, solemnly. "Personally, I have never heard of it. Well, well, we shall let that pass. Four shoes you shall have, with four holes in each. The usual rule is eight, but there will not be room enough for that. If you would be content with the holes alone I could let you have them at half price . . . but I suppose that would never do? . . . Well, well . . . That I might almost have guessed for myself. I am not quite such a stupid! . . . Do you see this bit of bar-iron here? Would you like to feel it? It is not handsome, it is red and rusty and has been thrown here as unusable . . . shall we see what the fire and Bjarni can make of it? Shall we?"

I was more than willing.

"The fire and Bjarni, look you!" went on Bjarni. "Two odd companions, don't you think? What one cannot do, the other can; that is the reason they are such good friends. Can I make iron glow by putting it into this mouth of mine? No! Am I, therefore, less skillful than the fire? . . . No! Can the fire hammer a horseshoe, shape it into a hoof and hammer it fast? . . . No! Is it, therefore, less skillful than I am? . . . No! I can hold the fire in check, light it when it suits me, put it out when it suits me; am I, therefore, the fire's master? . . . No! The fire can be too strong for me, burn me to ashes. Is it, therefore, my overlord? No! . . . That is what the fire is like, that is what Bjarni is like. Unless they agree, there will be, for example, *no horseshoes!* . . . And how would you get on then, you and Red?"

During this long speech the fire had several times heated the iron to a white heat, and as many times had Bjarni hammered it black. It was strange watching how, like a soft dough, it was shaped by the hammer and the anvil so long as it glowed red-hot—and even more curious to see how the hammer and anvil gave up as soon as the iron blackened and became hard again. I must confess that I was a little sorry for the iron; first the fire burned all the obstinacy out of it, then Bjarni grasped it with a pair of tongs and forced it to conform and obey. And yet I was not quite sure about my sympathy, for, though this may sound incredible, it seemed almost as if the iron were smiling and enjoying it. True, it doubtless grumbled while it was being hammered and pounded, but a newly beaten horseshoe looked much more satisfied than a piece of bar-iron! It had almost the appearance of having just got out of bed and washed itself! And Bjarni would not deal so high-handedly with the iron if he did not know that he was doing it a service.

When at last I stood there with four small horseshoes in my hand I burst into laughter in which were mingled both sobs and tears. The shoes were so incredibly small and sweet that I could scarcely believe they were real. I felt as if I were living a fairy tale instead of being told one. . . . I was overcome with emotion, my heart danced in my breast and I felt quite giddy as I pulled at Bjarni's arms, got his head down and kissed him fervently on his hard lips.

"Thank you, dear Bjarni!" I whispered. "Thank you, thank you, thank you!"

"Well, well. Thanks is something generally given in addition to payment," Bjarni informed me sedately.

"I will be sure to pay you," I promised confidently. . . . "Do you know the story of the boy and the wishing-moment?"

"Yes, thank you!" answered Bjarni, seriously. "Do you intend to pay me with horse-dung?"

"No, with gold, dear Bjarni!" I informed him, feeling aggrieved.

"Say rather with hoped-for gold," Bjarni advised me thoughtfully. "Then you will not promise more than you can fulfil."

"Hoped-for gold—what is that?" I asked doubtfully. "Is it better than other gold?"

"Both better and worse," answered Bjarni, craftily. "That is the peculiar thing about hoped-for gold. But you must not pay for those shoes at all, for they have one fault. . . ."

"A *fault?*" I repeated incredulously, and looked at them with pleasure . . . in my eyes they were more than perfect.

"They have the fault," Bjarni informed me impressively, "that you will not get a single living person—not even me—to shoe Red with them."

"Why not?" I asked, puzzled.

"Simply because one does not shoe a colt," laughed Bjarni, suddenly gay. "Not even if God Himself demanded it . . . yes, I must be careful . . . but I would hesitate even then."

"Why did you make those shoes then?" I asked, both disappointed and relieved.

"To please you, I suppose!" smiled Bjarni. "Can one shoe a colt? A colt's hoof is as soft as a child's nail—if it is scratched, it bleeds. No, for a horse, four shoes; for a colt, none. . . . That's the rule! But now you have the shoes and can show them to Red!"

I thought that excellent advice. We could play with them together—Red and I.

3

BESIDES the two south windows—the windows giving onto the courtyard—the loft had one window in the turf roof facing east.

When it was summer and clear weather the sun began to glint in through this window very early. If I woke I could see it standing there shining to itself, wonderfully quiet. What amazed me more than anything else was that the sunbeams followed a direction they never took during the day. I thought to myself that the sun was bored because no one else was up, and that it therefore took the opportunity of looking round the room a little—examining the pictures on my mother's chest of drawers between the two south windows and admiring our pretty washstand. I lay very still so as not to disturb it . . . then I slept again.

Not until the sun shone straight through the east window, right across my mother's and Veiga's bed and also on my father's and mine, did I wake in earnest. And if I was the first to wake, I used to sit up at the end of the bed and begin the day.

I was almost always the first awake in the loft, and for this the fact that I fell asleep so early in the evening was to blame.

Every evening sleep claimed me for his own. There existed nothing on earth, and scarcely anything in Heaven, there was not a human being or a story known, that could keep me awake after six o'clock. Whether I was dressed or undressed, hungry or replete, sorrowful or glad, at six o'clock I slept! The sleep which attacked me then did not come slowly and gently, as sleep generally does, and was not heralded by either drowsiness or weariness. It simply took possession of me and carried me away without so much as a moment's warning. If it found me absorbed in a game, it cut the game short. If it found me sitting on a stool, it rolled me quite calmly off it and left me lying on

58

the floor. If it found me with food in my mouth, it never gave me time to swallow it. If it found me in the middle of a laugh, I was never allowed to finish that laugh.

This sleep which took possession of me so summarily was not one that I could go in and out of, as through a door. It was a sleep which had become a tradition, a sleep which had even originated a saying. If anyone at Ofeigsstadur found himself up against what seemed an impossibility, he would say: "No, I would just as soon try to wake Uggi between the hours of six and twelve."

"It is because you are descended from Egill Skallagrimsson," Old Begga—Sunday-Begga—informed me. "Egill's grandfather was called Ulfur and was nicknamed 'Evening Ulfur' because it was useless trying to get anything out of him in the evening. And I can tell you that when he was a child he used to be just like you. In that family there were always the most beautiful women and the ugliest men. That does not apply to the men in your father's family. But look at your mother's father—Ketilbjörn-of-Knör! . . . Both the families, they say, date back to that good-for-nothing Borg rabble."

"Borg rabble?" I asked inquisitively. I gathered that Old Begga had a grievance against these people, but that "rabble" was a disparaging epithet was not quite clear to me at once.

"Yes . . . I call them a rabble," answered Old Begga, hesitating a little. "Heathen dogs they were, anyhow, Egill and his race—that at any rate I am sure of. But they were also ungodly in other ways. The slightest disagreement led to murder; they hid their gold in the bogs, or buried it somewhere so that no one should benefit from it. And they knew nothing of Our Lord, although He had, at that time, been born for over nine hundred years."

Old Begga stopped abruptly. She sat there rocking herself backward and forward from sheer annoyance.

"Tell me a little more about the Borg rabble, dear Begga," I implored.

"On a Holy Day!" shouted Old Begga. "Pray God in Heaven

to forgive you! . . . Besides, you are far too small to understand such things. I suppose you would only want to do the same yourself. One thing, though, you shall know: these ancestors of yours were terrible bandits, hot-tempered and wilful, selfish and cruel, whom you must never wish to resemble. The heritage will be heavy enough in any case. When Egill was only seven he murdered a man. And do you think he was satisfied with that? Murderers and robbers—that is what those people were! That is the sort of blood you have in your veins! . . . Since, of course, there have been good people in the family—that is true. But one must pay attention to each drop of blood—or it may lead to evil. But perhaps you want to be a murderer?"

I disclaimed with disgust any desire in this direction, and then I asked Old Begga why the Borg rabble were worse than others.

"I would not exactly call them worse," she answered, after some thought. "They were loyal friends to their friends, and now and again they displayed human feelings toward their own kinsmen, although far from always. Once Egill's father would have killed him, if a girl on the farm had not thrown herself between them . . . and then he chased her into the lake! And if they behaved like this to their own children, is it likely they would love their enemies? Do you think they would hesitate for a single moment to kill a man if they were angry with him? Do you think they would turn the other cheek, as the Scriptures tell us? I have often thought that if my Jon Vidalin had lived then all would have been different."

"Wasn't he alive then?" I asked.

"Bless you, those were heathen times!" Old Begga corrected me, exasperated. "Those people did not know their Saviour . . . of course, one should always remember that."

"Would Jon Vidalin have known his Saviour?" I asked perseveringly.

"If you knew what you were saying it would be pure blasphemy!" Old Begga corrected me sternly. "What a question to ask! Do you wish to be wiser than older folk?"

"Oh, no, dear Begga, certainly not," I piously assured her.

"Well, then, hold your tongue," she counseled me mild-ly. . . . "Did I tell you that Egill was a great poet? Some say that he is Iceland's greatest, but I think more of Eystein and his *Lilja,* and of Hallgrimm Pjetursson. . . . Once Egill was about to be put to death, but during the night he composed a poem which saved his head. He was in England at the time and it was Erik Bloody-Axe who pardoned him. He had a job to finish the poem in time. One of his friends had to keep watch beside him, for there was a bird sitting on his windowsill all the time and trying to disturb him. . . . That bird was none other than Gunhild, the Queen Mother of Inglehamm—the ugly old witch!"

The whole picture rose before me. But I saw most clearly a bloody axe . . . a little bird with human eyes . . . a large, sol-emn head. My heart beat violently and I turned away to hide from Old Begga the tears in my eyes. For some time I was not in a condition to ask any more questions.

Old Begga too was silent for a while. Then she added, darkly triumphant: "Whether Egill has been able to deliver his soul out of Hell with his poems—well, *that* we do not know."

"Do you think I might become a poet one day, Begga?" I asked shyly.

"No one can *become* a poet; that is something one is either born or not born," answered Old Begga, importantly. "And, moreover, it is a heavy burden. Let me look at your tongue. A long tongue is the first condition. . . . Put it out farther . . . is *that* all you can do? Out with it . . . farther, farther. Try to reach your nose with the tip. No, Goldilocks, you will never be a poet . . . or in any case only a poor one. But be thankful for that. All poets are unfortunate; they are no good for any-thing. The girls won't look at them and then they take to the bottle, die early, and leave nothing behind them but ele-gies. . . . In olden times they sang of their own and others' heroic deeds; now they sing only of sorrows and disappointments. The one who is the most unhappy is considered the best."

"Had Egill a very long tongue?" I asked. Nothing else interested me at all.

"Egill?" repeated Old Begga, looking seriously at me. "For poems such as his the words must be fetched from far away and then thrown together ingeniously. To write poems is like weaving a beautiful pattern; so you can see for yourself how long and supple the tongue must be. For that matter, I know nothing about Egill Skallagrimsson's tongue, but I know something about his face. When he was not very pleased about anything he could make one eyebrow shoot right up into his hair, and the other hang down almost in a line with the tip of his nose. What sort of tongue do you *think* could have belonged to such a face! It would not surprise me to hear that he could lick the corners of his eyes."

"Can't one make one's tongue longer by stretching it a little every day?" I asked, discouraged.

"Where there's a will there's a way," answered Old Begga, soothingly, "but as for you, I should not advise you to imperil your head if you hope to save it by a poem."

Before I left her on this occasion Old Begga had taught me a new morning prayer (evening prayers were wasted on me); and she adjured me to be on my guard against taking after my heathen forebears more than I could help.

"Remember," she finished, putting the hand in which she held a piece of candy behind her back, so that it might not distract me: "Get it well into your mind that Jesus Christ is the Spotless Lamb, and the Devil a sly fox!"

When I had absorbed this sufficiently I was given the candy, and went away to my farm to speculate further on my newly acquired knowledge. . . .

The morning hours, whether the day was sunny or a gray, quiet one, were delicious times. I had been told that I must not make a noise, or wake the others; but the injunction was quite unnecessary, for I had not the slightest inclination to do either. There was enough to look at, and it was good to have time to look at everything undisturbed.

The objects of my attention varied, and my mood was often in tune with the morning. These objects were almost innumerable. . . . There was the wainscoting with its knots, its grain and its marks. There was my father with his curling beard, ring on finger, a network of wrinkles all over his face, on the palms of his hands and on his knuckles, and with a chest which, when he slept, rose and fell like a pair of bellows. There were the whole and the worn-out pillow slips. There were my father's braces, when he had hung his trousers over the end of the bed. There was the ceiling covered with faces and odd beasts. There were my mother and Veiga in the bed exactly opposite ours, and Beta in her cradle.

There were the flies, the small and nimble ones as well as those whose wings must never be pulled off. There was the chest of drawers with its keyholes, each with its own particular expression, that winked and leered at me. There were the chairs, one standing empty, looking injured, in a place where it did not belong; another with my mother's clothes folded neatly over one arm and reminding me, without rhyme or reason, of my cousin Greta; a third peeping at me with one eye, and patiently sagging under the burden of my father's coat. There were the photographs and the knickknacks on the chest of drawers; there were my own clothes, looking as if they were either just going to begin a game or had stopped in the middle of one, and seeming to hold various forgotten parts of my body—half an arm, a leg, or various other round bits of me.

There were the misty windowpanes down which small drops made their devious ways in sudden bounds. There were the clear panes through which could be seen the grass outside, thickly powdered over with tiny, sparkling, silver-white drops of dew which became many-colored in the rays of the rising sun when it reached them. There was the same grass when it was dry and moved a little in the wind, or when a strong gale bowed it down toward one side. There were the blue sky, the clouded sky and the gray lack of sky—the dreamy and the lashing rain—the singing wind and the growling storm.

There were our shoes that stood in pairs on the floor and waited for our feet: decrepit or eager, tired and downtrodden with toil or erect and pugnacious with toecaps still undamaged. There were the buttons and folds, holes and patches, colors and patterns, worn parts and new parts, of the many bits of clothing. There was the washstand with the big washbasin where blue swans swam over blue water, blue butterflies flew over blue grass, blue people stood on a blue bridge over a blue stream, blue birds sailed over blue woods, and blue bees flew backward and forward between the blue scenes. Finally there were the pictures on the walls, the frames round the pictures, the nails they hung on and many other things. . . .

And then there were also the picture books given to me by Sigga's papa. These picture books I used to hide early in the afternoon under my pillow so as to have them when I woke up; and more and more often in the mornings I would sit and gaze as if hypnotized, not just at the pictures, which I knew well, but at the writing beneath and at the side of these pictures. I realized more and more that the best way to get at stories was to read them to myself rather than to rely on having them told; and, further, that in books there were stories to be found which neither Old Begga nor anyone else would tell me because I was still "too small." I could doubtless steal a chance to read them—if only I *could* read!

One day as I stood talking to Old Begga I suddenly let slip that I wanted to learn to read. Unfortunately, it was Weekday-Begga with whom I was talking, and she answered me shortly: "*You* learn to read! . . . You'd better learn to button your own trousers first, you rascal!"

These words offended me to such a degree that they suddenly transformed my long-cherished thought from a beautiful dream to stern action.

I had always imagined that the greatest difficulty with reading would be that most of the letters were so small and were printed so close together. Therefore I did not begin with a book but begged for a number of the weekly paper *Isafold* and started with the title. When I had managed the title I set to work with the headings. It was a long time before I reached the text itself.

I acquired my knowledge by the tiresome method of going round with the journal in my hand and asking anyone I met what this or that letter was called. Then I followed this letter through the whole paper and as soon as I considered myself sure enough I shut my eyes, opened them again and pounced upon the letter in question like a hawk upon a ptarmigan. This hunt for letters was very exciting and, furthermore, not particularly troublesome. It became worse when, after having collected a supply of letters, I began to tackle the actual words. I would choose a word consisting only of letters I knew, and yet it would be almost impossible to discover what the word was. For it appeared that the letters were able craftily to disguise themselves: their sounds in a word might be quite different from those they made standing alone. Most words were, therefore, very difficult riddles and it was only a few of them that I solved without help, even when I knew all the letters by name.

The greatest difficulty of all lay neither in the letters nor the words but in my surroundings. My mother, my father, Nonni, Sigga's papa (whom I seldom dared approach) were the only ones around who answered me properly, and, of these four, only my mother was always near, now that the summer had come. And she was generally busy.

It was no use asking Old Begga.

"To be sure Adam and Eve ate of the tree of good and evil, but can *you* distinguish a good book from a bad?" she asked me angrily. "There you are running about with a sinful paper both on weekdays and Sundays! Do you think *that* will lead to any good? . . . I can tell you of a boy who began to read in the cradle; now he is sitting in a wooden cage and does not even recognize his father and mother! . . . No, if you want to be like

other people you will learn your alphabet in a couple of years'
time, and for that you will use an ABC."

And Old Begga did not leave it at good advice alone. So far
as she could, she saw to it that I was never alone with Nonni and
the paper, and she had strictly forbidden Nonni to answer me if
I should ask him anything. We had, therefore, to be very
careful, Nonni and I.

My cousins, and especially Cousin Greta, helped me a great
deal. But hers was expensive tuition. A letter might easily cost
a sheep—a word, a cow or a horse or a particularly attractive
stone from my farmyard. My fortune dwindled away without
my becoming very much wiser in return.

Bjössi, whom, of course, I had also asked for help, scorned and
mocked me when he heard that I wanted to learn to read, called
me a bookworm, spat after me, and advised a course in oaths.
Maria Mens was willing enough, but was generally quite unable
to see the letters for tears (or, as she said, "dew in her eyes").
Sigga Mens confused me by giving quite innocent letters rare
and awe-inspiring names. And Bjarni the blacksmith showed
himself to be almost as ignorant in the art of reading as I was
myself.

"I have never had much use for this Latin lettering," he confided to me with a thoughtful look, scratching his neck. "That
learned folk and such-like should go in for it I have nothing
against. But I, who have spent three years of my life learning
black lettering, have had enough of letters to last a lifetime,
that I can assure you! And then there is horn-spoon lettering;
yes, that I also had to learn, seeing that I make horn spoons.
But can one keep everything in one's head? One day you will
learn that that is impossible—wait until you have to learn your
catechism on your five fingers! In your place I should think
twice before I took a book into my hands unless I were forced
to. But I expect it is the clerical blood in you; you take after
the wrong side. . . . Well, let's look at it."

He spread the paper out on the anvil, carefully, as if it were
made of glass. The bulges and knots stood out in his fore-

head and his fingers made a rough sound as they moved over the page.

"There is a capital *B* for you, and there is a capital *A;* I know *them*. Do you know what they say when they are put together? Bjarni Andresson, they say—that is my name: Bjarni Andresson. An *S* and a *U* I recognize also. They are a pair of well-behaved letters which never put on airs because they are growing up! And *S* and *U* stand for Sigbergur Uggason; I know that from the branding irons. Shall we look at the branding irons for a moment? Here they are."

We looked at the branding irons. Bjarni the smith seemed to know them by surer marks than just the letters.

"Those over there are your father's," he continued. "*G* and *U*—Greipur Uggason. When you have some of your own one of these days it will only mean putting the *U* in front of the *G;* so much I can reckon out. But now look at this. On this long end of rope I have to put the whole of 'Ofeigsstadur,' all in one. The name begins with *O;* what all the other little oddities are called—well, ask someone else. Not because I do not know—I am both confirmed and married and can write my name. But when it is a question of Roman lettering, I have to stop a moment and think, and I have not the time for that, you see. With all I have to arrange it is better to spare one's head a bit, and therefore I prefer to go in now and take my little afternoon snooze. Thinking and Roman lettering—those are things that require learning or else they give a man the headache. I have always held with black lettering; it suits the eyes better. But lawgivers and children are all alike: anything new is always the best! I cannot understand why the King agreed to it. What will he get out of it? . . . Now do you remember all I have taught you—*B* and *A* and *S* and *U* and *G* and *U* and—what was its name now?—*O*? What were they like— can you show them to me? . . . Right, right. If that is wrong you can summon me before the magistrate and have me fined! Do you believe me? That's right! . . . Besides, you yourself have seen the branding irons."

The summer passed . . .

At its close I had used several copies of *Isafold,* but if the lines had been roads and myself a traveler I should not have got very far, as I moved slowly, like a lame person, or someone with a wooden leg and as good as blind. I "read," to be sure, but my reading consisted principally in knowing the letters, both the capitals and the small ones, and in finding my way through most of the words I met but generally without grasping more than a fraction of the sense they made.

The bright mornings had gone the same way as the summer. When I woke now in my warm nook between my father and the wall, it was not to sun and daylight but to one of two other well-tried friends: darkness and moonlight.

To wake up in the dark and lie alone and undisturbed was as good as listening to a story, and far easier than reading one out of a book. Staring into the darkness I could see the most wonderful pictures, yes, I could see almost anything I liked, and not only make up stories but see them happening in front of my eyes. In the darkness the improbable became probable, the impossible possible—by doing away with the visible the darkness seemed to do away with all limitations.

So I was very fond of the dark. And I was no less fond of the moonlight, in whose pale radiance things looked almost as they did in dreams.

One calm moonlit morning I woke to find something that I instantly recognized—the frost had drawn his gay patterns all over our windowpanes. But why did not the moonbeams melt the ice? . . . Another day the panes were covered with thick hoarfrost that reminded me of plush. The glass could be seen only here and there where the frost was not so thick between the panes and the window frame.

By degrees it became cold up in the loft, cold in all the houses.

The cold, which made romping games a necessity, kept us children together more. When the weather and the state of the ground allowed it, we tobogganed and had snow fights. We made snow men and built snow houses and agreed that we far preferred the winter to the summer. When the weather was bad, or when the frost bit, we had to stay indoors. We found an empty stall in the warm cowshed where we played "grown-ups" or told each other stories; or we collected round the open fireplaces, baked bread from flour we had begged, fried bits of fish-skin and spat into the fire; or we stayed in the living room where, if we had not been able to get Old Begga to tell us a story, we played hide and seek, blind man's bluff and many other games.

Everything was different in winter from the way it was in summer. Old Begga sat all the time in the living room spinning fine yarn, the youngest servant girls having been put to do the kitchen work. Bjarni Smith was scarcely a smith any longer, but had turned weaver and sat pounding his loom in a workshop beneath the living room. And Old Begga was only one of many in the living room, where the whole day through they carded, spun, knitted, wound spools, plaited ropes and twined saddle-girths; and Bjarni was only one of many in the weaving-room, where the farm's four dogs each laid claim to a corner, while the puppies sprawled all over the floor. Happily, from Bjarni's seat he could reach the door when he had to shut or open it for one of his many companions, which happened pretty often.

"Dogs not only give warmth and comfort," he explained to me, while he knotted a thread that had snapped, "but they are the earth's wisest, most blessed animals among four-footed beasts. Some people are fondest of horses, others of sheep, and one or two like cows; but the dog is *my* animal. You must beware of people who are fond of cats—'birds of a feather flock together,' says the proverb! But dogs, you see, are wise, and gay and faithful animals. They understand every word you say; they lack only the gift of speech. And what would they do with speech? Which is best: a clumsy tongue or a clumsy heart? And can you tell me of what use the gift of speech would be to a dog? A dog can show plainly, with his ears, his tail, his eyes, his mouth and his whole body, what he is thinking—what need has he for speech? Just look at Gryla, your father's bitch—see how she lifts her ears and listens if her name is but mentioned! Of all our dogs Gryla is the wisest. Watch her carefully for a moment and you will see for yourself. . . . Gryla, you are going to be shot! . . . Ha, ha, ha! What an expression that dog can put on—can you believe that she is only a dog! She knows well enough that I do not mean what I say, but all the same she does not like such talk. There must be no light chatter about so serious a subject—that is what the lady feels. . . . There, there, Gryla, my little one! Do not misunderstand your old friend Bjarni. Do you want to go out? This evening you shall have *all* my scraps. . . . What is that? You want to go out after all? Very well—so long!"

Twilight came as early as between two and three in the afternoon, and then the spinning wheels fell silent and most of the workers in the living room took a nap. That was the time to catch Old Begga and badger her until her sleepiness forsook her and she gave in. If we were successful, we children would sit on stools at her feet, for she had to speak very low for fear of disturbing the sleepers. If my sister Veiga was absent she did not confine herself to tales of elves and fairies, but told us, now and again, stories of outlaws, and even some of the more harmless ghost stories.

If we begged for *real* ghost stories, she answered inexorably: "Uggi is still too young for that sort of thing."

I could not but consider it an insult that my cousins were thus classed above me, and I answered in an offended voice: "No, I'm not! You'll never guess how much *I* know!"

"Tut, tut," said Old Begga, clicking her tongue scornfully. "What do *you* know, my little sparrow?"

"I know a *lot!*" I answered with forced superiority, already afraid that these hints would force me to perjure myself.

"If you can get your mother to tell you ghost stories, then I will too." Old Begga cut further argument short and fished up out of the depths of her memory an outlaw story which soon held us all spellbound.

But my mother was no more disposed to tell me about ghosts. She refused with a smile and a hug, and made me forget her refusal by telling me about herself and her brothers and sisters when they were children.

"The farm stands on a slope near the sea," she began, God knows how many times . . . and whenever she told me anything about her childhood her voice would become soft and vibrant and so warmly emotional that all she said assumed a peculiar flavor of adventure. "Down below the slope we children had our 'house,' an old dinghy which lay with its keel in the air. We had knocked the stern out of it, and had lifted it up by putting stones in under the gunwale; so we were able to sit up comfortably inside it, and the smallest of us could even stand upright. You can't think how lovely it was in our 'house'! We had mussel shells, and conches and starfish, and we carried off all the broken cups and plates we could lay hold of and brought them there. Then we used to beg biscuits or syrup from Old Papa, and play visitors. Sometimes we invited children from other farms, and had a wedding or a funeral, collected firewood, fried herrings on half a frying pan, cooked vegetables in a broken saucepan. . . .

"When I was a little girl I used to lie for hours in our 'house,' looking out over the sea. There is nothing so lovely as the sea on a summer's day, with the red and white sails gleaming out there. . . . Many a time the French fishing sloops came to do business with Old Papa. You should have seen those people. They were always so polite to us children: gave us sweets and many-colored handkerchiefs, and when we grew into young girls they bowed to us so low that we could never keep from laughing at them, and then they laughed too and chattered like children. Not a word did we understand, but Old Papa—he could chatter too! And although he generally chattered in Icelandic they seemed to understand him! It was very entertaining. . . . But the best of all was to lie alone on the shore and watch the water, and the birds with their young. The eider ducks near us were so tame that they allowed us to stroke their backs if our arms were long enough and we did not go too near. It will be such fun when we can visit Old Papa, little Uggi. You can't imagine how lovely it is at Knör!"

"Can't we go now, this summer, Mama?" I suggested, and laid the palms of my hands against her cheeks.

"No, no!" she smiled, and I discovered to my surprise that her eyes were wet. "Why, child, it takes three whole days to ride over there. Besides, this summer we are going to be very busy getting straight at Hjalli—you know that we are going to move, and have our own farm? Besides, don't you think you would rather wait until you can visit Old Papa riding on your own horse, with a whip in your hand, and in riding boots?"

"I can easily ride alone on a horse now!" I tried to convince my mother.

"Do you know what Old Papa has promised me?" she asked, still smiling, and ignoring my last remark: "He has promised to bring biscuits and syrup with him for you children next time he comes, and perhaps—perhaps—but no, I mustn't tell you!"

"Oh, do tell me, Mama!" I begged, getting up and throwing my arms round her neck and laying my cheek against hers.

"Perhaps . . . some mussel shells!" she laughed, kissing me.

Then both of us shouted together with joy at the thought of seeing Old Papa, whom I had seen once before, but about whom I could not remember anything except a peculiar nose. . . .

One day conversation was not as free as usual in the living room. Instead, there was whispering and giggling from bed to bed, as if there were something we children must not hear. All this secrecy whetted my curiosity, and after some patient eavesdropping I managed to discover that the talk was about a man called Geitastada-Gvendur, who was expected at the farm that afternoon.

"As he was at Kambar yesterday, he is certain to arrive today," somebody had it reckoned.

When visitors were expected they were generally spoken of in quite a different manner—openly, and with happy expectation. And generally their arrival was discussed with an entirely different expression on everybody's face.

"What sort of a man is it who is coming?" I asked Old Begga, excited and disturbed.

"I do not know of anybody who is coming," she said peevishly, trying to put me off. (Old Begga, Nonni and Maria Mens were the only ones who had not taken part in this odd talk about Geitastada-Gvendur.)

"Who is Geitastada-Gvendur?" I asked again, unabashed, more interested now than ever.

"Go on with your games," Old Begga advised me harshly. "If he comes, he is the sort of man it were better for you not to see; you can learn nothing good from him. So do not take any notice of him."

"Surely he ought to take notice of his own kith and kin," said Sigga Mens, with a shrill laugh which roused several ill-restrained echoes round the room.

"The relationship you speak of is so remote that most people would not count it when it concerns well-to-do folk," answered Old Begga, with a sudden flush on her wrinkled cheeks. "If your master's household nevertheless acknowledges it, *you* need not be ashamed of it, you baggage!"

Old Begga's imperious words and sarcastic tone of voice caused more than one occupant of the living room to drop her eyes and become absorbed in her work.

"As there is no shame in being related to Geitastada-Gvendur, why should not the boy know it?" shouted Sigga Mens, innocently volatile. "The poor wretch can hardly help being such a down-and-outer. Perhaps he has *not* done what everybody says he has."

"Don't listen to her," Old Begga admonished me, again speaking in her usual calm voice. "Geitastada-Gvendur has not been in prison; that much is certain. What he has done is, therefore, between God and himself—and so it is with most of us! That Gvendur is an unfortunate person, who is at home nowhere, but who wanders round and lives on the generosity of God and man, that we all know; but more we do not know."

"Ha! His hungry face and coarse speech are known, at any rate," shrilled Sigga Mens, still unquenchable.

"Who are you to talk of his way of speech, Sigga Mens?" answered Old Begga, with a gravity which turned the words into stones. "Let us hope that on the Day of Judgment your heart will be set on the scales against your tongue!"

After this speech Old Begga started her spinning wheel again, making, intentionally, such a noise with it that conversation was impossible.

With the first light fall of dusk Geitastada-Gvendur came to the farm. I had been looking out for him and was, therefore, the first to see him. I stood just inside the door into the yard, he just outside it. I do not know whether he saw me, for it was impossible to catch his eye. But he thundered with his long staff—three mighty strokes—on the door, seeming to look straight through me all the while.

Thus he stood and waited, ignoring me entirely. I also stood and waited but, far from retaliating, I devoured him with my eyes. He was like no other person I had ever seen, and yet it was difficult to say clearly what it was that made him different from others. Certainly he was taller, heavier, and more even all round than most of the men I knew—but it was not that. Nor was it his begging-bag, his legs like posts wound round with string, his queer clothes mended with many-colored patches, or the cat-skin cap shaped to his head, that made him so eccentric. His coarse, broad face, its sinister features surrounded by long, dirty-colored tufts of hair which stuck out everywhere from under the edge of his cap, was horrible to look at; but that was not it, either. Suddenly I realized what it was; it was his eyes—those eyes whose glance it was impossible to catch. My heart beat in my breast; suddenly I felt afraid. I longed to run away from the strange emptiness of his look, but I could not move a muscle. . . . Still, after all these years, my blood runs cold at the remembrance of those vacant eyes—which, since then, I have seen in many others, and which, whenever I meet their all-embracing misery, call up my innermost fears and severely test my hope and faith. . . .

When the spell was lifted I was standing hidden behind the still open door and peeping furtively at Geitastada-Gvendur. Somebody must have asked him in during the interval, for he was standing in the broad passage bending down and scraping the snow from his long legs, still without giving me even the fraction of a glance.

Nor did he pay the least attention to my cousins when they crept in. Only when Madame Anna appeared did he mumble something—without, however, lifting his head or interrupting his scraping.

Madame Anna went straight up to him in her dignified way, stretched out her white, plump hand, and said with gay friendliness: "Welcome, dear Gudmundur! I am delighted to see you again."

"Stop giving yourself airs," answered Geitastada-Gvendur, shortly, and for the first time I saw a look in his eyes—a look so evil and ill-tempered that it was almost worse than the vacant stare.

"Yes, you have always been full of jokes, in *your* way!" smiled Madame Anna. "Don't you see I am holding out my hand to you?"

"I am not joking," answered Geitastada-Gvendur, sulkily. "And what have I to do with your hand? Give me something to eat; that's all I want."

"You shall not starve, dear Gudmundur," answered Madame Anna, still gaily and with dignity. "Where have you come from today?"

"What does that matter to you?" sneered Geitastada-Gvendur. "I never bring any messages or greetings. And anything else, people would hardly trust me with."

Before Madame Anna had collected herself for an answer, Sigga's papa came into the room. Madame Anna smiled at him very significantly and, more than willingly, left the field to him. Erect and calm, she went away.

"Good day and welcome, kinsman!" Sigga's papa cried, and slapped Geitastada-Gvendur on the back—apparently he knew that it was no good offering him his hand.

"Shut your cursed mouth and leave out all this hypocrisy!" growled Geitastada-Gvendur, without raising his head, and still continuing to scrape.

Sigga's papa sent my cousins out of the room with a wave of his hand—me he fortunately had not seen.

As soon as Greta and Sigga were out of ear-shot, he altered his bearing and his tone a little. "I beg of you, dear Gudmundur, to be careful what you say here—and, indeed, wherever you go—when there are children present," he said gravely.

"Hold your damned mouth!" answered Geitastada-Gvendur, in the same defiant tone which he had been using all the time. "In all my days I have not lied as much as you do every Sunday in the pulpit."

"I thought you knew that you cannot offend me," smiled Sigga's papa, and was friendly again. "Your angry words are only a kind of habit you have—you are not as bad as you want us to believe. But isn't it really very foolish of you to do yourself harm in this way? Would it not be more pleasant to be liked?"

"No," answered Geitastada-Gvendur, fiercely. "It is your food that I care about, not your false friendliness."

My father came in hastily from the yard. The quick flush that colored his cheeks betrayed that he had caught, if not Geitastada-Gvendur's words, at least his tone of voice.

"Well, so you are here again, you plague of the neighborhood!" he said, with the cold, two-edged playfulness he very seldom used.

Geitastada-Gvendur was suddenly, as it were, transformed—interrupted his scraping, rose to his full height, and even stretched out his hand. "Well, it will soon be a year since I was here last," he said humbly, in a curiously friendly tone.

"I should like to see the person who would not have had more than enough of you if he saw you only every tenth year!" my father continued, teasingly. "Where have you actually come from now, monster?"

"From Kambar last of all," Geitastada-Gvendur hastened to answer.

"What had Sigurjon to say for himself?"

"Sigurjon was in bed," answered Geitastada-Gvendur, with a gloomy laugh.

"What was the matter with him?"

"Ram sickness."

"Has the old ram King Frode died?"

"Yes. King Frode died yesterday morning and knows his children no longer—neither to the third nor fourth generation. His lungs, heart, and kidneys tasted no different from the insides of any other sheep, so far as I could tell."

"And so Sigurjon is lying there apparently with an attack of the gout?"

"Well, yes, he called it gout—God knows he had plenty of pain."

"When you have finished being witty, go and creep into your little corner—you know the way," my father interrupted him shortly. "If you contaminate the farm with your language as you did last year, I shall set Gryla on you—and you be careful, for she is a year older than she was."

Geitastada-Gvendur slunk off. Sigga's papa had been a silent listener. When Gvendur had gone, he asked my father with an uncertain smile, which suddenly seemed to do away with their difference in age: "Do you think it is absolutely necessary to take him in that way, Brother Greipur?"

"That is how he prefers it," answered my father in his ordinary voice—just a little uneasily, it seemed to me. "It will probably be best for me to keep my eye on him until I see what sort of mood he is in."

We children watched Geitastada-Gvendur (at a suitable distance, of course) and wanted neither stories nor any more play that day. It was not because Gvendur was entertaining that we could not leave him alone; he was, indeed, anything but entertaining. Most of the time he sat there looking sullenly in front of him or furtively glancing round the room. The odd thing about these glances was that they never seemed to go straight, but crept around by-ways toward the floor and about the walls, or slid down from the ceiling like small agile spiders.

I could see clearly that Geitastada-Gvendur would have liked to grumble if he had for a single moment thought it safe to do so. It was not by his own wish that he sat there without saying a word except when my father spoke to him. He answered my father willingly and promptly, and there was always a peculiar friendliness in his tone. In this friendliness there could be detected a trace of fear, but certainly no more than a trace.

Sleep caught me while I was still sitting staring at Geitastada-Gvendur. But no sooner had it released me than I hastened into my clothes and into the living room to stare at him again. Speak to him I dared not, but the longer he was silent the more I longed to hear him say something—preferably something really bad.

Madame Anna entered in her stately way. When she came in I noticed there was sunshine in the room. "Good morning, dear Gudmundur!" she smiled cheerfully. "It is lovely weather today."

Geitastada-Gvendur's face contorted itself into a cunning grimace. "It's all the same to me—I shall not go before the food is ready," he drawled crossly.

When he left us later in the day his bag was bulging with the food, clothes, and new shoes and stockings which Madame Anna and my mother had given him between them. Geitastada-Gvendur did not thank them and only reluctantly said goodbye—as for me, he had neither noticed me nor addressed a single word to me, although I had stayed faithfully by him all the time.

When, after seeing him off, I turned back into the farm again, I was gripped by a peculiar fear lest he should have left his look behind him, and lest it might suddenly meet me out of some corner or other. . . . Sigga Mens found an opportunity to tell me something very bad about Geitastada-Gvendur, but for my tongue's sake I do not dare let it go further.

Perhaps my memory is at fault in placing Simon Daleskald's visit immediately after Geitastada-Gvendur's—perhaps there were months, possibly years, between them. However, in my memory they are linked together inseparably. The chief reason for this is doubtless that I do not remember Simon in any particular incident, probably because I was so absorbed in listening to his talk. Perhaps another reason is that Simon and Geitastada-Gvendur were both wanderers, and yet were so little like each other that a contrast was inevitable. If they had been less different they might have been merged together in my memory as one figure. Now they stand separately, but holding each other by the hand.

In no detail did these two tramps resemble each other. Gvendur's face was coarse and swollen, Simon's thin; Gvendur was extremely fair, Simon dark; Gvendur sulky, Simon cheerful; Gvendur dirty, Simon clean; Gvendur had ignored us children, Simon saw little else; and then there was, of course, Sigga Mens.

Before Simon went on to the next farm he had composed a poem about every single person on the farm, even my sister Beta in her cradle—but about Sigga Mens he wrote a poem every half-hour. He praised her hair, her eyes, her hands, her feet, her arms, her bosom, her cheeks, her nose, her forehead, her ears, her lips, her teeth, her gait, her speech, her laughter, her brains, her heart! Sigga Mens laughed at him, and Simon went on extolling her. He was so busy writing about her that he had scarcely time to offer his books of poetry for sale. When at last he could find nothing more to praise, either on or about her, either seen or unseen, he still did not give up. On the contrary, he soared still higher, called her "the undying glory of the Island of Ice," "the gentle flower of womanhood," "the poet's

familiar spirit," "the golden goddess of autumn." Sigga Mens
continued to laugh.

Yes, Sigga Mens laughed, Simon sang her praises, and I
followed the journeyings of his tongue behind the ramparts of
his teeth as best I could. I begged him to show me whether he
could reach the tip of his nose with the end of his tongue (this
I could not quite manage myself, although the desire was not
lacking). I did not doubt that he could do so.

Before he had given me *my* verse, I asked him: "How do you
set about making poetry, Simon?"

"It is a gift from God," answered Simon, and smiled gaily.

"But how do you manage to write poems so quickly?" I
asked.

"It is a special gift from God," answered Simon.

"Yes, but can't all poets write them so quickly?" I wanted to
know.

"The greatest poets I have ever heard of were now and again
able to write a poem on the spot," conceded Simon generously.
"I can always do it."

My admiration was unbounded. To strengthen it still further
I asked him: "Could not Egill Skallagrimsson do it?"

"Egill Skallagrimsson . . ." Simon drawled the name in a
tolerant voice. "He was the man who sat for a whole night over
a single poem, and still had not finished it. Pah! I should never
give much for those poets who have to reflect so long. From
those gifted by God the verses flow as water out of a tap."

"Don't you have to think at all?" I asked admiringly.

"Listen to this," answered Simon:

> *"On to fortune marches sure,*
> *Rapt and undefeated,*
> *Fair-haired Uggi Greipsson,*
> *Gay but not conceited.*

Did I have to reflect over that?"

"No," I admitted, as if a miracle had been worked.

"Don't you think it is a beautiful poem?" asked Simon expectantly.

"Yes," I answered honestly. "But my hair is not fair, it is red."

"Is it red?" exclaimed Simon, opening his eyes wide. "Golden, *I* should have called it, if the word had not been too long; but fair or golden, both come to the same thing. In real poetry things are never taken quite literally. But listen to this:

> *Sigrid, daughter of the Sun,*
> *Simon longs to marry;*
> *Day and night the beauteous one*
> *In his heart doth tarry."*

"Teach me that," I begged.

I missed Simon very much when he went. For a long time I always had some verse or other of his on my lips, and I never tired of hearing others recite his poems. As Old Begga was the one on the farm who remembered them best I stayed with her a great deal. Once when something had gone wrong for her, or I had tried her too far, she burst out vehemently: "Yes, some of Simon's verses are very nice, but you must not think he is a real poet! He is only a poet of clay."

In answer to my questions, Old Begga explained the difference between a real poet and a clay poet: Good verse was inspired, bad verse only kneaded into shape; and Simon was a "kneader." What she said about Simon distressed me very much. My only consolation was that I did not think she was right. In order to test me she quoted "real" and "false" poems to me all mixed up and asked me whether I could tell the difference. But that I could not do. We argued backward and forward a little, especially about Simon.

"You always come along with objections," she interrupted me reproachfully, in her curtest tone of voice. "By now you should have cured yourself of this habit of wishing to be wiser than the wise!"

After that, she positively refused to say another word. . . .

And then all at once it was Christmas.

Suddenly one day I was dressed in a new green suit and stood in the middle of the floor, so grand that no one might touch me or even come near me. I dared not move, as I knew from experience that the only way to keep immaculate was to stand perfectly still without stirring. My head, which I turned and twisted all the time so as to inspect my own glory as far as possible from all angles, was the only part of me that was not put out of action.

Candles had been placed in all the windows and in all the corners. Even in the passages there were candles on little pegs stuck into the wall. The coming Feast was a very great one and we were all ready to receive it dressed in our best clothes. Even the animals on the farm had been given an extra feed and were included in the Feast. And as soon as the Holy Day began we were all—Sigga's papa, Madame Anna, Bjössi, and all of us—to collect round a long table in the living room to eat rice porridge and roast ptarmigan. I was looking forward to the banquet with great delight; but unfortunately the Feast* did not begin until six o'clock. Six o'clock the lights were to be lit, six o'clock the meal would begin—and it was just at six o'clock that sleep generally claimed me! I had determined that this evening it *must* not happen nor *should* it happen. But I knew only too well with what I had to contend, and my heart was full of apprehension.

My mother sat busying herself with little Beta who, like the rest of us, was to be so grand, so grand! Although she was busy, she glanced at me now and again.

"You must not be unhappy about it, little Uggi!" she suddenly said sweetly. "This year you shall at least see the candles lit before you fall asleep. Last year I had only just got you dressed and put you down on father's bed—and away you went!

---

* The Feasts of the Church begin at six o'clock on the Eve, i.e. the evening before.

Can you remember? But this time we are not so late, and I have arranged for the lights to be lit just before six o'clock. As soon as I have finished you all, Mother will take Beta in her arms and Uggi by the hand, and then we shall go round and look at all the lights. When we have seen enough, then little Uggi shall have his food—that will be all right, for you can sit with us at table if you can keep awake—and then if there is time when you have eaten I will tell you a story."

When we had been round and made sure that there was not a dark corner in the whole place, my mother took me on her knee and gave me my food.

"Will it soon be six o'clock?" I asked, with sobs in my throat.

"You are *not* to think of the time!" my mother admonished me, kissing me gently. "It will only make you sleepy. Think of something else, and try to forget that there is anything called six o'clock!"

I pulled myself together, and followed her advice. "Why have the cows got candles?" I asked. "Can they sleep when there is a light in the cowhouse?"

"Oh, but the cows never sleep on Christmas Eve!" answered my mother in her gentle "I-will-tell-you-a-story" voice. "You know that Jesus was born in a stable and laid in a manger? Not only people, but animals, keep his birthday holy. Has Old Begga never told you that at twelve o'clock on Christmas Eve the cows are given voices and speak like human beings? No one really knows what they say, for they do not like anybody to hear them. Therefore, one must never stay in a cowhouse on Christmas Eve at twelve o'clock. Anyone who has heard the cows talk together is never the same again. If they do not gore him to death, he always becomes strange, and goes about taking notice of nothing."

"Doesn't *anyone* know what they say, Mama?" I whispered, enthralled.

My mother smiled at me and kissed me. Her eyes were a little moist, though I could not understand why.

"What they say when they are alone we do not know, of course," she answered, and pressed me to her, rocking me backward and forward. "But there are rhymes about the things they have been heard to say. Listen to this," and, sinking her voice, while an odd golden twilight filled our loft, for once so well lit, she sang softly:

> 'Tis now midnight, says the cow that is white;
> So it's time to chat, says the cow that is fat;
> There's someone within! says the cow that is thin;
> Let's gore him dead, says the cow that is red;
> I'll deal with the lad, says the bull that is bad;
> Where can we build snugly? says the cow that is ugly;
> Down by the brae, says the cow that is gray;
> On the highest down, says the cow that is brown;
> The place I will find, says the cow that is blind;
> My milk has run out, says the cow that is stout;
> I can't eat in this box, says the bad-tempered ox;
> I'm fatter by half, boasts the little calf.
>> He sleeps so sound,
>> The bull's little son,
>> With his nose on the ground,
>> And for him sings no one.

4

I WOKE from my Christmas sleep, as far as memories are concerned, six months later, and then I found myself, not in our loft at Ofeigsstadur, but in the living room at Hjalli.

This living room, which was small and not very light, was divided down the middle by a partition. In the one half there were two fixed beds and a window in the gable facing south; here my parents lived with us children. In the other half there were four fixed bedsteads, and there lived Old Begga, Nonni and Maria Mens, our servants. The fourth bed was a spare bed.

Hjalli was only a small farmstead. The houses were small and in bad repair, and the meadowland tufted and stony. It lay, like Ofeigsstadur, up against a steep rock wall, but the wall was steeper and the houses stood closer to it. In contrast to Ofeigsstadur, which was in a fertile valley and from which many other farmers' dwellings could be seen, Hjalli lay by itself in a narrow and barren offshoot of this valley. The only other buildings we could see were at Vidiveller, a farm lying on the other side of the snappish, clay-colored glacier river. This river, flowing along its rocky bed, rushed precipitously along the steeply sloping hillside, so close to Hjalli that it was possible to stand on the edge of the cliff at the southern end of the yard and peer straight down into its swirling eddies.

It seemed to me now that during the year we lived at Hjalli we did little else but pull down houses and build them up again, that it was always windy and that I always had my eyes, nose and mouth full of dust as fine as snuff. It also seemed to me that I never wore any other clothes than my "working clothes," which were always crusted with mud, could stand all sorts of weather and could not be spoiled by anything. It was a happy year.

Even the first morning was like none other I had ever experienced.

I was in the company of my father and Nonni in the yard, and we three men were making a tour of all the outbuildings, shaking our anxious heads and discussing the wretchedness of it all. Although only one of us was chewing tobacco, we all spat plentifully (we had also, all three of us, our hands buried deeply in our trousers pockets, and when we paused we stood solidly, with our legs well apart); but, on the other hand, we were sparing of words. Now and again we drew one hand out of a pocket and carefully felt a bulging wall; now and again we laid our heads back and counted half aloud the holes in the roof; now and then we disdainfully kicked a half-rotten plank, or anxiously inspected a rickety door—but otherwise we expressed our feelings of disdain by long-distance spits.

"Never have I seen such buildings!" said my father, and as he was the most experienced of the three it was only reasonable that Nonni and I let the remark pass unchallenged.

"There is not one building on the whole farm that is safe," my father went on with a short laugh. As neither Nonni nor I could find anything appropriate to say, we contented ourselves with accepting the remark as it stood.

"Hell!" muttered my father, kicking at some bits of horse-dung.

"Hell!" agreed Nonni, in his piping voice.

And not wishing to be left out I mumbled, almost inaudibly: "Hell! . . ."

My father looked at me sharply and I quickly obliterated myself behind Nonni and escaped further remark. We went on.

"There's a hell of a lot to be done here!" sighed my father, with that kind of complaint in his voice that Old Begga had when she bewailed visitors and having to keep the "pot boiling hot" the livelong day.

"Yes, the devil of a lot!" agreed Nonni, with a genuine and sincere sigh. These words I thought good enough to repeat myself.

As far as the outbuildings were concerned, all three of us agreed that they would probably fall in "one of these days," and that they would hardly be considerate enough to do so during the day, but would naturally choose the night for this dark deed, as they could then mutilate and bury our cattle at the same time.

There was another thing we all agreed on: the whole place must be rebuilt.

"What we haven't time to pull down and build up again before winter, we must just strengthen a little and smack a few bits of sod onto!" shouted my father, trying to drown the sound of the river, when we were again back in the yard. "But who the devil can do anything with such rubbish? And yet we simply must do something about the living room at once."

"Yes, that we must," agreed Nonni, in his thin falsetto. "As soon as we have seen to the lambs."

Meanwhile, without saying anything, I had run off and chosen the worst of our spades.

"May I borrow this, Papa?" I asked piously.

" 'Seen to the lambs'!" snorted my father, without paying any attention to me—"What is the use of keeping lambs alive, since we have nowhere to put them this winter? . . . Well, let us go and see to the lambs, then, Nonni—Uggi, run in to your mother."

A little later the same morning I lay crying on my father's bed.

"I want to go home to Ofeigsstadur," I wailed to my mother, who was tidying up. "I don't want to stay here at all! It's a horrid place—it's so dull! I want to go home to Ofeigsstadur."

"This is our home now, little Uggi!" my mother comforted me kindly, stroking my neck.

"Now be a big boy! What do you think Father would say if he heard you?"

I swallowed my tears, sat up, was given a piece of sugar for my hiccoughs and reflected.

"But, Mother," I said persuasively, "I—do—not—want—

to—live—here—at—all. I want to live at home in the loft at Ofeigsstadur!"

"Would you rather live there alone, than here with your father and mother?" asked my mother seriously.

"But *why* have we got to live here?" I said, to avoid answering that difficult question. "I can't even remember how we got here."

"How could you remember?" smiled my mother, and sat down and took me onto her knee. "You were asleep, Uggi child."

"Was I asleep?" I asked uneasily. "Where did I fall asleep last night?"

"Under Sigga's papa's writing-table!" laughed my mother, and leaned her forehead against the top of my head. "Can't you remember it?"

"No," I answered.

"Can't you remember that all yesterday you were in Sigga's papa's room playing with your cousins?"

"Yes," I answered, "I remember now."

"When you had fallen asleep in your sudden way," my mother went on, with an oddly lowered voice, while her warm breath tickled my neck comfortably, "your father picked you up, wrapped you in a blanket and rode with you here. I rode with little Beta, and Bjarni Smith, who came with us to take Sigga's papa's horse back, carried Veiga. That's how it all happened."

"And all our things?" I asked.

"Most of them Papa and the others had moved here earlier in the day," answered my mother, and pulled at my hair with her lips. "The rest we brought with us."

"How far is it to Ofeigsstadur?" I asked.

"An hour's ride," answered my mother.

"Will you take me with you when you go over there, when you go there to church?"

"Father will take you over there now and then, I expect," my mother comforted me.

"Who is living in the loft now?" I asked after a little pause.

"No one . . . yet," whispered my mother.

"It was so lovely in the loft," I whispered back.

To this my mother made no answer.

"It's not lovely here," said I.

My mother was silent for a time. Then she blew her nose—she had kept her head behind my neck all the time—and said mildly:

"You will enjoy being here, you'll see. It is only in the beginning that one is a little unhappy in a new place. Why, I was unhappy to begin with at Ofeigsstadur! And yet I was grown up, while you are only a child. But then, of course, I did not know a soul—had only spoken to Madame Anna and Siri Sigbergur once when they stayed the night at Knör."

"Why did you leave Knör? Were you tired of it?" I asked, wonderingly.

"Because Old Papa always sent us children away from home when we were old enough," answered my mother. "And then I was only to be away for a year."

"Why did you stay away longer?"

"Because I met Papa!" answered my mother gaily.

"And you're not tired of it?"

"No," laughed my mother.

"Didn't Papa want you to go home again?"

"No, because we married and then our little Uggi came, and little Veiga and little Beta—and now we have three children."

We both laughed.

"The morning I left Knör," began my mother, suddenly, in her low "story-telling" voice, "I was up long before anybody else and crept out of doors. The dogs wanted to come with me, but I did not allow them to, because I wanted to be alone. . . . It was in the month of May, as it is now, and it was such a lovely dewy morning, and the shadows were long as at sunset, except that they lay the other way about. . . . You know how dew looks on the grass, don't you, little Uggi—but have you ever seen the sky when it is dewy too?"

I shook my head quickly, not wishing to interrupt her.

"Then I went round and touched everything," my mother continued. "Our old tools, doors, windows, walls, mounds, stones—I wanted to touch everything—wasn't it stupid of me! Then I went down to the stream that ran through the meadow at Knör—I had so often lain at the side of that stream, damming it up, sailing ships on it, catching baby trout. As I was now going away it seemed to me that I must drink a little, although I knew the water was cold and would set my teeth on edge. . . . Have you ever seen yourself in a stream? It isn't like seeing yourself in a mirror. There are such strange shadows in your face—and there is heaven behind your head—and it is almost as if you were alive down there, lying on your back and looking up at yourself. And then when you drink, it is as if you were kissing yourself—as if you were drinking from your own mouth. . . .

"Well, so then I went on farther. Do you know that you can write in dew? Yes, listen now: wherever you walk you leave a dark streak, and you can write your name in the dew and draw houses with windows and doors, or people or animals. I will teach you all that one day. . . . And do you know what Mother did then? Why, she went and picked flowers. I found purple saxifrage and lady's mantle and primroses. I will show them to you one day, they are packed up in a box where I also put shells and small stones from the shore . . . for you see, I could not rest until I had been down to the shore to say goodbye to our 'house.' I should like to know if the old boat lies there still."

"Yes . . . and then what?" I whispered.

"And then there was nothing more," smiled my mother, and hastily dried her eyes. "For then I went home . . . and then I went away . . . and Old Papa traveled with me. More years have passed than you have lived since then, and in all that time I have only seen Papa twice and Mama not at all—who would have thought it possible!"

She was silent. I raised myself up on her lap, clung closer to her and we neither of us spoke. . . .

We cannot have been long at Hjalli—at any rate we had not

yet roofed the living room—when my grandfather Uggi Greips-son of Fjall came to visit us one day.

I called him Grandpa-from-Fjall to distinguish him from my other grandfather, Grandpa-from-Knör. I knew him very well, as I had seen so much of him at Ofeigsstadur, but here at Hjalli he first, as it were, comes to life in my memory.

At Ofeigsstadur he was generally surrounded by churchgoers or had grown-up, uninteresting things to discuss with my father or Sigga's papa. For us children he meant at the most a knee, a little petting, a few sweets and, above all, a beard. This beard was white and shining and reached to the middle of his waist-coat, and with it Grandpa-from-Fjall satisfied once and for all every reasonable demand. It was not easy to sit and talk to a man whose beard claimed all one's attention, nor was one very interested to hear what he had to say. Instead, one longed to put out one's hand and feel his beard a little.

At Grandpa's first visit to Hjalli, it fell out very fortunately for me. My father and mother had just gone out to "have a look at the land," and Nonni was sent off to fetch them. Maria Mens had stockings to wash and besides she was shy, and Old Begga felt it to be her duty to make a cup of coffee immediately.

All this combined to leave Grandpa-from-Fjall to me to be entertained, and so at last we learned really to know each other.

From the outset I behaved as his equal. If he stroked his beard, I stroked my chin; if he put his hands behind his back, I also put my hands behind my back; if he crossed his legs, I also crossed my legs; and when Old Begga—who thought that a "drop of coffee" could not harm any living creature—brought two cups and told me to keep Grandpa company, I suddenly felt it to be my duty to act as host, offer sugar, offer cream, offer cakes.

Grandpa-from-Fjall appreciated my politeness and returned it in full measure.

"I hardly know what to call you," he said, wrinkling his forehead thoughtfully. "You are no longer a boy—may I call you 'younker'?"

I nodded solemnly—that would do, I decided.

My esteem for Grandpa rose every minute. Without realizing it, I suddenly penetrated behind the beard. I realized that his voice was calm and beautiful. I saw that his blue-gray eyes were gentle and deep.

"How are things going with your lambs?" I asked over the second cup of coffee.

"Oh, thank you, they might be worse," answered Grandpa-from-Fjall, and his glance with its almost invisible smile could not possibly hurt my dignity. "We have lost seven. How many have died here?"

"Only three," I answered as modestly as possible. "But, of course, we look after them so very carefully."

When we had finished our coffee I offered to show him the farm and the outbuildings. Grandpa-from-Fjall thanked me and went with me very willingly. This time he was the only one with his hands behind his back—my own I stuck ostentatiously into my trousers pockets, out of which I now and again drew first one then the other, when I thought it necessary to feel a bulging wall. Otherwise I conscientiously counted the holes in the ceiling, kicked the rotten doorposts, inspected the worst of the doors on the wrong side and spat vigorously, first in this direction, and then in that. I confided to Grandpa that never in my life had I seen such houses, that they were dangerous to inhabit, that all the timber on the farm was completely rotten, all the walls were on the point of falling down, every single ceiling riddled with holes like a trout-net—and Grandpa nodded agreement, with his little smile so deep at the back of his eyes that it could not possibly embarrass anybody.

Therefore, when we passed a clump of horse-dung, I kicked it without thinking, spat over my shoulder and burst out fervently:

"Yes, damn it all!"

When after this outburst of "manliness" I at last dared to steal a glance at Grandpa-from-Fjall, I immediately understood quite clearly that this time I had gone too far; the smile was right to the fore.

My cheeks burned and I bent my head so that he should not

see my face. It was some time before I dared remark that there was plenty to do here.

"Yes, now I am beginning to understand!" answered Grandpa-from-Fjall, half aloud—from a faint difference in his distant smile I understood that this time it did not concern me. "This is something for my son Greipur."

"The living room we shall have to start on at once!" I said with greater daring.

And Grandpa-from-Fjall nodded and agreed, nodded and agreed.

But suddenly he turned to me and said, with his hands hidden under the tails of his black frock-coat:

"Shall we agree that you will never swear again?—and I, for my part, will promise to give you a watch at your confirmation?"

Again I felt my cheeks burning. But his smile was so gay and friendly, and so free from all reproach, that at last, without a word, I put my hand under his coat-tails and took hold of his hand. We went on—I, a little boy; he, my grandfather.

"You must always remember," said Grandpa-from-Fjall a little later in a tone that sounded as if he were giving me a present, "that you bear one of our family's greatest names, and that you are the fifth Uggi Greipsson, in the same line in which your father is the fourth Greipur Uggason. . . . Do you know, little younker, that my eldest son was called Greipur? Yes, your father is my second son with that name. My eldest died when he was eighteen years old, and lies buried in the churchyard at Ofeigsstadur. . . . Well, well, you must not cry about that. He is happy, we are happy—what is there to be sorry for! If I had not had another boy whom I could call Greipur, then perhaps there would have been cause for sorrow. Greipur Uggason, Uggi Greipsson—those names have so far been borne with honor. And God gave me another Greipur, so now I can die happy."

We walked along silently for a time.

"Is Father like . . ." I began gently, but came to a standstill.

"Is your father like my other Greipur?" Grandpa-from-Fjall kindly helped me out. "Well, yes, perhaps—all my boys are like one another to a certain extent! The family likeness is there, however different they may be superficially. The two Greipur brothers would now have been about the same height, and in manners and coloring your father has much in common with his namesake. There is no picture of the elder Greipur; nobody imagines that an eighteen-year-old boy is going to die. But doubtless I shall show him to you some day, and then you can judge for yourself."

Suddenly I thought of Sigga Mens. Grandpa-from-Fjall smiled at the expression on my face.

"Why do you look at me like that?" he asked, and patted my head. "Some day, I hope, we shall all gather in the presence of God, and then I shall show him to you."

The trustful, matter-of-fact tone in which he spoke made a deep impression on me. I had often heard death and "the other life" spoken of, but never before as everyday things.

"When some time or other we meet at Ofeigsstadur I shall show you his grave," said Grandpa-from-Fjall gravely. "It is extraordinary to think that, whereas I have lost only one child, my son, Sira* Sigbergur, has three under the soil. God has tried him hard; He does not spare His own."

Grandpa-from-Fjall looked at me and stopped.

"Didn't you know that before?" he asked gently. "Yes, all three of them died in one and the same week, of diphtheria—a boy and two girls—they lie in one grave. That is to say, their soulless bodies lie in the grave; they themselves are running about and playing with the angels in Heaven."

My father and mother returned home, gay and in good spirits.

"He tried to make me ride up and down perfectly perpendicular rocks!" complained my mother, playfully, to Grandpa-from-Fjall, giving him a welcoming kiss. "We were out looking for meadows . . . we found two or three fields about the size of a pocket handkerchief!"

---

* Sira—the title given to a parish priest.

"I have told you that the real fields lie higher up in the mountain and cannot be reached on horseback," answered my father, suddenly turning red.

"But how are you going to get the hay home when you cannot get up there with the horses?" asked my mother, smiling. "I thought you were making fun of me."

"The hay is stacked on the spot," explained my father, with forced calmness, and a hasty glance at Grandpa-from-Fjall. "In winter when snow has fallen and is frozen, the hay is put into sacks, thrown down the mountain-sides and collected at the bottom. It is quite simple."

The smile in Grandpa-from-Fjall's eyes was there when he looked at my father, just as when he looked at me.

We went in and Old Begga had another cup of coffee ready. I was allowed to sit at the table, but this time there was no coffee for me.

"Uggi has shown me over the place," Grandpa-from-Fjall said genially.

My father cleared his throat, hastily stirred his coffee, but said nothing.

"Uggi does not seem to have any great confidence in the durability of the buildings," added Grandpa-from-Fjall. "But he is, of course, only a child."

"The buildings are just as God and anybody else can see them," answered my father, hastily, and his side-glance at me was anything but encouraging. "But otherwise Hjalli is a good little farm, more or less as it was described to us. The meadows are not big, I confess, but on the other hand there is better winter grazing for the sheep than on any other farm round here. And as far as the house and the outbuildings are concerned, they have this advantage, that they can be pulled down and built up again!"

"Quite so," Grandpa-from-Fjall conceded with a smile.

"Quite so?" repeated my father, growing red right out to the tips of his ears. "What do you mean?"

"What should I mean?" answered Grandpa-from-Fjall, and

drew the smile farther back into his eyes. "I agree with you. That is all. Then what I hear is correct, that the living room is going to be done first?"

"Well, yes," answered my father, evasively, and glanced at the leaking wainscoting. "We have not quite decided yet, but this is the room we live in. Another couple of windows, one here and one there, would be a great improvement. Besides, these walls cannot stand a new roof, and a new roof there must be before winter."

"Timber is said to be at a high price this year," Grandpa-from-Fjall said calmly.

"Yes, a damned high price," admitted my father, unsuspiciously. "Can't be done!"

"Well then, how are you going to get on without it?" asked Grandpa.

"Without it?" my father answered in a surprised voice. "Why should I do without it? My brother has sent Bjarni Smith off with five horses—but five horse-loads will not go far."

"They will go pretty far on the bill," said Grandpa-from-Fjall, casually. "Who is going to do the carpentry?"

My father smiled at him suddenly right into his eyes and answered frankly:

"I had thought of my brother Arni!"

"Well, you might have thought worse," smiled Grandpa-from-Fjall, benevolently. "I must arrange to spare him for a few days. . . . I was indeed rather afraid that you had gone off on the quiet and hired a man whom you would have to pay. For you must not pay Arni, not behind my back—I won't have it! He gets his yearly wage from me and shall have no more, although if you particularly wish it you can stand him a little tobacco. I will send him along one of these days. You can keep him until the haymaking, but no longer."

Not only with my tongue, but with my hands and my feet, did I express my joy over the fact that Uncle Arni was coming to stay with us for many, many days.

"Yes, it is really very fortunate," Grandpa-from-Fjall agreed with me. "In the winter I cannot lend him for you to play with. He speaks of sailing in the autumn—he wants to perfect himself in carpentry," he explained to my father rather unhappily.

"But does he want to go abroad?" my father asked in surprise.

"Wants and wants," answered Grandpa-from-Fjall, good-naturedly. "There is scarcely a thing Arni does not want to do if only he could manage it. What he *does,* on the other hand, is known only on the day it is actually carried out!"

We had not been many days at Hjalli before I suddenly became good friends with Maria Mens, whom I had scarcely dared speak to before.

It happened in this way. As she passed me in the yard one day where I was gazing down into the eddying river, Maria Mens softly patted my cheek.

I stood for a moment and stared at her in surprise; she was on her way down to the stream with a wooden bucket to fetch water. Then I ran after her, took her free hand and went with her.

We glanced rather awkwardly at each other and I asked her, just for something to say:

"How big is the ocean, Maria Mens? I expect one can see the mountains on the other side, can't one?"

"No, no, that one cannot," answered Maria Mens, and smiled shyly at me. "That one certainly cannot do."

"When I am grown up I shall go sailing," I boasted, so as to make a good and courageous impression.

"No, surely you mustn't do that," said Maria Mens, terrified.

"Yes," I insisted. "I shall be a carpenter and go abroad."

Maria Mens took her hand away from mine and blew her nose, dried her eyes, gave me her hand again and said in a subdued voice:

"You must never think of that, little Uggi. In foreign countries there are so many dreadful people. Besides, you might drown."

"No, no!" I exulted, omniscient. "One does not drown on board a ship."

"Everything that sails on the ocean may go under," answered Maria Mens, scarcely audibly. "Many, many people drown every year. My father and my two brothers drowned one day from a boat. We found them on the seashore, my sister Sigga and I. . . ."

We had sat down on a mound by the stream. Maria Mens sat there with dry, frightened eyes, staring straight in front of her.

"Is that why you are always crying?" I asked in a whisper, and squeezed the forefinger she had left me.

Maria Mens gave a little nod—and soon the tears began to flow again from her red-rimmed eyes.

Now that I knew the meaning of her tears I could not help crying with her. Maria Mens heard me, looked at me despairingly for a moment, hugged me violently and we cried together.

"Dear, good little boy," she mumbled, and kissed me with cautious lips. "Dear, good little boy . . ."

These words had the twofold effect of delighting my heart and redoubling my tears.

Another day I told Maria Mens that she need not be so unhappy, as Grandpa-from-Fjall had said that we would meet all our relations in the presence of God.

"Don't you know, child," answered Maria Mens, uncomforted, "that not only all that we say and do, but also all we think and desire, is written in a book? It is only if we have never done, or thought, anything evil that we attain to God."

We discussed the matter further. Her prospects of becoming "blessed" she considered to be exceedingly small. . . .

One day I heard Gryla barking with her visitor-voice, and rushed out.

Above the slope leading to the courtyard there came into view, first of all, a pack-horse, carrying on one side a wooden trunk and on the other a mighty sack; then my Uncle Arni's smiling face with its spreading mustache, and finally his beautiful gray horse, appeared. Uncle Arni dismounted by swinging his right leg over the horse's mane and jumping down. The first thing he did when he stood on the ground was to pick me up and whirl me round and round; the next thing was to light his pipe, and the third to free the pack-horse from its burden.

"Well, comrade, what fun we shall have," he shouted to me while he unsaddled his horse. "Have you begun to smoke yet? . . . No? . . . Have you forgotten how to eat sweets? 'No' to that also!"

The next day we started on the living room. We began early in the morning, and, as there were four of us, we were all in high spirits. There remained nothing of the room by the evening but the timber-work and the leaky skirting board.

"Now is just the moment for a week's rain!" laughed Uncle Arni, contemplating himself in his pocket-glass and arranging his mustachios to his own satisfaction.

"No nonsense there, or you will soon be lying on your back counting stars in broad daylight!" threatened my father. "You have been lent here to work, my boy—not to call down misfortunes on us with your forebodings."

"It would be worse if the wind rose," mumbled Nonni, so low that my father could scarcely have heard it unless he had taken the trouble to listen.

"The boy is right!" shouted my father, and spat far and accurately. "A nice state we should be in if the whole lot came down over our heads, or each peg were blown away in the morning when we woke and we found ourselves in the open air! We must tether the animal."

We tethered the animal. We stretched all the rope on the farm over the living room, crossways and longways, and bound it to the beams in the other houses and to large stones.

As the living room stood in the center of the group of rooms, its walls were also the walls of some of the other rooms. The only building on the whole farm which had its four walls intact was the cowhouse. All the rooms lacked either a whole or half a wall, or at least had a corner taken away. It was, therefore, almost more airy indoors than out, if one could call it "indoors." Uncle Arni pointed out that in the living room, as it now was, one had "a free choice of four different kinds of draughts." Old Begga was the only one of all the servants on the farm who did not take it in good part—but who had time to worry about what Old Begga mumbled?—Old Begga, who sat all day as if nailed to her bed, just spinning, spinning, spinning, leaving us in peace as we left her. But in the humming of her spinning wheel there was an undertone which could not be mistaken.

The new walls grew apace. Nonni handed the stones; my father put them in place, and I helped—in my own eyes—by shoveling up earth for stuffing. Uncle Arni had enough to do with hammer, plane and saw. He replaced the worst beams altogether, and onto others he nailed planks for support. He nailed strips of wood over the cracks in the paneling, and into the sloping roof he put new windows. My father wanted the new window in our room to face west, I wanted it east for the sake of the morning sun; Uncle Arni solved the problem by putting in two windows, and neither my father nor I raised any objections.

"One should spare neither windows nor tobacco!" Uncle Arni instructed me one day. "Light is the source of life, tobacco the source of good humor. Whisky is also good, but it makes one drunk, and unfortunately there is not time for that every day of the week. Besides, our holy brother has pushed both your father and me into a Temperance Society, which we even have to pay to belong to! So now it is up to us to keep our mouths shut and go softly, so that there is no clucking, when we have something either in our heads or in our pockets. You be thankful that you are not the youngest, for you are let off with just a father and a mother. He is really very dear, is Beggi—it is not out of malice that he is so strict—but Brother Greipur and I are not sucklings, after all. If we happen to come home to

Ofeigsstadur in rather a happy mood, we might just as well try to move the church as the priest. And if one can't settle a difference of opinion with a wrestling bout, how the devil can one do it?"

Uncle Arni had this peculiarity, that if he chanced to touch a spider or any other vermin he hopped round the room on one leg and shrieked. When it seemed to him that we had amused ourselves often enough over this comedy, he suggested one day that we should wash the outside of the living room. My father considered it an excellent idea; and as neither Nonni nor I was the sort to make difficulties, the thing was as good as settled when the noise of the spinning wheel inside the living room suddenly stopped, and was replaced by Old Begga's voice, full of anxiety.

"God help you, Greipur."

"Did you say anything, Old Begga?" asked my father, and winked at the rest of us.

"Yes; I begged God to help you, and I repeat it!" answered Old Begga, gloomily.

"But why now more than at other times?" my father asked gaily.

"Because you are going to call down rain on this unhappy house before you get it under a roof," answered Old Begga, with prophetic weight.

My father and Uncle Arni laughed loudly, and I laughed too. Nonni hopped about, his face distorted, pinching his cheek with one hand and his thigh with the other.

"Are you laughing, too, Jon?" asked Old Begga, who in certain moods refused to use her son's pet name.

Nonni tried to answer, but had to give it up. We others looked at him and laughed louder than ever.

"Are you laughing too, Jon?" came again from inside the living room—and this time the voice was so awe-inspiring that something had to be done. "Why do you not answer, boy?"

"No, Nonni is not laughing with us," my father informed her as solemnly as he could.

"Why doesn't he answer, then?" asked Old Begga, suspiciously.

"He hasn't time!" answered my father, and looked sternly
at Uncle Arni and me to make us stop laughing: "Well, look
alive, boy! Here I am waiting for stones! I suppose you are not
crying because we are smiling a little at your mother?"

The spinning wheel began again, my father winked at us
and we contented ourselves with making faces at each other,
making signs with our heads and laughing noiselessly.

On the day when the walls were finished and only the roof
was lacking, my father defied the weather gods: each man was
given a wet rag, and we began merrily to wipe off the mildew
and the spiders' webs. No sooner were we well under way than
the day's face was suddenly darkened and it began slowly to
blow up for rain. My father dropped his rag, a deep frown
appeared in his forehead and he stood for a minute gazing incredulously at the threatening banks of clouds; then he suddenly spat out his tobacco, swung himself up onto the wall and
began to roof. Without a word he signed to Uncle Arni to come
up to him. Then he sent Nonni for Maria Mens, and told
me shortly not to "get in the way." With Nonni and Maria
Mens as assistants, and me as an unwillingly passive spectator,
my father and Uncle Arni raced the touchy weather gods. Heavy
scuds of rain could be seen to the south of us, to the north
of us, to the west of us and to the east of us. I kept the workers
fully informed of their capricious courses. If I saw new scuds
suddenly appearing I announced them and prophesied their
probable course, and also, as long as I could, kept count of the
drops which fell in my neighborhood. But I cannot claim
that I was warmly thanked for any of this information, or
that anyone paid any particular attention to me. Just as the
last sod was laid and the last flat stone placed upon it to
hold it in place until it had taken root, the weather broke and
chased us indoors. Of course, I had not the slightest doubt
that my part in the fortunate result was by no means the least.

The smell of coffee and newly baked cakes greeted us inside the house and, although it was long past breakfast time and almost dinner time, we men were soon sitting round a table on which were enormous plates with rolled sugared pancakes and biscuits sprinkled with sugar or cinnamon; and fortunately there was also, as well as coffee, chocolate, so that both Veiga and I also had our cups while little Beta drank with Mama.

"Well, we won, Old Begga!" teased my father and winked at the rest of us.

Old Begga growled something into her cup without lifting her eyes.

"What do you say, Old Begga?" asked my father, gaily and very loudly, as if he were speaking to someone deaf.

"I am saying that this is not the first time that we are all enjoying ourselves through the forethought of my blessed Cecilia," Old Begga answered impressively.

During the ensuing laughter Old Begga looked only at Nonni, who sat there, his colorless but pleasant and gentle boy's face quite expressionless, stirring his coffee convulsively.

"Even if you still have some coffee in your cup, is there any reason to go on stirring?" asked Old Begga, her voice trembling.

"I have a little—at the bottom, Mama," answered Nonni, blushing, and hastily emptying his cup.

There was coffee after the chocolate. And as the conversation passed on to other things and my mother began to need Old Begga's help particularly, her expression slowly relaxed and became more natural. But it was not until my mother began to feel a little cold and put a pretty shawl Old Begga had knitted over her shoulders, and this had led to our admiring my father's gloves, Nonni's latest pair of slippers and my cap—all of them knitted by Old Begga—that she thawed enough to allow herself to take part in the conversation.

Outside the house the rain beat down so furiously that I thought it must be angry with itself for coming too late. But in the living room it was calm and pleasant and we kept holiday.

Uncle Arni and Nonni shaved, and Nonni hastily made me a razor of wood so that I should not feel out of it.

Old Begga sat at her spinning wheel, which was angry no longer but on the contrary purred like a peaceful cat. When I asked her for a story she was more than willing.

The story she told me was about a courageous boy and a loathsome troll. The boy was at home alone, sitting in the kitchen. Suddenly he heard a voice from the smoke-hole: "May I fall?" "Yes," answered the boy. And down fell a long hairy leg which remained lying on the floor of the kitchen. "May I fall?" came the voice again from above. "Yes," answered the boy. And down fell another leg, the mate to the first leg. "May I fall?" said the voice, again. "Yes," answered the boy. And in that way there flopped down, one after another, a body, two arms and a head, and then all these parts united into a frightful troll. But what the troll did, or what happened to the boy, I have, unfortunately, never been able to remember.

Even in those days Old Begga used often to scold me for my forgetfulness.

"You are not specially gifted, my good child," she once said, when she had had proof of my forgetfulness. "Or if you are, I doubt whether your gifts will be of any use to you. You only remember the unimportant things in the stories I tell you, seldom the most important. . . . You remember that Bukolla says, 'Pull a hair from my tail,' and that the troll says, 'May I fall?' but what's the good of that when you have forgotten all the rest, so that no story can come of it?"

I realized myself how unfortunate it was, but what was I to do? It was just as impossible for me to forget the unimportant details as it was for me to remember the main points.

"If you cannot remember things, you must be a little silly," Old Begga added. "What's the good of telling you stories at all? It's like pouring water through a sieve."

But when she saw that I had tears in my eyes she softened at once.

"There, there, there—let me think a little—would you like a piece of sugar candy to suck for a while? Have I told you the one about the trolls in the mountains? . . . No? Well, listen. . . ."

In the morning, when I was feeling most lively, Uncle Arni often looked tired and depressed. Eventually I found out that this was because he slept badly during the night.

When we were alone we talked a great deal. One day I asked him:

"Why can't you sleep at night, Uncle?"

"I don't know at all, Uggi boy," answered Uncle Arni, and braced himself up to smile. "I think it is my heart. You see, I wake and find it hammering and hammering, and then I can't get to sleep again."

I was so sorry for Uncle Arni that I felt quite tired myself. I sat down on a pile of planks.

Uncle Arni was busy with his work and did not look at me, but went on in a friendly voice:

"So then I lie and think of all sorts of things, and that is not a good thing. I ought not to do so. I ought rather to pray."

His tone and expression filled me with a strange uneasiness and an odd painful curiosity. But I could not bring myself to ask anything more.

"If I had Brother Beggi's power in prayer," continued Uncle Arni, "*then* God would hear me . . . though I don't know . . . He took the children."

The day he was leaving us I was very unhappy. He tried to cheer me up by playing with me—put me on his shoulders and was a horse.

"And so we trot!" he shouted, and set off down the field. "And so we gallop! And so the hack stretches its legs! And so . . . there you lie!"

We laughed very much, but in the middle of our laughter I burst into tears, and Uncle took me in his arms and carried me home.

"We shall see each other again in the autumn at latest," he comforted me from his horse, when my father lifted me up for a last kiss.

A last kiss . . . yes, years passed before I saw Uncle Arni once more. Would I had never seen him again!

I woke one morning and found myself alone in bed. Where had my father got to? Yes—now I remembered. He was living in a tent far, far up in the mountains, with Nonni, Old Begga and Maria Mens.

The sun smiled at me, and seemed to know that it was thanks to me he could get into the room so early. Outside one corner of the window a spider's web glittered, closely set with tiny dewdrops. I could see a sunbeam slyly trying to tickle my mother's nose; and the sunbeam and I winked at each other and were both amused at the result. My mother shook her head a little—the sunbeam did not move; my mother lifted her hand, but the sunbeam refused to be frightened.

So when my mother suddenly woke with a sneeze, I burst out laughing. My mother looked across at me with such a comical smile that I had to lie down to finish laughing, and when, with her hand, she told me to be quiet so that I would not wake my sisters, I stifled my laughter in my pillow. While we quietly and quickly dressed ourselves, I told her in a whisper why I had laughed, and she whispered back:

"What fun! He will be sure to tell his mother!"

My mother carried me out of the room, as she did not quite trust me to get out without making a noise. From the store-room she fetched a wooden stool, a milking pail and a strainer, and carrying these things we set off to the cowhouse. When we opened the door our two cows got up, flicked themselves with their tails and greeted us in a friendly way with short moos. All this noise woke the calf in his stall. He sprang up, shook himself so that his ears flapped round his head, shuffled toward me so as to tempt me over to the stall, made a couple of clumsy leaps with uplifted tail and, when I advanced and stretched out my hand toward him, began to suck it greedily with his soft gums and rough tongue.

"Bring me his basin, little Uggi," said my mother, sweetly. And the calf was given a little milk, and I had my mug filled, and both of us gulped down the warm frothing milk greedily.

When my mother had finished milking she loosed the cows and I loosed the calf—which, just in fun, poked me and pushed me if I came anywhere near it—and then we all went out into the dewy morning. As the cows walked away with a faint clatter of hoofs, their stiff joints giving little clicks, my mother and I stood hand in hand, my mother murmuring half aloud a morning prayer, and making the sign of the cross—*"in the name of the Father and of the Son and of the Holy Ghost."* She stood there for a moment breathing in the air, which was fresh and cold like water in a mountain stream.

"I think it's going to be a fine day," said my mother. "Shall we hurry and get ready so that we can all go out into the lovely sunshine?"

We went back into the storeroom, humming a little tune, and there my mother strained the milk, filled the milk cans, poured the rest into a couple of flat pans, took the two milk pans with yesterday's milk, separated the skim milk and the cream, put the cream into a small churn, let it stand while she made up the fire in the kitchen, put a large saucepan of water on the fire and then began to churn. The comfortable squelching sound from the churn filled the room while I, stooping, swept with a little twig broom. Now and then my mother sent me to the bottom of the bedroom stairs to "listen," but I still heard no sounds from up there other than Veiga's morning snores. My mother rinsed the pails, the pans and the churn with the boiling water from the saucepan, put them out in the sunshine to dry, took hold of the bread-trough, put some handfuls of flour into it from a chest, made a depression in the middle of the flour, gradually poured water into this depression, carefully stirring it round and round, kneaded the dough, put it out in handfuls onto the board, flattened it out, taking care that the cakes were nicely rounded, pricked holes in them with a bodkin, squatted down on her heels in front of the fire, fetched an old, thick, burned piece of dressed leather from behind a stone and, using it as a fan, baked the bread on the glowing cinders. A lovely smell of fire and warm bread penetrated everywhere. My mouth watered and I suddenly felt so hungry, so hungry—warm bannock with newly churned butter is the best thing I know of.

When my mother had finished baking she made porridge; and as my sisters were still asleep in the bedroom she cleaned out the cowhouse in a trice, while I followed behind her with a little wooden spade that Nonni had given me, and sprinkled the sand. We talked gaily of how deliciously hungry we now were. My mother poured the porridge into our bowls, put them on a tray with the bread, butter and a jug of milk, and then we went into the bedroom, woke Veiga and Beta and before they were really awake my mother began to put food into their mouths. Veiga was cross and hit out, Beta cried a little; but it was not long before we wheedled them into a good temper, and then we all smiled and sang little songs, and my mother told us about herself and her brothers and sisters—we had heard the same stories again and again, but they were always just as interesting to us, yes, almost more interesting the oftener we heard them.

When we had finished our breakfast, and Veiga and Beta were washed and dressed, my mother took Beta on her arm and we went out. When we were outside my mother took Veiga's hand and so we went for a long walk. We walked slowly and made many detours. Veiga and I were soon running about picking flowers and collecting pebbles. My mother did not know the names of all the flowers. "I never saw that flower at Knör," she would say thoughtfully, and look long at it. In return we searched for flowers she described carefully to us, saying they were everywhere at Knör; and we were all—with perhaps the exception of little Beta—surprised that we could not find them, and supposed that they did not grow here at Hjalli.

At last we reached the rocks above the farmyard. The sun blazed down, and the gray mossy stones were very warm on the sunny side. The still atmosphere was heavy with the sweet, narcotic smell of herbs and heather. It was cool only where our little stream came jumping down over the cliffs in a slender waterfall, murmuring to itself softly and tenderly, as if it had something to tell us.

We sat down and looked out over the valley. Little Beta was already asleep, and Veiga had scarcely sat down before she too had gone off. My mother busied herself with them, whispering soft little endearments. I sat and tried to pick out our cows and calves, and our horses, tried to count the strange horses on the other side of the river and also to count the people who were moving busily in a long row and turning over the hay at Vidivellir.

"I wonder if Torgrimur is there?" I asked my mother softly—for it was at Vidivellir that Torgrimur, that old sinner, lived.

"Torgrimur?" asked my mother, astonished. "What do you know about Torgrimur, child?"

My cheeks grew hot and I wanted to ignore the question; but when my mother repeated it I answered hesitatingly that I had heard Old Begga speak of him.

"Oh, well," said my mother, mollified, and began to count the people and check up. There were seven of them.

"Yes, Torgrimur must be there. What an incredible amount of life there is in the old man! He must be at least eighty-five—and there he is, turning over the hay. . . . How lovely it would be up in the fields with the others today—wouldn't it, Uggi child? They will be very busy today."

Whether I went to sleep at this juncture, or how we got home, I have not the slightest recollection. There are sure to have been many summer days like that. . . .

But now it was winter, deep snow over everything, the air very still and bitingly cold, the sky clear but no sun to be seen. I ran in and out—in when I could bear the cold no longer in

spite of gloves, scarf and cap, and then out again as soon as I
had warmed up a little at the fireplace or in the cowshed.

The reason why I thus braved the tingling frost again and
again was that my father and Nonni had set off before daybreak
for the fields to fill sacks with the summer's hay. These sacks
were to be sent sliding down the precipitous mountainside slippery with frozen snow. As it was already well after midday
the sacks ought soon to be appearing. When at last I saw
something dark against the white snow come gliding down from
high up, I thought at first that it was a bird. But when I
saw this dark something give a mighty jump as it came nearer,
nearer, I was convinced that it was the first sack of hay. And
just as I had made up my mind that it was so I suddenly went
cold all over—for what if it were not a hay-sack at all, but my
father who had lost his footing? I rushed in, clung, sobbing, to
my mother and for a long time could not say a word. When at
last she understood me, her expression changed suddenly, and,
taking hands, we went out. The first things we saw were three
or four sacks which seemed to be running a race down the
mountainside.

My mother smiled in a queer, hasty fashion and said cheerfully:

"You silly boy! Why, if anything had happened to Father,
Nonni would not go on sending down the sacks!"

Then, still smiling, she lifted me up, hugged me closely to
her and ran indoors with me.

Nevertheless none of us was quite happy until Father was
home again. But in the evening when he was sitting on his bed,
talking as if through a funnel, loosening big bits of ice from
his beard and suggesting that we should help him off with his
shoes and stockings, we all laughed at nothing until we had
tears in our eyes.

And then there was another day.

It was blowing hard outside. The wind streamed down the
narrow valley, a roaring torrent of cold and discomfort. It was
not snowing, but the storm brought with it clouds of drifting

snow like fine sand that dashed against the windows in flurries.
The window panes were heavy with hoarfrost, we were all rather
cold, and Veiga and I had to run over to Mother again and again
to have our hands warmed. My father and Nonni had finished
the work early and now my father was sitting on his bed, reading, in an unnecessarily loud voice, a story out of a thick hand-
written ragged book. Opposite my father sat my mother, knitting with long, yellow, wooden needles and balls of wool of
different colors. The door to the servants' room stood open and
in there sat Old Begga, spinning today with a quiet, well-oiled
spinning wheel, Maria Mens who was carding with vacant eyes,
making it difficult to tell whether she heard more than she saw,
and Nonni who had put Maria Mens' trunk on top of his
own and stood high up in the air winding fine yarn onto a reel.
On one side of my mother sat Veiga with one cheek bulged out
by her tongue, imagining that she too was knitting. And I knelt
leaning against my father's back with my head on his shoulder,
my interest divided about equally among the story, the book and
Nonni—whom I expected and hoped would fall down. Beta
slept.

Suddenly a cold shiver passed through me. I looked at the
others to see whether they had heard anything, but it did not seem
as if they had.

"What is the matter, little Uggi?" asked my mother, in an
undertone. "Are you cold?"

"No . . . I just thought there was someone calling," I whispered, and another shiver went through me.

"What nonsense!" my father burst out, impatient at the interruption. "Who could be traveling about in such weather? It's
only the storm, can't you understand?"

He searched down the page with his finger for his place, and
again lifted up his voice:

" 'But Hjalmar, who had now got the better of the giant,
turned hastily to the giantess and said: "Now you have
talked enough, and more than enough," and chopped off her
head. . . .' "

I jumped down from the bed, clung trembling to my mother and when she looked at me questioningly, I whispered:

"There it is again."

My father testily put the book aside and said shortly:

"Well, then, go out with Nonni and see with your own eyes that there is no one there! I will wait a minute if you will hurry up!"

Nonni laid the reel aside, bent his knees for a jump, but straightened himself suddenly and listened.

"Something *is* there," he muttered, growing pale.

We all listened.

The frozen roofs droned with a hollow sound; the storm howled vindictively and shook the house. Maria Mens sat there quite pale, with rigid eyes. Suddenly she whispered:

"A ghost!"

"Ghosts would scarcely walk at the height of the day!" Old Begga snapped, and started her spinning wheel again.

But we heard a scraping on the window over my mother's bed; Veiga and I gave a yell and then came a thin, pitiable voice:

"God's peace to this house."

"God's peace to you," answered my father, and the other grownups all mumbled something too.

Then the voice shouted again.

"Will Farmer Greipur please come to the door for a minute?"

"Yes, I am coming," answered my father, and as he went out through the room he murmured: "Who can it be?"

Again the roofs boomed with their hollow sound.

"At the worst a ghost!" laughed Nonni, suddenly, in a shrill treble, and attempted his jump at last.

"I think it is a woman's voice," said Maria Mens, in a relieved tone, as if it were quite out of the question that a ghost could be a woman.

Old Begga, who was rather behind-hand with her comment, because she had been absolutely obliged to give Nonni a long, reproving look, said mumblingly to her spinning wheel:

"It is not usual to be so pious in the middle of the day, whoever it may be . . . I should not be surprised . . ."

My mother looked from one to another of us and said
calmly:

"It was the voice of Maggi from Vidivellir, Sigrid's son—
either alive or dead. Hurry up, Maria Mens, and get the kettle
on—I almost think he may be alive."

I tried, in spite of my terror, to forestall my father in opening
the outer door, but my fingers stuck to the frost-drenched iron
and as it took time to loosen them I was told a few home truths
about my uncalled-for zeal. Nevertheless I was the first to put
my head outside, and my eyes were blinded by the icy, dry, sharp
flurry of snow as fine as flour. A minute later the same thing
happened to my father and Nonni. It was therefore some time
before we saw, a little way off, a lanky boy, leaning on a long
stick, who seemed to be afraid to come any nearer.

"Good day!" called the thin voice. "I am to greet you from
Torgrim of Vidivellir and ask you . . ."

"Is that Maggi?" shouted my father, surprised. "Come in,
boy! Have you stood there shouting for long?"

"Yes," answered Maggi, swallowing hard. "I was to greet
you . . ."

"Why didn't you knock?" shouted my father, reproachfully.

"Torgrim said I was not to knock."

"Come inside, you will die of cold."

"Torgrim said I was not to come inside."

My father laughed impatiently.

"Is Torgrim mad? What has happened to the old devil?"

"He is dying," Maggi piped back.

All this time the storm had been talking too, emphasizing
certain words, cutting out others, so that they had to be guessed.

My father opened his mouth to say something, but gave it up,
took his tobacco pouch out of his trousers pocket, bit off a quid
and chewed vehemently.

"I was to greet you from Torgrim and ask"—the thin boy
began at last to tell us his errand—"whether you, Farmer Grei-

pur, will follow him to his grave next Sunday, ten o'clock, from Vidivellir, or whether another day would suit you better?"

"Greet him and tell him that I will be sure to come," answered my father, in an oddly sympathetic voice. "Say also that he has made sure of a funeral procession in good time," he added with an attempt at cheerfulness.

"He wanted to be sure, he said," explained Maggi.

"That is just like him!" answered my father, with the same rueful cheerfulness.

"He also said," the voice piped from outside, "that you are not to take anyone by the hand, or embrace anybody, either at Vidivellir or in the church, nor go into any of the houses, nor take off your gloves except to play the psalms on the organ, and that you must go straight home from the grave. He said that unless you promised this, you must not come."

"What does he mean by all this?" asked my father, half-smiling, half-annoyed.

"He says that there is a dangerous children's illness about in the valley, and that he does not want to be followed into the earth by any of his *friends'* children."

"Well, I suppose that is the reason why he has forbidden you to come in, and forbidden you to knock."

"Yes . . . I must not touch anything or get close to anybody," he said.

"Very well—greet him from me, and say, 'God bless you.' "

"I daren't."

"Daren't you greet him?"

"Yes—but not the other! . . . Goodbye."

"Well, well, leave that out! . . . God be with you, boy."

I rushed in so as to be the first with the news.

"Begga, Begga!" I shouted, when I had only got as far as the stairs. "That old sinner is going to die!"

I noticed that Old Begga looked at me rather peculiarly as I passed her, and became unusually "young" in her cheeks. I did not take any notice of it then, but repeated the same words to my mother.

My mother looked at Old Begga, Old Begga looked at my mother and my mother said:

"Whom is the child talking about? Is Maggi ill?"

She had already stood up before I had time to explain to her who the "old sinner" was and that Maggi had already gone.

My mother and Old Begga looked at each other again, and then my mother sat down, while Old Begga gave the spinning wheel a hasty turn. She spun in jerks and loosed the thread. . . .

I suddenly felt very unhappy. I just wanted to creep up onto the bed behind my mother and begin to cry.

My father came in. He told us shortly what Maggi had said. Otherwise few words were spoken. . . . My father hid the story book away, brought out a half-finished horsehair rope and plaited silently with a sure hand.

"Do you really think he will die?" asked my mother, quietly. Old Begga's spinning wheel lowered its voice and we all listened to my father.

"Old Torgrim does not usually make a mistake," answered my father, casually.

Again there was silence, again Old Begga's spinning wheel hummed.

"Do you know Torgrim well?" asked my mother, when Maria Mens, followed by Nonni, came in with the coffee. "Why did he send to you?"

"To begin with we are neighbors," answered my father, in a grave and quiet voice. "Secondly, I suppose I am one of the few who have not quarreled with him."

While my mother stood and poured out the coffee I sat and listened to Old Begga's spinning wheel. It seemed to be talking to me, telling me about Torgrim. . . . I could not understand what it said, but by degrees it seemed to me as if I knew Torgrim very well—better than many of the people I had actually seen. . . .

"Come in here, Begga and Nonni," called my mother. "We must drink our coffee while it is hot. Oh, how cold it is today! Poor Maggi!"

When the coffee had been drunk my father got up, took down
the book of sermons and the hymnals from the shelf over the
gable window, handed round the hymn books, turned over the
leaves of his own, gave out a number. . . .

When the hymn had been sung, the sermon read, and another hymn sung, my father said the *Our Father* with folded
hands and closed eyes. When he had finished, he and the other
grownups sat for a time without moving or opening their eyes.
Then my father crossed himself and so did we all.

Outside the howling storm washed over the trembling,
coldly-creaking house. It grew dark. . . .

Old Begga's spinning wheel told me that now Torgrim was
dead. Then suddenly it began to repeat again and again, as if
to torment me: "that old sinner! . . . that old sinner! . . . that
old sinner. . . ."

5

WE WERE living again at Ofeigsstadur. . . . Not in the loft, for Sigrid-from-Vidivellir lived there now with her son Magnus, but in the two rooms that Sigga's papa and Madame Anna used to have.

Sigga's papa, Madame Anna and my cousins had gone—over land, over water. The same day that we moved from Hjalli to Ofeigsstadur in the morning, they left Ofeigsstadur in the afternoon.

I remember that day so well. We got up earlier than usual, were given only fresh milk to drink, and said a hasty goodbye to Nonni and a couple of men from Ofeigsstadur who were to follow with our belongings. When we rode away, the small short-stalked dandelions in the yard had tears in their eyes. When I saw this, tears came into my eyes also, although, in my heart of hearts, I was very glad to exchange Hjalli for Ofeigsstadur. The sun shone, white clouds floated across the sky. The air was cool. My father rode on Brunka, I sat on the pommel of his saddle and Red, no longer a foal but a young horse, trotted all the way so close to us that my father's leg became covered with his red hairs. In front of us rode my mother with Beta on her lap on a fine-looking gray horse—and behind us was Bjarni Smith with Veiga, who slept. My father was angry with Red because he ran with his head stretched forward. He predicted that he would become "rein-heavy" and therefore no good for riding. I was sorry for this, but felt quite certain that he was mistaken; and when he suggested that I should change and have a colt, perhaps Brunka's next, I refused with great firmness. We came to a river that was as clear as a pane of glass and which snapped at the horses' legs, hissing with foam-flecked mouths.

Sigga's papa received us in the courtyard of Ofeigsstadur,

kissed me, lifted me down and put me on my legs. I was very
stiff, very hungry and very happy. My cousins, who were so
grand, so pretty and so friendly, overwhelmed me by present-
ing me with their farmyard and all the animals belonging to it,
kissed me and let me take as big bites as possible from their
slabs of chocolate. Madame Anna was as gay and dignified as
usual, gave me some chocolate, filled my pockets with fragrant
cakes and openly admired my big brass buttons with anchors
on them which, to my very great satisfaction, she called "offi-
cial buttons." Sigga Mens found an opportunity to whisper
a horrible greeting in my ear. Maggi from Vidivellir, whom I
met in a doorway and immediately recognized, stopped and
looked at me silently. I looked at him, also without a word.
Then he contorted his thin gray face into a vile grimace, blew
at me rudely and left me standing. Björssi, whom I sought and
found behind the farm, where he was shoveling the contents
of a wheelbarrow onto the top of the dunghill, patting it smooth
after each shovelful, looked at me for a moment astonished,
rushed at me with the shovel, landed me one and roared in a
voice which was breaking:

"Oh, hell! There you are again, you wretch, you vile
wretch!"

There was a note of innate kindness both in the words and
in the blow and, when he had at last mastered his emotion, we
were both rather out of breath. Björssi helped me to deal with my
bleeding nose and rub the marks off my clothes. Then we divided up my cakes and my chocolate.

"I suppose you have forgotten how to swear?" asked Björssi,
with his mouth full of cake, evidently ready to give some return
for the sweetmeats.

"No-o-o," I drawled. "But I have promised Grandpa-from-
Fjall to leave off."

"Brrr," scoffed Björssi, "one promises so much! Do you really
trouble about what you have promised an old graybeard like
that? You will promise other things that you cannot keep, as life
goes on."

"He is going to give me a watch at my confirmation, if I leave off," I excused myself.

"That's quite another thing," answered Bjössi, thoughtfully. "I will give you a good thrashing one of these days, the Devil skin me if I don't, you tail of an ass!"

They called me, and Bjössi and I parted in great friendship. Through a mist of tears I saw Sigga's papa, Madame Anna and my cousins ride away from the farm. My father, who was very grave and whose eyes were red, rode with them. He intended to accompany them as far as Fjall, where they were going to spend the night. My mother was crying, and everybody who had collected in the yard was crying. I hoped to the last that they would turn back, but they did not. My mother took my hand and we went in. I sat on her lap and she rocked me backward and forward, humming softly. I was very tired, very unhappy, and soon fell asleep. . . .

Many days passed. So many days that my father and mother said that now Sigga's papa and his household must have arrived in Skerjavik. All that I knew about Skerjavik was that it lay far, far away. All that I knew about the future of my relations was that they would probably never come back to Ofeigsstadur to live, but that possibly they might be expected here on a visit once in a while in many, many years. I had cried about it and had reconciled myself to the thought. Now, when I thought of Sigga's papa, whom, by degrees, following my father's example, I grew to call "Brother-in-Skerjavik," I was mostly occupied in wondering what Skerjavik was like, what sort of mountains were there, what sort of houses, people and animals. I could not bear to think that I knew nothing about all this. It was as if this lack of knowledge separated me from these people whom I loved so much. I felt as if I must get to know what Skerjavik was like. But how? No one seemed to know.

"If Sira Sigbergur were sent to the underworld he would take a blessing with him," was all that Old Begga had to say about the matter.

There seemed to me to be very little comfort in that—almost

as if Skerjavik lay very much nearer that evil place than did Ofeigsstadur. I looked at Old Begga, and considered. "Who has sent Sigga's papa to Skerjavik?" I asked wonderingly.

"God has sent him!" answered Old Begga, crossly, and blew her nose into the fire. "Who else?"

As it was Weekday-Begga I was talking to, I was not quite bold enough to ask her in what way God revealed Himself to Sigga's papa—whether He called him up into a mountain, spoke to him from a fire, or merely sent him a big letter, closed with red sealing-wax. While I pondered over it, something quite different came into my mind.

"Then it is God who is sending Sveinn Olafsson here?" I asked, and looked at Old Begga expectantly.

"No—that, I should say, is the work of man!" answered Old Begga, and looked at me sharply and rather suspiciously. "Commend me to this chit of a thing! Does he think he can put me right? . . . A *little* boy can be a *big* nuisance—now you know that. Is it like God, do you think, to saddle us with Sveinn the Little Devil? No, Mr. All-Too-Wise; because God sends the one, it does not follow that He sends the other. No, maybe, He has left it to man, or even to the Evil One! I can never believe that God has anything whatever to do with Sveinn the Little Devil and his affairs. Anyhow, this I say, and this I am going to keep to—rather than receive my Saviour's blessed Body and Blood from *his* hands, I shall go for a year without communion, however sin-stained I may be. Every morning, every evening and the whole of Sunday I pray to the Almighty that I may not die in this Year of Sorrow when it will be the duty of Sveinn the Little Devil to 'consecrate to the dust' here in Ofeigsstadur Churchyard! '*In Jesu's name I daily live . . . In Jesu's name I die . . .*' "

I let Old Begga sing the hymn through undisturbed to the end. Not until I was certain that she had quite finished did I ask her whether she had ever seen Sveinn the Little Devil. That, thank God, she had not. I asked her whether she knew why he bore that name. That she neither knew nor wished to know. I asked her what she did know about Sveinn the Little Devil. Nothing. I refused to believe that, and went on with my questions.

"Well, since you will not believe me," answered Old Begga, impatiently, "I will tell you that once he put a sheet over his head to play ghost, and almost frightened the life out of a pair of servant girls! . . . You shudder—you have reason to shudder! Is that the way for a priest to behave? If I had been a Dean or a Bishop, I should have stripped his shirt off him at once, in the view of the whole congregation, and deposed him in disgrace."

To please Old Begga I said that I should undoubtedly have done the same if I had been Dean or Bishop.

"There was a person who is very nearly related to you who did not do much in the matter," said Old Begga, scornfully.

"Oh, who?" I asked inquisitively.

"None other than your blessed *Altings Man,** Dean Sira Sigbergur Uggason!" Old Begga informed me angrily. "Sira Sigbergur is a remarkable man, he is a good preacher and he has an excellent heart. But he is not stern and zealous, like my Jon Vidalin—pah, I say, pah!"

I, also, said "pah," and repeated it several times, but even this did not bring me, as I expected, Old Begga's approval. On the contrary she looked at me with still greater displeasure; and when a little later I was indiscreet enough to disclose that I was looking forward to seeing Sveinn the Little Devil, she took up the stick and I took to my heels.

I soon became very much absorbed in "Sigrid-in-the-Loft," as we called Sigrid-from-Vidivellir, and I was quickly on good terms with Maggi also.

"To begin with you looked to me like a damned wet-blanket," he confided to me one day. "And you are rather simple, I must say. Still, you are neither a tattle-tale nor a cry-baby. . . . Give me that spade!"

---

* Representative to the *Alting,* the Icelandic legislative body.

I handed him the spade willingly, feeling honored. Maggi was in my father's service. At first he was not quite satisfied with his work.

"What that fool Bjössi can't get through, and the other men won't take the trouble to do, they pass on to me!" he complained to me. "But I'll be damned if I'm here for the servants to abuse and send on errands. And your father knows that very well. I am old enough to do men's work—look at my muscles!" He pulled up one of his shirtsleeves right to his shoulder, and turned and twisted his bare arm about. "You can see for yourself!" he said, and hastily pulled down his shirtsleeve, blushing a little. "Do you know what is wrong with your father? He is too peaceful—does anything to avoid a row! He never speaks out, even if he is angry! But I will soon settle those chaps—as truly as I am called Magnus Bachmann!"

"Are you called Magnus Bachmann?" I asked, puzzled. "Haven't you a father?"

"Didn't I say you were simple-minded!" exulted Maggi, pityingly. "My name is really Magnus Jonsson Bachman—my father was as good as a German, and that is a very grand thing. In a few years' time, perhaps, I shall be visiting my family in Germany. I must just get a little money in my pocket. Magnus Bachmann would not care to meet his relations as a pauper, you understand."

I nodded—I understood perfectly—and Maggi added:

"My father died year before last. Poor old man, he had grown so old. . . . Then we came to Torgrimur at Vidivellir. He was also old. . . . But that didn't come off. . . ."

"What didn't come off?" I asked cautiously.

Maggi looked at me hastily.

"You must not get in the way of sticking your nose into what does not concern you!" he said sulkily. "I'm not going to make you my Father Confessor."

I shook my head very vigorously, for, although I had no idea what sort of a Father a Father Confessor was, I did not want Maggi to suspect that I was considering plans to marry his

mother—a thing that I fully realized could not yet take place
for a number of years, and about which I therefore did not
wish to speak.

In a surprisingly short time, with the help of his sharp and
dangerous tongue, Maggi carried his point—namely, that the
boys' work that Bjössi could not get through should be divided
out among the men.

"Didn't I tell you so?" Maggi one day appealed to my memory. "There's not a tongue like mine in the whole world!"

Another day he confided to me he had no need to exert
himself. The words lay on the tip of his tongue; he only had
to utter them. I immediately remembered Old Begga's remark
about "my Jon Vidalin," and whispered, fascinated:

"I expect it is God who puts them on your tongue."

"Not exactly God, I think," Maggi rejected the suggestion in
an expressive tone. "Not exactly God, old man. . . . The Devil is
also a good one to have as a friend, I can tell you; besides, you
can always take him in! He is so simple, so stupid. I hope that
you know the story of Saemund the Wise and the Devil!"

I acknowledged, ashamed, that I did not. It was, therefore,
Maggi who initiated me into the many legends about the wise
priest, Saemund, whose chief occupation seems to have been to
outwit the Devil.

Sigrid-in-the-Loft supplied her own food. Maggi, on the
other hand, ate with our other servants. My mother had several
times offered to arrange for him to have his meals with his
mother, but he always refused. This astonished me very much.
But what astonished me even more was that Maggi, who was
usually so full of fun, became sullen and moody as soon as his
mother appeared. . . .

I visited Sigrid-in-the-Loft much oftener than she cared to
see me, because I was fascinated by her. She was tall and slim,
had a narrow face, gray eyes and heavy fair hair. If it had been
I whom she wished to pat on the head or embrace, I should certainly not have turned away my head or squirmed away from her.
But Maggi did. In all possible ways he showed her his dislike.

If she asked him a question he only answered her reluctantly or after a long pause, if he answered at all. If she sent him on an errand he very seldom came back. This was grist to my mill. Sigrid, who did needlework, needed among other things to have irons heated for pressing, and I liked nothing better than to run errands for her and to be at her beck and call. . . .

"When Sveinn the Little Devil comes I will ask him to put the sheet over his head and publish the banns of marriage for you and Vidivella-Sigga," Sigga Mens teased me.

I felt that Sigga Mens saw through me but I did not care, and did not stay away from the "loft," which I never willingly left. Either someone had to fetch me or I stayed until Sigrid told me to go.

Unfortunately I was not at all amusing company. I found it difficult to open my mouth when I was with Sigrid. It was enough for me just to stand with crossed legs and my arms on the table, my head on my arms, looking at her. But Sigrid's talk was almost always of the kind that needed no answer from me except "Yes, yes," or "No, no." Very often she teased me, but to be teased by her was a pleasure.

When by degrees it dawned on me that my father owned the whole of Ofeigsstadur, the horses, cows, sheep, dogs, cats, tools and furniture, I realized that a farmyard such as mine, even after I had inherited my cousins' farm with its stock, was not worthy of my dignity as the son of my father. First of all, I must have a house, a real house, with walls, roof, windows and doors. I went to my father and asked him if he would assign me a place where I might build.

"You may build where you like—but it must be outside the home field," answered my father, with a smile. "Definitely not in the field."

I found a spade, put it over my shoulder as I had seen the men do and set off to find a building site. I had not been walking long before my shoulder became sore from carrying the spade. When I had made my other shoulder equally sore, only to keep up appearances to myself, I let vanity go, and contented myself with dragging the spade, first with one hand and then with the other and finally with both. After a search I found a place which suited me, and stuck my spade into the ground—that is to say, it was my intention to stick it into the ground. Unfortunately, either the ground was hard or the spade blunt, or both. I tried once or twice, but without success, threw down the spade and disconsolately continued my walk. Suddenly I thought of an old, broken-down sheep-pen above the smooth, steep, so-called "potato slope," down which we children used to roll when no one was watching us and we wanted to get giddy. I went off and looked at the pen and my good humor increased. It was overgrown with the most delicious grass and the walls were still high enough to allow me to creep around inside, even if I put a flat roof on top of it. As soon as I had decided for the pen I settled that Veiga should be my wife and little Beta our child. In the next few days we all three worked hard dragging bits of plank and any wood that we could get hold of across the field and up the steep slope. It was not quick work. Veiga and I wasted a good deal of time trying to be parental to little Beta, who would not acknowledge our authority. Happily it was Sunday, so we gave up altogether and Nonni came to our assistance and roofed in the pen with sods. So at last we had a proper house.

We called the farm Fjall, and Veiga and I lived there with our child, Beta. We collected household goods, moved our animals over there and with all this work the summer began to pass.

We had other things to see to besides the farm, Veiga and I. It was our duty to bring Beta up in "the fear of God and with good habits," and we were both very zealous about this. If she had been particularly naughty we would hold a service. I would put one of my mother's old chemises over my suit and be the priest. Veiga would take the many-voiced part of the sobbing congregation. But that was the smallest part of our work. We had to hunt for birds' nests and mark the place where they were, we had to look at them every day and we had to keep Beta away from them. We had to listen to the curlew's trills and admire the black breast of the plover. We had to chase butterflies, fly from bees, and find snakes and beetles to make each other shudder. We had to milk the stems of dandelions so as to have milk in our pails, and make chains of the stalks. We had to collect flowers and sweet-smelling grasses for Mama. And finally we had to find time to lie on our backs and drink in the strong fragrance of sun-baked heather on the hot stones, and trace the shapes of faces and animals in the clouds.

There were, especially for me, other things that must not be neglected. There were Old Begga with her stories, Sigga Mens with her horrors, Bjössi with his eternal longing for a fight, Sigrid-in-the-Loft with her beauty, Maggi with his practical jokes and his sharp tongue, Maria Mens with her shy friendliness and many tears, Bjarni Smith so cheerfully garrulous, Nonni with his pale quiet smile and his eagerness to help, my father with his manners and gait so worthy of imitation— and my mother, who had so much time to tell me about herself and her brothers and sisters when children and about the life at Knör.

"What is *your* mother like?" I asked her one day—for she seldom mentioned her mother.

"Mother scarcely ever spoke," answered my mother, with a strange light in her eyes. "But she could never pass us children without patting us. We were very fond of her. If we felt that we had vexed her we were inconsolable. My sister Halla is like her . . . poor Halla!"

"Is she dead?" I asked; that was the worst thing I could think of.

My mother was silent for a moment. Then she said:

"She married a man whom Old Papa could not tolerate. . . . They are so poor, and Old Papa will not help them."

She made a movement with her arms, and although I was sitting with my back to her I knew well that she was drying her eyes and did not want me to see it. As I thought that she did not want to talk about Halla any more, I asked her about something else.

Early one morning I met Bjarni the smith in the yard with his beard and eyebrows covered in soot, a twinkle in his eye and his scythe over his shoulder.

"Where are you going, dear Bjarni?" I asked him ingratiatingly, as I saw that he did not have his dinner basket with him.

"Off to hack down the grass on the Devil's own hummocks west of the hayfield," answered Bjarni Smith. "Are you coming too, scrap? Shall we have a look at the Outlaw's graves?"

I was more than willing, and hand-in-hand we set off westward across the field.

The Outlaws' graves were three oblong mounds. I knew them very well. My father once shortly forbade me to play there, and he never allowed the grass which grew on them to be cut. Not that it mattered—it was no great loss. Except for some high grasses between which enterprising spiders stretched the finely-meshed webs in which they lived, only low grasses and short-stalked flowers grew there. It always seemed to me that there was a strange kind of stillness round these three grave mounds.

"Look there, now," said Bjarni Smith, when we had been standing silent for some time looking at them. "Look there," he pointed with a sooty finger. "There lies Bessi, there Ofeigur, there Bjarnhedinn. Ofeigur is in the middle, he was the leader. And look up there—on the mountain above us, I mean. There is Bessi's cave, there is Ofeigur's cave and there Bjarnhedinn's cave. They were each of them caught in his own cave, that they were. Why anyone should go to the trouble of digging them a grave apiece, that is more than I can understand. . . . Well, perhaps the people who lived here were afraid that they would rise up and fight among themselves if they were put too close together. What do I know! Anyhow, look how these graves are turned at right-angles to those at home in the churchyard. A Christian grave lies east and west, a felon's grave from north to south. That's the rule."

"Shh!" I whispered uneasily.

"Ha, ha, ha!" laughed Bjarni Smith. But his laughter did not ring quite true. "Are you afraid that those down there will hear you? . . . Well, well, well! In those graves lies only their dust. Their souls have been burning for long ages in Hell, or at any rate in Purgatory. Death is bitter if one has been a monster in life, especially the part after death—that's the rule! . . . But let us suppose that they are lying down there listening to me—what could they do to me, a Christian, washed in the blood of the Lamb?"

He got rather red, and I had an intuition that these last words were said as much to the three in the graves as to me.

"Well, whatever can be said against Ofeigur, it was he who gave the farm its name," he conceded in quite another tone of voice. With a scowl at the graves he turned away more calmly. "One can't get away from that! . . ."

"Hadn't it a name before, dear Bjarni?" I asked, surprised.

"It probably had some name or other," answered Bjarni Smith, a little flustered. "Perhaps it was called Stadur. Now, at any rate, it is called Ofeigsstadur!"

"Do you think they were very wicked?" I ventured to whisper when we were a little distance away from the graves.

"Bad they certainly were," answered Bjarni Smith, talking on purpose in a low voice. "Why else should they have been out-lawed, tell me that? And even if they had not been very bad be-fore, they must have stolen the farmers' sheep to keep body and soul together. . . . To steal money is very bad, but to steal sheep is still worse. You can understand that. A man can look after his money; he can bury it in the ground, if he has nowhere better to put it. But how can a man look after his sheep in the mountains? It is not worth while to make a fuss about a little pilfering and that sort of thing, you see; a little butter, a hand-ful of flour, a piece of smoked meat can be stolen by a poor man in God's name if he is very hungry and has nothing to eat. But sheep stealing, that is a regular crime, that is. . . . These three here were either hanged or beheaded or both; God knows what they did to them. At any rate they were captured in the caves I showed you. And now there they lie."

Bjarni Smith winked quite unnecessarily toward the Outlaws' graves, to show me exactly where they lay.

"Would they have stolen sheep from the houses?" I asked, insatiable.

"Stolen sheep from the houses?" repeated Bjarni, pulling a long face so that he looked just like a horse. "How can I know that? Most certainly they *wanted* to. A thief always *wants* to steal. Whether they had actually planned it, though, I do not know. . . . First and foremost, I suppose, they went to the church to hear the Word of God. Can you believe it—these robbers and sheep-killers trooped calmly into the House of God just as the priest was beginning the service. Rabble of that sort have absolutely no shame. The farmers looked at each other—they could guess what sort of folk these strangers were even if they did not know them and had never seen them before. Did they therefore spring up and attack them? No! What should they spring up for? The murderers stood hugging the doors, and, besides, the service must not be disturbed—one must never disturb a service. . . . They winked at each other, they agreed. Some understood, some did not. When, therefore, the last holy word was spoken and the outlaws took to their heels to save their lives, then those who had misunderstood ran after them, and tried to overtake them, while those who had understood, leaped onto their horses. And now the outlaws, you see—well, they did not only take to their legs, they also took to their hands, they turned cartwheels, as it is called, and a man who turns cartwheels cannot be caught by any devil on two legs. . . . What are cartwheels? Look at me! One turns oneself into a wheel. . . . One rotates along the ground . . . like this!"

Bjarni Smith, with the optimism of old age, turned himself into a wheel and tried to "rotate" along the ground. He wanted to demonstrate the impossibility of catching an outlaw who is turning cartwheels. Unfortunately, he did not even manage his first revolution, for, to his own great astonishment, he flopped over onto his back before he had got his legs properly off the ground.

"In my young days I could do it—you should have seen me!" Thus he tried to relieve the situation while he slowly gathered himself together and got to his feet. "Well, well, chicken, take your hand away from your mouth and laugh out freely. Ha, ha, ha! Was it very funny to see me? Ha, ha, ha! I quite forgot my years and my stiff legs. Ha, ha, ha! . . . But if you can turn cartwheels you cannot be caught, except, of course, by a horse! And that was just what I was saying. Those who understood and were not asses did not run after the rascals, who naturally separated immediately, each of them running in a different direction so as to separate their pursuers. No, you see, those who had brains, they sprang onto their horses, gave themselves time to arrange who should follow whom; and in that way Ofeigur, Bessi and Bjarnhedinn were captured.

"What did they want to go to church for, since they had not come to repent and take their punishment? I repeat: What were they doing there? . . . To steal sheep is just as bad as to make a bargain with the Prince of Darkness in one's own name and with one's own initials, *B. A.,* Bjarni Andresson. . . . No, you see, it was certainly fate. And it is not by turning cartwheels that one can escape fate—that's the rule! All is written in the book of life . . . I have often wondered whether in Heaven they use the Roman type of lettering, black lettering or runes—it can scarcely be a question of hornspoon writing. . . . In any case, what is written is written, and somebody must be able to read it. There must be some order in things. Suppose there were a confusion with another man who died on my death-day—what would happen to *me?* No, you will see, it will stand there clearly—*B. A.,* Bjarni Andresson. And if it is written in the books that I am to freeze to death one winter night, I don't want there to be a muddle about it. I have *my* destiny just as much as the King has *his.* . . . That's the rule."

While I was still standing talking to Bjarni and neglecting

my home, my wife came running and asked what I was doing
and begged me to come home at once and "hold a service" over
Beta.

"She is quite unmanageable today, the little lass," my wife
complained, sobbing. "She has broken up our bannock! She
has spilt the milk in our storeroom! She has overturned my
cupboard! She has pulled down my shelves! Now she sits
there spitting into the porridge! . . . Say a prayer over her, dear
husband!"

"Certainly, my dear," I answered with dignity, and went off
obediently with my spouse.

I prayed over Beta, and she improved, and allowed herself to
be persuaded to take her right place in the family. Her mother
put our only, but quite unbreakable, "teat," a red stone, into her
mouth and said:

"Suck that, my dear child, but don't swallow it!"

While Beta sucked, Veiga and I set about restoring order in
Fjall, knocked pegs into the walls for shelves, made bannocks
from mud and water, baked them on sun-heated stones, filled
our pails with dandelion milk and cooked a spit-free portion of
mud porridge. . . .

Suddenly extraordinary things began to happen in the world
around us. Old Begga came out of the house and shouted and
beckoned vehemently and very angrily, not to us, but to Bjarni
Smith. And Bjarni Smith looked scared, threw down his scythe
and ran, terrified, westward over the slopes, not turning his head
once. Old Begga was pacified and disappeared into the house.

I was sorry that Bjarni Smith should have to run so fast, to no
purpose. I made a funnel of my hands and shouted after him
at the top of my voice:

"It's all right. She has gone in, good Bjarni!"

Bjarni Smith was too far away to hear me. With bent back
and arms akimbo he rowed himself forward through the air and
disappeared behind the hill. Before I had quite recovered from
my astonishment he suddenly reappeared on Brunka's back, with
two other of my father's horses galloping wildly in front of

him. . . . What was the man thinking about? Was he so angry
with Old Begga that he had fetched the horses to trample her
flat and even her with the ground? No, but there came Old
Begga, not pursued by anybody, with a bundle in her hand—and
there went Bjarni Smith off from the farm, still on Brunka, but
with saddles on the two other horses now. . . .

Many remarkable things happened that day. It happened
that Old Begga's bundle turned out to be cakes and sugar candy
which we children were given on the condition that we were not
to come home, whatever happened or whatever we might see,
before we were called. It sounded like an adventure, and of
course we promised. Furthermore, Old Begga refused to know
anything about Bjarni Smith's journey, and in answer to my
questions informed me that there were many things children did
not need to know and that it was not at all necessary to be able
to read to have part in God's mercy and the Bliss of Heaven.
More extraordinary still was it that a little man, who did not
look quite like a groom, came riding on one of the horses which
Bjarni Smith had taken with him—that Bjarni Smith some time
later came galloping with lifted whip, driving before him a
horse on which rode a woman—that I had a glimpse of my
father, who I had thought was out in the fields with the har-
vesters—that Old Begga brought us our dinner, but oddly
enough continued to "know nothing about anything"—that the
chimney at home smoked very heavily the whole day as if a feast
were being prepared—that the little man rode away again in
company with Bjarni Smith—and that, at last, Old Begga appeared, beckoned to us to come home and came to meet us. . . .

I rolled down the slope, completely forgetting my wife and
child, rushed over to Old Begga and asked breathlessly:

"Who was that little man?"

"The little man," repeated Old Begga, heavily, "that was
the district doctor. Can you tell me why a man such as he
should come and visit a married man's house as soon as his wife
is in labor? He ought to know better. Weak coffee and burned

pancakes were all that man got from me. He won't return to this house for the sake of its hospitality. . . . But there, now, one more has been added to this household since you got up this morning, goldilocks. . . . Has that woman Bjarni Smith fetched come for good? God knows—she is sure to stay longer than she need! However, you ask according to your understanding. A midwife all the year round—such a thing has never been heard of before! . . . But, would you believe it, midwives must be trained now. Well, well, the old methods are no longer any good. Not a few little ones have I helped into this world, and they have turned out very well—most of them, at any rate—but now practically the whole parish has to be fetched because your father is to have a daughter and you a sister. . . . All right then, run on ahead, poppet; you are bouncing about as if you were on hot bricks. I expect we can find our way home without you!"

In the south room, our bedroom, lay my mother in her bed, smiling but pale and her hand hot. My father sat on a stool beside her and looked very happy. A strange woman moved busily about the room. When I wanted to throw myself onto my mother, she warded me off, carefully lifted a corner of the sheet and showed me a little baby face and a pair of very, very small hands. So that was my little sister. . . . She opened a pair of dark blue eyes and looked at me, looked at me intimately. I stood there at first fascinated; then tears came into my eyes; then I laughed, and finally I asked gently:

"What is her name, Mama?"

"She isn't called anything yet, Uggi child," said my mother, and smiled. "What do you think we should call her?"

"Madame Anna." It tumbled out of me—her mouth looked so masterful, I thought.

My mother laughed, my father laughed and the strange woman laughed.

"Papa and I decided long ago that if it were a girl we would call her Anna," said my mother. "Now she will never be anything but Madame Anna, whatever else we decide to call her."

Sleep no longer pursued me as relentlessly as of old. If any-thing particular were happening I could keep awake until a little later in the evening. But I still missed various interesting events by sleeping through them. One of these was the arrival of Sveinn the Little Devil.

"What horse is that, out in the home meadow?" I asked my father one morning.

My father looked out.

"Oh, he's that sort, is he!" he said hastily. "Wants to be out in the home field! We must soon cure him of that—other-wise he may ruin the other horses for us! . . . He belongs to the new parson, and he is like him."

"Has he come?" I asked subdued.

"Came last night," answered my father, shortly.

"Where is he sleeping?" I asked.

"In the gable room," my father informed me impatiently, dipping his head in the basin.

I got into my clothes in double-quick time, shirked my morn-ing wash, hastened out of the room and settled, after a few moments' indecision, on inspecting the horse a little more closely before I ventured in to its master.

The horse, to put it mildly, did not look reassuring. He was piebald, white with black markings, and his mane was very badly groomed. Besides, he had a broad muzzle, shaggy fet-locks, flat hoofs, and a white ring in one eye. He gave the impression of having been used for all sorts of things and not always having been treated well. His back was roughened with great sores, the hair on his sides was, in several places, worn down to the skin—and God only knew whether he was a real horse.

Thoughtfully, and as unobtrusively as possible, I slipped away from him, went back to the house, went along the passages, and, with my heart in my mouth, approached the living room stairs.

Eh—pouff! . . . I heard heavy breathing from above. *Eh—pouff.*

That must be the parson: Sveinn the Little Devil. But what could he be doing? Was he really black and white and dirty, just like his horse, and with a ring in his eye? The sounds seemed to confirm this.

Eh—pouff . . . eh—pouff, breathing and panting. It must be he. *Eh—pouff . . . eh—pouff.*

Perhaps he was fighting all alone with a crowd of small devils, or what could it be? Was the Evil One carrying him away? Would I die if I peeped in through the knothole in the paneling at the side of the door? . . . Noiselessly I crept up the stair, noiselessly I stole through the empty living room over to the wall between it and the gable room and, holding my breath, looked through the little knothole.

Eh—pouff . . . eh—pouff . . . eh—pouff!

Sveinn the Little Devil was sitting on a chair in his room doing nothing. He had no ring in the white of his eye, but otherwise he was undoubtedly like his horse. I was even certain that he had sores on his back! He was black, he was white, and he puffed and he blew. Now and again he took a pinch of snuff out of a great black, brass-bound snuffbox. Otherwise, he just sat, fat and shapeless, on his chair, rolling a pair of big, black-and-white eyes round the room as if he were searching for devils in the corners, breathing hard: *eh—pouff . . . eh—pouff . . . eh—pouff!*

His eye rested on my peephole, he listened, he got up. . . .

I did not wait for him; I dashed toward the stairs—but there he was standing in the door, fat and short and almost neckless in a stained black coat that reached to his ankles. I stared at him as if paralyzed. Now he raised a thick, short finger and said in a thick, short voice, after an *eh—pouff . . . eh—pouff:* "Don't break your stairs falling down those necks!"

To my ears this simple injunction sounded entirely mad. Giddily I let myself slide down the stairs, without paying any heed to the bumps I was getting, and when I reached the floor I did not even give myself time to get onto my feet but crawled off on all fours to save my life.

That very day Sveinn the Little Devil visited my mother. Madame Anna had finished her meal and had fallen asleep, and the midwife had just gone, when there was a knock at the door. I was alone with my mother, sitting on a stool and holding her hand. So as to save her the trouble of answering, I got up and hurried to the door and opened it, but as soon as I saw who the visitor was I rushed back with a shriek, meaning to save myself by climbing onto the bed and hiding behind my mother. However, before I got as far as that, my mother looked at me very gravely; and when I understood that she was not in the least frightened I suddenly felt very much ashamed and my fright died down.

Sveinn the Little Devil came through the door as awkwardly as it was possible to come through any door, got his coat-tails caught when he was about to shut it, puffed and blew, blushed and rubbed his hands together. At last he reached the bed, held out his hand and stammered:

"You are glad that I am so well . . . *pouff, pouff!*"

"Thank you," answered my mother, with a smile. "Welcome, Sira Sveinn! You *are* Sira Sveinn Olafsson, aren't you?"

Sveinn the Little Devil blushed still more at my mother's words, and his white puffy face became stained with red.

"Yes indeed, yes indeed," he answered eagerly. "Sira Sveinn—*pouff, pouff!*—I wanted . . . I did not want . . . *pouff, pouff!* . . . I just wanted to let you say how do you do to me—No, no, I mean . . . Will you have a pinch?"

Very much flustered, Sveinn the Little Devil tried to push his snuffbox into my mother's hand, as if it were very important that she should accept that pinch of snuff.

"No, thank you, Sira Sveinn!" answered my mother, sweetly. "It is very kind of you, but I have not yet learned to take snuff. Won't you sit down a minute?"

"Yes, thank you . . . no, thank you—*pouff, pouff!*" answered Sveinn the Little Devil, and put his snuffbox first into one pocket and then into another and finally into a third. "Did you hurt yourself?" he asked, relieved, suddenly turning to me. *"Ouff, pouff,* you need not be afraid of me."

"No, I'm not afraid any longer," I answered truthfully.

"Good," said Sira Sveinn. *"Pouff, pouff.* What is your name?"

When I had told him my name my mother smiled at me. It was not until afterward that I understood it was because I had spoken in friendly fashion to Sira Sveinn. In a way I was glad of her smile; but at the same time I felt hot in the face, and tears came into my eyes, because she had divined that quite suddenly I felt an affection for him.

Sveinn the Little Devil brushed my shoulder with his snuffbox, blinked at me with his uncertain eyes and said: *"Pouff, pouff ...* When you visit me next time, come inside the door."

I blushed still more. Sveinn the Little Devil saw it and touched my shoulder repeatedly with his snuffbox. Then he turned toward my mother, evidently to put an end to his visit.

In the meantime my mother had uncovered Madame Anna's face and looked at him with happy eyes and an expectant smile.

"Eh—pouff," groaned Sveinn the Little Devil, uncomfortably, looking toward the door. "A lovely girl ... is it a boy?"

My mother shook her head smiling, lifted Madame Anna up in her arms and proudly mentioned her weight. Sveinn the Little Devil stood there shuffling his feet, saying everything the wrong way round; we generally understood nothing but his puffs, and when he went he first of all knocked his head against the door, then pinched his fingers.

"Poor man!" said my mother, softly, putting Madame Anna back in her place, and she lay with a thoughtful, anxious expression on her pale, radiant face. "As long as he isn't quite so unfortunate in the pulpit!"

Sveinn the Little Devil was not quite so unfortunate in the pulpit. If only he kept to his notes, always very dirty and very ragged, things generally went well. But if he was rash enough to try to make an impression with gestures or looks, everything went to pieces and his only hope of saving himself was in returning to his papers as quickly as possible, no matter where. But so long as his mind was not agitated he spoke, on the whole, fairly well.

However, it did not take much to upset his equilibrium. He was as self-conscious as a child. Maggi, who asserted that he had

inherited his sermons from some old predecessor, insisted that
a glance from a woman down in the pews was enough to make
the words "jump about in his head." There was some truth
in it at any rate. So far as women were concerned, Sveinn the
Little Devil was no gallant—if he fell in love he put a sheet
over his head. There were, of course, innumerable stories about
his solecisms in the pulpit, but most of these were inventions.
On the other hand, weddings, confirmations, baptisms and bur-
ials were matters of chance with Sveinn the Little Devil at the
altar. Once a newly married couple had suggested being married
again by another parson, because the wife was not certain
whether she had been married to Sira Sveinn or to her husband.
Things were very near to going wrong at Madame Anna's bap-
tism. My Grandmother Elizabeth had given her name, Anna,
and all was well until Sira Sveinn dipped his hand into the water
and said: "Madame Anna I baptize thee . . ." Happily, my
grandmother was quick enough to hold the wet hand away from
the child's head—and Sveinn the Little Devil was given a towel
to dry himself with and, trembling, just managed to get through
the rest of the service.

When he left the church afterward most of the congregation were standing with their backs toward him, very busy drying
their eyes.

That day, as on many others, I was very sorry for Sveinn the
Little Devil. When I, a little later, looked him up in his room
his pantings were very disconsolate and I had to use all my
powers of persuasion and call my obstinacy to my aid before I
could get him down to drink chocolate.

As far as I know, I was the only one who ever visited Sira
Sveinn in his room without a definite errand. My visits were,
therefore, not unwelcome, and I often repeated them. There
was a tacit agreement between us that on these visits the door
to the living room was left open and that he did not go between
it and me. Since saying that I was not frightened, I had seen
new sides of him; but I never felt quite safe with him and he
did not seem to expect it. It was the silent internal laughter

which shook him now and again, and his habit of eternally look-ing into all the dark corners, that kept my distrust of him alive.

Sometimes we went for walks together. Alone, Sveinn never left his room unless it was necessary, although I seldom found him reading and still more seldom writing. He seemed to do little else than sit on his chair, pant, and scowl. Only once did he say, "Shall we mouch about a little?" And so we mouched. Even out of doors I did not like going with him very much unless I could see people. This weakness of mine he also bore patiently.

One day when the folk were at home drying hay he said openly:

"Today we can go right up the mountains if you would like to. If we keep near the edge of the ravine you can see the people, and they you, the whole time. *Pouff, pouff*. . . . What do you say?"

I went.

By degrees we talked more and more openly to each other, both when we were alone indoors and when we went for walks.

"What sort of one you are, I am sure I don't know," said Sveinn the Little Devil at last one day, and looked curiously at me. "*Pouff, pouff*. . . . Perhaps you are laughing at me just like the others? Alas, people are not so good as they ought to be. *Pouff, pouff*. . . . Neither am I. I know very well that you all call me Sveinn the Little Devil. Well, well, to everyone his deserts. Anyone else but you would shake his head; anyone else but you would swear that he had never made fun of me, and had never heard that name. *Pouff, pouff*. . . . So they do laugh at me when I am not listening?"

"Sometimes I laugh, too," I answered very unhappily, and felt burningly hot all over my body.

Sveinn the Little Devil was silent for a bit. I was very anxious to know whether he was angry with me, but I could not see, for I was walking with my head bent down so as to hide my wet eyes.

"Laugh too, yes! *Pouff, pouff*. . . . Well, I never," said he, at last, calmly and without sounding at all reproachful. "And why exactly should you not laugh too? Even I sometimes laugh at myself. . . . But I expect they ask you a lot of questions?"

"Yes—but I never tell them anything of that sort," I answered him happily, looking him straight in the eyes.

Sveinn the Little Devil immediately cast down his own eyes (not once in all the years I knew him did I manage to hold his glance). We walked along silently for a time after this candid exchange of home truths. Then he tapped me suddenly and amiably on my shoulder with his snuffbox, took a pinch, tapped me again on my shoulder—went on tapping me on my shoulder. . . .

On the day that Madame Anna was baptized, Grandpa-from-Fjall showed me his eldest son's grave.

"Here he lies," he said with his sincere and simple gravity, stopping beside a grave where an unostentatious stone had been fixed in the firm greensward. "Here he lies. . . ."

Grandpa-from-Fjall bent down and parted the high grass that drooped over the stone, and read quietly:

" 'Greipur Uggason. Given us by God on the 3rd November, 1844. Called home in the flower of his youth on the 5th May, 1862. May the Lord God be to him as merciful a Father as he was to his parents a good son.' . . . That is what we had put on his stone. The next year your father was born. That is now over thirty years ago—and to me it is only as yesterday that we lowered him here."

Grandpa-from-Fjall stood up. Now he bowed his head, put one hand over his eyes, the other on my head and stood for a time immovable. The wind played with his beard, and white as his beard were the belts of fog gliding hastily across the sides of the mountains toward the glaciers. When he at last took his hand from his eyes he crossed himself slowly and with dignity, his head held high, and then he made the sign of the cross for me. There was a look in his eyes that I have never seen either before or since in the eyes of any other human being.

"Well, little younker," he said, taking my hand again. "Do you know that here, where we are now standing, Grandpa- and Grandma-from-Fjall will lie one day side by side? We shall have my brothers and sisters on the right, my eldest son on the left. Here we shall sleep well—it could not be better. God who has not grudged us good parents, good brothers and sisters and good children will not grudge us a good sleep. . . . Ah, here comes the companion of my rest."

My Grandmother Elizabeth—Granny-from-Fjall—came toward us among the graves, tall, thin and dignified, with her face glorified by age and courageous experience, and framed by snow-white hair. Grandpa stretched out his hand to her, smiling. They kissed and stood for a moment with closed eyes, their old heads leaning against each other. When they again lifted their heads their eyes met in a long gaze, and then they turned and looked at me.

"Who, in our family, is he really like?" asked Granny-from-Fjall, and turned her brilliant brown eyes toward Grandpa. "His hair—where has that come from?"

"From God!" Grandpa-from-Fjall smiled and patted my cheek. "He has his father's eyes and hands. The forehead is also ours, and the nose—that, at any rate, does not belong to Ketilbjörn! His skin he seems to have fetched from somewhere very far back. I wonder whether Great-Grandfather Greipur did not look something like that. . . . Where he has got his mind from is more important; but that will scarcely be revealed before we lie here where we now stand, Elizabeth."

Granny-from-Fjall laid her hand on my head, bent it backward and looked me long in the eyes.

"What do you want to be—a farmer like your father and grandfather, or a priest like your uncle Sira Sigbergur?" she asked when she had looked at me long enough.

I answered eagerly, "I want to be both!"—and added, beaming:

"And then I want to be a carpenter, too, like Uncle Arni, a

poet like Egill Skallagrimsson and a smith like Bjarni." I paused.

Grandpa-from-Fjall laughed loudly. Granny only smiled and asked:

"Isn't there anything else you would like to be?"

"Yes," I admitted hesitatingly. "But that is something not easy to become."

"What is it?" Granny asked gravely.

"A Viking or a sea-robber," I whispered with my eyes on the ground.

Grandpa-from-Fjall laughed louder than ever, and now Granny laughed too. Grandpa said teasingly:

"You got a lot out of that, Elizabeth!"

Granny-from-Fjall stooped over me, drew me to her, kissed me and said:

"Whatever you become, whether a groom or a big farmer, you will become through the grace of God. . . . Am I not right, Farmer Uggi?"

"Right as always, Elizabeth," answered my grandfather and namesake, with his cheerful gravity.

Granny-from-Fjall bent down and passed her fingers through my hair.

"Shall I ask your father and mother to let you come and stay with us for a few days next winter?" she asked kindly.

"Oh, yes, Granny, do!" I said, jumping up and down with joy.

"You shall bring the *Sagas of the Kings of Norway* back with you," Grandpa promised me, smiling. "When one is going to study to be both a priest and a Viking, one must begin early."

Granny stood up. The smile slipped away from her face and from Grandpa's. They turned to the grave and stood for a moment looking at it. . . .

Quietly we left the churchyard.

6

ONE Sunday, outside the church, I saw a little girl with a great deal of yellow hair and very blue eyes. She stood by the side of her father, an elderly farmer in a pepper-and-salt coat, who looked as if he had put on his bedding under his waistcoat before he left home.

The little girl and I stood looking at each other for a long time while my father talked to her father. At last they went into the church without paying any attention to us, and we let them go. How it happened that we were suddenly standing there holding each other's hands I do not know—but we were.

"There are fish in the stream—would you like to see them?" I asked her anxiously.

"Yes, very much," she answered hesitatingly and glanced toward the church door. "Do you think we may?"

"I only go to church when I want to," I answered in a manly way.

She looked at me. . . . I looked at her.

"Now it is too late," I sighed, relieved as we heard a quavering note from the church. "That is my father playing the organ."

"Oh."

"Don't you think he plays well?"

"Ye-yes."

Brook, church, hymn-singing—all disappeared from my consciousness. I saw nothing but her eyes.

"What is your name?" I asked at last.

"Sigga," she answered softly, while her long dark eyelashes slid down and hid her blue eyes. "What is yours?"

"Uggi Greipsson," I answered loudly, emphasizing each syllable of my name. "My father lives here at Ofeigsstadur, my grandpa is Uggi-from-Fjall. And then I have another grandpa who is called Ketilbjörn-from-Knör, but my nose is not like his."

"Oh."

"No. What is your father's name?"

"He is called Sigurjon," answered Sigga, shyly.

"Where do you live?"

"At Kambar."

"Is that far from here?"

"No-o . . ."

"Why is your father so fat?"

"He has leaf-fat on his stomach."

"Is leaf-fat the same as ram-sickness?"

"I don't know . . ."

"Shall I show you my farmyard?"

"Yes, please."

We went off, still holding each other's hands. When we were well outside the churchyard we began to run. We got in among some large grassy mounds, fell over, laughed heartily, and all at once became quite natural and unconstrained.

I showed Sigga my farmyard, but refrained from telling her that I already had a wife. I taught her to roll down a slope. I took her round my empty birds' nests and told her, in great detail, about every family of birds, their number and their fate. I told her about Skjoni who kicked me and was killed for it, which impressed her very much. Naturally I did not forget to touch on the fact that I was now a horse-owner, and I did not belittle Red.

Tired and untidy, we at last came to rest in a whortleberry patch, where we lay down and gathered the fruit—I in my cap for Sigga, Sigga in her pinafore for me. How warm the sun was! How the rivers and streams shone! How pleasantly the field stretched out before us! How mellow were the brown rocks, how refreshing the breeze, and how good the fruit tasted that day! When Sigga asked me for a story I could, however, think of nothing but the one about the troll who asked the boy: "May I fall?" Sigga thought that it was a good story, and I went on telling it without worrying because I had no idea how I was going to finish it. For each bit of hairy troll which I allowed to fall down through the smoke-hole, Sigga came nearer to me, and this led me not only to divide the said troll into a large number of pieces, but to provide still more frightful trolls for division. From the remarks that Sigga let fall, I could see that in the depth of her heart she had identified me with the courageous boy, which misunderstanding I did not consider it necessary to rectify. When I had filled up the kitchen with trolls' limbs, some of which matched, while others did not, Sigga asked me at last, with much sense, how the boy escaped. I led her to understand that it was a small thing to fling the bits of troll out again the same way that they had come, or, better still, to command them to get up and sneak away, and Sigga shuddered and thought the story wonderful.

When I had finished, she began. In the course of an incredibly short time I learned something about the cat, the dogs, the sheep, the cows, the horses and the people at Kambar. Sigga was no longer dumb, and in everything she told me there was something we could laugh about.

We sat and ate berries and laughed at each other.

"What a lot of Siggas there are in the world," I burst out suddenly. "There is my cousin Sigga, and there is Sigga Mens, and there is Sigga-in-the-Loft—and now there is you. Four Siggas."

"My name isn't Sigga," answered Sigga, sulkily, and looked at me coldly. "Sigga is only something I have been called."

"Oh, I know that," I insisted accommodatingly. "You are all called Sigrid."

"Yes, but *I* am called Sigrid Maria Sigurjonsdottir," Sigga informed me, unappeased, and turned her back on me. "If there is anyone else called that, then she has stolen my name."

"No, there isn't anyone," I stammered pacifically. "It is a pretty name. . . ."

"Do you think so?"

"Yes."

There was a pause. Then Sigga said:

"Uggi Greipsson is a pretty name, too."

"Do you think so?"

"Yes."

"You are very, very much prettier than all the other Siggas," I whispered, with my heart in my mouth. "Much prettier."

"Do you really think so?"

"Yes."

When we had finished our berries we went down to the stream. Chattering we followed the busy prattling stream downward until, in a slight dip in a field, it broadened out and, as it were, took a rest.

There, I took off my shoes and stockings and turned up my knickers and waded out to try to catch some fish. My courage was so tremendous that I thought I could catch fish with my bare hands. I was used to catching the small stream-trout, with backs as gray as the water, and stone-speckled sides, in a pail, a scoop, or an abandoned osier basket; but as no such tool was to hand, I thought it would be waste of time to postpone my triumph by going to fetch one.

When Sigga had followed my fruitless attempts for some time, she could not restrain herself any longer, but suddenly stood beside me with bare legs, slipping on the slippery stones, and giving little cries when the sharp ones pricked her. We tied her skirt up with a piece of yarn which I found in my pocket, and then we went for the little fishes hand in hand; but all this noise and shouting had frightened the trout, and, like scurrying shadows, they rushed through the water so quickly that we could scarcely see them. Then we gave up all thought of catching them and only splashed and dabbled—and thus Sigurjon-from-Kambar found us.

"Sigga, Sigga," he groaned, out of breath, his arms hanging helplessly at his sides. "What a church-going! What a way of going to church!"

"Oh . . . but it has been so lovely, Papa," laughed Sigga, quite unconcerned, and remained standing still.

"Do you think your mother will think it lovely too?" asked Sigurjon, shaking his round head sedately. "Sigga, Sigga, are you a child, or are you a fish?"

"A fish," laughed Sigga.

"Now, come ashore, both of you," said Sigurjon in an imploring tone of voice, and we followed him. "Sigga, Sigga! . . . and you have eaten all the berries."

We dried our mouths and did not deny it. Sigurjon continued for a time his half-gay, half-despondent reproaches. Then he promised to forgive us if we brought him my cap full of large, black berries with no leaves mixed up in them, and he went toward Ofeigsstadur, shaking his head.

"Sigga, Sigga!"

When we reached home with the fruit we found Sigurjon in the guest-room talking to my father and mother. It struck me, although it did not surprise me, that he sat on the settle between the windows, and not, as most people did, on a chair. His legs did not reach the floor, and he kept them far apart, as if they were enemies. I let Sigga give him the berries, while I did my part by accompanying the transaction with a very polite "if you please."

"I can see that you would like a bowl of skyr,* Papa!" laughed Sigga, as Sigurjon put the first handful of berries into his mouth.

"Isn't it a little early for you to play the part of hostess at Ofeigsstadur?" mumbled Sigurjon, despondently, with his mouth full. "Sigga, Sigga! . . . Is Uggi going to study—has he been promised the living? . . . It would be just like you if everything were already cut and dried."

I fetched my books and showed them to Sigga. That I could read did me, as I had expected, no harm in her eyes. Between the pages of one of the books lay a golden, gleaming, highly colored tobacco-label.

---

* Sour milk—an Icelandic dish.

"Oh, oh, oh!" cried Sigga, fascinated. "What a lovely label!"

"You may have it if you like," I said, as indifferently as possible, to hide my pleasure.

"May I?" answered Sigga, delighted, and smoothed the label carefully with her small supple fingers. "Thank you, thank you, darling Uggi. I will never forget you!"

Naturally thinking that words like these would bring a kiss with them, I put up my face for one, and received it.

"Sigga, Sigga," admonished Sigurjon, sitting there stirring the berries into his plateful of milk, which my mother had fetched him, amid a great deal of laughter. "Your mother would weep her bitter tears if she saw how her daughter is behaving."

It was not with the idea of hiding my light under a bushel that I invited Sigga to write her name on the back of the "label" so that everyone might see to whom it belonged.

"Can you write, too?" whispered Sigga, lifting me, as if in a chariot of fire, into the clear blue heaven of her eyes.

"No," I answered modestly. "Just print."

Sigga did not, however, seem to consider that art less clever—rather the opposite. I borrowed a pencil from my father, put my elbows well out, and, with my tongue in my left cheek, I began to print—while there flitted through my head bits out of the letters which I had heard Old Begga read aloud to the less educated members of our household.

"To the young girl Sigrid Maria Sigurjonsdottir, said to be living at Kambar in the parish of Breidale. Good day—farewell. Your sincere Uggi Greipsson. Forgive scrawl."

While I composed and wrote down this letter, Sigga's blue eyes passed rapidly from my face to my hands and back again. Long after I had read it aloud to her she gazed at my printing as if bewitched.

"Is that what it says?"

I nodded.

"Is it a letter—to me?"

I nodded.

When I handed her the label she scarcely dared to touch it, or walk across the floor with it, for fear something might happen to it.

"Will you hide my letter in your pocketbook, dear Papa?" she asked her father in a low voice.

"Sigga, Sigga!" groaned Sigurjon, troubled, but his eyes followed her with a smile.

When Sigurjon in the early dusk at last mounted his horse, while my parents and we children collected round him in the courtyard, and my father was going to lift Sigga up in front of him, she suddenly ran away, shouting:

"I won't go home! I want to stay with Uggi."

"Sigga, Sigga!" groaned Sigurjon, helplessly. "Think of my rheumatism."

But Sigga refused to think of his rheumatism. My mother offered to keep her, but Sigurjon opened negotiations, promised to bring her to church again—in fact, the very next Sunday, if the weather permitted. Yes, even if the weather did not permit; and to these conditions, Sigga at last, although unwillingly, agreed, and allowed herself to be taken home.

"It seems that I must secure Uggi if I want to keep my daughter at home!" sighed Sigurjon, as he rode away from the farm. "Oh, Sigga, Sigga! . . ."

From that day, I waylaid every traveler who was going to Kambar, or in that direction. Even the very next day I managed to send off another label that I had found at Bjarni Smith's. On the back was written, in addition to the address:

"Here is another label. May it be of use to you for a long time. The kiss can wait. Your sincere Uggi Greipsson. Excuse scrawl."

A few days later, I received a letter, my first letter, a brilliant label, with the following words printed on the back:

"To the young man Uggi Greipsson, living at Ofeigssta-
dur in Breidale parish. Papa is writing, and I tell him what
to say. Thank you for the letter. Our cat has had kitttens.
Here is a label and a kiss. I am coming on Sunday. Your sin-
cere friend, Sigrid Maria Sigurjonsdottir. Forgive scrawl."

Sunday came, but no Sigga. On the other hand, there came
a letter which was answered that very day. It was written with
"bitter tears," and ran: *"Are you happy? I am happy. Do be*
happy." A few days later came a letter which said: *"Now the*
nights are getting longer."

Sigga did not come very often to church, and still less often
was I allowed to visit her at Kambar. But I could not get her
out of my mind, and we kept up the connection, and were tireless
in sending each other "notes," labels from tobacco, packets from
coffee substitutes, from wine- and other bottles, from soap boxes
and all other sorts of boxes, and, in fact, from everything that
came to the house bearing a label. And we always finished,
"Your sincere friend," and "Forgive scrawl."

The nights grew longer. It was autumn. Over the early, still,
light-blue evening sky played the long golden flame of the
northern lights, which gladdened me, saddened me. The water
was no longer friendly—it bit if one stepped into it. The
stream slunk away, thin and crestfallen and shivering between
the edges of thin ice. Many mornings the mountains were gray
with snow right down to a line just above the farms. The
grass paths spread before us yellow and sere. Heather clumps
and heather slopes flamed crimson and blazed with many colors.
The air was light and sharp, the darkness very black. Veiga and
I had undertaken to pick whortleberries and cowberries for
Mama to make jam, but it was cold picking berries and they
tasted good, and we did not always feel so happy when it came
to bringing home the day's harvest. But my mother laughed
at us, pretended to scold us, accepted our promises of penance
and improvement just as seriously as we gave them, kissed
us and warmed our frozen fingers. Nonni, Maggi, and two other

men rode one Sunday up into the mountains, and stayed away for several days—the sheep were being collected.

The day that the slowly-moving flocks of sheep were driven down the mountain slopes toward the great communal sheep-pens at the bottom of the valley, I was allowed to go along. This concession had been gained for me by my good friend Bjarni Smith, and I went in his charge, sitting in front of him on Brunka. My mother told me to be careful not to be kicked by the horses, bitten by the dogs or butted by the rams. Sigga Mens confided to me, without demanding any promise of silence, that she had known several boys who had been trampled into cripples in the sheepfolds. Old Begga prayed God to be with me, although she was not sure that He had any power in such a place on such a day, and furthermore thought that I should hardly endanger my salvation if I waited another year before going up there. And Maria Mens whispered in my ear that if "anything went wrong" I was to keep close to Nonni.

I got off at last, greatly excited over what the day would bring forth. What I found at the great sheep-pen in no way disappointed me. Never could I have believed there were so many sheep in the world, or so many dogs, or so many horses, or so many people, or so much noise, or so many echoes of noises, or so much gaiety, or so much movement, or so many bottles, or so much liquor.

Over the wall of the fold there cascaded a full chorus of bleatings in every possible key. The dogs barked in different keys, the horses neighed and the men shouted. But that was the least of it all. Rams with spirally twisted horns as long and thick as my arms butted each other with a booming noise. Horses advanced toward each other on their back legs and bit at each other, shoved each other and uttered piercing shrieks. Dogs fought either with one another or in gangs, surrounded by a shouting crowd. And the men's vociferously cheerful, or emotionally tearful, bottle friendships (for each man had at least three half-pint bottles of drink in his pocket) were relieved now and then by small, quick skirmishes. During these battles a drop of blood might be spilled now and again, but never a drop of spirit. For, however hot-tempered a man might be, he never forgot to deposit his flask before he fought. I was very anxious that nothing of all this should escape me, but, in the long run, it was quite impossible to keep count of everything that happened. Sometimes I was so giddy and confused that I could not find a person, a horse, a dog, or even a sheep that had anything at all to do with Ofeigsstadur, and felt very much alone and neglected in this motley and turbulent world.

In the great communal sheepfold there was always a large crowd of cheerful men wading about, feeling for the sheeps' ear-marks, reading out the branding on their horns,* or pointing them out from a distance as their property because they recognized them by their color, horns, the lay of their wool or their shape. These busy fellows then made off in all directions with the sheep they had recognized—the most skillful with one straddled across the shoulders, and one in each hand. The sheep were taken to the small side-pens where they were collected by their owners or by several farmers going the same way. With beating heart, I made my way into this sea of sheep, which pushed, shoved, made room for pugnacious rams, trod on my toes with sharp hoofs, lifted me like a wave and moved me hither and thither. My object was to find a sheep which belonged to my father, and bring it to the fold where our sheep were being collected. As my father's mark, in contrast to the marks of most of the other farmers, who so often mutilated the whole ear, was only a small slit near the base of the ear, I took it for granted that all the sheep with whole ears were his. When, therefore, at long last, I found a sheep with undamaged ears, I clutched hold of one of its horns, which was very warm at the roots, and tried to drag it in the right direction; but, instead of dragging it, I was myself dragged in the wrong direction. In a manly way, I tried to force it my way by sitting astride its back, with the result that I had a ride

* The Icelandic sheep are a special breed bearing horns.

forced on me, an unwelcome ride, which roused much laughter around me.

While the battle between me and my unwilling sheep was still undecided, there suddenly appeared a very angry boy who asked me what the hell I meant by riding his father's sheep to ruin, and if I would be so kind as to come with him outside the fold to take one in the eye. Brought up as I had been to refuse no kind of entertainment, if it were only offered me in an honest spirit, I went with him willingly. There were numerous hands which, in anticipation of a good fight, were more than willing to help us out of the fold. When we had found a battlefield we rushed at each other in "the name of God and the Devil," as my unknown opponent expressed himself. My many bouts with Björn now stood me in good stead, and, fired by the criticism which hailed down upon us from all sides, together with my remembrance of my distinguished descent from the "Borg rabble," I soon went berserk. How it happened that our "expert critics" suddenly became part of the battle, I had not time to inquire. On the other hand, I could not but notice that there were no longer only two of us fighting, but a whole crowd—a floundering crowd in which I was sometimes on the top, sometimes at the bottom. Suddenly Björn appeared on the field of battle, and as he could not manage to drag me out immediately from the entangled mass, he ran amok with such a stream of bad language that a group of grownups noticed us, separated us, and held us fast while our ardor cooled.

My father arrived. He was very gay and quite in his element, laughed heartily when he saw me and was entirely willing to consider the matter closed. Bjarni Smith found me where I was sitting putting wads of grass into my nostrils to stop the bleeding, pointed out that this had happened because I did not follow his advice and stay close to him (which advice he had never given me) and took me off with him to a stream in the neighborhood. Bjarni walked very oddly, spoke very oddly, and moved his hands so oddly that the water he scooped up caught me everywhere but on my face. I asked him if he was ill, and he found my question very amusing and answered that he probably was, but that it was a very odd illness—ha, ha, ha!—and very infectious, very infectious! These words he repeated again and again, and each time seemed to find them funnier than ever. But suddenly he changed completely, became very sorrowful, remembered his responsibility for me, asked me if I could recall that it was he who once made horseshoes for me, informed me that he was both confirmed and married, and also a widower—a widower—and finished by saying that we'd better get home now and get to bed, in the grave—in the grave—preferably in the grave. . . . Then his frame of mind changed again, and when, hand-in-hand, we returned to the fold, he sang gaily the old nonsense rhyme:

> Pour a caskful in my grave
> 'Mongst earthy stones and sandy,
> For my bones will always crave
> The tart delicious brandy.

Many things happened, and the day passed. When, toward evening, the sheep had been divided up into the different pens, the crowd began to break up. In all directions small flocks of sheep departed, carefully guarded, and the air was full of their pitiable bleating, the deafening barking of the dogs, song, laughter and bad language. I found Bjarni with his saddle on his back, staggering from horse to horse confiding his sorrows to their friendly, twitching ears, but quite unable to find Brunka. We decided to leave the saddle and concentrate on finding Brunka, but when at last we found Brunka we could not find the saddle again, and Bjarni stated that it was his definite opinion that the Devil himself had taken it and hidden it behind his great-grandmother's back. "I will shoe her—I will shoe her," he kept on repeating. Perhaps he did not dare direct his threats against her great-grandson.

I was just about to give up in despair when Nonni fortunately came to our rescue, found Bjarni's saddle, put it on Brunka, helped him up onto his horse, but refused, in spite of his tears and pitiful pleading, to put me up in front of him—remarking that "Uggi would be safe enough" with one who was in full possession of his five senses, and that Bjarni might "lose" me on the way. Bjarni Smith asked whether he had ever lost his heart, whether he had ever lost his soul, whether he had ever lost his eyes out of his head—to which Nonni answered that he knew nothing about all that, that perhaps he had not, but that it was more than enough that today he had lost his reason. Bjarni asked whether Nonni had found it then, as he seemed to know so much about it. Nonni answered that he had not, but that even if he had he would leave it where it lay, as it was not worth picking up. In this way they wrangled until we caught up with our own and Sigurjon-from-Kambar's people who had gone on in advance with the sheep (as to whether my father and Sigurjon had ridden on in front, or were still behind, opinion was divided).

I was very sorry for Bjarni Smith, and I was rather inclined to attribute the extraordinary gymnastics he practiced so industriously on the way home, standing on his head in every ditch and in every stream, to Nonni's hard-heartedness. However, Nonni would not hear of giving me up to him, and as Bjarni, except for these futile attempts to break his neck, took life gaily, I did not worry any more. Bjarni did not worry either. Every time he was helped onto his horse he struck up—in the deepest bass—the song which was being sung in many parts, by many men, on many horses, and which went as follows:

> *Gladly will I all endure,*
> *Fire, ice, and trouble sore,*
> *As long as thou my ills wilt cure,*
> *Bottle of my dreams!*
>
> *Oh, thy mouth is soft and round,*
> *Soft and round, soft and round,*
> *Oh, thy mouth is soft and round,*
> *And more I cannot say!*

It was getting dark. Our progress was slow. But incessant was the bleating of the sheep; incessant the barking of the dogs; and incessantly did the men sing. Only the horses and I were silent. Before we reached home I was asleep. . . .

On a day of shifting snow squalls in the mountains, fitful sunshine which was driven away by cold clouds, and a bitter wind which froze bones and marrow and made teeth chatter, my father and the men went round the crowded home fold, choosing out the sheep to be driven to the nearest town for slaughter, and marking with tar those that were to be killed at home. I had been allowed to choose the sheep I wanted, and had at last come to a standstill before a black-and-white one, which I thought was the prettiest sheep I had ever seen. I called my father and pointed out to him my choice, and he winked one eye and asked me:

"Don't you know that one gets more for white wool than for black?"

"Yes," I answered, and felt my cheeks burn.

"Wouldn't you rather have one that is quite white?"

"No . . ."

My father laughed, shook his head and went away.

Just after that, Nonni came carrying one of his lambs, a very pretty brown ewe lamb which I had stood for a long time admiring. He said:

"You can have this, Uggi. Here you are."

"Why?" I asked, but he only blushed and did not answer. I kissed him. Bjarni Smith laughed.

"Two sheep, one horse—but no earmarks, no registered marks. That will never do," he said, and shook his head. "One of these days I must have a few words with the fire."

Next day four of our men went off with the sheep for slaughter. The following day Bjarni and Maggi followed them with our horses, and the day after that my father rode away and said that he would be the first man there. The time they were away seemed to me interminable. Although I both wrote and received "notes," although my mother patiently told me all that she knew about life in a market town, although Bjössi had plenty of free time both for fights and games, although Sigga Mens cheered me up by informing me that one must always be prepared to have one's father brought home drowned or drenched to the skin, although Old Begga told me real ghost stories until I did not dare to go alone in the dark without first having crossed myself and said an *Our Father,* the days moved along at a snail's pace and it seemed impossible to kill time.

At last one brilliant, sunny day we saw a caravan approaching, which, from the color and number of the horses, we decided must be ours—and then the hours, then the minutes became as long as days. Finally the horses came into the yard, laden with flour and corn in sacks, planks, iron bars, and many boxes and trunks in which were packed groceries of all descriptions. The unpacking, at which we children were more willing than useful helpers, began at once. For Veiga there was a kitchen range with saucepans, for Beta a doll with real hair, for Madame Anna an India-rubber doll, for me a tool chest—and besides that, Nonni had sneaked a sack full of horns onto one of the horses, so that Veiga and I had our stock of sheep doubled in one day.

The following days were great days. The only things we lacked were hands and pockets—for where could we put all our raisins, all our figs, all our sweets, all our chocolate, all our prunes, our pieces of sugarloaf as large as our fists, and our toys?

In the wake of these great days followed other great days, for now the sheep for home use were killed. It was a busy time salting down the meat, hanging up the legs and sides for smoking, cooking the lungs and the meat for pasties to be stored in large skin bags, making blood, liver, and fillet sausages, and preparing sheeps' heads and bones for pickling; melting down suet, sewing up meat rolls; shaving, dyeing and drying the sheepskin; and all the other autumn work, which it was just as important for children to watch as for grownups to do.

In the kitchen, where Old Begga, Weekday-Begga, reigned supreme, all the kitchen fires were alight both day and night, and if we children came and asked for a story we were given neither a story nor a scolding, but were bundled off with a kidney, a fragrant blood sausage with raisins in it, or a sheep's bone. The sheeps' heads and sheeps' bones were "sweated" over the fire in Bjarni's smithy and then treated with a piece of glowing iron, and Bjarni Smith went about, gray and peevish, blowing the stench out of his nose, and refusing to cheer up until he had got his smithy well aired, and had begun to make spiked shoes for horses and men.

"There are one or two things that God in His wisdom has not foreseen," he confided to me one day when I visited him. "Apparently, it never occurred to Him, the Blessed One, that horses would need shoes, much less that they would have to use two kinds of shoes, or he would have made their hoofs harder and arranged for hobnails to grow on them during the winter.

"Well, I suppose one must excuse Him, as He had so much to do in so short a time. If one of us had created the world in six days, I wonder what sort of a world we should have started going. I wouldn't care to be born into that world! But why six days? That I have never rightly understood. Either God must be lazy or He must have had a great deal else on hand as well. . . . We will leave the matter of a horse's hoof; but that God had so little understanding of farming that He could not say to Himself that all foals cannot become stallions, nor all lambs rams, that I cannot understand. . . . And why did He not alter it again later? Can it be pleasing to Him in some way, as things stand, that stallions and rams have to be castrated with much pain and misery? One would never have believed it. Loose people have tried to make me believe that those dogs of Turks even castrate men. But who can believe that? In any case not yours truly, B. A., Bjarni Andresson. He has seen a lie grow in traveling a shorter distance, he has—and no—God would never have allowed that.

"But that this world of His is imperfect, *that* He can have in writing any day. Ought not tobacco to have grown here in Iceland? Tell me that. In other countries they can go and pick tobacco and put it in their pipes without its costing them even a threepenny bit with a hole in it. Therefore, I find it strange that tobacco does not grow here. Why should we pay for it? . . . I am now just saying what *I* think. God Himself has created truth, so surely He can stand hearing it. . . . And what do you think of this, chicken—that we who live so near the North Pole have to *buy* spirit? You can say what you like about spirit, but it warms the stomach in cold and sleet. To one who has lost his wife it is a good gift. Some are simple enough to think that it is on the contrary a gift from the Devil himself, but if that were so you would think that God would long ago have sent it back. There is no doubt that God created spirit. But He did not consider carefully enough how to divide it up. But then the whole thing was a rush job. Do you think it would have done any harm if one of the many mountain streams here in Breidale had been filled with something good which would be a real comfort and refreshment, instead of that eternal water? If I were God I should not be so sparing of miracles.

"I, for my part, enjoy a happy day—many happy days—in this life. In the grave we all behave properly. Once your uncle, the blessed Sira Sigberg, wanted me to join his Temperance Society, 'Hope.' Do you know what I answered? I said, 'I am only going to join one Temperance Society, and that is the one called "Death." ' Then he laughed and left me in peace, for he is a young man, and I am an old one. No, you see, in the grave you get neither tobacco nor spirit—that's the rule. It may be all right for whoever is laid to rest here in the cemetery of Ofeigsstadur, where the earth is good enough, dry and clean; but in a cold and damp cemetery it might be different, and it may be a long time till the Last Day. I don't care a fig for Sveinn the Little Devil's prophecies about the end of the world. Sira Sigberg was very careful when he touched on that subject. But what I would like to say is, that I have reckoned out that if only I had not been obliged to buy either tobacco or spirit, I could have been a rich man with my own farm. At least three sheep a year for sixty years makes a hundred and fifty sheep, and with lambs and wool it would have been a lot of money. If only every other Icelander had saved that much in the last fifty years we would now be a rich nation able to hold our heads as high as anybody, anywhere. But still I say, even if the country does not flow with honey and spirits and mead and oil, let us at least have tobacco growing here."

In this way Bjarni Smith instructed me in religion and patriotism. It pleased him very much and lifted me high in his estimation that I agreed with every word as he spoke it. . . .

Short sunless days, long, starry moonlit nights, storms of frost and storms of thaw, with and without snow. A sun returning new and radiant—and the winter was past.

On the whole, I do not remember very much from that winter. I remember that my mother, one gloomy day, made candles, and that I held the ball of yarn while she stretched the wicks in the molds; that the gray tallow in the pot bubbled, impatiently anxious to be poured out, and that when we took it out of the molds as long smooth yellow candles it appeared exceedingly proud, ornamental and sedate. I remember my father's sitting under the paraffin lamp in the middle of the living room and reading aloud from a book while we children were quiet and attentive, the servants worked, Sveinn the Little Devil panted and puffed in the dark in his room, and all the time we heard the beat of Bjarni Smith's loom below us, and heard him speaking now and again to his good friends the dogs. I remember that on Christmas Eve Sveinn the Little Devil sat in Father's place under the lamp and read—*pouff, pouff!*—about the Child who was born, and that Veiga and I went round with long candles in our hands dripping tallow onto our fingers, and that everybody was very quiet, friendly, and had water-combed hair; and that Old Begga, who used to frighten us with the troll-wife Gryla who went round stuffing naughty children into her sack, taught us a rhyme to the following effect:

> *At Christmas give the children bread,*
> *Give them candles and frocks of red*
> *So they can get up out of bed.*
> *Give them mutton from sheep that fed*
> *High in the mountains—for Gryla is dead!*
> *Wicked old Gryla is dead!*

I remember further that on a dim day when the south wind blew, soft and heavy, my father and mother rode away to Fjall, that I sat with my father on his shining brown horse and that my mother's gray seemed pleased to have her on her back again; that the crackling of the ice under the spiked shoes of the horses crept pleasantly into my bones and marrow; that my father hummed and sometimes sang, and that my mother, who was so happy and smiling, talked about the groups of houses which stood out so darkly in the snowy waste, and from which the smoke rose leaning in the direction toward which the wind blew it—this, she said, reminded her of steamers on the sea.

I remember from Fjall that the farm was very quiet, very light and friendly and very clean, that Grandpa and Grandma told me many stories, that I found I had a young Aunt Beta who was rather like Grandma and who was soon going to be married, that I was always being asked what I liked and did not like, that my answers gave rise to a great deal of merriment and some shakings of the head; that my observations in the manner of Bjarni Smith were not well received; and that there was divided opinion about my future in that my father considered that I ought to "uphold the name" and become a farmer, while my grandpa and grandma thought it best that I should "keep to my book" until I showed "what there was in me." But my mother only kissed me, while I, myself, being descended from Rolf the Ranger, thought a little of making my title valid in Normandy. I remember that on our way home we spent the night at the neighboring farm, Kambar, that Sigga's eyes were bluer than ever, Sigga's hair more golden in reality than in my dreams, that to my amazement Sigga's mother turned out to be a little, mild, smiling woman, who had nothing but kisses and caresses for her daughter, and that the first words, the last words, and the words which I heard Sigurjon say most often were: "Sigga, Sigga!" . . .

It was spring and very restless on the farm. Much was about to happen; some came, others went.

Sveinn the Little Devil had gone. I did not see him go, because Sveinn preferred to travel at night—it suited both him and his nag best. Nor did he leave any message for me, which saddened me and made me conscience-stricken. If only just once I had shut the door when I visited him! But now it was too late—he had gone. The attic room where he used to sit and puff and pant, used to lie and puff and pant, where he spent the evenings, mostly without a light, for the greater part of the year he "served" Ofeigsstadur parish and "consecrated to the earth" in Ofeigsstadur churchyard—that attic room had now been scrubbed out, fumigated with sulphur and thoroughly aired, as if he had died of typhoid fever there and not as if he had just left it in the ordinary way. Happily, he had not seen it done, and was not, therefore, wounded by it. He had gone, no one missed him. . . .

Sigrid-in-the-Loft and her son Maggi, whose full name was Magnus Bachmann and whose still fuller name was Magnus Jonsson Bachmann, were also going away.

They were both very sorry. We were all very sorry, but nothing could be done. The new parson and his family were to come into the "parson's lodgings." My parents were, to my great joy, going back again to live in the loft, and, as Sigrid would rather be buried alive than take over the attic, even after it had been cleaned with sulphur, she had to go.

The next to the last time I visited her, I was busy making a list of the goods that I was going to ask my father to buy when he went on his half-yearly journey to the town, although it was yet some weeks before my sheep would be sheared. I had noted down "1 lb. of figs, one hat with gold buttons, 1 lb. of raisins, 1 lb. of prunes, one flute, 1 lb. of barley sugar, 1 lb. of cinnamon sticks, one pair of reins." When I showed Sigrid-in-the-Loft this list she cried aghast that I had forgotten the most important thing. I asked her what it was. She said that the most important item was a corset. I asked her what a corset was. She said it was something that would make me handsomer than ever. I wrote down "1 corset." I asked if there was anything else. She thought that a box of powder would be good for my freckles. I put down "1 box of powder." The laughter from everybody on the farm, Bjössi's and Maggi's teasings, which these additions to my list brought me, caused me to contemplate Sigrid's departure without any particular sorrow. Once I had decided to marry her—now I found it difficult to see that she was at all pretty.

The last time I visited her in the loft, the last time I saw her with my eyes, was the day when she and Maggi were leaving us. Only after a great deal of persuasion had she made her son put on a flannel vest with red stripes; now she was standing in front of him with a shining white shirt in her hands. She had spent a great deal of time making the shirt, and much care in ironing it. Now she was trying to get him to put it on. I had seen the shirt being made, had followed it through all its stages, and, although Sigrid's looks left me in no doubt as to how very unwelcome my presence was at this moment, I was determined to see with my own eyes that Maggi put it on. This time, however, he would not allow himself to be persuaded. He yelled, he roared, he hit out with his arms, did not want to be togged up, would have his own shirt on—his old shirt. But if Maggi was adamant, Sigrid was no less so.

At her wits' end, with a hopeless look in her gray eyes, a pitiful expression in her long, hard face, she stood and looked at Maggi, holding the shirt ready to put on him, and not daring to touch him with it.

But Maggi was on his guard; he incessantly hit out with his

thin stick-like arms, and continually shouted with his thin voice:

"My old shirt, my old shirt!"

Sigrid still went on trying, then she gave up. She looked at me sternly, but I did not mean to budge. If she began hitting Maggi, which was what I feared, I had decided to rush off and fetch my father.

But Sigrid did not hit him. After she had made an untold number of attempts either to persuade Maggi or to outwit him—an endless battle without any apparent victories—she suddenly flung the shirt onto the pillow of his bed and said in a shaking voice, which she tried to keep calm:

"There it is! If you don't put it on, I shall leave you behind."

Then she went. She herself was ready all but her riding clothes.

Maggi sat immovable on his bed and looked straight in front of him. Behind him lay the shirt, sunning itself. It lay there contented as a dog that has laid himself on his back to be scratched. I saw all this out of the corner of my eyes. Maggi, the shirt—none of us wished to meet one another's eyes. This, I understood. Sigrid stuck her head through the door, looked at Maggi, went away again. Sigrid came back the second time, came right into the room, stood for a minute in front of Maggi's bed looking at Maggi (who would not look at her), said nothing, avoided looking at the shirt, and paid not the slightest attention to me.

I noticed suddenly that the room was empty; her things had gone.

My father came in, silent, with a hidden half-comical interest in his cheerful, gray-brown eyes. He pulled at his beard, looked briefly at Maggi, a long time at the shirt, briefly at me, a long time out the window, tugged and tugged at his beard—went.

For the third time Sigrid came in, this time in her riding clothes and with her whip in her hand. She went with short steps over to the bed, said a short goodbye to her son—whom she had great trouble in kissing, and who returned neither the words nor the kiss—said goodbye to me with a short passing kiss, and, without meeting my eyes, swept out of the room, leaving the door open. . . . Maggi sat as he had been sitting. The shirt lay where it had been lying. I stood where I had been standing. There was Sigrid riding away. Time passed, nothing happened . . . then I crept out. . . . And thus were my parents given another son, and we children a brother—Magnus Jonsson Bachmann.

7

It is not only about events that my memory is capricious, it is so also about people. Some features or personalities stand out sharply in my remembrance; others are entirely wiped away. . . . Far back in the twilight of the years I glimpse indistinctly a tall and powerful, fair and merry man. It is Sira Halldor Jonsson, our new priest. His wife I can remember only as the shadow of a picture, and their two daughters, our playmates for a year, I can recall just as a pair of fair, red-headed little girls, one about my own height, the other a trifle smaller.

My father and Sira Halldor were together a great deal, especially at first. They were always good friends and were always very busy. They divided everything up. They divided the fields, they divided the meadows, they divided the winter pasture, they divided the outbuildings, they divided the dwelling-houses, they even divided the kitchen—although only with an imaginary wall—divided all that could be divided into two halves. They were always to be seen moving about together, either riding or walking; the fresh spring wind filled out their coats, the warm showers drenched them, the sun warmed them pleasantly, the light sky was stretched out peacefully above their heads.

When we were all reunited in the loft in the evening (how happy I was to be living again in the loft, and how well I knew each knot, remembered each nail!) my father always had a great deal to tell us about what had happened and had been discussed between him and Sira Halldor during the day. Once when my mother disagreed with his choice in a particular case, he answered in his good-humored, confident way:

"But you do realize, don't you, Cecilia, that as far as grass-plots, fields, and grass paths are concerned, we are going to change round again next year?"

"And what will happen the year after that?" asked my mother. "Are you going to change again?"

"Yes, of course!" answered my father, proudly, as if the idea were his, of which I was not so sure. "In that way neither of us can ever grumble."

My mother laughed heartily at this Solomon-like division, and, although I did not really understand what she was laughing at, I laughed too. But as my father, who had become a little red about the forehead, did not seem to appreciate our laughter, and definitely refused to share in it, we ceased abruptly.

"Will you soon have finished?" asked my mother, and could not quite give up her teasing.

"It has to be done," answered my father, shortly.

It certainly had to be done, and it was done. They also divided up the farm servants, with the latter's consent. My father kept Old Begga, Maria and Sigga Mens, Nonni, Maggi, half of Bjössi and three-quarters of Bjarni Smith, while Sira Halldor had those servants that I can remember only as shadows, without faces and without names, together with the remaining bits of Bjössi and Bjarni Smith.

Meanwhile time passed. The grass grew and became green. Long-legged lambs with their tightly curled coats played gracefully on the slopes. My parti-colored sheep appeared with two other little parti-colored creatures, and this gave my father occasion to remark that what I lacked in "farm-sense" was perhaps counteracted by something better, namely, "farm-luck." However, he took back these words when one of my lambs died, and I thus lost all at once "half of my lambs and a quarter of my sheep," as he said. I cried a little over my lamb, but soon comforted myself by thinking of what I could buy with its skin. The sheep were deprived at one and the same time of both their wool and their lambs. The lambs were driven, bleating piteously, to the mountains, along with the wethers and the rams; while the ewes which, during the first few days, missed their lambs so much that they were really ill, were handed over to Bjössi and his dog Little Devil (Bjössi had had a soft spot for Sira Sveinn).

The wool was washed and divided into wool for home use and wool for sale, and after that my father and Sira Halldor went off to town together a day after the wool caravan had started. . . . They came back. Nonni had my "goods" in a special case which was shut extra tightly. Maggi had a two-bladed knife for me, and this laid the foundation of a long and lasting friendship. Bjarni Smith had been what he called "light-fingered" when it was a question of "labels," and brought me a whole bundle. All of us children received from our parents mugs with golden writing on them, "For a good girl," "For a good boy." When from my riches I honored Bjössi with a flute, a pocket handkerchief with pictures of children and animals on it, and some sweets, he cried, called me all the worst possible names, gave me a good sound thrashing, told me that I was a silly fool, promised to remember me even when he was burning in the depths of Hell, and offered, if I cared about it, to call his lamb after me. . . . In this way the spring passed. One day the scythes sang round the farm, and my father and Sira Halldor went about in their shirt sleeves and saw that their boundaries were carefully respected. They themselves had not time to work, too, as they used to do; they still went about dividing up, agreeing, bargaining, dividing up again and chewing a lot of tobacco.

When I woke the next morning there was the first scent of hay in the air and it was summer—rich, sweet summer. . . .

I remember Mr. Howell very clearly—but no, it is really only the man's luggage that I remember.

He arrived one day in a pouring rain at Ofeigsstadur, and dripped in through the door—a little man with much luggage, completely incomprehensible to all except Sira Halldor and my father. His luggage was enormous. To my mind his red trunks, which were divided between the guest room and the two outbuildings, were innumerable. These red trunks Mr. Howell opened and shut, opened and shut all the time he was staying at Ofeigsstadur, except when he sat on one of them and scrawled something in a book—and where should I be, whenever Mr.

Howell opened a trunk, but close at his side? And where should I look while he rummaged round in it, if not right down into it? And what did Mr. Howell's innumerable trunks contain? As far as I could understand there were boxes of biscuits, chests of biscuits—biscuits that looked as if they were exceedingly eatable, yes, more than eatable. . . . The other contents of the red trunks, which consisted to a large extent of boxes in different sizes, were to me, as far as clothes were concerned, a riddle, but the labels on his boxes were very pretty and very easy to understand with their many-colored pictures of sea animals, land animals and rare fruits.

One day I ventured to ask Mr. Howell for a label that was loose. He looked at me with his big eyes and growled for a very long time in English, seemed to expect an answer, pointed down into the trunk and, when I could find no answer except to shake my head, he shook his head too and promptly banged down the lid. Then he immediately opened it again, emptied the biscuits out of the tin box and handed it to me with a beaming smile. I whispered "Thank you," and he nodded and nodded. I gave him my hand and said "Thank you" again. But it was certainly a disappointment that he had emptied the box so carefully there were only a few biscuit crumbs on the bottom. Of these crumbs, most went down the wrong way and the rest tasted a little of dust and a little of rust and a little of tin, but were otherwise extremely good and foreign.

Among the secret things in Mr. Howell's trunks there was a sort of box on three heavy legs which he manipulated with great care, and always wearing a black cloth over his head. When my father told me that this was a photographing apparatus, "a picture machine," I understood fully Mr. Howell's respectful attitude toward it. My father and Sira Halldor seemed happily prepared to share Mr. Howell, too—how else would they have found time to look after him, show him the neighborhood, its birch wood and other things worth seeing, and get themselves photographed on horseback or with large rams (which had been brought down from the mountains with a great deal of difficulty) held by one twisted horn? Mr. Howell stayed for a week at the farm and then he went on farther into the country accompanied by my father, various trunks and most of the farm's horses. I do not remember how long they were away. The time seemed to me long, but at last they came back, both very elated, both very brown from the glacier sun and the mountain weather; and the following day Mr. Howell, Sira Halldor and my father seemed to compete as to who could chatter most madly in English. My father had scarcely time to tell my mother and us children about their great and gay exploits, about how they had gone through a snowstorm, photographed each other in snow up to their waists, "discovered," photographed, and—as far as Mr. Howell was concerned, described, the place where our river broke out from the glacier; how they had almost lost the three-legged picture machine in the river, almost lost themselves in the river while rescuing it, and much more of the same sort of thing, all of which can be such fun in good company in the mountains. My father finished by saying that on the whole he found Mr. Howell to be an "excellent neighbor," and then off he went to seek out his neighbor.

Mr. Howell stayed a few more days at Ofeigsstadur, photographed graves, photographed churchgoers, photographed Sunday-Begga, photographed Björssi with all his sheep—an oath in his mouth, and Little Devil standing on his hind legs beside him—photographed me on Red, with my father holding the bridle, photographed everything we could think of and wanted to photograph Weekday-Begga and my mother, but was not allowed to. He ended by giving me his empty tin boxes and tin cases, allowed me to peel off many valuable "labels," and rose in my estimation with every day, with every box, with every case and with every label. He would have seemed to me a still more perfect "neighbor" if among the crumbs at the bottom of the boxes and cases he had left as much as an eighth of a biscuit. At last he gave my father his address on a piece of paper, which still preserves his English writing, promised to send him the photographs, and at the end of the year an illustrated travel book about his journey, scarcely escaped the salty fate of Lot's wife when Weekday-Begga, from whom he had bought some knitting, gave him a kitchen kiss when he said goodbye, and departed disconcerted but happily unharmed with all his red boxes and the remainder of his biscuits back to his poor, queer-tongued fatherland. My father asked him to give Queen Victoria his love—there was no one who asked to be remembered to Mr. Pickwick. . . .

The home field had been cut and the hay brought in. A heavy vapor from the open barn door spiced the alternately sun-drenched and wind-cooled summer days. In our part of the farm only my mother moved about during the day. When Madame Anna was not sleeping in her cradle my mother had her in her arms. We children played in the home field and outside the home field. Far away in the meadows my father and his farmhands worked. I knew where they were and visited them from time to time, for now I could sit alone on a horse. When on dry days Maggi brought the hay home, I was often allowed to go with him and stay out there as long as I liked. On the journey there we rode very quickly, and I clung to the pommels of my saddle and laughed and thought it huge fun. I did not stay out in the fields for very long, as even my father had no time to answer my questions; and I soon felt lonely and neglected and preferred to make a few trips to and fro with Maggi.

On the journey back to the farm, the horses were laden with great bundles of half-dried hay reaching almost to the ground. Maggi rode in front on my mother's gray (riding horses never carry pack-saddles), while I sat up among the bundles of hay on our quietest horse, an old reddish-brown plodder. As the crow flies, it was half an hour's ride home from the fields, which lay along the river in the middle of the valley, but I was not sorry it was so long, for I was very comfortable on my perch. I sat looking at the sky where the light changed so whimsically, at the driving belts of cloud that made the tops of the mountains look as if they were suspended in mid-air, at the mountains themselves which slowly, slowly altered their outlines and at Maggi's narrow back there at the head of the swaying tunnel formed by the swaying bundles of hay; I listened to his thin "gee-up," to the creaking of the ropes and the saddles, to the breathing and the groaning of the horses under their heavy loads, to the rising and falling of the earth under their hoofs, to the far-distant burbling of the stream that was suddenly transformed to jingling ill-temper when the horses waded heavily through; to the often raucous voices of Bjössi and his Little Devil, and the often raucous echoes from the mountain crevices above the farm; to the chattering wind and the piping blast; to the small voices of my sisters and playmates which reached us only as we neared the home field—and I composed in my mind a note to Sigga, whose farm I had seen in the distance from the meadows, and looked forward to the delicious bannock and fresh butter which I thought I would beg from my mother, and was happy, very happy. . . .

In sun and dust and with three horses Ketilbjörn-from-Knör, Ketilbjörn Hranason-from-Knör, came one day into the courtyard. In spite of his gray hairs and stiff back, he leaped lightly out of his saddle, waved to me who was standing looking at him from a window in the loft, smiled with a mouth which was like a cleft in the iron-gray beard, and walked with small light footsteps toward the front door.

As far back as I can remember we had been expecting Ketilbjörn-from-Knör. Every spring, every autumn, every summer, every winter we had expected him, and said that now he would surely come soon. Nevertheless, I was so surprised (I had recognized him at once from his nose) that I turned speechless from the window, looked dumbly at my mother who was sitting there playing with Madame Anna and singing childish songs, looked dumbly at Veiga and Beta who with laughter and shrieks were running in and out of the tunnel which our table made when both its leaves were let down—and it was only when the

door opened that I managed to whisper an explanation of the
strange steps on the stairs:

"It is my grandpa-with-the-nose."

In the doorway stood my grandpa-with-the-nose—and what
a nose! One might think that it was made from dough so soft
that it had run down as a joke from the narrow forehead, and
then stopped to think, and only decided that it was a pity to leave
him *quite* without a nose after it had begun to drip in a big lump
down over his mouth. . . . My grandpa-with-the-nose stood in
the doorway, laughing. "Ha, ha, ha!" he laughed, enjoying our
surprise. "Bless you, darling one! Bless you, children! Here
I am at last, here is Old Papa, here is Grandpa-from-Knör!"

My mother jumped up and threw herself on him, laughing
and crying.

"There, there, my dove . . . there, there, my dove," said
Grandpa-from-Knör, and patted her soothingly on the back,
chuckling his silent inward laughter, "Ha, ha, ha!" He blinked
the tears from his small, deep-set, steel-gray eyes, and mumbled,
half-embarrassed:

"Mustn't cry. Mustn't cry, no ground for tears . . . Mama
sends her love, Mama is very well, was to kiss you for her . . .
there, there, now it is done, now it is done."

"Oh, Old Papa!" whispered my mother tenderly and dried her
eyes. "I am so glad to see you. Why have you let all these years
go by? I have missed you so . . . welcome, Old Papa!"

"There, there, my dove . . . there, there, my dove," muttered
Old Papa, both troubled and satisfied. Freeing himself, he went
farther into the room, and the words continued to tumble forth
like small stones down a slope: "Let me look at your children,
say how do you do to your children. . . . Well now, that must
be Uggi, big boy . . . that is Veiga, have a present for you from
my Veiga, ha, ha, ha! . . . that is Beta, red hair . . . that is Anna, fat
like her namesake—nice children, good children, not de-
formed—you are not afraid to kiss Old Papa, kiss his mouth,
here right under his nose—dare you kiss Grandpa, kiss Grandpa-
from-Knör?"

We dared—all except Madame Anna, who began to howl when Grandpa put his bearded face close to hers.

I considered that I must excuse her and said:

"Madame Anna is always so afraid of strangers, Grandpa dear."

"Madame Anna—do you call her Madame Anna?" asked Grandpa, and repeated the name several times with much laughter and applause.

"Good idea, ha, ha, ha! Is exactly like a parson's wife, three chins, important, will stand no joking, won't kiss Grandpa, won't kiss old Grandpa. . . . Who is it unloading hay from your father's horse? It must be your father's groom, I suppose. May he unload my luggage, bring me my handbags, Celia? No, let me, let me."

Grandpa-from-Knör threw open the window, put out his head and the whole of his body down to his waist and shouted and waved to Maggi, who was standing loosening the bundles of hay from the patiently waiting horses—he was too small to lift them down.

"Boy, boy," shouted Grandpa-from-Knör. "Maggi, Maggi," he added when I had whispered the name to him. "Hurry up, you wisp, you whipcord, you shoestring—what have you been given two hands for? If you do not hurry up I will come after you, Ketilbjörn-from-Knör will come after you, ha, ha! So listen, you cow-ear, you goose, you stalk of rhubarb—when sometime in the next eternity you have finished loosing those hay bundles, unload my horse, bring me my bags, take the horses out to grass, and give them proper fetters. If you let them escape you will have to fetch them back, even if you have to follow them all the way to Knör, all the way to Knör."

Maggi, who at the beginning of this tirade had stood there with open mouth, beaten for once at his own game—Maggi did not think of answering back, but as soon as he understood what Ketilbjörn was driving at he put all his energy into unloading the hay bundles, full of zeal and desire to please.

Grandpa-from-Knör smacked down the window, smiling. He

asked my mother where he was to sleep, where he was to have his boxes brought, and we went down and waited for Maggi and the boxes in the guest-room. Grandpa would not hear of a cup of coffee, would not let my mother out of his sight, called her Celia and his dove again and again, and to everything in the way of refreshment which she suggested to him he replied, "It can wait, it can wait."

He would not hear of sitting down. With both hands buried in his trousers pockets, he walked restlessly up and down, backward and forward.

"As a matter of fact, I have a reason for coming," he said suddenly in an altered tone of voice, and stopped in front of my mother, who had sat down with Madame Anna on her knee.

"Why else do you think I should come in the middle of the haymaking, in the middle of the haymaking?"

The look in my mother's eyes changed. She regarded him closely.

"I have an errand," Grandpa-from-Knör went on, and began his wanderings again. "An errand to you, to your husband, to you both. Frederick-of-Grimsstadir is dead. . . . What did he die of? What a question! Do you think I have ridden all the way from Knör to tell you what Frederick-from-Grimsstadir died of? *I* did not infect him, *I* did not kill him! 'Do you know what he died of?' I suppose he died of some weakness or other, as most people do. . . . Frederick-from-Grimsstadir is, as I have said, dead. His foster daughter, your friend Sophia, still unmarried, not even engaged, does not want to keep the farm. Cannot keep the farm, has no understanding of farming. . . . Now do you understand why I have come? Why Old Papa has come? . . . You can have the farm from next quarter-day; you shall have it rent-free. Think it over, Celia, talk it over with your husband. Four or five hours, a quick ride from Grimsstadir, and you will be at Knör. At Knör with your brothers and sisters, with your Mama and Old Papa. What is the good of staying here where only half of Ofeigsstadur is yours? As soon as Sira Halldor can manage it, he will take the whole farm, and then, there you will be without a farm. Is it sense? Is it foresight?—I am only asking."

"I think, Old Papa, that Greipur would be very reluctant to leave Breidale," said my mother, gently.

" 'Reluctant to leave!' " shouted Grandpa-from-Knör. "The old people at Fjall are bound to die one day. Sira Sigbergur has gone away, and is not likely to come back. His brother Arni has gone to sea, has gone to sea—will he come back to land again? So Greipur has only one sister left here, and I have always heard that of all his brothers and sisters he was fondest of Sigurveig, Sigurveig-at-Fagravik in Hamrafjördur—scarcely a good hour's ride from Grimsstadir. . . . You shake your head? Because he has a priest for a brother, a priest for an uncle, a priest for a grandfather, a priest for foster brother, surely it does not follow that he must have a churchyard to look at every day? . . . Well, if you don't want Grimsstadir, then take whichever of my other farms you like, except Knör. They are all of them nearer to me than Ofeigsstadur. I could doubtless get the tenants out. Speak to your husband, or shall I? . . . there, there, you let me, you let Old Papa."

Maggi came in at this moment dragging the trunks, and when he put them down the incredible happened—he pulled his cap off his head.

"Oh, there you are, you rake-handle," Grandpa-from-Knör greeted him. "Come to Knör and learn how to move, drink liver oil and get a little flesh on your bones! I only hope that Greipur gives you a wage, gives you a wage. What is your name, you willow wand? . . . 'Magnus Jonsson Bachmann'? Why, that name stands up around you like a clerical collar around a sparrow! Can you carry it round the room? Let me see, let me see, well, well, here's a dollar for you—if you let my horses break loose or get sores from their tethers, you will have to give me new ones. And besides that you will have me, Ketilbjörn-from-Knör, to deal with. Well, run away now."

My mother retained Maggi with a look, and after my grandfather had finished with him she told him as soon as he had put

Grandpa's horse out to grass to take my father's and Old Begga's
saddles and ride as quickly as possible down to the meadows and
ask them both to come back as soon as they could.

Maggi ran off quite breathless with eagerness. Grandpa-from-
Knör was already on his knees in front of his sealskin boxes,
opening them.

"Now what do you think I've got here for you children, ha,
ha, ha?" he asked, and winked a laughing eye. "Now what do
you think I've got here, besides what you are most longing for —
of course—I mean liver oil, cod-liver oil! Are you not glad to see
this lovely liver oil, yellow and clear, cod-liver oil, a bottle for
each of you packed in wool? . . . Uggi can have the wool, sell
it for money, put the money in the savings box, become rich . . .
if you don't fancy cod-liver oil, then look at me, look at Old
Papa, look at Grandpa-from-Knör—all his life he has drunk
liver oil, cod-liver oil, half a pint a day. That's why I am so
young in mind, though old in skin, that's why I jump about like
a flea in spite of my fifty-three years! That's why I can out-talk
ten parsons put together, eat and drink more than ten parsons put
together, keep awake longer than ten parsons put together, ride
better than ten parsons put together—in short, live better than
ten parsons put together and cheat ten parsons and half a French-
man put together!

"Have you ever seen a man like me? No, never? . . . I thought
so. The people you see around you every day live on suet, on
mutton fat, and mutton fat congeals, congeals in the veins, congeals in the brain, makes the blood thick. Cod-liver oil does not,
cod-liver oil does not, cod-liver oil, dear children, slips loosely
through you, makes you tough and wide-awake and crafty. People who eat only meat and corn are different from those who eat
fish. A fish, you see, darts lightly through the water, goes through
the water like a shuttle, while a sheep, a meat animal, only jogs
along and gets out of breath, jogs along and gets out of breath.
Do you think I ever get out of breath? Ask Celia, ask Celia.
Can't I hold my breath just as long as a whale, Celia, can't I
breathe out as slowly as a whale can, Celia?"

My mother smiled, nodded gaily, stood up with a smile in her eyes, which somehow went right through her, kissed Grandpa-from-Knör on his forehead, stroked his curly hair and said warmly:

"You are just like your old self, dear Papa . . . I should like to be a sister to these youngsters and sit on the floor at your side and listen to you."

She hastily dried her eyes, and kissed him again on his wrinkled forehead.

"There, there, my dear . . . there, there, my dove."

Ketilbjörn warded her off and added teasingly: "Can't you leave us in peace? Why don't you go out and make coffee, make coffee?"

"No, now I'm going to stay, Old Papa," laughed my mother, and sat down on the floor between us. "I also want to know what you have in your boxes."

"Ho, ho! You think I've got something else—ha, ha, ha!" laughed Grandpa and winked. "Isn't liver oil, cod-liver oil, enough for you? . . . Well, well, let us see. First of all there is a present from old Veiga to little Veiga, from Grandma-at-Knör to the apple of her eye, whom she has never seen—a work-basket with needles, reels of silk, many silks, many colors, silks to sew with, to sew a rose, to sew a letter, to sew Grandpa's name. Then here is a present for Uggi, a book, a book with pictures, *Pilgrim's Progress,* godly but harmless—you read it, read it aloud to Mama, to Grandpa, read all you can—but don't be a priest, but don't become a priest, be a lawyer, be a magistrate, be a judge, take charge of Grandpa's lawsuits, win a case for Grandpa. Grandpa is always having lawsuits, masses of lawsuits, perjury, lies and wrongs—if only the money they cost could remain in the family, we should not lose by them, not lose by them. . . . But now what have I got for Beta? . . . A music-box! Tra, la, la! Tra, la, la! Don't peep, Celia, don't peep! . . . For Madame Anna, I have a bib, two bibs, they ought really to have been hidden until you had a daughter called Celia, called Celia. . . . There you are, Madame Anna, there you are! . . . Do you all want more? Do you want some fruit syrup? Yum, yum! Do you want brown sugar, moist sugar? Do you want biscuits? Do you want French biscuits? Do you want mussels and starfish? There, you are, there, you are! . . . Now shall the big girl over there have something, Celia have something, Old Papa's little girl have something! Shall she have a shawl, silk, yellow and blue, with flowers and birds, foreign flowers, foreign birds, silk, real silk, spun from silkworms, bought in France, ordered from France—a present from Mama and Old Papa! . . . There, there my dove . . . there, there, my dove! . . . For your husband I have dried fish, shark— six-year-old shark!"

My mother sat there with the gorgeously colored shawl draped round her shoulders and looked at it with faraway, dewy eyes, stroking it carefully with her hand.

"You have been in Hamrafjördur, Old Papa?" she said at last.

Grandpa-from-Knör got up abruptly and began walking up and down.

"The road goes through Hamrafjördur, as you know," he answered in a changed voice, and looked away. "Drank coffee at Grimsstadir, ate pancakes, good pancakes, good tough pancakes, wasted an hour, Sophia sent you her love, Tordis sent you her love. You remember her, old Disa?"

"You did not go to Fagravik?" asked Mother, gently.

"Too far away, too far away!" answered Grandpa-from-Knör, unwillingly. "Why should I go to Fagravik? Your sister-in-law can both read and write. Letters can be sent by post. One doesn't grow fat on greetings! . . . You are a nice sort of daughter, mixing yourself up in Old Papa's affairs, saying Fagravik, meaning Fagravigurfjara."

I understood that they were talking of my mother's sister Halla, who had married a man whom Grandpa-from-Knör could not abide. My mother had told me that they lived at Fagravigurfjara, a little farm outside Fagravik. A shadow seemed to pass over my book.

My mother got up, went over to her father and said gently, with trembling lips:

"Don't be angry with me, Old Papa. . . . It hurts me so . . . I am so fond of Halla. She is like Mama—you have said so yourself, and you know that Mama . . ."

Grandpa-from-Knör stopped her sharply.

"How do I know what I have said? I haven't said anything, I don't know anything, don't want to know anything—and so enough of that, enough of that, women are intolerable, never any peace, always trouble, trouble with my sister, trouble with Mama, trouble with you, trouble with your sisters, I feel inclined to bring an action, bring an action against you all, make you all pay fines, put you all in prison, punishment and fines, fines and punishment! . . ."

During the four days that Ketilbjörn-from-Knör stayed at Ofeigsstadur—as he said, "to spoil the horses and finish the veal" (my father had killed a calf on the day of his arrival)— I did not willingly, when I was awake, leave his side for a single moment. As soon as I woke in the morning, I stole out of my bed—I had been given leave to do this—took my clothes over my arm, crept down from the loft, and stole barefoot through the deserted passages to the guest-room. In the evening I fell asleep on Grandpa-from-Knör's breeched knees. My alertness, which almost equaled his, brought me the praise that I was the "only man on the farm." As to my precipitous manner of going to sleep in the evening, he said that I went to sleep faster than "a duck dives," and this expression I have used for many years when I want to make an impression of speed on anyone.

We had great fun in the mornings, Grandpa-from-Knör and I.

"Is that you again, hoppity?" he generally greeted me, and I kissed him in his tousled beard—which long ago seemed to have recognized the hopelessness of trying to endow him with any kind of dignity—and jumped up into his bed, and there we lay for a time and took snuff before we got up; that is to say, he took snuff and I sneezed.

"Why do you always wear flapped breeches, dear Grandpa?" I asked him one morning.

"I shall live and die in the breeches in which I was born—

ha, ha, ha!" he cackled in answer. "You ought to wear flapped breeches when you grow up, kinsman; all else is improvidence and corruption, soft bones and spittle."

Another morning I asked him where he got syrup.

"What's that? Ha, ha, ha!" laughed Grandpa-from-Knör. "Are you asking about syrup, not about liver oil, not about cod-liver oil! Don't you know, redhead, that syrup gives you stomach-ache, whereas if you take liver oil you will become strong, as strong as Ormur Storolfsson, strong as a giant? Some have become so strong from liver oil, cod-liver oil, that they can take a barrel of oil between their hands and drink it off as out of a bowl, a bowl! Wouldn't you like to be as strong as that?"

"Yes," I answered, sneezing and drying my eyes—and thought to myself that if I were as strong as that I would use my strength in a different way.

"We will pretend that I have two barrels standing in my store-room, one with syrup and one with liver oil, and I lead you up to them," Grandpa-from-Knör went on. "Which of them would you drink from if I were standing there looking on?"

"The oil barrel," I answered after some thought.

Grandpa-from-Knör laughed.

"But supposing I gave you the key and left you alone with the barrels, alone with the barrels, which of them would you drink from then?"

"The syrup barrel," I answered, jubilant at the thought.

"Ha, ha, ha!" laughed Grandpa-from-Knör. "Where do I get syrup from? I buy it from the Frenchmen! Sell them sheep, sell them calves, sell them mittens and socks—get in return syrup, moist sugar, brown and white, French wine, red and white, French biscuits, many other things, many other things. Grandpa, Grandpa-from-Knör can trade with the Frenchies, sell high, buy cheap! One must know French, that is all—curse in French, that's all—say 'diakelnong,' say 'saccerbloy.' What do those mean? Have never known, never known. But they answer, they burst themselves laughing, they let themselves be cheated, are only too pleased, only too pleased! . . . When you come to

Knör sometime I will let you row out with me to see them . . . decent people . . . like children, are kind to children."

Later in the day Sigga Mens called me to her where she was standing rinsing stockings in the stream. It was with reluctance that I left Grandpa-from-Knör—but Sigga Mens never called in vain.

"Funny old bird this grandfather of yours," she said, and looked through me, knowing everything. "Do you like him very much?"

I nodded. The sudden beating of my heart made me think of a baby ptarmigan which I had once held in my hand.

"You ought to know what *I* know," said Sigga Mens, dryly.

"What do you know?" I asked softly.

"No, my good child—you're not going to walk over me with your dirty shoes," answered Sigga Mens, coldly, and let a little time pass before she asked: "Has he invited you to visit him at Knör?"

I nodded.

"Has he asked you to come with him on board the French fishing boats?"

I nodded. Sigga Mens was effectively silent. . . .

"Poor little innocent!" she said at last. "Poor little victim!" . . . An indefinable fear went through me.

"You should know the Frenchmen as *I* know them," whispered Sigga Mens, ominously. "You should know how many red-headed boys they have stolen along the coast, or won by barter. You should see them—black hair, black beards, black eyes, black eyebrows; their souls too are black, or else why would they not rather go without fish than fish with human flesh on their hooks?"

"Do they fish with human flesh?" I questioned her, and made sure of my hold on the corner of her apron.

"Only with boys' flesh," she told me in a whisper, lest anyone should hear us. "Only with the flesh of red-headed boys. . . . But the Frenchmen might at least kill them properly, instead of hanging them up by the heels and flaying them alive; perhaps you do not believe me, but I myself have heard the shrieks."

I caught a glimpse of Grandpa-from-Knör in the yard and set off at a run without paying any heed to Sigga Mens' shouts—I had in mind to investigate the truth of her statements this time at any rate, and did not want to be hindered by a vow of silence.

With a smile on his face which reminded me of a mountainside in strong light with deep shadows, Grandpa-from-Knör listened to my recital of what Sigga Mens had told me, and when I finished by asking him how much of it was true, he answered, with his mischievous laugh:

"One often hears queer sounds from out there . . . but I will look after you, look after you."

So, I thought, Sigga Mens was right after all, and in the back of my mind I determined that Grandpa should have no opportunity of looking after *me*.

The very first evening Grandpa-from-Knör told my father that Frederick-from-Grimsstadir was dead and that the farm would be available from next quarter-day. My father answered that doubtless a tenant would turn up. The next day Grandpa-from-Knör asked my father whether his sister Sigurveig still liked Hamrafjördur? My father had not heard anything to the contrary. It was not until the third day that Grandpa-from-Knör said definitely:

"Listen, Greipur, is not Grimsstadir exactly the kind of farm for you? Have you ever known a suitable farm fall vacant here in Breidale, here in Breidale? Are you not getting tired of being here at Ofeigsstadur as half-parson, ha, ha, ha! half-parson? Take Grimsstadir and then we shall have Celia nearer us. You will be almost next door to your sister Sigurveig. At Knör you can buy dried fish cheaply, you can ride to the town in twenty minutes, and therefore you will need only half the horses, half the horses."

"Grimsstadir?" answered my father, hesitatingly, in his maliciously joking tone. "Is not Grimsstadir one of the farms over which you and your sister are engaged in a lawsuit?"

A hasty blush spread over Grandpa-from-Knör's face.

"What of that, son-in-law, what of that? . . . when that case is settled sometime in the next fifty years I shall win it, I cannot but win it. It is to be carried right up to the higher courts as truly as I am called Ketilbjörn-from-Knör, Ketilbjörn Hranason-from-Knör, and should I lose it I have other farms, Greipur Uggason, other farms."

"I know that," answered my father, with the same sharp reserve. "You have farms enough, Ketilbjörn—and another son-in-law too."

Grandpa-from-Knör glanced at him hastily, walked up and down. . . . "Then we shall say nothing more about that," he said a little later. "As the houses have to be rebuilt, you could have had Grimsstadir rent-free and with pre-emption, with pre-emption! . . . But you can scarcely have earned any money with your building activities at Hjalli. You've had enough of building, enough of building, ha, ha, ha!"

"Yes," answered my father—but immediately asked with unwilling interest: "I suppose driftwood is quite cheap in Hamrafjördur?"

"Driftwood!" shouted Grandpa-from-Knör. "Cheap! Driftwood! I should think so, more than cheap, gratis, for a song, it is given away to anyone who takes the trouble to fetch it, sledges full of it the whole winter at Hamrafjördur! Timber, whole trees, planks of ships, masts can be split up for beams, for boards, split up for rake-handles, or tools, can be split for the devil knows what. . . . But do what seems best to you, I shall not press you, shall not entice you . . . I shall not rent out the farm, shall leave it till the first winter night. No. . . . Well, I shall do nothing with it at present. I shall keep it free in case you change your mind. If you think that you would like it, just send a message, send a message."

The next day Ketilbjörn-from-Knör rode home, in sunshine and dust, with his three horses.

Time passed, many things happened.
One Sunday evening my mother gave birth to a little boy.

The next Sunday she was up, the boy was baptized and was given the name of Sigbergur. . . . The third Sunday we children were no longer allowed to see him, but I knew that his little body lay on the table in the guest-room, the windows of which were shuttered, and that his soul was with God. The fourth Sunday, after service, Bjarni Smith and Nonni lowered him, in his little black coffin, into his little grave which they then filled with earth. I stood by, watching it all. I held the hand of my Grandpa-from-Fjall whose eyes were so old today. On the other side of the grave stood my father and mother side by side, crying, with heads bent, and looking so strange. Several people stood round the grave. There were many horses on the home meadow. Nevertheless the day was desolate.

Desolate were now the days, desolate the weeks.

It was so quiet up in the loft. Even Veiga and Beta were subdued; only Madame Anna chattered and laughed as usual. When we children told her to be quiet, my mother smiled at us, kissed us and burst into tears. . . .

One morning my father sat with wrinkled brow at our table and wrote a letter. At his side sat my mother with Madame Anna on her knee. Softly he read her every sentence he wrote, and now and again my mother nodded and reminded him, also softly, of something else. Out in the courtyard Bjarni Smith and Nonni were shoeing Brunka and another of my father's horses for a long journey. Around them flew the yellow and dun-colored shavings from the hoofs. At noon Maggi, proud and silent with responsibility, rode away from the farm with a thick letter bearing a red seal in his pocket. He was going to Knör.

When he returned that day week, my mother told me that in the spring we were going to move far, far away to a district called Hamrafjördur and live on a farm called Grimsstadir. I nodded. My mother looked at me a little surprised, and asked me whether I was sorry to leave Ofeigsstadur now that we no longer lived here alone, and I replied that I did not know.

I sent a "note" to Sigga at Kambar: *"We are moving to*

Hamrafjördur. Can you move too? Your respectful friend, Uggi Greipsson. Forgive scrawl." Her answer ran: *"We own the farm, dear Uggi, and cannot move. Your respectful friend, Sigridur Maria Sigurjonsdottir. Forgive scrawl."* . . .

It was winter. Bjarni Smith had rough-shod Red, had clipped his mane and round his ears, had clipped a narrow channel along his back, clipped where his belly and his legs met, had made him into a regular riding horse. When the weather was good my father rode him to break him in, but he did it without gaiety, without laughter, without jokes, and if Red was headstrong or clumsy he was given the whip so that he stood trembling on his thick, and anything but agile, legs. If I saw my chance to pet him a little after such an event, he put his angular head close to mine, hanging it down miserably with a trembling underlip and looking like a child about to burst into tears.

And then things happened.

The day we said goodbye to Ofeigsstadur the sun shone and the air was mild.

I was dressed for a journey and stood at the side of Red, whom I had tied to a ring outside the smithy. It seemed to me that I had stood there for a long time, and, although I tried hard not to show it, I was impatient to be off. The farm and its surroundings had already taken on a queer strangeness. The red house seemed to have become paler in color, and since Bjarni Smith and Nonni had come and put our bedclothes into sacks while we were still dressing I had lost all desire to stay within its doors.

The bustle of our departure was increased by the horses and men who were being lent to us by neighbors, friends and relations, and who were moving about among our own horses and men. On all sides strange voices were heard among the familiar ones, and, as the latter were full of unusual emotions, they also did not sound quite familiar.

At last all our loose property, which had been tied up in bundles to be fastened onto the pack-horses, lay spread about the courtyard and the home field; but still the people went in and out, talking, laughing, shouting, crying and scolding, and although the horses had stood saddled almost since dawn, it seemed that we were far from being ready to set out.

Old Begga, Maria Mens and Nonni were to travel with us. Maggi was already at Grimsstadir. He had gone when our sheep were driven there a fortnight ago. I had said goodbye to the other farm servants except Sigga Mens, Bjarni Smith and Bjössi, whom I could not find. When I caught a glimpse of Sigga Mens I called her over to me. I stood with my mother's whip in my hand because, for some reason or other, I did not dare let go either of Red or the whip.

"Is there anything I can do for you, my little friend?" asked Sigga Mens, in a harassed voice—and in her great blue eyes, for the first time in my life, I saw tears.

"No, dear Sigga," I answered her, and pulled her head down toward me and kissed her. "Goodbye, dear Sigga, and thank you for being so kind."

Sigga Mens wished to say something, but now there was a lump in her throat. She hugged me close to her, put her mouth to my ear and whispered at last:

"Forgive me, Uggi, if I have not always been as I should to you—most of the things I've told you were untrue—think kindly of me!" Then she slipped away. At the moment her confession made no impression on me. Again I stood and looked at all that was going on around me.

Sigurjon-from-Kambar, who had come over with his man and his horses to bid us farewell, went perspiringly round among our things, shaking his brown head again and again and groaning every time he looked at my father.

"What a to-do, Greipur Uggason, what a to-do!"

Veiga and Beta, wrapped up in shawls, were put up on the sod wall that ran round the courtyard, and were each given a piece of candy to suck, together with commands not to move lest they "get mislaid." . . . My mother and father went side by side into the churchyard. My mother had some wild flowers in her hand which she and I had picked in the dewy grass that

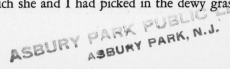

morning. When she came back she no longer carried the flowers. . . .

Bjarni Smith came over to me, wiping the perspiration from his forehead with his shirt sleeve.

"Shall we try once again and see whether the stirrups are the right length?" he suggested, blinking, and lifted me onto my horse. "Yes, yes, could not be better. . . . Well, I must say you look splendid. You set each other off, you two red boys."

He lifted me down again, bobbed me up and down a little, but did not hurry.

"Well, well," he said, then, oddly affectionate, he stroked my cheek with his hard hand. "Meet and part—that's the rule. Willingly would I have followed your father and you to Hamraf-jördur, but I have not long left to live, and I would rather rest my bones here in Ofeigsstadur churchyard where the earth is so dry and good. . . . And then—it seems to me that I have dug so many graves for others in this churchyard that it would be strange indeed if I could not lie here myself. I should feel alone in any other place, I think. . . . No, chip, we shall not see each other again. I could wish I had been kinder to you, that must be allowed, and especially I ought not to have got drunk on that day, you remember? . . . have you forgiven me that, will you think kindly of your old Bjarni?"

"You could never have been nicer to me, dear Bjarni," I whispered, and dried my eyes. Bjarni Smith also hastily dried his eyes.

"Well, well," he roared, angry with himself. He kissed me hastily and shamefacedly. "So I will say goodbye to you, my chicken. May God always look upon you with his right eye."

So Bjarni Smith went away. . . . I do not even know whether my good friend now lies companionably among all those for whom he had dug graves, in "the good dry soil" of Ofeigsstadur churchyard, or alone and cold in the damp soil of another place.

It was suddenly arranged that Sigurjon-from-Kambar and I should ride on in advance so that I could say goodbye to Sigga. My father lifted me into my saddle, begged me jokingly to "spare the foal," asked me if I had now said goodbye to everybody, suddenly gave me a kiss. When I was free, I started Red—not a very easy undertaking.

Bjössi, who had apparently been hiding himself until this moment and was rather grubby, appeared, his youthful face bluish-red and rather the worse for wear. He was fourteen years old and about to be confirmed at this time. He walked across the home field at Red's side, holding my left stirrup. We said nothing and avoided each other's eyes. When we came to the end of the field, Bjössi growled in a deep man's voice that now he would go no farther. Nevertheless, he still continued to walk alongside Red and me, waded through a stream without noticing it and not until we reached a place where the path was so deep that his head was on a level with mine did he stop Red by pulling at the reins, kissed me for the first time in his life, stood for a moment with downcast eyes, tried to say something, and at last stammered out that I would have been all the better for some more beatings if there had been time for them. Then he turned sharply round and ran full tilt back to the farm.

I never saw him again, never heard his name, have no idea what good or evil may have befallen him.

For a long time Sigurjon rode silently in front of me. Not before we were nearing Kambar did he rein in his horse and allow me to come up alongside.

"Sigga will miss you," he said as if he were beginning a long conversation; then he suddenly came to a standstill, shook his head and said: "Oh, Sigga, Sigga!"

Sigga and I were put side by side on the red plush sofa in the guest-room in Kambar. Then both Sigurjon and his mild little wife left the room so that we could "talk a little together in peace and quiet." Perhaps it was for this reason that neither of us could think of a word to say to each other. We could only sit and hold each other's hands.

Sigurjon stuck his head through the door, came right in and said to us kindly: "Why do you say nothing, children? . . . Oh, Sigga, Sigga!"

He went away, he came back.

"Say something Uggi, Sigga, are you dumb?" he groaned, breathless. "It will be years before you can visit each other again. Don't sit there like a pair of wooden dolls. Kiss each other at any rate . . . What a parting! . . . Oh, Sigga, Sigga, you are not like yourself today!"

Sigga's mother laid the table in front of the sofa with many kinds of cakes, as if Sigga and I were grown-up visitors, gave us chocolate in thin gold-bordered porcelain cups, and begged us to eat and drink, but neither of us could do so.

Sigurjon announced that the horses with the movables had passed, that my parents and the other riders would now have started from Ofeigsstadur and that we must hurry ourselves a little unless we wished them to wait for us at the cross-roads.

When I kissed Sigga goodbye she opened her mouth for the first time.

"Thank you for the labels," she whispered almost inaudibly.

"Thank you too," I whispered back. We both had tears in the corners of our eyes; neither of us cried. "Oh, Sigga, Sigga!" groaned Sigurjon, and lifted me into my saddle.

There in the courtyard in the glad sunshine and the soft air "Sigga-Sigga" and I parted. We were never to see each other again. . . . Twenty-three years later my father wrote to me from Grimsstadir—I was at that time far away: *"We have now a new neighbor at Skulastadir, one Steven Gislason from Breidale, the son-in-law of Sigurjon of Kambar, nice people with three small children."* When I read the letter I said to myself, "People from our old district." I gave it no further thought. Two years later, almost a quarter of a century after this parting in the courtyard, my father wrote to me: *"Our neighbor Steven Skulastadir has had the great sorrow of losing his wife. She was called Sigrid, and was the daughter of Sigurjon of Kambar."*

"Those must be the people from our old district that he wrote about before," I thought, and suddenly the name struck me: Sigrid—daughter of Sigurjon at Kambar. That must be "Sigga-Sigga," my sincere friend. Sigga of the "labels," so near, so far, dead—and I did not even lay a "label" on her coffin. It would have been so easy to write the "letter": *"Sigrid Maria Sigurjonsdottir, sleep well. Your sincere friend, Uggi Greipsson. Forgive scrawl."* That and nothing else. . . .

Red traveled proudly with his light burden, and if Red was proud, the burden was not less so.

At the cross-roads Sigurjon-from-Kambar and I met my father who was riding with Veiga in front of him, my mother who was riding with Beta on her lap, and Old Begga. We learned that Madame Anna was lying in a box on one of the pack-horses, which Nonni was leading by the rein, with Maria Mens riding at its side.

My father and Sigurjon got off their horses, embraced and kissed each other farewell, and then Sigurjon kissed my mother, kissed Old Begga, kissed us children, hoped that luck would follow us all, wished us a good journey and then stood there breathless and waved to us when at last we gave the horses the rein.

We rode on through the warm day. The few words spoken between my parents and Old Begga were gay in form but uncertain in tone. My mother rode all the time in front on the gray, my father at the rear on the brown, much against the latter's will.

We came to Fjall where we stopped and were given a meal of which none of us, not even Grandpa, could eat very much. Grandpa sat at the table and looked at each of us in turn. His eyes were old, as on the day when my little brother Sigberg was buried. My grandmother herself waited at table and could not be prevailed upon to sit down even though we children were not eating. Now and again she stopped, put a hand on my mother's shoulder and said a word or two. Then my mother's mouth always began to tremble. The conversation was light but with long pauses. Veiga and Beta sat there with an uncertain expression on their small faces, looking at their elders. Now and again they laughed loudly and shrilly at something funny, but always pulled themselves up and stifled their laughter.

Grandpa and Grandma accompanied us when we rode "to the boundary stream, Elizabeth," as my Grandpa said. . . . At the boundary stream we found our servants who had eaten and had rested the horses and were now loading up again. Madame Anna shouted with joy in her box when she saw my mother, and my mother took her up, kissed and hugged her and let her say goodbye to Grandma, who surreptitiously dried her bright eyes.

"When you cross that stream over there, you will, for the first time in your life, have crossed the boundaries of Breidale, kinsman Uggi," said Grandpa-from-Fjall to me, and put his hand on my shoulder. "You and Red."

He looked me in the eyes for a long time. "You will have many other boundaries to cross in your life," he added in a tone half gay and half grave. "Cross them always with as light a heart and as good a conscience as you are crossing this one, and then the last, and the greatest, will not seem to you so difficult. . . . Since Uggi won't eat any food, he will have to ride on my good advice," he said laughingly to my father, who was standing close to us—red-cheeked, but otherwise pale, violently chewing his tobacco. Then Grandpa kissed me goodbye, kissed me many times, mumbling blessings, apparently not troubling whether I understood them or not.

A little later we crossed the boundary stream, the boundary of Breidale. The men with the pack-horses had gone on in advance. When we reached the edge of the gully that the boundary stream had dug out for itself during the centuries, my father and mother and I pulled up our horses and waved to Grandpa- and Grandma-from-Fjall, who were still standing on the spot where we left them, holding their horses by the rein—and each other's hands, I felt sure.

But little did I guess that this was the last time I should see the breeze blow out Grandpa's great white beard, or see Grandma's black-clothed form standing erect on the green earth.

We rode on. . . .

We overtook the servants with the pack-horses and from then on we kept with them. We rode beside a broad, broad river whose surface, sparkling in the sun, was now and again ruffled by capricious bursts of wind, reminding me of the shells that Grandpa-from-Knör brought for us children the year before, and which we had forgotten to bring with us. The day passed. My legs began to grow stiff and I felt more and more sorrowful that we had forgotten our shells.

We halted on grassy land beside a river where the horses could get something both to eat and to drink. My legs were so stiff I could hardly walk. Veiga was peevish; Beta and Madame Anna were asleep. I ate the food my mother gave me with a good appetite, and sat on a little mound and looked back the way we had come.

How extraordinarily broad, flat and expressionless our lovely valley, Breidale, looked from here! How far away and low the mountains behind Ofeigsstadur already seemed! The secret picture of our home valley which I had until now carried in my heart was shattered with one blow.

As we rode on, a deep melancholy crept into my mind. It seemed to me that all the birds that passed us were asking us where we were going and why we were leaving Breidale. . . . A depressing creaking noise came from the pack-horses, and the only words spoken were the men's "gee-ups." Our leaf table was helpless with its legs sticking out at the side, and so were our chairs with their legs in the air; and everything was swinging, swinging—swinging a great emptiness into my heart.

As step by step we drew nearer to the strange farm where we were going to spend the night, the sun went down. Those mountains which once were Breidale were now no more than low, formless mounds. The air had grown chill. The broad river was now a little to the side, and might well have been carved in stone. The sun-glow had faded, and all the colors were dead. The cold blast whispered cold words in our ears, and blew past us with insolent laughter.

Had I not been a man riding my own horse—though not actually booted and spurred, yet with a whip in my hand—I might possibly have wept.

PART TWO

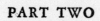

PART TWO

1

THE stones along the road had been awake since dawn. They were as different from one another as the members of a congregation in church on a Sunday morning. Some were smooth-surfaced and lay there with an expression of peace and wonder, like a child at the breast. Others were rugged, harsh, dark and unreasonable. Still others stood erect, with dented faces, and moss in every wrinkle. But they all followed our progress with an attentive gaze, for the day was very still and without sun and every eye could discern what it desired and every voice could be heard.

The streams talked and chattered, some of them eagerly, hesitating over their words like Grandpa-from-Knör, others with slow dragging speech like Geitastada-Gvendur.

"A dead one rides on a red one," sepulchrally declared one sinister muddy-bottomed brook, and a shiver passed through me; for surely it must be Red and me he meant.

"Gray carries—gray tarries," whispered a well-nourished streamlet ominously. And this time I was seized with anxiety, for the "gray" that "carried" must be my mother's gray, and the "gray" that "tarried," the glacier river. Perhaps the bridge over it was not quite safe, or my mother might grow dizzy and fall.

"Worship the Lord, but Jon is adored," sang a third blasphemously, a thin little wisp of a stream with stones like warts all over its body. He must be meaning Old Begga with her eternal talk about Jon Vidalin.

But how did all these streamlets know so much about our affairs? Have our cows been gossiping, or our sheep—or Magnus Jonsson Bachmann?

"Look at little stump—he has a sore rump," a pert little bit of a stream flung at me rudely, and burst into a roar of laughter.

My cheeks burned at having my secret revealed thus, and I scowled over at the others, especially at my father, ashamed not only of myself but of the stream.

". . . Shies?" laughed my father. "New-Skjoni? I should think he does. Now and again he has almost run his hoofs off from terror at his own shadow. He has cracked his neck three or four times . . . well, almost, then. However, he'll soon be knocked into shape. . . . Will he carry the chairs? Why, he is carrying them as meekly as a sheep its wool!"

New-Skjoni twitched his ears and sweated like a stone at daybreak.

"I have been a bit of a mutt all my days," drawled Matthias from Melar, the farmer with whom we had spent the night, and who was now accompanying us on our way. "Especially with horses—but the beast is sweating heavily."

"Let him sweat the marrow out of his bones, if it pleases him!" joked my father, and spat brown. "But Matti, are you by any chance coming with us all the way to Grimsstadir?"

"Who knows?" smiled Mela-Matti. "On just such a morning as this my grandfather Björn rode away from home, from his wife and six children, wearing his working clothes, and riding a horse without a saddle, to return three years later, bringing with him six more children who were all his own, fairly and honorably come by, as he worded it. 'There's your full dozen, Valgerda, whether you want them or not!' he said, and kissed my grandmother and showed her the children, whom he had packed down in a couple of wheelbarrows, generally used for peat, three in each. 'Yes, indeed,' answered my grandmother, and looked at the children. 'Because you, to further your own ungodly will, Family-Björn, have begotten these children in dishonor and shame, that will not prevent me from bringing them up in honor and decency!' And that she did—one was my father. From that day my grandfather was called 'Family-Björn,' and that was all he got out of that story."

"Didn't he call himself so too, the scoundrel?" asked my father, gaily.

Mela-Matti turned over the quid of tobacco in his mouth. "He did so. . . . Twelve children did he desire like the twelve apostles. One of the boys was to have been called Judas. But that was not allowed. Jesus, then. Not allowed either. Sirak, then. Why the hell not! So by that name the boy was baptized. Soon afterward he died."

"What about you?" asked my father, winking. "Have *you* reached the apostolic number?"

Mela-Matti glanced at him sideways, and arranged Beta more comfortably on the pommel. He had taken her for a short time, so my mother might have a rest, and she now refused to leave him.

"I am afraid I am altogether too great a bungler for that, good Greipur."

"Yes—a bungler—" laughed my father, and they all laughed except my mother. "I think I have already heard something about that."

My mother was riding silent and unencumbered, lost in her own thoughts. A faint light as from an inward smile rested on her face.

"How many children have you, Matti?" asked Geir, one of Sigurjon's men, innocently.

Mela-Matti looked at him mildly. "Six—like my grandfather."

"I suppose you never give up your children to the parish as you do your sheep?" asked Geir.

"Now, now, my good friends," said Mela-Matti, "I have always been a great duffer when it comes to answering back."

"Dear Matti," lisped Beta, with her thumb in her mouth, leaning backward against him so as to look up at him, "if you will be my husband I will mend your stockings so well that it will never show! I have needles and thread which Grandpa-from-Knör gave me, and the cat is mine."

"Does kitty give plenty of milk?" wondered Mela-Matti. "So much milk that we can give up cows?"

Such deep ignorance made Beta laugh, and even Veiga, who

was a little vexed with her husband-hunting sister and very embarrassed on her behalf, laughed too. But she pulled herself together at once and whispered reproachfully to Beta:

"Aren't you ashamed to carry on like that with a married man!"

I felt as if my mother were so far away that I whispered her name. She did not hear me. Where was she off to? What could she be thinking of? Why was she smiling? Like tiny puffs of wind brushing lightly over the grass and disappearing imperceptibly as they arose, a vague, shy feeling of sorrow swept through my mind now and then.

Nonni and Maria Mens were looking after the pack-horse on whose back Madame Anna was rocking in her basket, lying with her face to the sky. As she lay there, gazing upward, the angels could not but keep an eye on her. Perhaps God Himself saw her blue eyes fixed on Him, smiled at her, waved to her and said to His angels:

"Listen, My angels, look after the little one there! If the basket is not properly strapped on, support it. See that the hack does not stumble. Her name is Madame Anna. You realize, of course, that it is Greipur Uggason who is moving."

I collected my thoughts and looked round me surprised. How strange; the sun was not shining today!

"Whoa! You lousy beast, you miserable hack, you jade of Hell, can't you keep to the path?" thundered one of the strange men who had come with us.

A feeling of rare well-being passed through me suddenly. The healthy neighing of the horses and their quick hoof-beats, the sharp creaking, the movement, the rank smell of horse, the gray unpretentious day, the raucous shouts of the men and their harsh voices, the childish prattle of my sisters, Old Begga's peevishness and even my mother's silence—all was as it should be.

"You and Rufus—you are a devil of a pair," grumbled Old Begga, drying her dripping nose. "When one is young, life lies in front of one, and one lives like a colt in the meadow.

But youth slips by and age comes on. A stone makes its own bed, and the longer it is left lying the more firmly it settles down. It's not surprising that I dug myself well in, in Breidale, where I was born and brought up. How could I dream that God would blame me for that? Could I have thought that it would be reckoned a sin?"

"No, dear Begga," I comforted her, for her eyes were very bleak, and her face, whose features were more flaccid than usual, looked desolate and forlorn.

"You speak as if you had understanding," she fumed, as though I had offended her. "Are you a messenger from God—a teacher? We think we know our own children. Do we? We know them about as well as we know tomorrow's weather! Until their reason is fully developed they should listen to their mother's voice, not to their own desires; and that my Nonni has always done—until now. In spite of all my prayers and entreaties he has insisted on leaving his home-district and following Farmer Greipur—yea—and of course Maria Mens was coming too! It seldom snows from the east if it blows from the west. None shall hear me say anything bad about Maria Mens—but in a house that lets in the rain the woodwork is bound to rot sooner or later. Well, well, one can delay fate for a time, but to escape it altogether is impossible."

The foremost horse suddenly ducked down into the earth. Then one after another all the horses ducked into the earth and disappeared. The heads of the riders rocked for a moment over the gray graveled edge as if they were rocking on the surface of water, and then they also disappeared.

When Old Begga and I reached the edge we saw a gully in front of us, on the other side of which the advance guard of the caravan was already outlined against the gray sky as if cut out of black paper: the horses with their round or square burdens, and the riders with their dangling legs breaking the delicate bow-line of the slender horses. Right across the ravine stretched the line of horses, wonderful to watch from up here, for they appeared to be crawling forward on unseen legs oddly broad and flat. Through clouds of grayish-yellow dust the line of human beings and horses could be seen extending along the path like a rope; and last of all came Old Begga and I, side by side, like a big knot at the end.

And Old Begga talked and talked.

"Well, well, just as God is Three in One, so there are three kinds of tears, the sweet, the salt and the sour. But what do you know about that, you and Red—such a pair of little saddle heroes? You know as little about life as a couple of stones buried in the earth. The sun has not burned you yet; the frost has not bitten you yet; you can shelter from the storm, and sleep through the night. Well, well, I myself am not much wiser. 'We weep for all imagined pain, and hurry restlessly for barren gain.' And yet we see each day that the river swallows the rain, time absorbs our tears—and God provides for the ravens."

Old Begga was silent.

The golden plover fluted his two gray-weather notes, and the curlew spun long trills out of his long beak. The ravens came in pairs and followed us silently, turning in the air so that it was difficult to be quite sure which was the back and which the breast. They said a short farewell and flew away with heavy wing-beats.

"I must be a great sinner for our Heavenly Father to lay on my rheumatic shoulders the burden of traveling over rivers, mountains and deserts to die in a foreign land where I do not know the courses of the sun, and where even the water tastes different," sighed Old Begga.

I looked around me. In among the stretches of sand and hummocks of heather, friendly grass paths wound along, and here and there I saw a farm surrounded by its green fields, smoking its pipe and following our journey closely to see whether we were going to stop or ride past.

"Is this really a desert, Old Begga?" I asked doubtfully.

"Never a word can one say to you but you turn it and twist it like a bride her wedding dress!" sneered Old Begga, screwing up her mouth. "How many times have I not impressed on you that to pick holes in words and sentences is a devilish habit? I pity the girl who will stand at the altar with you one day. It doesn't matter about red hair if the heart is pure and you bridle your tongue! Well, well, my little dandelion, don't worry about what *I* say. Perhaps this isn't a desert after all. But in any case it is a very ugly district to *my* mind; *I* think so at any rate, and just you wait till we cross the Butterwater Moor tomorrow—just you wait, I say!"

I had thought a great deal about this moor and the lake known as Butterwater from which it had taken its name. I liked butter very much, and the combination of the two names seemed to me infinitely alluring. Old Begga's terrifying statements made no impression on me; I understood that she knew the Butterwater Moor as little as I did. If only I had a gigantic ladle and a churn I could easily marry Sigga-Sigga, build us a hut at the side of Butterwater and skim the cream, churn it and sell the butter in the summer and skate in the winter. What fun it would be when I came back from town in the autumn and Sigga-Sigga unpacked all that I had bought for her! "But haven't you bought anything for yourself, my dearest friend?" she would ask, and put her arms round my neck. "Yes—a gun," I would answer offhand. "I thought you would like a little game in the pot on important occasions, and besides it will be useful to have a gun by us in case white bears come." "You think of everything," Sigga-Sigga would shout joyfully. "Come over here, my husband, and share the figs with me. God knows I cannot eat them all myself."

"If these were only the Breidale ravens I should know most of them." Old Begga broke in on my dreams with her brittle ageing voice. And suddenly I remembered how it felt to go into a kitchen full of smoke.

"Don't you call it hard that now I have to grow accustomed to new ravens?—I, poor wretch, who cannot abide strange ravens. There are no creatures more easily infuriated by dogs and children and old people whom they do not know than ravens. Much rather would I be in my grave than obliged to

fight those damned black carrion birds the rest of my life—
as well as my rheumatism and other plagues. But death will
be neither enticed nor frightened away."

I heard my father's happy laugh and Mela-Matti's neighing
voice in the distance, and I thumped Red's sides so as to catch
up with them, but Rufus would not better his gait.

"The air at Breidale was lovely, so healthy and clean and
mild to the lungs—soft as milk," Old Begga went on. "In
Hamrafjörd we shall have a land mist in the morning, and a
sea mist in the evening, I expect. It will be like coming from
Paradise into Purgatory, even for the poor innocent speechless
animals. Alas for Breidale! . . . In proud recklessness and
without fear for the future you make your entry into Hamrafjörd—and on your own horse too. Pah! 'Many ride into the
yard in full blossom, and ride away like dying flowers!' . . .
Well, well, don't let me prophesy evil for you—all may turn
out for the best. But you will never live to see in any other
part of the world such splendid, close-growing wool and such
gleaming hair on two- and four-footed animals as there were in
Breidale."

"Well, soberface—shall we run a race?" cried a gay little
stream beside me. But I had not the time, though I should have
enjoyed taking it down a peg or two.

"Hamrafjörd!" Old Begga savored the name, but without
appetite. "Does it not speak more of rocks than of mountains?
A bad district can always be recognized by the fact that the
mountains keep away from it; they don't feel at home there.
In a land without mountains both thoughts and animals stray
away, for what is there to keep them together? And how anyone
can sleep at night in a flat country is more than I can guess."

My mother pulled in her gray, speaking kindly to her and
patting her broad mane; and although she was very unwilling
to be seen among such slow companions as Old Begga's Brunka
and my Red, she could refuse my mother nothing and only
showed her dissatisfaction in her eyes and by dragging at her bit.

"Well, little Uggi," my mother cried gaily, "can't you even get through a day's traveling without a story?"

Old Begga's withered cheeks suddenly flamed red.

"I have known the *Psalms of the Passion* by heart for over forty years, my dear mistress, and yet I have not learned to bridle my tongue," she hastened to come to my rescue. "You imagine that I am telling your child stories, Celia, but the truth is that I am riding here and spitting fire and brimstone out of my mouth like a volcano. Now I begin to realize my sin and to understand my punishment!"

My mother had not been listening; she was again absorbed in her own thoughts.

"All that God allows to happen to us is always for the best," Old Begga turned toward me and continued instructively, "even if it is difficult to understand at the time. Otherwise, why should He allow it to happen?"

I could not take my eyes off my mother.

"It will be pleasant to see Sophia again," she said to Old Begga and me together. It sounded almost like an answer.

Like a thirsty man who finds a stream in the mountains I threw myself upon those words, absorbing their tone; and I went on listening to them long after their sound had died away. Sophia—why, that was her friend from childhood days, who was said to be so good-looking. It was Sophia's foster father who had died. It was she who was to live with us at Grimsstadir. Was my mother really so glad to be seeing her again? I listened and listened. . . . No, it was not that.

I thumped Red's sides. My mother and Old Begga must not see that I had tears in my eyes. Suddenly I felt so unhappy. In his tiny grave in the churchyard at home lay my little brother. How could we have left him? Had my mother quite forgotten him? Who would remember him? Who would sit and cry upon his grave? Of course, he had Granny- and Grandpa-from-Fjall; no doubt they would stop beside his grave on Sundays. But if it had been one of us others, if it had been I, would my mother have gone away and left me? Would she still have been happy and smiling today?

At the side of the road a gray man held a gray horse aside to let us pass. A strange man and a strange horse. As each of us passed him he lifted his hat with an odd jerk, only just showing the top of his head, which was quite bald like a new-born child's. And to each of us he murmured a short greeting in a gray, toneless voice, without showing more expression in his face than a fish snapping at the air. Some of us answered his greetings in a friendly way, others shortly, still others in an unfriendly manner, and everybody, except my mother, showed a more or less obvious embarrassment in voice or manner. Rufus, who was always ready to avail himself of every opportunity for play and gossip, stopped immediately and nosed at the gray horse; but the horse was as sullen and queer as its rider. It laid back its ears, and angrily refused Red's friendly advances. Suddenly, however, it thought it would like to follow the other horses, but that the gray man would not allow.

"What is your name?" he asked, while we both struggled with our horses.

"Uggi Greipsson," I answered shyly, for his eyes seemed to me so sinister. They were the color of river water on a cold and dreary spring day.

"Oh, indeed. My name is Sigbjörn Arnason," he said when at last he had turned his gray horse in the right direction.

"We are going ever so far away," I shouted after him, thinking that by saying this I should free myself from my fear of meeting him again.

"Where have you been wooing today, Simbi?" Geir's coarse voice rang out in the stillness.

I looked back anxiously at the gray man, to whom the shout was evidently addressed. He was sitting in his saddle almost apologetically, and his gray horse was moving its legs as if it were begging the path to forgive it.

"What did he say to you? Was he asking you about Maria

Mens?" laughed Geir, when I caught up with the others. I pretended I had not heard.

My father was in very good spirits, and told us, with the shy gaiety he always assumed when he spoke of his young days:

"I shall never forget the winter when he tried his luck in Sildarfjord and returned home without a hat—and without a hair on his head. He had wooed a rich widow whose husband was scarcely cold in his grave, had old Simbi. That time he escaped without his hat. He insisted he had lost his hair before."

The men all laughed, and even from Old Begga there came some odd little sounds which certainly represented laughter.

"We kept him warm," my father went on. "We sent him out on a wooing expedition at least once a month. There were girls enough of all ages, and Simbi was tireless. Once we made him as good as propose to Jon of Teg's unborn daughter—only it turned out eventually to be a boy. There was not a thing we could not, with a little pressure, make Simbi do. He thinks nothing but good of everybody—as long as no one tries to borrow his books."

"Or his money," Geir giggled, and let his whip swish over the nearest hack. "A confounded miser is Roadside-Simbi, a money-hoarder."

"Have you tried him too?" laughed my father. "Yes, Simbi is careful. But he cannot have a great deal of money, surely."

"Oh, he's got plenty," said Geir.

"One's neighbor has always plenty," my mother observed casually, but without a smile.

My father, wishing to stand up for Geir, who was a stranger and unknown to us, said in a tone that closed the matter:

"Well, he's probably got a copper or two in his coffers."

Suddenly we heard the men shouting:

"Whoa, whoa, whoa! . . . Look out there! . . . Look out there, I say . . . what the devil!"

It was New-Skjoni, our New-Skjoni with the chairs. He was galloping as if eighteen little devils were after him.

My father slid Veiga down onto the side of the road and set off in the same direction. They disappeared to the sound of the heavy hoof-beats.

Around us laughter and crying were mixed with all sorts of other noises. Veiga, Beta and Maria Mens wept loudly. Nonni stood with Madame Anna's basket close by him and sometimes cried and sometimes laughed. The men swore, whistled, joked and coaxed their horses with a false show of friendliness, and the horses themselves snorted, neighed and were inclined to shy.

"We shall see Farmer Greipur again," shouted Nonni, in a treble that was just about to break. "Perhaps we shall see New-Skjoni again. But the chairs, never."

"There, there, Jon," soothed Old Begga, with dignity. "All is in God the Father's hands."

"Yes, yes, Mama," acknowledged Nonni, shamefacedly, and burst out again into tear-filled laughter.

On top of all this laughter and shouting there followed, as soon as the horses had been calmed, a queer, awkward bustle. The men swore long and loud, thumped the horses without reason, kicked them, used their whips for nothing at all and were then angry with the result. Old Begga, who was too annoyed with Nonni to notice him, prayed loudly to the Father of Light. My mother, who had taken little Veiga up in her lap, whispered calming words into her little ear, which was a deeper red than her tear-sodden face.

"It will be bad enough to lose your chairs, dear lady," Mela-Matti consoled her, and the bushy brown beard moved in a queer shaggy smile, "but it would have been worse if it had been one of the children."

My mother slowly lifted her head and looked at him, listening, thoughtful. A helpless expression spread over her sweet face. Then suddenly she crumpled up, sobbing heavily, inconsolably, wearily.

Mela-Matti whipped his horse and moved away at a gallop, cursing himself.

"A damned fool!"

Something like dread seemed to be gnawing at my heart. But so far as I knew I had nothing to dread. God knew whether it might not be a mouse that had slipped down my throat one night while I lay and slept. But, of course, it might also be a water-beetle that I had swallowed without knowing it, or perhaps a sort of snake. Or could it be a tapeworm? Perhaps I was going to die of it! But I didn't quite feel as if I were going to die just yet. Probably it would eat its way out of me in the end.

My father returned with the offending New-Skjoni. The ends of the ropes were neatly looped round the pommel of the packsaddle. They looked blameless and carefree. New-Skjoni, on the other hand, trudging along without the vestige of a chair on his back, looked like a dog returned from burying a stolen bone. My father was very cheerful, and I realized suddenly, to my immense relief, that chairs are not the sort of things a man cries about.

"My only regret is that I left my millstones behind. Sira Dori got them much too cheaply!" he shouted from a distance. And thereupon he gave New-Skjoni a loud smack over his loins and said, as if a more bloody revenge could not be thought of: "Well, well, now you shall carry nothing but air for the rest of the day, and be thoroughly ashamed of yourself."

"Is that all there is left of those blessed chairs?" asked Old Begga, in a tone she tried to keep indifferent.

"Yes, just a couple of backs, but neither of them any better than yours," laughed my father, unmoved—and then an idea occurred to him. "What a fool I was not to exchange with Simbi! New-Skjoni is on the whole no worse than the hacks he manages to dispose of."

"I thought at the time God must have had some reason for setting up that apparition at the side of the road," exclaimed Geir, in real annoyance. "It is not too late yet. I will saddle the spare horse and ride back after him."

My father enjoyed the thought, but, when he understood that

Geir was entirely serious about the matter he replied, in a banter-
ing tone:

"Haven't you enough to do, taking in people on your own
account, my good Geir?"

Many times since, the thought of Roadside-Simbi and his
queer steed has given me strange shivers down my spine.

"Gray carries—gray tarries!"

A noise that reminded me of the buzzing of a bumble-bee
in the distance, a noise with a sting in it, quivered slowly toward
my ear, and suddenly the air was full of a deep, monotonous
note. This note increased continuously and grew at last into a
dull heavy roar that hammered at my ears with cold persistency.
Not as if it wished to do me any harm, nor as if it wished to
do me any good—only so that I myself and all around me,
human beings, animals, the sky, the earth, might be absorbed
into a very simple melody played on a single string.

We were nearing the glacier river known as "River-under-the-
Bridge."

In a short time we reached the edge of its deep rocky chasm.
A slender bridge, with spaced horizontal railings, spanned it
from side to side in a homely, comfortable sort of way.

Deep down at the bottom of the cliff, the walls of which
were black from the smoke of the breaking waters, the river
made its way, foaming, gray and turbid, giving hasty glances
from its angry, icy eyes. Was it a snake wriggling down there
between the rocky walls—some fabulous monster-snake? No,
it was water; and strangely enough it was the same river that,
over there near the horizon, spread out into a broad, still
stream—upon which there fell, from a rift in the clouds, a
shimmer of faint evening light.

A shiver passed through me, my teeth chattered as if in fear,
and yet I was not cold, or really afraid; a queer kind of excitement, suffocating, joyful, tore at me, where before it had only
gnawed.

For the water down there was not water at all. . . . What did it want with me, that gray monster thundering past, foaming with ice-cold life? Why was it calling me? Why was it dragging me toward it with unseen hands?

Suddenly someone came and grasped my arm hard and pulled me away from the abyss. Thank God, it was my mother.

"Are you frightened?" she asked with a little laugh, as soon as we could hear ourselves speak. Then suddenly she became serious, unhappy. "How could you go and stand there so near the edge of the abyss? Think if the river had taken you, child."

I pulled myself away, ran over to my father, who was loudly and cheerfully giving orders, and clung, shivering with fright, to his legs. At the same time I looked up into his face with a smile to hide my fear.

The horses were led by their bridles one by one over the bridge, the less reliable ones without their loads. In the center of the group walked Maria Mens with her eyes bandaged, led by Nonni. Behind them tripped Old Begga with her skirts lifted high, singing hymns. My mother held my hand in the fond belief that she was looking after me. Everyone got across at last except our New-Skjoni. He would not budge.

His eyes were bandaged like Maria Mens's, but still he refused. He ate all the sugar and all the bread we offered him, but over that bridge he refused to go. Neither caresses nor blows had any effect. There was a long consultation as to whether it would be advisable to send him down to the ford, where it was supposed he would be willing to swim across; but it would be difficult to spare a man to ride down with him, and the end of it all was that Mela-Matti arranged to take charge of him.

My father took me back across the bridge so that I might say goodbye to him and, with tears and sighs, New-Skjoni and I divided up the last bits of sugar my father found in his pocket.

When we left my father patted him affectionately and said sadly: "Well, well, old man, we shall miss all the fuss and bother we have had with you."

New-Skjoni slowly turned his head, looked at him ques-

tioningly, twitched his ears. I understood that they were now
reconciled, but I could not understand why New-Skjoni did not
come trotting after us toward the bridge.

"Now we are only waiting for you to finish saying your
prayers," shouted my father to Old Begga, when Mela-Matti
had gone off with New-Skjoni and the men had got the horses
started.

Old Begga hobbled up to him and was helped into her saddle.

"Old women and old saddles are both very solid," he panted
jokingly, giving her the reins.

"Alas, all is but transitory, Farmer Greipur," she answered
with dignity.

"Even Vidalin's *Book of Homilies?*" asked my father, and
managed at last to get old Brunka, who was clearly showing
her disapproval of both her saddle and her rider, to begin
to move.

A good deal later we reached the farm where we were to
spend the night.

Close up to the house, an ill-tempered little stream was
chasing down the field between large stones and fallen bits of
rock. A rope had been fastened across the stream, on which
a boy of about my own age was walking as easily as a spider
mounts its thread. The stream was shaking with anger, and
snapped at the back of his trousers, but never managed to
catch him.

"Can you do that, boy?" he asked me calmly, after he had
once or twice demonstrated this daring climb to me.

"No," I answered with sincere admiration. "She is angry
with you."

"Who?"

"The stream."

"Oh, her—she has good reason to be," he exulted. "She
wants to catch hold of me, but she won't. I cheat her often,
every blessed day. You should see her when the thaw begins!
She carries stones and small rocks along as if they were bits
of ice. But she won't frighten me. When she is fussing her

worst, I spit in her face! She drowned my brother, the devil!"

"How old was he?" I asked.

"Old?—he wasn't old. He had not learned to walk."

"I too have lost a brother," I confided to him sorrowfully, "but he died of sickness."

"Pyt! Of sickness—there are many that do that!"

I realized, without annoyance, that here I could not gain ascendancy in any way. We stood there in the dim twilight and looked at the river and said no more.

"Come, little Uggi," called my mother, "we must go to bed. We have to be up early tomorrow morning."

She took my hand and sighed, as we walked away:

"If only we were safely across Butterwater Moor!"

When I lay in her arms and the twilight was about to close in around us, she said in a subdued voice:

"This evening we are halfway to Knör. I have thought of little else all day. Are you glad you are going to see your Granny? . . . How your heart is beating, child! Perhaps we shall visit Mama and Old Papa this summer, and perhaps you will be allowed to come too! . . . Don't cry. Are you feeling ill? Have you a pain anywhere? . . . There, there, that's all right—rest yourself—you are so tired. Doesn't it comfort you to think of Old Papa and his formula: biscuits and syrup?"

"And liver oil," I laughed through my tears.

"Yes, liver oil—cod-liver oil," said my mother, imitating Grandpa-from-Knör's voice.

So we lay there and laughed.

From the deep places of my sleep a voice came to meet me, which I recognized instantly. It was the glacier river speaking, stern and stimulating, fascinating in its rude relentlessness. This strange river with its strange name—River-under-the-Bridge.

"Now I know you too," I murmured to myself. "Soon I shall know the whole world." . . .

Grass reaching to the horses' bellies, bushes as high as men, with trunks as thick as my father's arm—thus its fat name had misled me into imagining Butterwater Moor. But on Butter-water Moor there was nothing but the solitude of waste places. Wide and wearisome it stretched in all directions. Stones, and endless undulating stony expanses with blades of grass nodding their heads sadly to each other, and here and there a few sur-prised-looking flowers that seemed never to have seen any other living creatures except flies and birds, and brave mountain tufts scattered like raisins in a cake made by a parsimonious woman, and here and there wild mountain grass, the honey-sweet flowers of which I shared with the bees while we were resting.

Poor Rufus was so tired that he scarcely had the inclination to nibble what was before him, and did not trouble himself to go off and search for greener hummocks. I was very sorry for him.

"I cannot do it for you, dear Red," I whispered tearfully in his ear. "I should not be allowed to, and then I am so stiff in my legs."

Red moved his ears and let me know that there were others besides myself who might be stiff in the legs, and perhaps with more reason; but he realized there was nothing to be done in the matter, and hung his head, his soft childish nose twitching with unhappiness and newly-gained experience.

The worst was, however, that whenever my father came any-where near us he nagged Red.

"A lazy fellow, your red foal!" he shouted to me again and again, and generally he was there with his whip. "And he won't learn any better, either, it seems to me. What a pair of dead ones you are! Odd ideas you both have of what is meant by a ride. You'll spoil every horse we put you on if you lack a horseman's grip. A horse notices it as soon as you get on his back. Do you think a whip is just for ornament, my son? There now, he can move along all right if he likes."

And Red really did get up speed, and perhaps the whip hurt him less than it did me.

But where was Butterwater? No one could tell me that. No one knew where it lay—no, not even in which direction. And no one seemed to miss it. Perhaps it belonged to those things that are lost just when one has most need of them. Perhaps it was one day here, another day there. Perhaps it could even make itself invisible. Perhaps even now we were riding on its edge. It was easy to imagine something of the sort. Perhaps the birds around us were not real birds at all, but transformed fish! Just think if Butterwater suddenly appeared again and we were all of us drowned!

Alas, there was nothing adventurous about Butterwater Moor. Even the "cairn" in the midst of it turned out to be only a large heap of stones. The piles of bones I had imagined reaching up to my waist (for I had never seen a cairn before) were reduced to a few pale bones which the dogs scarcely troubled to sniff at, and which they treated with great disdain. And then it was so cold up there. The sun looked now and again to see where we were, but it did not give any great warmth. There was snow lying in most of the hollows, brown snow as coarse as cooking salt.

We rested at the cairn, as was, of course, meet and proper. We ate our food and drank our milk and cold coffee. There was a flask of brandy which went its round among the men, and they were very merry and made all sorts of jokes about the flask and about Maria Mens.

"Not for you, Jon," warned Old Begga, every time the flask reached Nonni, and like an obedient boy he let it pass him by.

"The flask and Maria Mens—that would be altogether too much of a good thing!" said his neighbor, taking a good gulp.

Geir bent down toward Nonni.

"Is that milk that I see in the corner of your mouth? My God, the old woman suckles him still!"

My father leaped to his feet with a short laugh.

"Come along, Geir, you old warrior—will you take a toss?"

There lay Geir. He fell hard. He got up and went back to his place. He did not say much.

When we were again ready to move on, we riders separated from the men with the pack-horses. Madame Anna was wrapped up in shawls and my father took charge of her. Veiga rode with Mama, Beta with Maria Mens.

"Now we are off again," shouted my father in high spirits. "Now then, Brunka, best foot forward! We must get there before nightfall, understand that. Trot or gallop—nothing in between."

Red considered this order a dreadful hardship and, as my father could not be after him all the time with his whip, and as I used mine only for appearances' sake, we dropped clear behind the others; even Old Begga forsook us.

"Are you lying asleep beside your steed, or what in the world is the matter, Uggi?" Nonni woke me up.

I looked in confusion at Red, who was standing there with his head hanging down, his eyes half-closed, snoring; and I looked from Red to the pack-horses approaching, enveloped in dust and sun, on the one side, and at the isolated riders disappearing toward the horizon on the other. But I could give no explanation.

"Now then, gallop after them, my friend, and see that you keep up with them," Nonni encouraged me gently, and very carefully lifted me up again onto my horse. "Here is a bit of barley sugar to keep you awake."

And Red and I scurried along as best we could, and nearly caught up with Old Begga.

"Are you lying there again?" Nonni woke me, and this time he gave me a bit of lump sugar with some drops of spirits of ether on it. "That will brighten you up, but don't you go anywhere near Mother, for she will smell it at once. Now hurry along and keep to the path, promise me that. The others are just in front, even if you cannot see them."

And Red and I started again and pushed on. Red trotted. I thumped him with my heels and flourished my whip until it whistled, and encouraged him:

"The sooner we get there, the sooner you will be free."

Red seemed almost to understand, snorted and put his best leg forward. Soon we saw no one either behind us or in front, and had only the path to keep to. The path was, of course, quite good and dependable, an old path with new hoofprints; even the square heads of the nails in the horses' shoes could be clearly distinguished in the firm clay.

"Work a little miracle, dear God," I prayed earnestly. "No one will see, and I will promise not to tell anybody. It is only to move Red from this ridge over to the next one so he will be let off the hollow in between."

But God did not seem to think it worth doing.

"You might just as well make yourself a little shorter," I said to the path. "You are not a cat, or an earthworm, so there is no need for you to stretch yourself out like that. I could tell you a story you have never heard before—but I won't do it so long as you make yourself as lengthy as all that."

"Yes, why not sleep when the bed is ready?" laughed my father, irritably, and shook me awake. "We could not imagine what had happened to you—but I might have known. Are you cold? Does your bottom hurt? . . . Good! Clench your teeth and swear to yourself, for now we are going to ride!"

We galloped! Gravel flew round our ears, the whip whistled, the faint smell of steel against stones smarted pleasantly in our noses, and Red was transformed, for now he was both angry and wild.

"You see he has temperament after all," laughed my father, appreciatively. "Hang on, and we'll take this ditch."

I clung to Red with my hands and feet, and Red took the ditch. He hopped like a flea over ditches and stones, and was entirely transfigured. In my heart of hearts I was not a little proud of him, and as my father was riding alongside the unaccustomed speed did not frighten me. I was proud of myself too.

We caught up with the others, who were waiting for us by a bit of a stream—a very tiny stream, a very silent stream, but its water flamed black and red in the evening sun.

My father helped me off my horse and told me to stir my stumps. Astonished and fascinated, I gazed round me.

"Oh, look at that great lake with the white birds! Is it Butterwater, Mama?" I asked, for my mother was standing there, gazing, gazing.

"It is the sea, little Uggi," answered my mother softly, in the voice she used when I asked her questions in church. "Those 'birds,' child, are sailing boats."

I looked at my mother, and from my mother to that thing, so far away—that thing which was the sea. There was something strange about them both, something puzzling in the obvious bond between the two of them. I saw the pale faint outline of a moon above the dark surface of the sea.

Maria Mens sat by herself and pulled and tugged at the grass, pulled up seedlings of dwarf beech by the roots, dragged all the leaves from the branches in one sweep of her fingers.

Down below the heath there was a broad valley which divided into two toward the highlands, and then came a long, low ridge with many small lakes blinking between the molds of gray lava. Behind the ridge was another valley, a green one, then a ridge again, then a blue valley and finally high mountains quite unlike the mountains I had been used to. The ridge with the lakes pushed a cape out into that great water which was the sea, and to the east of this point there seemed to be red, green and yellow flowers between the rocks.

"That is the town," said my father, in answer to my question, and then he bent down over me and pointed. "Do you see that little lake, there just below the middle of the next ridge? Just above it you can see something green and white in the valley behind. That is Grimsstadir."

"Can you smell the sea?" asked my mother. "And the seaweed?"

But she was the only one of us who could.

The green and the white over there in the distance were the fields and the gables of our future home. I stood gazing at them. . . .

"I am so hungry, little Mother," I whispered, and slipped my hand into hers.

But when I was given a piece of bannock and butter, my favorite meal, I could not swallow a bite.

My father had taken the saddles off his brown and my red, and both horses had immediately found a piece of flat ground where they lay down and rolled from side to side with all four legs in the air, neighing with delight. He went round among the horses, felt their backs, looked at their legs, put ointment on old Brunka's saddle sores, patted each horse pleasantly, sympathized with each and praised them all.

Then he got them together and led them all, in a cluster behind him, toward us—five of them, like the five fingers of a hand. He saddled them, spat, and hummed a little tune:

What can be happier than the meeting of good friends?

My mother stood caressing her gray, who transformed her soft dark muzzle into a trunk, seeking her way into the pocket of her mistress' skirt, pushing her gently and begging for sugar.

"There, there, Grani," she laughed gently. "You must behave properly in a strange place."

The playful words brought tears to my eyes. This was certainly not Breidale. Would I ever go back there again?

2

STEP by step we rode down the slopes, and every moment the buildings came closer and became more real. The grass paths stood out more and more clearly from the clumps of heather, the stones and the gravel hills. Here and there we saw people on horseback, cattle grazing, sheep on the mountainsides. But even these familiar things seemed strange. Smoke was ascending from most of the farm chimneys, telling of supper and evening milk. A dog barked somewhere or other, amazed, reproachful. A foal that had been busy playing, and now could not find its mother, was frightened and called her insistently. Its mother answered. That was all right, but the foal was offended and let her know she must not stay away like that another time.

We approached the first farmstead and passed by.

There were people in front of it standing in a row and looking after us. A dark, bearded man, a woman with her arms crossed, another man tall and fair, and two or three more men, young and beardless.

These people did not greet us, nor did we greet them. They only looked at us, and we rode past.

It seemed to me there was something odd about these people, something frightening and mysterious. I felt I would like to know what the farm was like inside, and what they all said to one another every day. For surely they did not belong to the "underground folk"? Surely this was not one of those farms that vanished if one but turned one's back for a moment?

Suddenly the fair man began to take long steps with his long legs. Hastily he struck across the field, obviously having it in mind to meet us where the path made a turn. The dark one looked after him, called out something in a weak voice, bent his head and went in through the low door and disappeared. Behind him followed his wife with her arms crossed, and after her the three young men. All of them looked after the fair-haired man before they bowed their heads under the lintel of the door. Perhaps they were transformed into shadows the moment they stepped across the threshold. Who could say?

The man with the light hair and beard was quite young. He walked very straight, and as soon as he saw he had plenty of time his gait became very dignified. He maintained this stiff dignity while he greeted us politely and very formally. In contrast to his calm bearing, his brown eyes shone with a wonderful brightness, as if there were lighted candles behind them. When he had greeted us all, he laid a long thin hand on the mane of my father's brown, stood for a moment with an expectant smile on his face, looked my father straight in the eye and asked in a restrained tone:

"How about that letter?"

"What letter?" asked my father, shortly, and looked at the stranger with a puckered brow, annoyed and puzzled.

"The money letter," answered the young man, and drew himself up. Then he lowered his voice confidentially and winked. "My name is Einar Bjarnason."

"Oh, indeed," said my father, unsympathetically. "I have no letter for you."

Einar Bjarnason stood for a moment looking down and thinking deeply.

"Haven't you?" he said with a bitter smile. "Haven't you brought even a greeting?"

My father shook his head silently.

Einar Bjarnason controlled himself, set the matter aside with a movement of his hand, bade us farewell, chucked Madame Anna under the chin, spoke nonsense to her, and made faces at her till she cried. Then suddenly he walked away, tall and dignified, talking to himself.

We rode on without speaking.

It was clear that my father was unpleasantly affected. The

thoughtful frown in his forehead was still there. Red was given a sharp rap.

"It need not mean anything at all, Cecilia mine," Old Begga comforted my mother, in a tone that contradicted the words. "On the whole this district looks very habitable."

"What is it that need not mean anything?" asked my father irritably. "Damned superstition, that's all it is. Old wives' tales. Tickle up the hacks, or they'll go to sleep."

"Greipur!" begged my mother, smiling a little.

We reached the river at the bottom of the valley—the Stada River. It was a strong stream, brown with melted snow, smooth enough on the surface but with a kind of false smoothness that hid strong currents underneath. There was something about this river that I could not bear. Even when I stood looking at it from the top of the moor, I felt glad I was not going to live close to it. It did not wind about in a friendly way, and at the same time it did not really run straight; it was unreliable with an ominous capriciousness.

We all dismounted. My father laid Madame Anna between the hummocks where my mother had spread a blanket. She was asleep, breathing calmly, her face as expressionless as a china doll's. Then my father rode into the muddy river to find the best place for wading across, paying no heed to my mother's prayers and entreaties.

"Promise me to be careful, Greipur!" she begged in a faint voice, and with tears in her eyes.

The water received the brown with a bellow. At the bank the foam whipped his gleaming loins. But the brown was safe and my father was safe. They leaned against the stream and held the bottom. I was not at all afraid for my father. I had seen him overcome all the difficulties of the journey, and I had never found anything he could not do. But I was anxious about my mother, who was standing so close to the river that the water was wetting her shoes. I went behind her and in all secrecy took a good hold of her skirt in case she should suddenly begin to wade out into the river.

"Do you think we can manage it?" asked my father, when he had come back to the shore and had poured the water out of his shoes.

"Not with the children, Greipur!" begged my mother, in a voice of fervent entreaty, with the strong, entirely honest look she had in her eyes—a look that most children have for a time, but is seldom seen in older people.

"The children!" mocked my father. "I'll take them over two at a time, as easily as drinking water. It is more difficult with some of you others who faint when you see milk flowing out of a trough—like the old witch who lay down seasick as soon as she saw a boat. There is nothing to be afraid of. I will answer for the horses!"

Maria Mens stated, with not a few tears and many interruptions, that she had nothing against drowning, nothing at all— her father had died by drowning, her brother too—it was only that she would *not* drown on horseback. She would rather throw herself into the water.

"But there is no need, Maria," answered my father, kindly indulgent. "If you drown at all you are more likely to drown in your own tears. But what do you say, Bergljot Sigurdardottir?"

"Since you ask me yourself, Greipur Uggason," answered Old Begga, with great dignity and a slight tremor in her brave old voice, "and since by so doing you seem to attach some importance to the opinion of such a superstitious wretch as I, I would only remind you of what you, as brother of a priest— may God preserve the pious Sira Sigbergur!—and as nephew of a priest, ought to know without any reminder from me: namely, that you should put your trust in God but should not tempt Him."

"Is that what Vidalin says?" asked my father, with the greatest gravity.

Old Begga straightened herself up.

"How can a true Christian like you, Farmer Greipur, mock in the hour of danger, and before the face of God?"

"Has it now become mockery to inquire into Vidalin's

opinion?" exclaimed my father, amazed. "And what danger is threatening us here on dry land, may I ask?"

Old Begga turned her back on him but did not yield.

My parents continued to discuss the matter a little longer, my father chaffing but annoyed, my mother gentle but determined. At last my father gave in and we rode up the river, rode and rode. At Stadur Parsonage there was said to be a ferry.

"There would be no harm in crossing ourselves before we get onto the ferry, and saying a prayer as we go across," suggested Old Begga, as we rode down the ferry slope above the parsonage.

"Yes, who knows?" answered my father thoughtfully. "Everything can be overdone, good Bergljot, but a priestly ferry such as this one must be blessed and consecrated so thoroughly that a few extra holy words can make no difference either way."

"Now you are being too bad, Greipur," laughed my mother, with a glance at us children.

Old Begga talked to herself half-aloud about the glorious blessedness of those who have witnessed even unto blood, and the many joys of the martyrs.

The parsonage ferry was a small flat-bottomed boat rowed by a thin, cheerful man. The rowboat with the thin man in it bobbed up and down on the river's slippery back like the float of a fishing net into which a pin has been stuck for a mast. The river was not particularly broad, but the ferryman was carried far beyond us before he managed to land. Then he came trudging toward us, dragging his boat, a tall, good-humored man.

"She is quite mad today—quite mad," he shouted when he was still some distance away, speaking of the river as a father does of a child with whom he has had difficulties, but of whom he is secretly proud. "The sun must have been very hot in the mountains, for yesterday she was so manageable. Today she is rushing about like a mad cow!"

With shrieks and yells, much piety and many tears, the

ferryman and my father at last managed to get us and our saddles over, and the horses chased into swimming across. When the poor animals came up out of the river they shook themselves like dogs, so that the water stood out like rain around them. They rolled on the grass, galloped up and down and kicked their hind legs.

The scene on the ferry bank was a curious one. Madame Anna slept; Veiga and Beta each sat on a mound and nodded; Maria Mens lay on the ground sobbing, alone and forsaken; Old Begga was loudly silent; my father and the ferryman went about saddling the dripping horses; my mother held the reins of her gray, talking encouragingly to her. Above us was a dark blue sky with the stars like solitary points of gold, for it was already night.

"Sira Björn will be angry," mumbled the ferryman, half offended, and for some reason this threat made a strong impression on me. "What is the good of all this hurry? The horses are hungry, the children sleepy, and Grimsstadir will remain where it is."

"But one cannot settle down for the night just outside one's own fields," answered my father, softly but decidedly; and with quick movements he tightened saddle girths, jerked the saddles to see if they were fastened firmly, felt the curbs and patted the wet bodies of the horses.

When all was ready and we were just about to mount, an old white-haired man, tall and powerful, dressed in black and followed by three young girls, who were also tall and well-built, came down the slope that separated us from the parsonage.

"What do I see?" a voice thundered as if God Almighty were speaking from His Heaven. "Do you intend to disdain my hospitality the first time the Lord has given me the opportunity of opening my doors to you? I should take that to be an ill omen."

"That's Sira Björn right enough," said my father, and went to meet him. Long before they had finished saying how-do-you-do to each other, the three cheerful girls had overwhelmed the rest of us with kisses and laughter and a warm welcome.

"I will take charge of the souls while you look after the beasts, Pesi," Sira Björn said to the ferryman, who contentedly led away our horses.

"The two old ones and my brown must be tied up," my father began, but the ferryman would not listen.

"I shall put them all in the night-pen, man," he shouted. "There they will have plenty of grass, and unless they grow wings they will stay where they are put. I have looked after horses here for forty years, and seven days onto that, so I ought to know my job."

The young girls and Sira Björn wanted to carry everything for us—Veiga, Beta, Madame Anna, our clothes, our saddle-bags—I was scarcely allowed to be a man and walk on my own legs.

"All the best places are like this," Sira Björn comforted us in his coarse voice, which was full of a singular heavy humor and open-hearted friendliness. "Thus it is with the Kingdom of Heaven, and thus it is with Hamrafjörd: hard to get to, and then hard to get away from. But once inside, one stays there; that is the best of it."

He told us the names of the mountains, the names of the hills, and as we approached the parsonage he finished by saying:

"There is the cemetery. It needs enlarging, but to do that we should have to take in part of the field, and the dead do not quarrel in their graves, even if they have to lie rather huddled together. The church itself, as you see, is an old house lately done over. Well, God might do worse!"

He herded us into the house as a conscientious shepherd herds a flock of sheep.

"Come along in. In with you all. My wife is expecting you, has something good to offer you, I'm sure. Eider ducks' eggs—what do you say to that—new, freshly-cooked eider ducks' eggs, and some schnapps in the bargain?"

We went through paneled passages into a large low room,

and Sira Björn pressed us down with his own hands into chairs and onto chests.

"Sit down, sit down, and we shall have a drop to welcome you with. Your brother is a temperance man, Greipur, but that's his own affair. Of course he's a parson, and it's all supposed to be so modern—all that water-drinking. But answer me one question: has not Jesus Christ, God's only Son, told us clearly how the Trinity looks at the matter?"

"Wet outside, dry inside—after all, that's the world upside down," laughed my father, and emptied his glass. "Thanks; that was good."

"The spirit of God is always present, as it is written, or ought to be written," continued Sira Björn. "But does it warm a cold church? I'm blessed if it does. To that end God has given us liquor, and he who disdains such a gift in pride and self-righteousness . . . well, he does himself a bad turn. God is long-suffering and forgives much. Perhaps even that."

"I don't think God is angered by trifles like that!" said my mother, smiling.

"God's mercy is infinite, good mistress, but when He is in wrath the stars flee before His breath like hoarfrost before the storm," shouted Sira Björn, laughing contentedly. "Well, *skaal*, Greipur Uggason; *skaal*, mistress! *Skaal*, old woman, and you too, you young fountain of tears; *skaal*, you blessed children— welcome to Hamrafjörd! May you live long in the fear and honor of God and die in His Grace in His good time. *Skaal!*"

Sira Björn fell silent, emptied his glass and suddenly bent down and kissed his wife with a loud smack. She had come in during his stream of words, and was small, plump and friendly.

"Can we begin soon, my dear?" he asked good-naturedly, and let his big hand rest on her round, well-brushed head, while he surveyed the table as a farmer does his sheep.

The active hospitality of the three daughters fully corresponded to their father's forcible speech. Before we knew where we were, our outdoor clothes had been taken off us, dry stockings had been drawn onto our cold feet and we were sitting at a table on which was enthroned a dish full to overflowing of blue-green eggs among mountains of all sorts of other food—a yellow cheese, large as a millstone; smoked meat, red as clotted blood.

After all these years, I still remember clearly that laden table in a room filled with the warm twilight of a summer night, and my keen delight in these good-hearted people, the sincere welcome they gave us, the spirit of simplicity pervading the whole household. More than once the memory of it has come into my mind during a moment of loneliness as something precious and unforgettable.

My father playfully remarked that now he was beginning to understand why everybody wanted to come to Stadur and no one wanted to leave it.

"You've said it, and it's true," laughed Sira Björn, and made no attempt to hide his enjoyment of the good food. "There are at least a dozen affectionate colleagues sitting about in the country waiting for Old Björn to drown, whether in the bottle or the river—it is all the same to them. And it's all the same to me too, so long as I die a natural death and am not obliged to wear out too many bedclothes in my last illness."

"Oh, Björn." His wife hushed him, putting the saltcellar in front of his plate with a look of rebuke.

"Oh, Holmfrid," mimicked Sira Björn, placing his hand on her head. For a moment I sat on tenterhooks for fear he would take her as one does a walking stick and stand her in a corner.

"How *can* you talk like that, dear?" asked Mrs. Holmfrid, looking round at us all.

"There, there, my beloved," answered Sira Björn, mildly, gaily pushing the matter aside. "Don't you think God will do just as He pleases, whatever I say, Holmfrid?"

"What a blessing these bird-islands are," said my father, with comical gravity, perhaps as a sort of excuse for helping himself to yet another egg.

"God's earth is full of God's gifts," answered Sira Björn,

filling up the glasses. "And each one has, according to his deserts and God's decision, free access to them, and many enjoy them with a good conscience—first and foremost, of course, His servants who faithfully work in His vineyard, but after them every honorable man whose hand is hallowed by toil and whose spirit is pervaded by the love of God. Only thieves and fools deserve to starve, deserve to die—to wither as the grass which is pulled up and trodden under foot. . . . *Skaal,* Greipur Uggason! May the Lord preserve you and your house, your wife, your children, your cattle, your servants, your ground and your property. *Skaal!"*

"Excuse me, good priest, for venturing to ask, but I should be glad to know what you really think of Vidalin's *Book of Homilies?"* broke in Old Begga, with a voice in which emotion and despairing courage each in turn took command.

Sira Björn lifted his glass.

"Inspired by the spirit of God, God's powerful . . ."

"And holy," hastily interposed Mrs. Holmfrid.

Sira Björn cleared his throat.

"Inspired by God's powerful and holy spirit—I was going to say, my beloved—like the Bible. What other opinion can anyone have of such a holy book?"

Old Begga looked round at us all. She tried in vain to catch my father's eye.

"The Vidalin sermons are Bergljot Sigurdardottir's most treasured possession," my mother informed the company quietly.

Sira Björn got up, fetched a schnapps glass, filled it and forced Old Begga to empty it.

"God forgive you and me, good priest!" she groaned, laughing awkwardly when, at length, she had stopped coughing. "But it warms one up. It is good to come among good people."

"God forgives all except the lukewarm, the weak, the spineless, those who steal time from themselves and the fruits of labor from their brothers," proclaimed Sira Björn, in his simple way. "Naturally those who please the Devil during their lifetime fill his pots when they die, for, as rewards and bliss await the good, so bitterness and destruction await the evil. All is ordered by the Lord. From the same earth out of which creep worms that hate the light, grow flowers and useful herbs. Yes, sweet-smelling flowers which stand among the grasses of our rich pasture-land like Saints' Days among our ordinary days."

Sira Björn went on eating for a long time, and we all did the same. Then he said:

"Everything has its uses, and its good and bad sides. Stroke the stone and your heart is gladdened; hit it and your knuckles bleed."

When we were all satisfied and could not force down another mouthful, he rose abruptly and kissed his wife.

"I thank you, beloved, next to God, for this good food. . . . Now you are tired, dear people. The children are already asleep like the apostles themselves. Are the beds ready, girls? . . . Good. Breakfast will be on the table at eleven o'clock to-morrow morning, and the horses in the yard at twelve o'clock."

My father thanked him again and again, but said we absolutely must set out earlier, as he had to speak to the men who had come with us, and he did not know how long they could wait.

Sira Björn agreed very unwillingly to such haste, wanted to send a message early in the morning, wished to arrange for a man to watch and stop the caravan so the horses might rest and feed and the men have food and ale. My father said that then the men would lose another day, and this was not allowed for in the contract.

"Very well, then," Sira Björn at last conceded. "Good night, everybody. God be with you. May the night give you sweet sleep, the morrow bread and butter. Give God the glory."

Between cool sheets in a broad bed I fell asleep as the light went out, like a lamp when the oil is finished.

The air was still, the sun scorched down calmly and blazingly, the horses panted and groaned in the heat, and sleepily we followed a marshy path over a bog, surrounded by strong vapor rising from ferruginous water and last year's grass and blended with a suspicion of perfume from flowering plants.

"A marsh," mumbled Old Begga, "a quagmire! Can this be called a proper path for churchgoers?"

We reached the ridge that still separated us from our future valley, Valadale. Slantwise and upward across the slopes the path wound in a friendly and cautious manner, stealing past precipitous slopes like a dog moving warily among strangers. We were met by a narcotic smell of bog myrtle, flowering ling and vernal grass, among the tufts of which one sleeps sweetly and dreamlessly. The mosquitoes were very bad. They got into our mouths, noses and eyes. The horses could not defend themselves against them, and the insects therefore drank themselves so heavy and sleepy in the sweet horse-blood that they let themselves be crushed rather than move.

The path did not hurry and we followed its example. It was early in the day and we had not far to go.

A tiny lake, surrounded by a bit of tufted meadowland, and outside that by moorland and gravel hills, lay there waiting for us. A bank of lava pushed forward its wrinkled face and mirrored itself in the dark waters, vain like all unnatural things. A drake with its sparkling green plumage and watchful swaying neck glided silently over the smooth surface, leaving behind it an arrow-shaped, finely ruffled wash, which softly rippled to its rest under bulging mossy banks. Where was the mother duck? Where was the nest with the eggs? The same thought seemed to have occurred to the dogs, for they set off with their noses to the ground. My father called them sharply, and they slunk shamefacedly back—Gryla with many insulted folds in her soft ears.

This lonely tarn on the ridge, the silent drake, the unseen nest hidden somewhere in the soft mossy bank—with an infinite sense of peace the whole scene sank down into my mind like a stone falling through water, and there it remained. It released captive longings as the bow awakes the hidden notes of the string. The sun-drenched day—the mysterious tarn with its birds and faithful, friendly banks—the perfume of brush-wood, heather and sun-baked stones—formed a harmony in the mind which died away, returned, and on its return was more than a note, was wisdom and happiness. Thus casually had God given me a gift greater than the so-called victories of life, more intimate than love.

The tarn is still there today. It has no name, for it is too small, but it freezes in winter, thaws in the spring, and in the summer has its pair of ducks and welcomes the young emerging from the eggs. The dogs may destroy the nest, the boys plunder it—God cannot keep an eye on all things everywhere. What does it matter? The tarn freezes, the tarn thaws. . . .

My father pointed out Fagravik to me. The fjord forced its broad and shining way past the farm, glittering in the mischievous sunlight, but the farm left the fjord to its own devices and kept itself to the mountain behind, a steep moun-tain reaching to the sky, streaked with zones of fresh snow and old.

"Aunt's house in Fagravik is smoking, all right," I said contentedly, for the smoking chimney was to me an earnest of the security I had always felt when I heard Aunt Sigurveig spoken of. "But where is Fagravikurfjara?"

My father answered shortly with a glance at my mother that "Fagravikurfjara lay on the seashore and could not be seen from here."

"Why is it on the seashore and not below the mountain like the other farmsteads?" I asked.

"Fagravikurfjara is not a farmstead but a cottage," answered my father, a little impatiently. "A little cottage."

I thought it sounded so nice, so friendly, so practical—something like the little house I had thought of building for Sigga-Sigga and myself by the side of Butterwater. Besides, it was always cottage children who, in Old Begga's fairy sto-ries, ended as princes and princesses. But my mother sighed, and the shadow of a sudden despondency glided over her face, which today was so grave and thoughtful.

"God knows how Halla is really getting on—poor Halla with all her little ones."

"Sister-in-Fagravik would hardly let them starve unless she has changed very much," said my father. "In the old days Veiga had all her wits about her. Neither Beggi nor I could stand up to her." He laughed at the memory. "You can imagine how sick we got of it, although she was the eldest. We had many a fight to the finish. She was a grand girl."

"I think we ought to arrange for Old Papa to see the children," said my mother. "Then he will be sure to give in," she added. But the doubt in her voice was stronger than the conviction.

"Well, I understand Ketilbjörn in a way, the flinty old man," observed my father. "Eiki is a fool—and what is the good of pouring water into a sieve?"

"Old Papa is not a flinty old man," answered my mother, blushing.

"Well, of course one's grandchildren are always one's grandchildren anyhow," said my father, soothingly, "whoever their father may be."

"Things are very different for Halla now from the time when we played farmyard, and fried small fishes in half a frying pan on the shore at Knör," my mother went on after she had ridden for a time in silence, surreptitiously drying her eyes. "God knows whether the fish she now fries are any bigger than those she fried then, or whether the frying pan is any larger. But now it is no longer pretense. One becomes hard-hearted with the passing of the years. I have thought very little about Halla and her difficulties, just because she has been living a couple of days' journey away. We must do something for them, Greipur."

My father, who preferred to settle a thing of this sort in private, gave no other answer than to hurry on the horses.

"How can we tell, Greipur, whether God will grant us life and health and give us bread for our children?" my mother went on insistently. "I had such a dreadful dream last night," she added after a few moments' silence.

"Now then, Cecilia, my dear," laughed my father, irritably, "don't grow like Old Begga, I beseech you."

"Dreams have often been a useful warning," murmured Old Begga, to herself.

As my mother said no more, my father at last said to her impatiently:

"Well, let's hear the nonsense you dreamed."

My mother rode on, staring straight in front of her, and, absent-mindedly caressing the gray's flank with her whip, shook her head.

"Isn't it part of your superstition that only the dreams one does not wish fulfilled must be told?" asked my father, with a mixture of mockery and curiosity.

"Oh, it was nothing but a lot of nonsense," began my mother, lightly. "I dreamed that when we got up from the table Sira Björn took me by the arm, led me out into the churchyard, showed me a grave with newly dug earth round it, and said: 'That is yours, good mistress—Glory be to God.'"

We were all silent until my mother suddenly laughed.

"Just nonsense, wasn't it? But it seemed so very real. . . . It was west of the church," she added in quite another voice.

My father, who had been growing redder and redder, suddenly burst out: "And you allowed yourself to lie there dreaming all that sort of thing! Well, well, it's over now, anyhow. That's something to be thankful for."

"To dream oneself dead means a long life, Cecilia dear; didn't you know that?" Old Begga comforted her, a reassuring look in her ageing eyes.

"There you are," shouted my father, in a relieved voice. "And there you sit, Celia, looking as if the Day of Judgment would be upon us before winter comes."

"The tears of the righteous turn into jewels on the Day of Judgment," Old Begga told me in a belligerent tone. "Some become diamonds; others crystals, rubies, sapphires and opals.

The tears of those whose hearts are as pure as the mountain stream become diamonds and are given a place in the Seventh Heaven—the Heaven of Saturn, as it is called by the wise men. That is where you will have to seek your mother when the time comes, my little red-headed knight."

I had no doubt it was Halla my mother was thinking of again, for she sighed absently.

"Happily she lives close to the generous sea."

"Come, boy. We will ride on," my father encouraged Rufus and me—particularly Rufus. "Only a little way to go now. There is Grimsstadir."

The valley that suddenly opened up before us was neither broad nor deep, but friendly and welcoming. The farms seemed to be comfortably situated on the sunny side, except one that lay between green hills east of the river. The river flowed slowly and peacefully in broad curves between the ridges, and finally, after innumerable windings, emptied itself into a great calm lake which filled the opening of the valley.

Grimsstadir turned out to be two farms lying close together, both of them immediately surrounded by meadowland.

"We are going to live on the East Farm," my father informed me absent-mindedly. "There is a stream for you to splash in, and a gully where you can break your neck and wear out your trousers. . . . Well, Cecilia," he said, turning to my mother, who had just arrived, "what do you think of it all?"

"I have seen Grimsstadir before," my mother smilingly reminded him.

"Tja!" spat my father, and continued, in a tone which was a queer mixture of pretended annoyance and a hidden boyish desire for approval: "Those cottages are not much to look at, but I shall be satisfied if they turn out to be half as good as they look from here. You will have to manage as best you can, Celia, until I can get it all in order."

"You know, Greipur, that as long as I have you and the children I am always happy," answered my mother, with a rare understanding in her sweet voice. "I long ago accustomed myself to do without the sound of the breakers on falling asleep and on waking—my dear wonderful breakers!"

"Think of your children, good mistress," Old Begga reprimanded her mildly. "Do not wish to live by the sea where there are sailors, sea monsters, sea apparitions and all sorts of other horrors just outside your front door!"

"At Knör we never noticed these inconveniences, good Bergljot," my mother smiled pleasantly. "Where the spirit of God rules, evil has no power, whatever shape it assumes."

"God's spirit in Ketilbjörn," laughed my father, but stopped himself.

"Old Papa read the Word of God aloud every evening during Lent," my mother assured him gravely. "I can remember no winter when the *Psalms of the Passion* were not sung from cover to cover."

"Where Hallgrimur* has a home, the Saviour is not far away," Old Begga stated her point of view. "But how he, such a man of God—I mean Hallgrimur—could go off and marry that infidel woman Gudda is more than I can understand. The hearts of men are strange as the Creator's ways."

" 'When I have shark's flesh and liquor, what use have I for porridge and whey, porridge and whey!' " said my father, imitating Grandpa-from-Knör's voice, and smiling teasingly at my mother. "Who was it gave that answer to his parson when asked why he was never seen in church?"

My mother laughed.

"Religion and churchgoing are two separate things, Greipur."

"Evil sea monsters have been seen by pious folk on all coasts," said Old Begga, returning to the attack.

"She is afraid of the mermen, the old dear!" laughed my father. "Heigh-ho—how these old tales live on!"

In front of us the path led down over the slopes, showing us the way. If we patiently followed its apparently so capricious direction, all would go well with us; but if we tried to take

---

* Hallgrimur Pjetersson, author of the metrical version of the *Psalms of the Passion.*

a short cut, we should come on gaping gullies, bottomless bogs and other impassable obstacles.

"For God's sake take a short cut if you want to," it laughed with assurance. "If you think you know better than I do! I, who have been here since the land was baptized. They must all keep to me, both dead and living, both ghosts and the Little People. The sea monsters gambol here at the new moon, and one icy winter I was visited by a polar bear. And I know Nökken,* you may be sure—and I know the difference between a horse and Nökken, even if they both have hoofs."

"So do I too," I answered.

"Are you talking in your sleep, you great traveler?" asked Old Begga, yawning loudly. "Pouf—it's warm!" she added, as if excusing herself. Then she lowered her voice, so that only I could hear her. "Never answer the voices you hear, promise me that, child! It is only when you answer them that they get you in their power. . . . Yes, it is warm right enough. . . . Aah-haa! I am yawning wide enough for a hay cart to drive in."

Behind Grimsstadir there was a long range of hills with steep slopes which culminated in a promontory facing west. Two cairns that looked like a couple of mounds broke the long line, which bent softly toward the sleepy midday sky.

"Grimur from Grimsstadir was buried in one, Brandur from Brandsstadir in the other," my father said in answer to my question. "They were probably brothers, or perhaps foster brothers. They have a wonderful view."

"We will go up there some fine day, children," my mother exclaimed. "You can see the whole district from up there, and the sea as well and your 'birds,' little Uggi. . . . I like the sea almost the best when it blows from the land before it quite gets to the point of thundering. The clouds drift, and the sun glints on the green crests of the waves—just think how lovely it all is!"

"It's farther than it looks and there is a bog between us and it," said my father, nodding toward the summit.

---

* A river-spirit in Scandinavian mythology.

Little did I dream that these calm words would, at a later date, fasten themselves in my mind like a thorn.

"Don't talk so much about the terrible sea!" wailed Maria Mens, suddenly, in shrill and uncontrolled tones. "Oh, if I only could do it some injury, for all the evil it has done to me and mine! My youngest brother, poor little Einsi, lying with his head quite buried in the sand when we found him! . . . The men that helped us laid him on the courtyard wall. My mother dug the sand out of his mouth with a wooden spoon and washed his face—and do you know what she said? She said: 'He must be able to breathe when he wakes up again; he must not stand there with a dirty face when the last trump sounds!' I stood and picked the sand out of his ears so he could hear, too. You cannot imagine how we cried and how unhappy we were. Little Sigga sat in the grass and rocked herself backward and forward, and cried all the time and kept on repeating: 'Einsi, Einsi! Einsi, Einsi!' . . . Tell me which is worse—life or death? I shall never forget that morning. *He* had got through his sufferings, Einsi had, but why did God let him be born since he was to drown so young? He had done nothing wrong—I can answer for that."

It was Old Begga who at last broke the silence which followed poor Maria's words and tears.

"Listen, Maria," she said in the rather gruff voice she always used when speaking to Maria Mens. "I will take over the milking while your finger is so swollen. But look after it well, my dear. For when we have the sheep too on our hands, you must be there."

But surely those were our cows approaching along the deep path between the tussocks of heather. They looked oddly different in these strange surroundings, but it was they.

"*Moo! mah! meh!*" we heard coming toward us, sorrowfully and reproachfully; and Skjalda, old Skjalda, who always walked at the head, undoubtedly had tears in her eyes.

"They want to get back to Breidale as sure as God is in

Heaven!" shouted Old Begga, moved to tears also. "Oh, you blessed speechless ones, you innocent four-footed animals, your faithfulness and good sense put many human beings to shame."

With wet muzzles the cows sniffed at my mother, at Old Begga, at Maria Mens, and recognized them in spite of their traveling dresses. The enlarged choir of cows was increased by the voices of the women and a consoling orgy of tears. Animals and human beings were all equally moved, and neither my mother, nor Old Begga, nor Maria Mens was in any way put out when the cows slobbered over them.

"Dear, good Skjalda," said my mother, fondling her favorite cow with her whip behind the bump on her forehead, "you will be happy at Grimsstadir, you may be sure. . . . Turn round now, my friend. Don't let us have to run about looking for you the whole summer. Remember it is from you I get my milk. If you are good, we will let your Christmas calf live. You shall have it in a stall beside you—*I'll* promise you that."

"Where's Maggi?" shouted my father, when at last he had managed to cut short all this welcoming and turn the cows round. "Is he sleeping in the middle of the day, the oaf! I'll sing him a tune that will wake him up! In bass and descant and up and down the whole scale."

Scarcely had my father finished speaking before we saw a thin line come rushing toward us, just a shadow in the landscape, a stick forked at one end. It was covering the distance over marsh and moor, ling and lava, with the greatest speed— Magnus Jonsson Bachmann in his own thin person.

My heart began to jump with joy, and then I remembered my father's threats and it sank again with fear.

"Greipur!" shouted Maggi, from far away. "Farmer Greipur!" he shouted, and swallowed the rest, for he had no more breath left in his body.

"Well, I never!—" began my father.

But now Maggi had reached us, and he looked only at my father, caring not a brass button for the rest of us.

"Sneggla has had two lambs!" he shouted, happy and out of

breath. "Two ram lambs. Shall one of them be called Sneggla-Halli?"

"Oh, indeed?" questioned my father. "Two lambs? Two ram lambs?"

Sneggla was his best sheep and came of a stock that was considered as old as our own. Sneggla was his darling, his idol, the apple of his eye.

"Are they both alive?" he asked uneasily.

"They were alive when I left them!" answered Maggi, importantly, "alive and kicking!"

"Where did you leave them?" asked my father, his forehead puckering uneasily.

"In the gully just by the farm!" answered Maggi, as happily as if the accommodation he had found them had been a stroke of genius.

"Did you leave new-born lambs beside a stream?" asked my father, sharply, and threw Madame Anna into Maggi's arms with such force that he almost fell over backward.

Away went my father on the brown. The path thundered under them, and they leaned obliquely outward as they took the sharp bends.

And there where a moment ago had stood our Magnus Jonsson Bachmann, now stood only Maggi, pale, hugging Madame Anna in his thin arms, while thin tears ran down his thin cheeks, so early furrowed.

"My damned skull," he wept angrily. "As empty as a meat bin in the autumn."

"Don't be unhappy about it, dear Maggi," my mother comforted him. "Believe me, Sneggla will take good care of her little ones."

"You are right, mistress!" answered Maggi, pulling himself together and wiping away both his tears and his sorrow with a movement of his hand. "Sneggla is wise, she is. I wish I had her head instead of my own."

"With horns and all?" I asked laughing.

"You're getting bumptious, young Uggi!" said Maggi, and gave me a foreboding look.

My mother took Madame Anna; Beta, much against her own and Brunka's wish, was put behind Old Begga; the cows trudged along in front, their tails swinging and their hoofs crunching—and thus we reached the brook.

Maggi got across in long leaps. The water splashed up round him, silver and gold, but did not reach him; and with shoes as good as dry he stood at the other side, laughing and waiting for us.

"The water runs off him as it does off a duck's back!" laughed my mother. "It must be because he is so thin. . . . A good boy is Maggi."

At that time I did not know why this statement struck so warmly on my heart. Now I know that it was made so lovable by its utter lack of logic.

"Well, there you are at last!" said the stream, as if it had been waiting for us, and its smile was so dazzling that it hurt my eyes. "Here is a good place for wading," it said, "but there is a hole. Have you seen my ducks and my watersnipe? Well, there go the ducks. But don't worry about that—they will come back as soon as I am alone."

How odd it looked to see all those strange horses lying flat and immovable on the ground, sunning themselves in the midday sun, with legs and heads stretched straight out almost as if they were dead! Only their tails moved now and again to ward off the mosquitoes. And now and again one of them would raise its head, shake it and look round.

"I expect the splendid animals are tired," said my mother, sympathetically. "Do you see our horses anywhere?"

Maggi pointed them out where they lay in a group by themselves, and I suddenly remembered New-Skjoni who was not there, and burst into tears. My mother rode up beside me to comfort me while Maggi grimaced at me behind the others' backs, and I was so ashamed of myself that I pushed aside my mother's caressing hand and made up a story about having a stomach-ache.

Then there was only a little bit of moorland left, and then we reached Grimsstadir.

3

THE farmstead stared at us with its many eyes, and we stared back. It did not yet know whether it liked us, and we did not know whether we cared for it. Its roofs rose one beside another, all small and green. There were many gables, and in the gables and in the slopes of the roofs there were windows, but both gables and windows were small, very small, and the panes were put together with bits of glass, and the gables were old. Outside the cluster of houses, half turned toward it, an outbuilding stood, wide and big, a house in itself. Behind the farm was a long barn sunk deep into the ground. A wall of sods about the height of a man's knee surrounded the farm on two sides and was useful as a seat and for putting saddles on.

At the moment it was altogether overloaded with pack saddles and riding saddles, with bridles and riding whips and with the belongings of the strange men who were with us, but there was not a single living creature to be seen anywhere. I looked round. East of the farmstead a grass wall sloped down to a cleft, at the bottom of which a little stream wound and wriggled, and played at being a river. At the edge of the slope there was a weather-beaten windlass set above a deep well of black water.

Our movables still stood together in a heap in front of the farm, chafed by their ropes and tired from the journey. They had not yet made friends with the farm. The door insisted it was too narrow to admit them; the houses looked at them with dusty eyes and refused recognition. The outbuilding had locked its door and held itself aloof. There was something clerical about it, almost as if it imagined that it was a church.

We dismounted, stretched our stiff legs, tottered about and laughed at ourselves and at one another.

Out from the farm came an elderly woman, thin and bent, looking as if she had been standing hidden behind the door.

She came toward us quickly with a queer hopping gait, keeping her eyes fixed on the ground.

"Who is it?" I asked my mother softly.

"Tordis," she whispered back hastily.

I felt rather depressed, but, still more, curious, at the sight of this old woman—who as a matter of fact was not actually old, though she looked it. Her thin weather-beaten face, her great prominent eyes behind the thin eyelids with the light eyelashes, her high nose which did not seem to get any lower toward the forehead, but only, as it were, sank into her face; the quick blush over her gray cheekbones, her lipless mouth, her narrow bony wrists and narrow freckled hands, her tight bodice composed entirely of colored squares of different sizes, her plaid skirt fastened with an elastic band round her waist so it did not reach more than halfway down her thin bird-like legs, her apron—all this made an indelible impression on me. Even now I can see her shuffling toward us, shy and incomprehensible, girt by a silence which one could almost catch hold of and feel.

Without lifting her eyelids she stared straight at my mother, kissed her fleetingly several times like a bird pecking, murmured something inaudible, and kissed the rest of us in turn in the same hasty way and at the side of the mouth, still mumbling to herself.

"Well, here we are, good Tordis—all that is left of us," said my mother, playfully. "I see your chimney is smoking. Seldom have I longed so for a good cup of coffee—such a cup as I know you alone can make."

Old Begga suddenly busied herself with taking off Brunka's saddle, and did not look as if she were doing it for love.

Disa leered at Old Begga, and leered at my mother with her grayish-blue eyes.

"It is all ready for you," she answered with a queer dusky voice, and a sudden smile passed like a whirlwind over her face and reduced the stiff features to disorder, so that it took some time to put them right again.

"Isn't Sophia at home?" asked my mother, who, following

Old Begga's example, had begun to unsaddle her gray. "These blessed animals must have any milk we can spare them. Thank you, my good horse, for having carried me so safely. But where is Sophia?"

The gray-blue eyes shifted.

"Sophia was sent for to town yesterday," Tordis answered slowly. "She ought certainly to be back this evening, but . . ."

"Well, then, I suppose we can expect her any moment—" my mother broke in, and her disappointment was evident, although she tried to hide it. She turned smiling toward a strange man who was approaching us. He walked stiffly as if on stilts, had pointed light mustaches and carried his fair head rather too consciously upright above a pair of crooked shoulders.

"I suppose this is Gudmund," she said pleasantly, and shook the hand he held out to her.

"Yes, Gudmund Jonatansson—that's right," answered Mundi, acknowledging his name. The joint of his forefinger was as thick as if it were a growth and gave his hands a queer flipper-like appearance.

"Welcome, mistress; I have already seen master. Let me take the horses. Well, children, I expect you are pretty stiff in the joints after your long journey?"

This last sentence was said in a bewildered, awkward tone that sounded odd, coming as it did immediately after the conscious superiority of his first words. This Mundi, who came as it were on the command of a king, was suddenly no more. Without anyone lifting a finger he had fallen as a dandelion before the scythe.

My father came toward us chewing his tobacco, spitting brown squirts, gay and laughing. "Sneggla has gone off. By my soul, she has taken herself off," he laughed, in a tone in which admiration and disappointment were fighting for the mastery. "When she goes off that way there is nothing to fear. Sneggla would never go to the mountains with lambs that had anything wrong with them. She'll bring me both her sons in good condition next autumn, you'll see, or I shall be very much mistaken in her, the little girl. I have no doubt she knows already where she belongs. Are you sure they both had white tails?" he asked, turning to Maggi and Mundi. "The whole tail? Well, well— that's the mark then. Where the rest of the white is, does not matter so much. They will probably be just as odd to look at as the rest of that family. It would have been fun to see them. If only we had not spent the night at Stadur! I felt that was a mistake all the time. Have some tobacco, Mundi—I can quite understand that you were not able to keep her; the Devil himself, hoofed and tailed, would not be able to keep Sneggla in bounds when she is in that mood. Well, now, we must see to loosing the ropes and getting the things into the house. Listen here. Have you any bread? Have you any milk? We must make some mash for the horses. You have done well, my brave beasts. Maggi, have you bought that corn and those peas? Fetch a little corn and put a trough of peas to soak!"

"Where are all the men?" asked Maria Mens. She always asked for Nonni in the plural.

"In the barn," answered Disa, who had stood there noticing everything. "They are sleeping, poor things; they were dead tired."

"And you rode from your child, Greipur, to save your lambs," joked my mother, and kissed my father, who showed plainly that he did not like being kissed in public.

"Shall we go and see whether we can get our whole bodies into the house at the same time, or whether we shall have to get in limb by limb?" he laughed, going on in front. "If I really want to stretch myself here at Grimsstadir, I shall have to lie down with my head in one house and my legs in another!"

Disa gave him a hasty glance, then drew away a little—just like a cat trying to avoid a drip from a roof—and busied herself with something by the wall, humming softly to herself.

We went in. A queer musty coldness met us even in the doorway. First of all we came to a little room, but found that the door was locked. That was Sophia's room, it seemed, and Disa knew nothing about the key. The passages which led to the rest of the rooms were dark, narrow and crooked. At each turn there was a door which fell to again after us, pulled into place by a stone fastened to the end of some string, the string being passed over a reel. "Extraordinary contraptions," Maggi called these doors, deeply impressed. In the small dark empty rooms the clay floors were uneven and in bad repair. Long-stalked yellow mushrooms grew in the corners, and the walls were gray with mold and covered with cobwebs that hung heavy with dust and dead flies. These rooms made me feel oddly weak in the legs and empty in the stomach. There was a desolate air about them all, desolate and empty, and it was as if shadows lurked in the dark corners, as if evil dreams and gloomy fore-bodings flourished in all this gray rankness.

We found a little staircase, up which we climbed, and which led us to a small bedroom with a window facing west and a smaller window in the sloping roof toward the south. There were two empty beds stretched along the short north wall, an-other one along the east side. There was only the framework left; even the bottom boards had been removed. A large kind of fly buzzed in the windows, ordinary house-flies abounded, and in all the corners hung thick spiders' webs, as if to hide something we must not see.

"This must be the best of the bedrooms," said my father, crossly, and clicked his tongue with discontent. "Frederick must have preferred three small rooms instead of a single good-sized one."

"Do let's go down and find some place where we can drink our coffee in peace and quiet!" My mother interrupted our voyage of discovery with a laugh that was a little too eager.

My father scratched his head.

"Coffee, did you say? . . . I must go and look after the sheep." He went. The dust whirled in the sunbeams.

My mother sat down on the end of the bed with Madame Anna on her lap. Madame Anna prattled gaily, but my mother paid no attention to her. Tears streamed down my mother's cheeks, large tears, falling quietly and unobtrusively.

When she noticed that I was looking at her she put out her hands to me and drew me to her, hugged me, kissed me on my forehead and said in a voice that she tried to make hopeful:

"I expect we shall have a very happy time here, little Uggi. Mama is just a little tired today. Nothing really matters so long as God allows you children to keep well and happy."

She got up quickly.

"Where shall we drink our coffee? Tell me that."

"There is sure to be a little place somewhere," I answered trustfully.

Whether it was my tone, or whatever it was, she suddenly bent down and kissed me.

"You must have inherited at least a few drops of blood from Old Papa—from Grandpa-from-Knör!" She laughed gaily again, and fresh tears came into her eyes. "They will not do you any harm, my boy, and you will find a use for them, believe me."

A long rusty lamphook hung down from the ceiling and from it, in turn, hung a spider on its delicate thread.

As soon as I saw it I hurried over to it, held my hand under it and sang as I had been taught:

"Up, up, if you bode good—down, down, if you bode ill."

My mother sought in vain for a window that could be opened from inside.

"Let's hasten out into the air," she said, and we went.

While she was serving coffee for the first time at Grimsstadir, out in the yard, with everyone sitting on boxes, I took the opportunity of getting to know Disa better.

I began by following her about wherever she went or stood, looking at her, watching all she did; she, on the other hand, seemed scarcely to see me, paid not the slightest attention to me and went on humming.

At last we reached a funny little flight of stairs at the foot of which a sack had been spread on the clay floor. Disa dried her feet on the sack and I did the same. Halfway up the stairs there was a little landing where another sack lay. Here we dried our feet again. Then Disa went up a few more steps into a tiny bed-room of which I managed to get only a glimpse before she—still humming—went in and shut the trapdoor behind her.

Had she seen me or had she not?

She could not have seen me. Anyhow, I remained standing there; she must come out again sometime. I heard her strike a match, I heard a primus stove being pumped, I heard it begin to buzz.

Suddenly the trapdoor above my head was opened again and Disa came down the stairs and passed me without seeing me, humming as before.

When she had gone I went up the steps, lifted the trapdoor a few inches and looked in. There were two large beds pushed close to each other; on one was a mountain of pillows, on the other was laid a board and it was obviously used as a table. These beds practically filled the whole room; nevertheless there was a great deal more to be seen. Two sacks and a dog's skin lay on the well-scrubbed floor. There was a little table with a drawer in it, the top covered with blue fringed paper, the fringe hang-ing over the edge. There were strips of paper fastened over the gable window and a skylight. There were various small cup-boards hanging on the wall, also ornamented with strips of paper. And everything was clean, pedantically neat and, except for the beds, incredibly small.

While I stood there staring round me, old Disa came back with water in a saucepan. She passed me still humming, and although she was so close that she almost touched me, she took no notice of me. She must be very absent-minded, I thought.

This time she left the trapdoor open and I remained standing where I was. The water was boiling and Disa made coffee in a tiny light-blue coffeepot. Never had any coffee smelled so good to me.

"Is this your bedroom?" I asked her at last and had to clear my throat once or twice before I managed to get the words out.

Disa glanced over at me.

"It calls itself so for the time being," she answered, and

poured the coffee again and again through the strainer. "I think your mother must be waiting for you. Hadn't you better go and have your coffee with the others?"

"I hardly ever drink coffee," I confided to her. "I am not allowed to. Who sleeps in the other bed?"

"Sophia," answered Disa, shortly, "when she is at home."

"Doesn't she sleep downstairs?" I asked.

"You had better come up and shut the door and then there will be more room," Disa invited me, in a voice which was not very friendly.

In spite of the tone I did not need pressing.

Disa sat and sipped her black coffee out of a basin with the greatest enjoyment. This basin was as many-colored as her blouse, and seemed to me larger than her coffeepot. One thin cheek bulged with a large piece of sugar which she kept thriftily between her teeth and cheek.

"Haven't you a husband?" I asked her.

"No, thank God," answered Disa, in a cold tone of voice, drinking noisily. "Don't you like coffee?"

"Oh, yes," I answered. "What is in all your little cupboards?"

Disa got up, took down a little bowl from a shelf, half filled it with coffee, put a few drops of water into it, pushed a trunk over the trapdoor—in this way giving me somewhere to sit—and handed me the sugar.

"Just you drink this," she commanded me, in a tone which sounded to me offended, but as if her resentment had nothing to do with me. "Black coffee is a healthy drink. Do you like it?"

"It's good," I murmured, and for a time we both of us drank loudly.

My little basin was very gaudily decorated, too. Round it there was a chocolate ring which I licked in secret, but it did not come off at all.

"Is that your child?" I nodded toward a picture on the wall. "I have never seen such a fine boy."

Disa took the portrait down from the wall and wiped the glass with her many-colored apron. Her stiff features relaxed.

"No," she sighed. "That is Dori, the dear child, Sophia's brother—a boy who would have brought honor to his parents and to his foster parents too. Doesn't he look fine? The photograph was taken in the King's town of Copenhagen."

The boy was actually strange-looking rather than beautiful; he had an extremely large head on a thin body—the rounded forehead particularly was quite overwhelming. I contented myself with nodding.

"He lay in that bed there, the darling child, and hardly ever got up, reading from morning to night," Disa told me willingly, and stroked the glass with her gray cheek. "He was only eight years old when his parents took him to America with them, but he knew as many languages as if he had lived for years and years. Blessed Frederick taught him German and Danish, the other languages he taught himself, and he was interpreter for the whole crowd of immigrants, that he was. They had to take turns carrying him, for his legs were so weak, but wherever he went he could speak the language of the country. Oh, he spoke so beautifully, slowly, and through his nose! 'How silly you are, Disa,' he used to say when I tried to express my opinion, for he knew everything so much better than I did, the darling child. It is not surprising that he is now a professor in a town they call Rio— Rio—something that I cannot remember. Sophia has it on a piece of paper. A town that lies in a country called Brazil."

"Oh, yes, where the raisins grow," I said eagerly and nodded several times to emphasize my geographical knowledge. "Why did not Sophia go with her parents?" I added peevishly, for I could not tolerate this Sophia whom my mother was so anxious to see again.

"She went as far as Copenhagen," answered Disa, in a noncommittal tone. "Then she could no longer bear to be separated from her foster parents, blessed Frederick and blessed Maria, and had to be sent back. Now she is here alone—that is the way of the world. Our relatives are in America, and we are here."

"Are you related to her?" I asked.

"Not more closely than the raven to the maiden," answered

Disa, shortly. "But she has a brother living in America, and cousins, too, and I have a brother and two sisters over there."

"Is that Frederick?" I asked and pointed to the picture of a man with a kindly look in his shrewd eyes, and a wreath of white hair and a beard round his head.

"That is blessed Frederick, and that blessed Maria," said Disa, and showed me a picture of a lady with sharp eyes, mouth, nose and chin, a lady who in my inmost heart I was treacherously glad I should not meet this side the grave.

And now Disa was like a spinning wheel that one has luckily been able to set going; she went on automatically.

"Look here," she said almost confidentially, and opened one of the cupboards, and then opened all the other cupboards in turn. "Just you look here, look at all these little bottles—all these different sorts of medicine. Blessed Frederick was a doctor, though he had not actually studied medicine. Many a life has he saved. Many an unhappy heart has he made happy again. Just look—here are the pills, there are the drops! All the cupboards are full. And if you will get up for a moment from the trunk on which you are sitting, I will show you bottles containing poison. But stand far away, child; you must not touch, for they spell death. Only a very wise man could keep all this in his brain, you understand that, of course? And so as not to misuse it, you must either have no enemies or else a very pure heart. How often has not blessed Frederick held the key to the door of death in his hand—and for such a man this farm was good enough! But now not one stone is to be left upon another, as was said of Jerusalem in the olden days. Never did I think that I should be forced to leave my little corner while I lived—but man proposes, God disposes."

"Of course you will be allowed to keep your little corner," I promised, and noticed how my heart seemed to jump into my mouth. "I will see to that."

"Well, we'll see," answered Disa, and did not sound very convinced.

I went down the stairs, Disa following me, and I found my

father, threw my arms round his neck and made my request about her "little corner."

"And so I suppose I must leave all these absurd passages as they are." He shook me off irritably. "They are regular rabbit warrens. Of course I can't agree to such a thing."

Quietly I put forward the suggestion that Disa's room might be left as it was, even if he pulled down all the rest of the place. It would only be necessary for a wall to be put up and a door to be made and I could do that myself.

"There, there, boy," laughed my father. "You think the matter is finished and done with by wishing for it. Then Disa would have to go out every evening to get home, and what would you say if she were blown away and frozen to death one winter night? . . . All right, all right, the impossible passages can stay where they are, but no more talk about the matter now."

It was with both hands in my trousers pockets that I sought Disa in her bedroom.

"We shall let the room stay as it is," I announced, spitting nonchalantly. "Papa and I have agreed about that." Disa suddenly flushed bright pink over all her gray face, kissed the side of my mouth, gave me both a big and a little piece of candy and then began to knit, her needles sounding a contented note. She hummed no longer. Then quite suddenly she began to sing, in a queer voice and certainly to a tune composed by herself:

Skarphedinn and Saint Paul are my favorite men. . . .

The next moment we were in the midst of a lively discussion as to whom we liked and whom we did not like among the heroes of the Sagas.

"Which king do you like best?" asked Disa, in a voice that had thawed and become quite friendly. "For my part, I like Olaf Tryggveson best—with the exception, of course, of the King of Kings. He was stern, but only for the sake of the Kingdom of God; and surely it is better for the heathen to be converted by torture than that they burn forever in Hell. Do you think

Olaf the King fell at the battle of Svolder? I don't. He was a holy man. Perhaps he still lives in a monastery, hiding the divine glory that surrounds him."

Maggi came and called Disa, and he and I remained standing below her staircase exchanging ideas about one thing and another.

"No one need die here, no indeed!" he burst forth when I told him about all the medicines. "Did she let you taste them?"

"Are you mad?" I answered, and returned to his first remark. "Do you think that all kinds of medicine help against all kinds of illnesses?"

"One can always try them," answered Maggi, and once again I had to acknowledge his superiority as far as common sense was concerned.

To reinstate myself a little I told him:

"Poisonous herbs lie soaking in a large bottle, and Death sits grinning outside the bottle."

"Not really!" laughed Maggi, and would not own himself frightened.

"But most of the bottles were nothing but small glass tubes with a cork at the end," I went on. "They were fixed in holes in the shelves. She has several cupboards full."

"Goodness me!" gasped Maggi. "Were there a hundred bottles?"

"More."

"Were there a thousand?"

"More, more."

"Were there a million, a billion, a trillion, a quintillion?"

"Oh, Maggi, there were a great many more," I assured him solemnly.

Maggi looked closely at me, then he shook his head.

"You're lying. Let me look at your tongue."

I put out my tongue as far as I could.

"You're lying, all the same," decided Maggi, cold-bloodedly. "There are not that many bottles in the whole world and Madagascar."

"But, Maggi, I saw them with my own eyes," I insisted, subdued.

"I don't care a damn for your eyes, I'm not a raven!" he mocked. "There can't be more bottles here in Grimsstadir than there are stars in God's heaven, you codfish!" And he left me, whistling.

As Maggi had left me alone, there was nothing for it but to try to find my own way out through the complicated self-closing door system of the farm. But as there seemed to me a large number of doors, and as some opened inward and others outward, while some had the hinges on the right, others to the left, it was not a bright prospect for me. Then I suddenly met my father, who was going about swearing small oaths to himself and lifting all the doors off their hinges and having them carried away. (Often since then I have dreamed that I was wandering in dark passages with locked doors in front of me and doors which banged to behind me, and that suddenly I met a man who went about lifting all the doors off their hinges, while swearing in a most unchristian manner. This man might appear in all sorts of guises, but he always had my father's knack with doors: one pull and away came the string, another and the door was off.)

Disa passed us, shaking herself as if she were cold, and humming.

"Do you want something to warm yourself with, you there?" my father called out cheerfully. "Here is firewood enough for half a hundred years and more."

I admired my father's resolute way of dealing with doors. When he had taken the last one off I followed him out into the courtyard. There all was bustle. Both the strange men and our own grooms were in full and cheerful activity, loosening the ropes from our belongings and carrying them indoors.

My father threw the last door down in the yard with such force that it fell whistling through the air.

"Well, that's the end of that spider's web!" he laughed proudly, and went over to the bottle which had been placed between the saddles on the turf wall for general use.

The men went over from time to time and took a gulp.

"Drink, boys, you have earned it," my father encouraged them. "But look here, Nonni, haven't you had as much as is good for you, my son?"

"He! he! he!" laughed Nonni, shrilly, quite unlike his usual self. "It shure tashtes damn' good, Farmer Greipur."

My father laughed doubtfully, but had not the heart to deny him a drop.

"There is the flask—stand close round him, boys, while he drinks, in case the old lady should come."

The men made a ring round Nonni and the bottle which he, after a quick glance over their shoulders, put to his mouth— whereupon both his head and the bottle disappeared. Through their legs I caught a glimpse of him crouching down on his heels while he drank, the group round him swaying as if all their legs and all their arms and all their heads were on one body. The eyes in the brown faces shone as if they were the glass eyes of dolls; but the men were dirty and covered with horsehair and were otherwise not at all like dolls.

Old Begga came past and threw a very suspicious glance at the group. Although she was dressed as Sunday-Begga, it was Weekday-Begga's voice that called:

"Jon, Jon!"

"Has your bishop deserted you?" asked my father, sympathetically. "Listen, boys, have any of you seen her Jon Vidalin?"

The men shouted with laughter, and said they thought they had seen something suspiciously like a bishop, slinking out of the farm and running as if the Devil were after him. But whether it was actually the ghost of a bishop, or just an ordinary farmyard ghost, they were not sure.

Old Begga went off shaking her head, murmuring something about wine and wit, whereupon the group around Nonni separated, laughing and joking, and each one went off to his job.

A tall, loose-limbed lout appeared, carrying a wool-winder— which did not look too happy, as its four arms were not crossed as a winch's should be, but two of them hung down slackly and the other two were stretched toward heaven in silent supplication.

"What shall I do with this-here thing?" he asked, and his voice creaked as if he himself were an ungreased wool-winder.

My father looked hastily round and then said softly:

"Put it in the barn—and don't let Cecilia see it."

The men shouted. The tag for the day had been found! They must drink on that. And they drank. And as soon as a bottle was empty, another stood in its place as if by miracle—no one seemed to know where it came from.

Maggi, who had also managed to get a gulp, began to bawl:

"It's better than blessed Frederick's medicine!"

Immediately the rest of the verse was there. The lines followed each other in quick succession.

> *It's better than you, my Bishop Vidaline,*
> *Better than forty winks*
> *Or kissing a minx—*
> *It's better than old brandywine!*

This verse was sung over and over a great many times, and every time it was brought to a finish the men added with energy:

"Glory be to God! *Skaal!*"

In the midst of all this shouting and hallooing a calm, thoughtful man suddenly appeared in the yard. His eyes seemed to dance in spite of himself, and were the only things about him that moved.

"Put him in the barn, and don't let Cecilia see him!" whispered the man with the wool-winder, but my father looked round sharply and the laughter died in the men's throats.

The thoughtful man had a heavy forehead protruding over his dancing eyes as if to keep them under control by its weight.

He was not alone. A little way behind him stalked a tall, stern-looking woman with a rust-red knitted shawl drawn tightly across her angular shoulders and thin arms. She walked with long strides, as if she wanted to get along but did not want to waste her footsteps on the way.

My father went forward to meet them, and the thoughtful man opened his mouth and said hesitantly, but without actually stammering:

"We . . . have . . . just . . . come . . . to make you welcome."

After this effort he shook my father's hand and kissed his beard; and suddenly I understood why it was so important to have a beard when one grew up. Then my father and the woman exchanged a kiss, as was only right between future neighbors— for these were the folk from the West Farm, Magistrate Toroddur and his wife Gudrun. While all this was going on, Geir had rushed forward, clasped Toroddur round the neck and begun to kiss him vigorously.

"How friendly of you to come, you old so-and-so!" he cried emotionally, with tears in his eyes, giving Toroddur's back a hearty thump. "One can see with half an eye that you are the best of fellows, and that your wife is a tower of strength. . . . But you've grown rather rusty in the jaws—I can hear that you need a little oiling. So take a drop, and don't be shy! Afterward we shall exchange knives."

"I . . . never . . . exchange . . . knives," answered Toroddur, and his eyes danced helplessly hither and thither.

"No?" said Geir, amazed and distressed. "Well, wife, is there anything I can exchange with you? . . . What about trading watches? I haven't one, but what does that matter?"

"I . . . never . . . trade . . . watches," answered Toroddur.

"How the devil do you make the day go then, old man?" shouted Geir, and left him.

"I shall soon have to deal with you, Geir, if you can't behave better," my father threatened him jokingly.

"Now, don't you talk, Greipur Uggason, you haven't been too sparing yourself!" Geir shouted back.

During all this time Nonni had been sitting on his mother's saddle, giggling helplessly. Every time he lifted his eyes he saw something or other that seemed to him so extraordinarily funny he almost died laughing at it. His body seemed quite incapable of anything but doubling up with laughter and then straightening itself out again. Every time he opened his mouth he laughed; every time a piece of furniture was carried into the house he laughed; whenever I went over to see what was really the matter with him he laughed. Maria Mens passed him, carefully averting her eyes, which were redder than ever with weeping. At this Nonni laughed immoderately. Old Begga came out and stood there looking at him sorrowfully. Then she left him without a word. And at this Nonni had such an attack of laughter that he fell out of the saddle and remained lying in the grass and continued to laugh, curled up like a worm that has been trampled on.

"Put him in the barn, and don't let Cecilia see him," Geir suggested, and Nonni was lifted up and carried away, still laughing out of all reason.

I hurried off to where my father and mother were standing talking to Toroddur and his wife; perhaps there would be something said worth hearing. As soon as I appeared, my mother took the opportunity to draw Gudrun's attention to the proud fact that I was her first-born, and that I bore my grandfather's name of Uggi.

"I always think the eldest children should be given the name of one or the other parent," said Gudrun from the West Farm, showing her teeth, which reminded me of the black and white keys of the organ, and staring relentlessly at my red hair. "Our two eldest children are called Turoddur and Gudrun—I wonder where they are? They were here a minute ago, both they and the children from Vegeirsstadir. Have you seen anything of them, dear?"

It was doubtless this sentimental way of addressing me that made me rush away without answering, although I knew how rude it was. Round the corner of the farm I found seven strange children gathered in a half-circle about Veiga and Beta, who stood with their fingers in their mouths and were waiting only to find a hole in the ring large enough to let them out so they could rush away and seek refuge in their mother's arms.

Even at that age I realized that witchcraft was a very rare

thing; but when one of the boys turned round and came toward me—an exact copy of his father, with his father's body, clothes, hair, nose, forehead and dancing eye—cold shivers went down my back, and if he had had a beard I should have taken to my heels.

"I . . . only . . . wished . . . to bid you welcome," he said in the same slow way, and we greeted each other with a handshake and a kiss.

It took time to exchange greetings, names and ages, but we went through it all. The children from the West Farm introduced themselves with their pet names: Doddi, Runa, No-No and Sigga. Runa was as like her mother as Doddi was like his father; No-No was an agile little fair-haired boy whose Christian name was Einar; Sigga astounded me by looking exactly like the kind of children my father had taught me to draw. Like them, her head was too large, her legs too short and fat, and, like them, she would certainly never become any different.

The children from Vegeirsstadir were Hjorleifur, a dark lively boy, and two golden-haired girls, Anna and Hildiridur.

Doddi, Anna and I were the same age; Hjorleifur, Veiga and Runa were of an age, and also Hildiridur. No-No and Beta went together, and Sigga was the youngest and had no one the same age, which for a long time made her quite unmanageable.

I could not take my eyes off Hildiridur. She was so sweet to look at, her manner so warm and friendly, so sincere and trustworthy, that my eyes no more wished to leave her than a bee wishes to leave a tuft of seaside pink. Never had I seen anything that moved me more. A happy intoxication seized me. My ears sang like distant bells. Every detail of her—her clothes, her manner of standing, her inability to say a single word, yes, even a little scratch she had on her cheek—all seemed to me perfect and more than perfect. A flood of light filled me as if the sun— which all the day had stood high in the heavens—had only just begun to shine. It was quite impossible to express what I felt. I can only say that she seemed to me wonderful to look at. She wanted someone to hold her hand all the time, someone at whom she could smile her flowerlike smile and at whom she could look with her big eyes, which were of the same shining blue as the forget-me-nots in the field outside the farm. Perhaps it was her need of someone to lean on and smile on that was the real cause of my infatuation. Full of desires as my life has been, I have never longed for anything so much as then—that the day might come when she would hold *my* hand and smile at *me* as she did at the others. And it is characteristic of life that I never attained either the one or the other.

Hjorleifur, who so far had scarcely opened his mouth, now exploded in a gloomy, devil-may-care voice:

"My father fell down a whole mountain and was dashed to pieces. He looked like the body of a ptarmigan after the fox has had him."

"Oh, yes, and then your mother died before you were born, or whatever it was, and your only brother is the eagle and your only friend the winter storm," mocked Anna, without the slightest movement of her cold regular features.

"If I were not too chivalrous to punish a woman, I'd go for you one of these days—you and your sharp tongue!" Hjorleifur snapped back. "But you can say what you like; the man who stands alone in the world, fatherless and motherless, forsaken of God and man—"

"Then Valdor and Sigurborg don't count?" objected Anna.

"—becomes hard as flint," Hjorleifur shouted her down, "cold-blooded as a raven, raging as a bull, thick-skinned and lion-hearted, false as a tiger, cunning as a snake, violent as a wave, hard-jawed as a crocodile, and strong as an elephant!"

"Oh, stop now, Leifur," begged Doddi, overwhelmed. But his remonstrance seemed only to act as fresh ammunition for Leifur.

"There is nothing in the whole world I don't dare do—not a crime, not a villainy I do not dare commit! I would dare to steal, to kill, to plunder, burn, murder! If I don't, it is only because I do not wish to cause sorrow to Valdor or Sigurborg, who are decent people and have been very good to me."

"Who are Valdor and Sigurborg?" I asked.

"Now don't pretend that you have come from so far away you never heard of Valdor from Vegeirsstadir and his sister Sigurborg," mocked Hjorleifur. "We are no chickens here in Hamrafjödur, I may tell you! We have seen a milksop before, and know what he's like to look at. You wait until Valdor and Sigurborg are safely under the green sod and I am free to wag my tail."

"Are you also a foster child?" I asked Anna. I felt I could not bring myself to speak to Hildiridur.

"When will you get into that square noddle of yours that Anna and Hildiridur are the daughters of Goldsmith Karl and Ingiborg?" said Hjorleifur, impatiently, although it was the first time I had been told. "I suppose that two farmers may live here at Vegeirsstadir as well as at Grimsstadir! Vegeirsstadir is in no way behind Grimsstadir or any other farm. Take my advice and don't begin running down Vegeirsstadir. If you do, you will meet at least one man who fears neither death, the Devil, nor Hell—his name is Hjorleifur, in case he should be out when you call."

"I'll fight you any time," I answered, feeling that I could not put up with more of this; not because the children from the West Farm and my own sisters were standing gazing at Hjorleifur with admiring eyes, but because there was one particular pair of eyes that seemed to admire him most of all—and those were Hildiridur's.

"Did he say anything?" Hjorleifur asked Doddi. "I thought I heard a cackle, but I may have been mistaken."

"Perhaps you don't feel inclined to take a toss?" I said in a voice which, to my annoyance, trembled slightly.

"You . . . had . . . better . . . not," Doddi warned me with friendly dancing eyes. "He is—"

"—agile as a cat, slippery as an eel, strong as a giant." Anna finished the sentence, while she lifted her strongly marked eyebrows. "Those are his own words, and so they must be true."

"Don't stand too near, and see that he doesn't land on your

heads," Leifur warned them, full of consideration for the other children. "The poor wretch! He is already trembling like a leaf. Look at him well before I begin. Perhaps you will have to swear to his identity. His own mother may not recognize him when I have finished with him."

It was quite obvious that it was not all boasting. Leifur was agile and strong, but I was more furious than he, and I had, as well as a year's extra weight, an undoubted advantage over him—Hildiridur. . . .

There he lay.

I had not much time for triumph, for like a steel spring he was up again and rushed at me, grinding his teeth and crying angrily and ignoring all the rules of wrestling.

"You cheated, you damned wretch," he shouted. "You butted * at me. I'll tear you to pieces like an old watch."

This time I had two advantages over him. The first was that he had lied, and this undoubtedly strengthened my position. The second was that he was quite beside himself with rage, and exposed himself to the attack again and again, so that it was not difficult to get at him. And I do not deny that I took advantage of the situation to the uttermost and was so worked up that, although I knew he would fall hard, I did nothing to soften the fall.

Leifur lay there and did not get up. I was very frightened, for he bled from the nose; his lips were cracked, and, besides that, he had a scratch on his forehead and his eyes were closed. It looked bad. My heart almost stopped beating. What had I done? Then a little tremor of one eyelid betrayed him and I, who would have gladly thrown myself on him and kissed him in spite of blood and dirt, my anger entirely gone, sniggered scornfully, and turned my back on him. In this way I thought to keep my dignity.

The girls fetched water in our caps and began to call Leifur back to life again, and Doddi, who also must have noticed some

---

* The Icelandic "glima," a particular type of wrestling, is governed by very strict rules.

reassuring signs, told him he was not dead and persuaded him in his sensible way to pull himself together and get onto his legs. No-No walked round and round me, giving me one kick after another. Only Hildiridur stood passive, gazing at me with tears in her great uncomprehending eyes—a blue, frightened gaze. At this moment she had no one to hold her hand.

Leifur came round from his faint, sat up, and looked at the world for the first time.

Doddi stood and watched us both, his eyes dancing.

"You . . . must . . . shake hands."

Then Leifur sprang up and limped away from the farm.

"I shall never come back here again, never."

And as if this were not crushing enough he added, looking me straight in the face:

"You are almost a murderer."

His voice was threatening, and hinted that it was still uncertain whether he would live or die. But he seemed to me alive right enough and I felt nothing but a little awkwardness on his behalf.

The children from the West Farm and the girls from Vegeirsstadir followed him at a proper distance—a quiet solemn procession. Veiga and Beta stood bewildered, looking after them. I tried to whistle a gay tune and as I did not succeed I began to sing at the top of my voice, stuck my hands in my pockets and walked away.

I found a solitary place close to the stream and lay down among the tussocks. "How silly you are!" laughed the stream, shaking its head, its eyes dancing. I turned my back on it, but it went on laughing behind me. I felt very lonely. I remembered some verses in which the poet said that he wandered alone at night through the barren desert of sand, and the North was far away, and he had no home. I sang this verse first of all calmly, then with freezing pathos and finally with a voice shaking with sobs like an old woman's at a funeral. I tried to make up verses in which I said that now Breidale was far away and I was in unfriendly Hamrafjördur, but Butterwater, which I wanted to introduce into the poem, would not work in at all; so I gave it up after a time and went on singing about the desert and the North—sang and wept, very unhappy, and very happy. A little wagtail was busy among his tussocks and took no notice of me, but a stonechat gave himself time to look at me and be sorry for me too.

"Poor boy, tst—tst—tst!" he said and shook his head and tail. Then he suddenly thought of a bit of advice. "Woo—her—now! Woo—her—now! Woo—her—now!"

Suddenly I noticed that all the forget-me-nots stood looking at me with Hildiridur's eyes. Yes, they reminded me so much of Hildiridur's eyes that my head became burningly hot as if she had stood there herself listening to my song and witnessing my agony, and as if she had heard what the stonechat advised me.

As a matter of fact I took the stonechat's advice very seriously, and decided after careful consideration that I had better follow it up, preferably as soon as possible. There was, of course, Sigga-Sigga. Perhaps she thought that we were going to get married—and I had thought so too at one time. But of course I was not really engaged to Sigga-Sigga, and, with regard to Butterwater, what did I actually know about that lake? Perhaps it had been possible to skim cream from it at some time or other, but that was certainly a long time ago. Besides, was there any Butterwater Lake at all now? And if there was no Butterwater Lake, how was I going to manage about marrying Sigga-Sigga? Although I tried to shift the greater part of the blame onto that unreliable lake, I was still not at all comfortable at the thought of my faithlessness. What worried me most was that I felt I could not depend on myself. If I failed Sigga-Sigga, might I not fail Hildiridur too? And that must not happen at any price. Hildiridur I must never fail. I must find a way to bind myself to her hand and foot, for time and for eternity, whether she loved me or not, and such a way was easy enough to find.

Out of my pocket I fished up a slip of paper which originally had been meant for a note to Sigga-Sigga. Then I took out my knife and made a scratch on the little finger of my left hand (why it was imperative that it should be that particular finger I cannot actually remember). Then I began to print with a straw. It took me a long time and cost me several scratches and a certain amount of blood, but blood it had to be; only blood was valid when one pledged oneself to the Devil. And even if this were not exactly a pledge to the Devil, it might happen—one had heard of such things before—that Hildiridur might somehow, by a miracle, see my pledge, and then blood would doubtless make the strongest impression on her. When at last I had finished, these were the words on the paper:

"I love Hildiridur Karlsdottir and will marry nobody but her. Uggi Greipsson, future priest."

With the intention of strengthening my weakening morale, I had suddenly decided to adopt the clerical calling.

When I had composed this document and signed it, there was still a little blood oozing from my finger. I used this blood to make crosses and mystic signs which I myself did not understand, putting them above and below the text. The whole thing smacked of witchcraft to such an extent that I began to feel very depressed and could think of nothing but how to get rid of the piece of paper. After much cogitation I dug a hole in a little sandstone hill which could be seen from the farm—I wanted to have the place always before my eyes—and hid it there, and smoothed away all traces of it.

Everything around me was silent, looking at me. It was impossible for me to find out whether they approved or disapproved of my undertaking. When the note had been buried my mood suddenly changed. I did not feel exactly sad, but I did not feel happy, and all these emotions which I had gone through produced a kind of emptiness in my mind. But then I pulled myself together. Now it was done, and done for life!

A strong evening sun lighted up the landscape, making long, sharp shadows, and the sky was crimson as if dripping with blood; the water in the stream looked as if it had suddenly turned into stone. Solitary, silent birds flew quickly past.

I wandered homeward. The yard outside the homestead

seemed strangely empty. All our things had been taken into the houses and the sod wall stood there, feeling lonely without a single saddle on it. There was not a person to be seen.

"Where have you been, child?" asked my mother, who, busy and hot, came to meet me in the doorway. "I asked Geir to give your love to Sigga. I thought you would have liked to send her a note? I hope he will remember it, the foolish fellow."

I must have looked rather odd, for my mother patted me suddenly on my cheek and added comfortingly:

"But you can put the note in an envelope and send it by post."

I stood and thought:

"Perhaps when I become a widower I shall be able to marry Sigga-Sigga."

4

THE sun streamed in through the west window in a golden torrent. My mother and I were alone in the living room, which shone white from well-scrubbed wood. The beds with their many-colored coverlets, the table under the window, our blue and red trunks, my mother's spinning wheel in one corner, her winder in another, bundles of wool needles and wool-winders on the wall, odds and ends stuffed between the rafters, the books on a shelf over the window—the whole room filled me with a calm content.

My mother sat on the bed nearest the window, my parents' bed, knitting soles of many-colored wools to be slipped inside our winter shoes. I was on my knees in front of the bed in which we children slept and which was next to that of my parents, looking at the pictures in my *Robinson Crusoe*. Madame Anna slept noisily.

"How I miss our pussy," said my mother at last, softly, and looked over toward the third bed in the room, on which there were bedclothes and a coverlet but which was used to hold carders and baskets of wool and yarn. "If only she lay there, purring! Oh dear, how stupid of me! I have actually forgotten the pattern. I was quite sure I knew it by heart."

I realized that she did not expect me to answer her, nor had I time to do so, for I was just in the midst of picturing what she would say and how glad she would be when, after many years, I returned home from the desert island where I would undoubtedly be shipwrecked sooner or later.

"I scarcely think we shall get to Knör this summer," said my mother, with a little sigh. "Tell me, Uggi child, which would you rather have—a brother or a sister?"

"A brother," I answered indifferently, trying not to be disturbed.

"What shall we call him?"

"Sigbergur."

My mother wiped a tear from her eye, and then she laughed.
"Why Sigbergur?"

"Like the one who died."

My mother went on knitting for a little while.

"How about Ketilbjörn—what do you think of that for a
name?"

"Quite good," I answered, and left my Robinson for the time
being, as I was not allowed to read in peace. "But then we would
have to have two, for of course we must have the one who died
again."

My mother laughed a little and cried a little—and dried her
eyes.

It was at this moment that Sophia Einarsdottir came in.

The swish of skirts in the passage, heavy footsteps, a voice with
a snap in it:

"But where is she? Where are you, darling Cecilia? In the
middle room? Oh, why of course!"

My mother got up hastily from the bed, counted her stitches,
shook the fluff from her apron and answered my look with a
hasty:

"It's Sophia."

Holding her very long, very wide riding skirt well above her
feet with both hands, a solid thick-set creature with heavy black
eyebrows came up the stairs. Her hair was dark and stuck out
in puffs from under her riding hat. Her eyes were dark and large,
her mouth big, with white teeth and full red lips. Her face was
smooth and fleshy, rather square, and to it was attached a
monotonous smile which, looking at photographs of her in later
years, I decided must have been assumed. Her hands were long
and strong, but soft and unused to rough work; the fingertips
were bent a little backward, reminding me of the feathers on
a raven's wing.

"Oh, so that's how it is with you?" were the first words she
said to my mother, letting her skirts fall and gathering her into

her large arms, the outlines of which were emphasized by her tight black sleeves.

These words made a strong impression on me. I saw in a flash how stout my mother was, and I felt a momentary resentment against this strange, corseted lady who talked so indelicately to her; but I could not but recognize that the strange lady was a very fine lady indeed. It suddenly seemed odd to me that my mother should know her so well, while I did not know her at all.

My mother and Sophia stood for a moment kissing and hugging each other, my mother silently, Sophia talking almost incessantly.

"Welcome, my darling! God bless you—how glad I am to see you! I longed to be at home to receive you ceremoniously and see that the house was fairly clean for you to come into—I suppose it was frightful. But then they fetched me to Rikka, Citizen Sigfur's daughter—you'll remember him. She fell and cut her leg, the silly child, and they would not hear of anyone's dealing with the wound except me. But you are still as energetic and clever as ever, I see—you've managed to get everything into order, my little one! What a madcap that Rikka is! It was a bad cut, right down to the bone. As soon as she saw me she began to howl and pulled the stocking off her leg. Well, the wound was ugly enough to please anybody. She's a dear child, I must arrange for you to see her. I will bring her over here some day—she's as good as she's pretty. They are all of them that, those children. But what was I saying?—You are very diligent in your way, Cecilia."

My mother, who was evidently touched by the meeting with her childhood friend, dried her eyes and said softly:

"We lost our last, as perhaps you have heard—a little boy."

"Don't cry about that, dear Cecilia," Sophia comforted her in the usual "comforting" tone, which always had in it a touch of rebuke and of impatience, but which was otherwise genuine enough. "He is doubtless happy with God."

"And so we must have another to call Sigbergur," continued

my mother, simply. "Then there is the name of Arni left—and after that we lack only a Ketilbjörn."

"Oh, are you that sort of family!" said Sophia, and lifted her heavy eyebrows a little. "What has happened to the old Celia I used to know? You did not use to take that kind of duty seriously in those days, my dear."

"And if you took the old Celia seriously you cannot have known her very well, Sophia dear," answered my mother, laughing, but with a glint in her eye which suddenly reminded me of Grandpa-from-Knör, Ketilbjörn Hranason-from-Knör.

"Oh, I quite agree that you have surprised me," laughed Sophia. "You who said you would never marry and would never have children. And then you went, at the very first opportunity, and broke the oath we swore to each other—and yet you were the younger of us two."

"But surely you did not take all that girlish nonsense seriously?" asked my mother, really surprised. "Did you never realize that I thought I was so plain, no one whom I could care about would marry me—and, on the other hand, that I thought you would be too particular to get anyone?"

"No—God knows it never occurred to me for a moment that that was your point of view." Sophia laughed loudly. "You've always had your head screwed on the right way, Cecilia; not for nothing are you your father's daughter!"

"There is just one thing I want to ask you," said my mother, and now she spoke simply and straightforwardly.

Sophia lifted her eyebrows expectantly.

My mother blushed. "It is only," she said, and hesitated a little over her words, "that you will promise to stay with me—until the baby comes."

"Why, of course I will, dear Celia," answered Sophia, with a smile which showed that she did not attach as much importance to the matter as my mother. "Besides, I live here. Surely you are not anxious about it, my friend!"

My mother hesitated. She stood looking straight in front of her, and her face was very serious.

"Yes, I am," she said at last, simply.

"But things up till now have always gone so well with you; why should they suddenly go wrong this time?" Sophia comforted her. "Now you must stop worrying about it. When the whole thing is over you will be the first to smile at your anxiety."

My mother, who was keeping her face under control by biting her lower lip, blinked the tears out of her eyes and said, in a subdued voice:

"I have always been so happy all my life until I lost my little Sigbergur. Now I am suddenly afraid."

"This is what one calls maternal hysteria, dear Cecilia," Sophia decided kindly. "I understand it so well: you have not yet recovered from the loss of your child. But why weep over a child who slips sinless right into Heaven? Life is not so delightful that there is any reason to weep for one who is released from it."

"No one who has not experienced it knows what it is to lose a child," said my mother, calmly.

"We must believe that the sorrows and sufferings God in His wisdom sends us are for our good," answered Sophia, piously, and yet not without a certain conviction. "No sparrow falls to the ground without His knowledge; you know that."

"Do you find any comfort in that?" asked my mother, with something like a smile.

Sophia burst into a laugh that sounded both surprised and pleased.

"At last I see a glimpse of the old Celia! So she isn't quite dead and buried—not quite smothered in all that clerical atmosphere?"

"Aren't you going to take off your riding dress?" asked my mother, again changing her tone of voice. "Run downstairs, little Uggi, and ask them to see about a cup of coffee."

"So that is Uggi?" Sophia stopped me, and after a short inspection she kissed me with her fat lips. "Well, as far as that color is concerned, Cecilia, you've certainly been paid in cash."

"Now I like that color better than any other," said my mother, and stroked my hair.

"Each one finds her own nestling lovely," laughed Sophia. "Is it you or Disa who locked my door and lost the key?"

"It was locked when we came," answered my mother, astonished. "Disa said you had the key yourself."

"Funny old thing," said Sophia, understandingly. "I expect she will find it. Can you see whether she's found it yet, my little friend?"

Just as I was going I happened to look across at Madame Anna's cradle. She had awakened without uttering a sound and lay staring at the strange lady with a frightened, wondering look in her calm blue childish eyes.

With the sweat of my brow I dragged stones to Veiga's and my new farm. Beta was our child, and had been told to cry and be naughty, which she seemed to do without much effort. When once in a while she stopped to listen to what we, her parents, were saying, Veiga would turn to her crossly and admonish her sharply:

"Howl, Beta. That's all you've got to do."

Veiga was uncommonly busy and quick in her movements today. She radiated heat almost like the sun itself. After going about for some time muttering to herself scornfully, she struck an attitude, her arms akimbo.

"There's just one thing I want to say to you, my dear husband; unless you get me a cow before the sun sinks below the wood, I am not sure whether I can keep life in our child till he rises again. Have you no heart, may I ask, or are you so deaf you don't hear how miserably she's crying, the darling? Not a drop of milk has found its way to her innocent lips since we left Ofeigsstadur."

"Our farm was not called Ofeigsstadur, it was called Fjall," I interrupted her rudely. When Veiga once got going one never knew when she would stop.

"It doesn't matter to me what it was called or not called," Veiga went on an octave higher. "That's not what I'm talking about. Call your farm 'Cow-town' if you like, but don't imagine that because of its name cows will grow up out of the earth. What do you mean to do about milk for Beta?—I should really like to know. Do you dare have her death on your conscience?"

"Yes, she can kick the bucket for all I care," I shouted angrily. "Then I shall get rid of her eternal whimpering."

"How can you talk in that blasphemous way?" sighed Veiga, clasping her hands, and indignantly shaking her head. "And then what is going to happen later on in the year? Has it entered your head that after the spring comes the winter? What are you going to kill? Tell me that. You have no sheep here. You could learn from Doddi what is needed on a farm—that man has enough and to spare."

"Well, go off and marry him," I advised her. "I don't care."

"I can well believe that," said Veiga, tossing her head. "I don't get much tender care from you. Do you want to put both your wife and child out to grass, like the cattle? Or are we going to live on air? Or if I want to enjoy myself a little on Sundays and go to the House of God, what is there for me to ride on? I don't suppose you want your wife trudging about the district on her own legs like any pauper."

"We've got Moldarbrunn, you baggage," I said angrily.

"Moldarbrunn?" said Veiga, turning up her eyes and clasping her hands. "Moldarbrunn, who has lost his head and whose hindquarters are rubbed off? Well, I've never heard such nonsense. Don't speak of it again, that's all I can say. I would rather sit astride a broom than on an animal like that."

I looked at Moldarbrunn, our brown hack, and a more pathetic imitation of a horse it would be difficult to find. I would not ride on him to save my life, but here in the East Farm where no children had lived since Disa's bedridden professor, that milksop in Rio, lay lapping up languages, Moldarbrunn was the only thing resembling a horse that, after an endless search, we had been able to find.

"I don't suppose you think I can create cattle?" I asked gloomily.

"That's your affair," mocked Veiga. . . . "There, there, my darling, thank God you are still too young to understand how badly your father is behaving. . . . That was not what you promised me when you were wooing me, Uggi."

"When did I woo you, you bag of bones?" I asked cold-bloodedly. "Unless you stop talking I will build a fortress for myself somewhere up in the gully where neither you nor Beta shall ever set foot."

"Tcha!" said Veiga.

However, my threat worked. She went over and comforted her child, and I had peace and quiet to think over what was to be done. Veiga was certainly right—without cows, horses or sheep, one could not run a farm. And that devil of a Doddi who would neither sell nor give me a single cow. "I am so fond of them all," he had said, even about the cow that lacked nearly all its feet. There seemed nothing else to do except fetch what we needed.

Over on the sod wall lay my father's whip, gleaming bamboo and silver. I went over and weighed it in my hand—the long leather thong whistled through the air. This whistle, which made Veiga and Beta huddle together, decided me.

"Now for war and plunder," I shouted, intoxicated by my own warlike mood. "You two are my army. Follow me close through blood and fire. I'll punish anyone who deserts me or tries to flee."

We borrowed one of my father's red pocket handkerchiefs from my mother's wash line, we tied it to a rake-handle for a flag and Veiga carried it. Beta made a trumpet out of a bottle. I marched at the head with my wonderful sword, "Whistler," which cut so easily through stones and water.

Doddi and his brothers and sisters, who were quite unpre-pared for an attack from a warlike and well-armed enemy force, cried, moaned, used coarse language and then fled at top speed before they understood what it was all about. But we had not come to bandy words; we had come to steal and to plunder and to leave no stone upon another; so we let them say what they liked. We had brought with us two ships, and these we loaded calmly and quietly. They were Veiga's and Beta's pinafores.

I cannot remember ever having been so elated with a single day's work, or feeling so absolutely master of the situation, as when we marched home across the grassy meadow with our plunder, shouting at the top of our voices:

> *My mother told me*
> *That I must purchase*
> *Ships with lovely oars*
> *To sail with the Vikings—*
> *Stand high in the prow,*
> *Steer the boat with courage,*
> *Land where I listed,*
> *Cut down and plunder!*

Scarcely had we put our stolen cattle out to grass and begun to name them before we saw Gudrun-from-the-West-Farm striding across the meadow with her apron to her face, sobbing and stumbling, a jealous Norn, an offended goddess of destiny.

"She didn't see us," spluttered Beta, when Gudrun had disappeared into the homestead.

"How silly you are!" I tried to keep up our spirits—for of course we could not be quite sure what my mother would say.

But our uncertainty did not last long, for there came Gudrun-from-the-West-Farm with her apron back in its place and apparently comforted, followed by my mother who, on the contrary, looked ready to cry.

"They just about frightened the life out of my poor innocent darlings," Gudrun complained, and blew the last bit of cry out of her nose. "My Doddi says that it is impossible to imagine their shouts and devilish tricks. 'They might have been the Turk himself,' says my Doddi. If he and the others had not had the sense to fly they might perhaps have been left on the ground like cold corpses, or crippled for life. I am so sorry for you, good neighbor, that your children show such a spirit—but let us hope that it is not yet too late to whip the wildness out of them, for otherwise it will only bring them to a bad end, believe me."

"Well, if they do I shall not ask you to weep over them, good Gudrun," said my mother, in a friendly tone, collecting, with trembling hands, the cattle we had stolen, and putting them into Gudrun's tear-stained apron.

When Gudrun-from-the-West-Farm had gone, my mother took Veiga and Beta rather hastily by the hand and went indoors with them. I saw how funnily they tripped along on their unwilling legs, but it did not amuse me. My mother immediately came back and stood in front of me and looked at me gravely. Large tears ran down her cheeks, and in order to stop myself from crying too I kicked down the houses I had taken so much trouble to build.

"Why are you doing that?" asked my mother, softly.

"They're *my* houses, I guess," I answered, in a voice I had never heard before.

"Didn't you know that one must never take other children's toys?" asked my mother, after a little pause.

"Yes," I answered, although it was not quite true, but I did not want to own this.

"And yet you did?"

"Yes."

"Aren't you sorry?"

"No."

"Not even when you see that it makes me cry?"

"You can stop that."

"You won't do it again, will you?"

"No—because I don't want all this blether."

My mother turned hastily away from me, but not hastily enough—I had seen a smile flash into her eyes. And what her gravity, sorrow and tears had not been able to do, this smile accomplished. I threw myself down, hid my face in my arms and cried—cried the tears of anger, disappointment, and repentance. This attack of weeping would doubtless have come sooner or later, whatever form our conversation took; but her con-

cealed smile released it, I think, because it showed me the hopelessness of attempting to appear superior. When I had cried for
a time I heard my mother go.

"I can't cry in peace here," I thought. "I'd better go behind
the barn."

And I went behind the barn, lay down in the short grass and
went on crying.

"As You did not leave cattle for me here in the East Farm,
You ought not to be angry with me because I took Doddi's," I
threshed the matter out with God. "And why did You make my
mother so unhappy about it? Don't You agree that Gudrun-
from-the-West-Farm is a regular devil?"

As usual Our Lord answered nothing, but I had a strong impression that He did not really approve of robbery; and I suspected it was He who, again and again, made me think that
now my mother was probably sitting somewhere, perhaps alone,
crying over me. I explained to Him that Doddi could very well
have defended himself and his possessions. There must have
been a stick or a whip somewhere at the West Farm, just as
there was everywhere else. He and No-No could easily have
punished me thoroughly and driven me home, my errand un-
accomplished. Then the whole incident would have been closed
and all this trouble avoided. The thought at the bottom of my
heart, which I refrained from expressing in so many words to
God, since He did not seem to acknowledge it, was that, as He
had supported me in my undertaking by allowing it to succeed,
He ought to have taken His share of the responsibility when it
went wrong. I had no doubt that Our Lord understood very
well what I was thinking, but He said nothing—withdrew Himself from the matter, as it were, with a smile.

Around me the eternally whispering grasses tittle-tattled. The
longest ones stood straight up like grownups in a group of children, nodded their heads condescendingly and allowed the little
ones to join in the talk. The whole field buzzed with conversation; only the flowers were silent—they never spoke unless everything around them was quite still. But even if the grasses knew

everything, yet, fundamentally, they knew nothing at all, for they could not tell a story. They certainly told me a great deal about Sophia and her brother, about Disa and the late Frederick, but they muddled everything together, and the only really amusing story was the one about Moldarbrunn who wanted to be a war-horse and after many adventures and much toil returned home, headless and tailless—and that story could not, of course, be any other than it was.

"I do not want to listen to all your nonsense," I shouted at last, and immediately every blade of grass anywhere near me began to tickle my face and my throat and my wrists. I turned over onto my back, then they tickled my neck and crept down under my collar. I laid my arms crosswise under my head— how blue the sky was!

Today, surely, one ought to be able to see the ships.

I gazed and gazed until I sneezed and my eyes began to water, but there were no ships to be seen. How odd that one never saw so much as a glimpse of those ships! If the world were really round—and everybody agreed that it was—then the sky *must* be an ocean, must be the waters that God had separated from some other land, and then the ships *must* sail round the world, sail right across this ocean sky with their masts downward, like flies crawling on the ceiling. But if this was so, why could they not be seen? Here I had been looking out for them for several days—but then of course the sky had often been overcast, and perhaps God always arranged for clouds when the ships sailed above the earth, so that those on board should not be frightened and fall down from sheer fright. Or perhaps the sky-navigators thought the great masses of land drifting above them were clouds over their heads. . . .

When I grew up I would buy myself a telescope and keep a close watch on the blue pieces between the banks of cloud. It would be delightful to lie and see what the ships had on board, but best of all would be when I myself became a captain and had bought myself a ship. Then I would be a real sea-king. What should I call myself? Uggi the Dauntless? Well, perhaps that would do. But Hugleik the Reckless Sailor sounded better still. That was what I would call myself: Hugleik the Reckless Sailor. I savored the name. Yes, that was the name under which I would certainly sail. My ship would have a dragon-head and a dragon-tail, and striped homespun sails as wings, and with this ship I would sail as no one had ever sailed before.

First of all, I would sail to that land, Brazil, and when I had spoken to Sophia's brother in all the eight languages that he understood, and eight others besides that he did not understand, I would fill the ship with apples, figs, and especially raisins, for my father liked them so much, and then I would take a trip on the blue sky; and when I arrived just above Grimsstadir, I would loose the whole cargo and shower it over the homestead (it would, of course, be best if it were in the middle of the hay harvest) and I would let red and yellow apples rain round my mother, raisins over my father, figs over Veiga, prunes over Beta, soft sugar over Madame Anna, biscuits over Nonni, barley-sugar over Maggi, currants, like sweet tears, over Maria Mens, coffee-beans over Disa and wrinkled oranges and books of sermons and other Words of God over Old Begga.

I wished I could be sure that Gudrun-from-the-West-Farm would not appear holding out her apron, which my mother would be sure to fill with all these blessings. Well, well, what did it matter? It would be just one blessing the less. But I suppose the West Farm brats would begin to shriek if just one raisin fell from above onto their heads, and then I should be blamed for that.

My mother suddenly appeared, looking for something in the grass, and though I was very short of time I got up and went over to help her search—the little cloud that had been between us seemed entirely forgotten.

"I suppose you haven't seen my bunch of keys, Uggi child?" asked my mother, when she saw me coming.

"No," I answered, and we took each other by the hand and hunted for them together, and when we had been searching for some time I asked her:

"Is sailing very difficult, Mama?"

"Sailing!" repeated my mother, and I didn't quite like her look, although it was friendly enough. "Why do you ask that?"

"Oh, nothing special," I answered, and began to swing her hand, and then I knocked against something hard in the pocket of her skirt.

I put my hand down into it and pulled up a bunch of keys.

"And here we have been hunting for it everywhere!" said my mother, gaily, and we both laughed very much.

We went in, and I was given newly-baked bannock and butter and we talked about Knör and about Old Papa, and Old Begga came in and said that we seemed to be enjoying ourselves, and my mother and Old Begga suddenly discovered that there was warm water in the kettle and felt the need of a cup of coffee. I was given a lump of sugar dipped in coffee, and my mother and Old Begga talked for a long time about the sort of things that interest grownups. When at last I was alone with Old Begga I asked her:

"Tell me quite truly, please, Begga, have you ever in your life seen a ship in the sky?"

"A ship!" repeated Old Begga, in a frightened voice, "in the sky . . . ? No. I must say this for the good God, that so far He has spared me visions and apparitions. Don't come and try to make me believe you have seen ships in the sky, child."

"No, I never said I had," answered I, sulkily, and thought to myself that probably grownups would never acknowledge that ships could sail across the sky, and that probably it would be a sin to see them.

So I gave up the attempt to get more out of Old Begga, and went away. Outside the house I met Maggi, who was trying to sort out some fishing tackle which he had found in the corner of the outbuilding.

"It's rotten and in a mess, like everything else here in Hamrafjördur, but it's the first sign of common sense in the late Frederick that I have yet discovered—or, for the matter of that, in the whole of Grimsstadir," he at last expressed his unvarnished opinion.

"Have you had permission to take it?" I asked absent-mindedly—and for answer I received a clout on the ear, which I immediately returned with interest.

Maggi looked at me amazed and rubbed his cheek. "How touchy you've become all of a sudden! Did you think I was in earnest?"

I admitted I had thought so, and begged him to forgive me.

"Oh, well, let's cry quits!" he answered magnanimously. "It's human to make mistakes. Take hold of this and help me a little. I must go off in a moment and see to the cows. Are you coming? I'll carry you over the stream so that you shall not wet your precious trotters. Otherwise we shall probably both of us get a lecture from mistress."

Before we went we collected a goodly supply of sorrel which we chewed as we went along, entirely at peace with each other and with life in general.

"I shall soon be having a dog, the Devil helping me," remarked Maggi, who swore more the farther he got away from the homestead, "and as soon as I have a dog, a real son of Gryla, then no damned native of Hamrafjördur will be able to put on me again. Can you stand any of the people in this district? Well, of course, you have not seen much of them so far. I myself have been here a week, so that there isn't much I don't know. But I ask you, is there any reason why I should be stared at like a monster or a ghost? I don't look any different from other people, do I? But wherever I go their eyes buzz round me like bluebottles. Every evening I look at the back of my coat to see whether any of them have got stuck to it or not. I should like to give them something to shout about—for instance, a pin or two in their evening porridge. Liquor has no effect on them, I have noticed. If they take a gulp they only go to sleep and make fools of themselves like Nonni Beggason. I suppose we shall have to

waste the best years of our life among these henchmen of Satan.
No thank you! And God knows whether or not in the end we
shan't get married to one of these vermin, one of these great
hulking creatures, one of these blockheads."

"Couldn't you lend me your dagger, so I might get even
with one of them?" said I, anxious for him to realize that
others beside him had their troubles.

"What good would a dagger be to you?" asked Maggi, in a
superior tone. "And especially such a dagger as mine? I dare
scarcely draw it out of the sheath myself, it is so sharp. When
I cut with it, it is not so much a matter of pressing home as
holding back. You don't know what you're asking, my lamb.
It slips through flesh and bone like sunlight through a pane of
glass. I often wonder whether it was made by dwarfs. I can
cut a stone with it as easily as if I were cutting cheese. Look
at this!"

Maggi took hold of a stone, halved it with one blow, and
played ducks and drakes with the two halves.

"Pray God to save you from having such a knife in your
hands," he advised me urgently, pushing the dagger back into
its sheath. "You are still too young and too beardless to go
about armed like this—and after all, why should you? You
have no enemies yet!"

"I shall soon have enemies on every blade of grass in Hamrafjördur," I asserted indifferently.

"You don't say," answered Maggi, appreciatively, and looked
at me with open and intense sympathy in his shrewd eyes. "Well,
you mustn't take to the knife unless it is a question of life and
death. It would be better to practice throwing stones, as then
you can go about with your pocket full. The round ones hit
best, you will soon find that out. If you can get hold of a
cotton reel for me I will make you a whistle that you can carry
on a string round your neck. Then you can blow it as soon as
you see war approaching, and if I am anywhere within earshot
I will soon be on the spot. Round stones are the hardest, remember that. If I had lived in France, in Napoleon's time, of course
I should most certainly have been a general. General Gruesome

would have been my name, I think. Then in the end I should
have been knighted Baron Bachmann. Doesn't that roll grandly
off the tongue? Doesn't it tickle the ears pleasantly? Do you
know that Magnus means the Great? Hell! How I should have
turned all the gentlemen and nobles upside down! I'm not too
sure I shouldn't have been called Magnus the Nightmare Rider,
or perhaps Bachmann the Firebrand. How Old Begga would
have crossed herself if anyone had told her about my dark
deeds! But seriously, if there is war and if I become a general,
what name do you think I ought to call myself."

"Maggi the Maggot," I shouted, and let my legs save me.

A little later we lay side by side on the bank of the river,
reconciled, looking for trout and minnows in a green hole.

"There are probably plenty here, although we cannot see
them," Maggi decided knowledgeably. Lacking sorrel, he
chewed eagerly on a blade of plantain. "I'll teach you something that you will be very glad to know if you promise on
your honor that you will never tell anybody the name you called
me just now."

With great solemnity the oath on my honor was carried out
and I promised never in this life, nor in the next, to allow the
name of Maggi the Maggot to pass my lips. When it was all
over I pointed out to Maggi that my oath said nothing about
writing either with my right hand or with my left, and to be
on the safe side I inquired whether it held in other languages
than Icelandic. A third oath was therefore necessary, an oath
which included even three languages. "What about writing it
on the ice with skates?" I asked, and this necessitated my legs
also being brought into the oath. When after various oaths I
was bound not alone by my hands and feet but with my whole
body, Maggi found a stone of the same kind that he had split
in two, and in a hand's turn he had scratched his initials on it.

"Now I know how to get animals for my farm," I shouted
excitedly, and thought that perhaps Our Lord had not done so
badly by me after all.

"I'll lend you my dagger," said Maggi.

"But where shall I find enough stones?" I asked.

"I'll bring you pocketfuls," Maggi promised generously.

We were late home with the cows, for which we were not thanked. I crept to bed crestfallen. That night I dreamed that some boards in the paneling behind my bed had given way, and that a band of robbers tumbled out onto me, clinging fast to my feather quilt. Onto the floor fell my blanket, with Beta, who would not let go her bit of it, and only Veiga was left lying in bed, shrieking at the top of her voice:

"Mother! Father! Hurry, the trolls have taken Beta, Uggi and the eiderdown!"

I woke and thought that at last I was really on my way to Hell. But then I rolled down onto the clay floor, and was that not Beta who was tumbling about? But surely the whole thing was a dream. Gryla sprang from her corner and began to bark, trying to bite our legs because we had disturbed her night's sleep, and then there was nothing for it but to rush up the stairs, and at the top of the stairs stood Mama and Papa looking quite strange and somehow half-blurred in the gray summer twilight—and what a lot of laughing there was when we lay in their arms and were comforted!

My mother made room for us in their bed. My father examined the hole in the wall.

"Somebody has been picking holes in the paneling," he said, and turned from my sisters to me.

"I only wanted to see what was behind," I said.

"Well, misdeeds bring their own punishment," he said shortly, and lay down. "But as a matter of fact, if one sneezes it's safer to do so outside this house than in. Every little bit of wood is as rotten as Ketilbjörn's old shark's flesh."

My mother whispered to me that now I must be a really good boy. What had happened was certainly a punishment for yesterday. Because my sisters and I had frightened Doddi and his sisters, God had frightened us. I thought this quite possible, and when I was alone I whispered to Our Lord, "How touchy You've become all of a sudden!"

Then, with a light heart, I turned over and went to sleep.

"Today we are very busy, little Uggi," said my mother, one morning, with a smile . . . and as the dandelion in the sun, so the child thrives in the warmth of a mother's tenderness. "The cotton grass is beginning to be blown off its stalk."

We all went off, each carrying a little willow basket (a present from Nonni), to collect the cotton grass which grew in a sphagnum bog.

High over the green valley, like a vault, stretched a gray sky. All round the farms the buttercups, kingcups and dandelions shone in their yellow glory like forgotten bits of yesterday's sunshine. The hills stood out clearly in the shadowless light, while the clefts and gullies faded away into the landscape. Cool and wonderfully intimate was the absolute clearness of the day, so free from mist. There was something in it that reminded me of Nonni.

"A wick of cotton grass is the very best thing for oil lamps," my mother told us, sitting on a little mound and picking all that she could reach. "I think this winter we must try to save the expensive petroleum in the kitchen and larder and in the cattle houses. At Knör we never burned anything but train oil when I was a child, even in the living room, and no light can be more pleasant to sit by, or more like the blessed fire. Oh, look! there is the marsh unquefoil. It will be out in a day or two. . . . What a lovely time summer is, with the scent of the flowers so strong that one almost forgets to miss the salty tang in the air! . . . Now, when we have filled our baskets we shall look at the little hill just above us. I am very anxious to collect some herbs—and isn't that bed straw lying like snow on the slopes over there? We must see. It is certainly rather early for lady's bed straw. We must come and pick it some other day. From the top of the hill up there we might be able to get a glimpse of the sea."

We picked many kinds of herbs and grasses on our way up the hill and arranged them very carefully in my mother's apron.

"Dear me! What a lot of cloudberries! We must fill your cap," my mother exclaimed, and we sat down in the wild thyme, inhaled its perfume and filled my cap with the berries. "When Old Papa had been to some festivity or other he always wanted cloudberry tea the next morning," she added, smiling, and began to mimic his voice, to our great delight: " 'Celia, Celia, girl, girl, where is that cloudberry tea, must I wait till Doomsday, till Doomsday?' "

We laughed so that the tears came. Longingly I asked: "When is Grandpa-from-Knör coming?"

"Old Papa will come and see us before the hay harvest, you'll see," my mother comforted me, and pulled a packet out of her pocket. "Here is a little bread and butter for us all. Oh, oh, children, don't knock me over! . . . I have seen a lot of different sorts of berries but I've scarcely seen any whortle-berries or stone brambles."

"That doesn't make any difference to me," I answered. "They are so sour."

"Don't you miss their long roots?" asked my mother, sur-prised. "They are so useful to tie up things with. But look here, we can easily use these fine roots instead. Just rub off the bark between a couple of stones—like this. Here you are, here is the true silver weed. My grandfather could remember a year so hard that people had to go and dig it up and eat the roots. . . .God often sends much want. He punishes our sins very sternly—remember that. . . . Look at this one with buds—this is the mead herb. Don't tell Old Begga that we found it, or I know what she'll give me to drink the next time I'm in bed!"

Suddenly my mother became serious. We walked on without speaking for a few moments; then she said:

"There is one thing we must try to remember, and that is to dry the herbs for poultices, in case my breasts should be troublesome—my mother always used them, I remember, and they were such a comfort."

The little cluster of whortleberries tasted both bitter and sweet; they tasted of honey and dew, and of astringent juices. My delight in the day was deep and calm. It was lovely even to fall down when it was flowering grass that tripped me up.

Over my mother and over the flowering slope there seemed to lie a rare and vigorous fertility. We were silent for long moments at a time and expressed ourselves only by a smile when we showed each other the flowers we had found. If we discovered a stone behind which a beetle had hidden itself we put it hastily back into place again, so that the creature should not be homeless.

"That's what Maggi really ought to have between his bed-clothes," laughed my mother, and showed me the swelling water avens which is so reliable for driving away fleas. "I cannot understand where that boy gets all his fleas from—whether it is because he is always playing about with the dogs, or because like goes to like! Oh, look, there's some heather! Oh, you faithful and unselfish one, you that keep green all the winter to nourish the hungry and persecuted! God will reward you according to your deserts. From your leaves also we get good tea—but *I* will not pick you. You should try sometime, little Uggi, to see whether a tuft of shepherd's purse, warmed in your hand, would not help your nosebleed. I don't believe it would, but who knows? God has not only given each herb its own taste and smell, but each also its own particular use. And each has its own peculiar attributes that cannot always be detected without knowledge. Who would think that a white flower would dye cloth red, and green would dye black? . . . How thirsty I am! What is your water like, little stream?"

She drank from my hand, and seemed to take kindly to its bitter bog-water.

"You will do better farther down," she comforted it, leaning over, and then turned toward me. "The Creator has put stones at the bottom of the streams so that we may have clear water, clean and clear for the benefit of His creatures. Look, the vernal whittloe grass has already sown its seed here in the barren sand. One would imagine that the good God would especially love such a humble plant. . . . Don't worry, Uggi love. I am only cry-ing a little because I suddenly thought of my sister Halla. . . . You and Nonni must get me a sack of crowberry branches one of these days so that I may have something to dress the leather with this winter. As a reward you shall each have a pair of socks for your Christmas shoes, and I will make your shoes myself. . . . All right, child, thanking in advance is like beginning backward, as Old Papa used to say. But tell me, where has that beacon got to?"

At last we reached the beacon—a good solid one, accustomed to stormy weather, standing on the highest point of a gravel hill. We could not see much of the sea when we got up there, just a few rocks and an inlet where there lay a couple of fishing boats with tanned sails.

"If a rock but turns its brow toward the sea, the surf beats on it immediately—it cannot stop itself," said my mother in a subdued tone, and there was a sort of listening quality in her voice. "If we were up there on the top we should have a good view, over both the fjords," she added, and looked longingly at the mountaintops of which we saw a glimpse behind the hill-slopes. "We shan't get up there today."

She stood a little longer looking out toward the sea. Then she suddenly collected herself and began quickly to descend the slope. She walked with her eyes lowered. We reached a slope on which dwarf birches grew, and there we sat down to rest.

The stream at the bottom of the valley seemed as abstracted as my mother was today; perhaps it was absorbed in its baby trout. In the fields round the farm our sheep could be seen grazing, and the lambs were playing, running about on one another's heels, knocking against one another, falling down, getting up, and running over to their mothers now and again. They knelt down and sucked with eager thrusts and bumps so that the ewes nearly fell over, and became annoyed and refused to have anything more to do with such naughty children. The thin bleating of the lambs and the deep replies of the mothers carried up to us, giving us a feeling of security.

My mother touched me softly, stroked my hand and showed me almost at our side a grayish-brown bird with black eyes ducking down among the birchwood. When we had sat there for a little, looking at it and smiling at each other, we crept away. It was a thrush.

"One does not often see them in this neighborhood at this time of the year," said my mother, softly, when we were far away from the bird.

"I thought it was only the ptarmigan that sat so faithfully on her eggs. She sometimes even allows herself to be stroked on the back. . . . Oh, dear, now the golden plover and the curlew are quiet, and the snipe has begun to cry. Is it evening already? Oh, shan't we sleep well tonight, Mother's only little boy! But what do you think Madame Anna will say to me for having neglected her all day long?"

On our way down we met my father holding down Yrsa, one of his best sheep; she was suckling a lamb. My father felt the lamb's belly.

"There now, I think you can manage till morning," he said, and let the sheep go. She turned round at once and sniffed suspiciously at her lamb.

"I cannot imagine what is the matter with Yrsa this year," said my father, angrily drying his forehead. "Went and killed her ewe lambs for me with her milk. God knows whether it's the grass here that does not suit her."

Yrsa sniffed and sniffed, and she had good reason for doing so. The lamb which they were trying to make her believe was her own was covered with blood over its head and round its throat, and down over its thin legs hung the bloody shanks of a lamb's skin which had been put over it. Dressed up like this the lamb reminded me of Maggi when he had once borrowed my father's vest, and neither my mother nor I could refrain from laughing in the midst of our tears—so pathetic and so comical did the little creature look.

My father explained to us that it was one of two lambs dropped by another sheep on which he had put the skin and which he had covered with blood from one of Yrsa's lambs. We stood for a moment to see what would happen. Yrsa recognized the skin and the smell of the blood, and had nothing against the lamb's seeking her udders, but as soon as the udders were in the lamb's mouth and it began to suck she shook it away.

"It tickles her udders," said my father, scratching his head. "She knows there is something strange in the way the lamb sucks. Well, I suppose she will settle down by degrees."

It was obvious that Yrsa was perplexed. Which was she to believe, her eyes or her nose? Clearly she felt more inclined to believe her nose. She sniffed and sniffed. Yes, the skin and smell were right enough. She began to settle down, pulled one or two tufts of green, juicy grass, looked suspiciously at her changeling, grazed busily for a time and then called suddenly, with a voice that was hoarse with sorrow, doubt and solicitude, for her child which was not her child and yet was her child, and away they went, side by side, Yrsa heavy and joyless, the child tripping along strangely solitary and homeless, with its bloody shirt, so much too large for it, flapping round its thin legs.

My mother and I walked home silently. My mother put away our cotton grass and our herbs; and when that had been attended to she collected us children in the living room, gave us our evening meal, and, sitting there with Madame Anna on her lap and the rest of us crowding round her, she sang:

> Ro, rah, rip,
> See the children trip
> Up into the mountain heights
> To look about for baa-lambs white,
> Ro, rah, rip.

That evening we felt that it was a very sad song and dried our eyes in secret, and my mother sang:

> Ro, rah, red oh,
> The lambs play on the meadow.
> The naughty tot steals up behind;
> On guard he finds our mother kind—
> Ro, rah, red.

We laughed at that and dried our eyes again, and Mother
sang:

> Ro, rah, ride,
> The little lamb that died
> Is now with God in Paradise
> Where seaside pinks and birches white
> Grow side by side in fields of light.
> Rest, rest, my love,
> Rest, rest, my dove.

And we cried and we sang, and the night came on apace.

5

A WATCHER for ships in the sky must always be on the alert, for it is when he least expects them that they sail past. On clear days he may lie from morning till night among the grassy mounds down by the river, moving only with the sun, without seeing a single ship. They must have passed while he moved, or when he forgot them for a moment, watching the red legs of the watersnipe. Who can tell when these ships will pass? For they pass continually.

"What do you do down there by the river the whole day long?" my mother often asked me; and the oftener she asked the less likely was she to get an answer, for one does not readily speak about one's ships, even to one's mother.

Besides, there were lots of other things besides ships in the sky—other things that were best dealt with in solitude.

Einar Bjarnason arrived one day, neat and tidy, on a curry-combed horse with an elaborately decorated saddle and reins which he had fashioned himself. He came to inquire about his money in case it might have been sent to my father. Every other minute he brought out his comb and his looking glass, combed his beard and hair, blinked, gesticulated with his hands, did not grumble about his disappointment. Now and again he made silent jokes to himself, jokes which he seemed to find very funny. When he rode away he winked at me, told me to visit him; if by that time he had had his money, ha! ha! he would show me something. He would make me a saddle and reins when he had the chance—hoped he would not have to skin me to get the leather for them.

This last I let pass as a joke. I nominated Einar Bjarnason as a sub-king under me, mostly for the sake of his hair and beard; let him have his own fleet and ascribed to him doughty deeds. Many a sea voyage did we make together, and often we came to each other's rescue at the last moment, although it was oftener I who helped him than he me. Wherever we went in the world he always inquired whether money was waiting for him, but nowhere did he find any.

I had many others on board as well, among them Roadside-Simbi.

I married him to the daughter of a king, and then his disguise fell off and he revealed himself as a shining prince, with beard and hair like Einar Bjarnason, and his gray horse became a mighty steed with a flowing mane and a waving tail.

Sira Björn was also in my fleet, converting the heathen. He drank heavily, and finished each sentence with "Glory be to God!"

Geir was there too, but things went badly for him, as he fell in the first battle. I soon began to miss him, and resurrected him with healing herbs and witch-songs. . . .

What a tremendous lot there was to do among the tussocks beside the stream! A minute ago it was morning and now evening had come. . . .

There were a great many things doing on the farm, too. Gryla had not been seen for several days. Where had she got to? Then one day a puppy crawled out from under the floorboard. Immediately Gryla appeared, caught him by the neck and dragged him back. She knew what happened to puppies when people got hold of them. For some time she held the fort; then one day the whole litter crawled out, seven of them, and she had to yield. She was entirely transformed, even her growl became gentle and kind, and she allowed us to make as much noise as we liked, even at dinner time. She did not chase us angrily indoors, and it never seemed to occur to her to bark or bite. But nothing saved her. The litter were put in a heap and she was allowed to choose. She took first a gray, then a black, then a black one with yellow spots. The test was repeated. This time she took first the gray, then the black-and-yellow. There was no doubt about it; she had picked out the best. The others were all put into a sack with a stone in the bottom . . . and there was the sack in the stream.

Maggi and I were told to come to an agreement about the two that were left. Maggi immediately chose the gray, and I was quite pleased at his choice. That evening we joined forces in a double christening feast of candy-sugar and currants. Each of us borrowed a white pinafore and a black shirt to hang over our shoulders, and we baptized our puppies from a tin pail. Maggi's was given the proud name of Dreyfus, mine was called Gaul; and as we could not agree which of the dogs was the prettier and the more intelligent, we began to fight. Nonni came in, parted us, and was nominated judge. He pronounced the sentence that Maggi and I must each take the whelp we liked the less and Maggi as the elder must say first. Maggi expressed the view that Dreyfus was inferior to Gaul in every way. As I expressed exactly the opposite opinion we were both satisfied and were reconciled, after which the arbitrator treated us to drops of spirits-of-ether on lumps of sugar—and some moral injunctions. . . .

While these and similar events were taking place, many ships might be sailing past in the sky.

In the kitchen Disa and Old Begga each had her own cooking-place, and these were separated by a low stone wall. It was a good thing this wall lay between them. They did not exchange many words, these two, even when they were both cooking at the same time; and when they had to speak they were as brief as possible.

"Has anyone been using the bellows?" asked Old Begga, and while she put her question she faced in exactly the opposite direction from where Disa stood.

"I have neither eaten them nor hidden them," answered Disa.

And then Disa hummed and Old Begga talked to herself in a low voice.

"Weren't the tongs here a minute ago?" asked Disa.

"If you saw them they must have been here," answered Begga.

"Well, then they must have made off on their own legs."

Old Begga mumbled, Disa hummed. But suddenly Old Begga lifted up her voice as if she were speaking to someone on the roof.

"These dung cakes are so wet they are going moldy; they could easily have stood a little more drying; they smoke instead of burning."

"N-n-n," hummed Disa, and banged the things about.

I endured the smoke.

Disa finished, covered her fire with ash, lifted up the saucepan and went away with it.

"Even the sheep-dung was better in Breidale!"

Old Begga stood up and turned round on her axle. Disa had gone. Calmly Old Begga fished up the bellows from Disa's chimney-corner and the tongs from her own. Thereupon she began to bake a bannock amid brightly glowing embers and a rain of ashes.

> *"Death like a solemn reaper,*
> *Severe and cold of mien,*
> *Moves on; and when he passes*
> *The earth lies bare and clean,"*

she sang loudly in her cracked voice, and I had a strong impression that she wished to inform Death that he had left too much between the strokes of his scythe—that he might well have been more thorough when he last visited Grimsstadir.

I tried to begin a conversation, but Old Begga—Weekday-Begga—cut me short.

"Disa has gone! Why don't you run off?"

I took no notice of her fretfulness. Whenever I spoke to Disa, Old Begga was peevish, and every time I spoke to Old Begga, Disa was annoyed; but it seemed to pass over if I were patient, and I was quite willing to be patient. I pretended that nothing was the matter when Old Begga did not answer me; I answered myself, carried on the conversation alone until it seemed to Old Begga that the time had come to put in a sensible and instructive word. Suddenly she went away, came back with a pat of butter between her fingers and spread it deftly with her thumb over a newly baked bannock which she handed to me.

"Eat, my little one—I can't say that I am happy at Hamra-fjördur."

"But there are so many flowers here, dear Begga," I said.

"Pooh! Flowers! Do flowers fill the udders with milk and the bones with marrow? No. All sorts of weeds grow in thin soil easily. I am unwilling to predict evil for anyone, but I shall be very much surprised if any luck awaits Farmer Greipur here."

"But yesterday Papa fetched a whole load of cod from the town," I insisted. "Don't you think cod tastes good?"

"In Breidale we lived well without cod, little curly-head," said Old Begga shortly, using the bellows vigorously. "How can one know what a sea-fish of that sort has eaten? Many a drowned man has been washed ashore with his bones gnawed."

"But we shall soon be having fresh sheep's milk," I went on, trying to cheer her up.

Old Begga slapped a bannock over as if it had been Disa.

"Wait until we actually see that milk and that skyr! Tordis has not grown exactly fat from the porridge made here on Grimsstadir, and Sophia's fat comes more from the warmth of her bed—and because she is fattened by those she visits at other places."

"But we've got a lot of houses at this homestead," I said unhappily.

Old Begga yawned.

"Perhaps, but I haven't seen them—not a house have I seen."

I cudgeled my brains to think of something to comfort her.

"But it is lovely being able to see the smoke from the ships that pass."

"Yes—if it makes anyone happy to see the air blackened with smoke."

"But don't you think it is lovely when the mist winds in and out along the mountainside?" I asked despairingly.

"What a blessed chatterer you are! But I feel to my joy that now the worms will not have to wait long for Bergljot Sigurdar-dottir, and, even if I would rather that it were the dew of night than the wet sea fog that lay on the grass over my grave, still it will be peaceful to rest and lovely to sleep."

With a sigh in which melancholy and relief were mixed, Old Begga shifted to a stanza from a hymn:

"*Whenever, Lord, thou callest* . . .

—all I know is, I'll be glad to go."

One scorchingly hot sunny morning I was kneeling by the stream building a dam, when a man with long gray hair and beard approached by an extraordinary path—he was riding down the middle of the stream, following each turn and bend in the gray glittering sun.

"You don't know me," he shouted, and heaved himself off his horse, thundering onto the ground like a giant. "I am Grimur-from-Ulfsstadir, your neighbor—the darling of all the women, the godfather of all the children."

"Why did you come that way?" I asked, taken aback.

"Why, you see, my horse had become rather hot in the hoofs, and I myself longed for shade. . . . Where the devil is your father, that villain Greipur?"

Grimur-from-Ulfsstadir could say things like that without offending anybody. He put me up on his horse and gave me the reins.

"Let him gallop, but don't strain him!"

I took a turn on his gray, a glorious creature, gentle and willing, with ears that expressed friendliness and good humor—all of which spoke well for his owner. When I came back I found Grimur sitting on the sod wall by the cowhouse enter-taining my father and the farm people (who were clipping sheep) with jokes that I could not understand but that made the men laugh loudly and the women blush and hide their eyes.

Apparently he had come to collect money for an altarpiece to be put in the church.

"Though what we want with an altarpiece I don't know," he laughed, waving a piece of paper in one hand and a pencil in the other. "I suppose it is really for the ladies. For not a man is born who would not rather look at the women's side of the church than at an altarpiece! If the parson did as he wished he would stop in the middle of his sermon, get down from his pulpit and go over to Maria Mens and chuck her under the chin, as I am doing now."

Maria dodged. Grimur tripped over the wool, fell down, laughed and remained lying there.

"Well, if I were a pastor I should have my Maria-lamb on every farm—but it would not be the sort of lamb that eats grass! And yet I am a pious man compared with my ancestor Sveinn. In his time things were different at Ulfsstadir; for every child his wife gave him he had another outside. The legitimate and illegitimate children often came at about the same time, and Sveinn always declared that it must be a case of twin mothers, as he called it, and therefore a sort of miracle.

" 'Next time we must be more careful, Jacobina,' he used to say. But when things had gone wrong twelve times, Jacobina wanted a separation and sent for Sira Björn. Sira Björn arrived in full dress with the sacraments and his 'Glory be to God,' but then Sveinn became quarrelsome and shouted:

" 'Twelve children in twelve years. What have you to complain about, Jacobina?'

"And he said to Sira Björn, pointing down the living room:

" 'Look there—one, two, three, four, five, six beds. You had better imitate me, Sira.'

" 'You should be more sparing with the wine and less with repentance,' answered Sira Björn, but Sveinn had plenty of liquor and was very hospitable. For Jacobina he stole the communion wine out of the priest's bag, and all ended in peace and good will. . . . How much will you give to the altarpiece, Maria of my heart?"

All gave to the altarpiece except Nonni. He definitely refused to have anything to do with it, saying he didn't hold with altarpieces. . . .

It was strange to see how small and thin the sheep became when their thick wool had been removed. It was almost impossible to recognize them and it seemed as if they scarcely recognized themselves. The lambs sniffed at them and gazed at them and then ran away terrified. The mothers ran after the lambs, bleating reassurances. A lamb would prick up its ears; it knew its mother's voice but had never seen that particular mother before, and would much rather eat grass than suck milk from such an apparition. Even toward evening one might see here and there a lamb running toward the mountains, amazed at its own loneliness and followed by a bleating mother.

I had the same sort of feeling as the lambs when, for the first time, I saw my mother without clothes. In Sophia's house there was a room where my parents kept trunks and hung their clothes—and it happened there one morning. We were busy, as we were going to Fagravik, and I had been washed in the tub and was dressing myself over by the window, when my mother suddenly took off all her clothes over there in the half-darkness at the other end of the long, narrow room, and twisted and turned herself while she washed. Never shall I forget her white distended body against the unpainted paneling, dark with age. The light of the sunny morning came in subdued through the west window of the room, but it was strong enough to show me her constantly moving body, strange and shining against the dark background of the room, and producing a dim, wild and vigorous warmth.

This incident made an extraordinary impression on me. I was in the same state as the lambs: I did not recognize my mother. The picture I had had of her in my mind was suddenly shattered, suddenly fell away from my eyes like scales. In its place came this image, never to be forgotten. If I had never seen her like this I might never have known what a mother is. She might, perhaps, have been always in my mind a shadowy picture, unreal, half-obliterated, smothered beneath clothes and plaited hair. . . .

We were all three going to Fagravik—my father, my mother and Uggi Greipsson, future priest.

The sun shone sharply in the heavens. The sparks from its flaming beams bounced off the mountain lakes like little balls of light. A pair of guillemots sailed proudly and silently through the heat-sodden air. As we rode down the other side of the ridge we passed a homestead pressed hard against the mountainside in the bend the river made, and overshadowed by a jutting piece of rock behind it. This homestead, Teigur, seemed to be cowering on its narrow ledge like a whipped dog. We rode down along the Stada River. Lifelessly its gray surface reflected the sun. Sparkling and flashing, a flock of terns attacked us with shrieks and flapping wings as we approached their hatching-place; they flew round us in curves and whirls, knocking our heads with their hard breastbones if we defended ourselves, and filling our ears with an indescribably angry noise which, in conjunction with the burning sun and the heavy thunder of the surf from the near-by fjord, made me dizzy and confused. The terns, white against the sky, were like ever-changing hieroglyphics traced swiftly on the blue sheet of heaven.

We rode along the fjord, and for the first time I saw the sea close at hand and absorbed its exciting, stupefying odor of salt and decay, its frank mixture of the nauseating and the fresh and invigorating. It made me breathless, drew me to it—foreign and challenging, full of infinite promises of achievement and of death.

The farmstead Fagravik lay beneath the mountain and awaited us proudly and hospitably; and broad and proud and hospitable was my aunt Sigurveig, "Sister-in-Fagravik," as she came to meet us. She lifted me down from the saddle with the words:

"Well, monsieur, I'll soon turn you upside down!"

To my great surprise she then lifted me down carefully, right side up, and kissed me again—and there I stood and felt that she had taken my heart by storm. Something secret had transpired between us.

A tall thin man, whom I took to be one of the farmhands, came over to me and kissed me kindly, averting his eyes. And then my four cousins and two other children (whom I later found to be foster children) surrounded me and, laughing and kissing, pulled me behind the homestead where we could be by ourselves. There we sat down, each on a mound, and looked at one another and laughed and beamed, as happy as the sunshine and the flowers around us. Never before had I met such frank, straightforward children, or children with whom I felt at home so soon. From the outset they treated me naturally and without reserve, and the confidence they thus showed me lightened my heart. It was as if my inner consciousness had been freed from all that weighed it down, and had been filled instead with the lightest cotton grass. When I laughingly told them I was quite sure that I could, without taking a run, jump right up onto the high mountain behind the farm, they laughed and attacked me with friendly pushes and shoves.

"Listen to him! Oh, you silly! Why don't you jump over the river and fetch us some sweets from the shop?"

And my eldest cousin, Björgvin, caught hold of me tight and swung me round and round until we were both dizzy, while he kept on repeating: "Uggi-Puggi, Uggi-Puggi."

Beta, the eldest girl, was graver than the other children. She only smiled when the others laughed; and she had a lot to ask me about Breidale. When she smiled she showed her upper teeth and a broad light-red strip of gum.

"You smile just like that man who kissed me," I said suddenly.

"Do you call my father 'that man'?" asked Beta, and I did not yet know her well enough to realize that her stern tone was only assumed.

I must have become very red in the face, for the children laughed at me so much that the tears ran down their cheeks. I can remember that I was very vexed at the mistake I had made, but still more surprised that Bjarni, the owner of Fagravik and the husband of Sister-in-Fagravik, looked so insignificant. I had heard vaguely that she had married him in spite of her parents' opposition, and I had involuntarily pictured him as broad and important as a magistrate. Having seen him, I should have understood better if she had refused to marry him except under pressure. However, I soon changed my opinion. Unassuming though he was in appearance and character, he was loving to his children, considerate and a good companion, grave and yet merry—especially when he had had a glass or two—and at the same time he was a daredevil and a real man. He crossed every river on horseback wherever he struck it; he sailed on the fjord even when the waves were high from shore to shore; and he came home from the most dangerous journeys silent and uncommunicative as always, and as if he had only been for a run around the farm. And then suddenly he would burst forth with a little laugh, a spasm of gaiety:

"What do you think? The rudder broke in my hand in the middle of the fjord!"

Sister-in-Fagravik's hand would go to her heart.

"The rudder?"

Bjarni would answer, firmly dismissing the matter, half-annoyed:

"Yes, yes, the rudder." And he would refuse to answer any other questions on the subject.

Later on I learned to know these characteristics in Bjarni, but even during my first visit he rose in my esteem the more I saw of him. In spite of the fact that he lisped, his grave friendliness made a deep impression on me.

We children did not, of course, sit for long just looking at one another. We started to play hide-and-seek, and I crawled in under our saddles where they lay in a heap. From my hiding-place I saw Sister-in-Fagravik put her head out of the farmhouse door, look round hastily, and then let out past her a man with a sack on his back.

"Be as quick as you can, good Lundi," she said quietly, "and don't let yourself be seen from the windows."

I knew at once where the man was going and, lying there, so well hidden among the saddles, I began to cry to my heart's content. . . . I was so sorry for my mother. It suddenly struck me that not once during our ride had she mentioned Fagravikurfjara or her sister Halla. I remembered my mother's heavy body on her swollen legs, her thin ankles and feet. I remembered her thin hands so full of tenderness. . . . In the midst of my crying I noticed that Jonina, the foster daughter, whose turn it was to be "it," was standing looking at me with one brown eye—where the other was looking it was always impossible to say. As soon as her glance met mine, she ran away, shouting:

"Where has Uggi hidden himself? I cannot find Uggi. . . . Uggi-Puggi! Uggi-Puggi!"

Had she really not seen me? I almost thought not. I began to rub my eyes with my sleeves, but found they had become covered with horsehair that stuck fast to my face, crept into my mouth, tickled my nose and blurred my eyes. Puffing and sneezing I crawled out. No one was so eager to help me as Jonina—she was sweet and helpful to all. It was always:

"Oh, Jona! . . . I can't find my scissors!" Or, "Jona, have you seen my cap?"

And Jonina found everything, had seen everything, knew where everything was. I thought it was because she could see in two directions at once, but my cousins told me that it was because she "could see farther than the tip of her nose."

My two youngest cousins, who were about my age, Hanna and Stina, were very pretty little girls, which they did not seem to realize, and their charm was further enhanced by their innocent, frank, entirely carefree attitude toward life. There was something about the children in Fagravik that reminded me of Grimur-from-Ulfsstadir's gray horse—the expression of one never exposed to ill-treatment or bad temper, and always well cared for. I have never met children or grownups so absolutely open to all sorts of emotions—joy, sorrow— sympathy, anger. If they imagined that they had hurt anybody's feelings they were inconsolable. They were always knitting something for one another, for relations, for the servants on the farm, or strangers. They were always happy if they could make others happy. Never did they purposely do anything they thought would grieve somebody else. The servants loved them, adored them, left very seldom, never wanted to go away from Fagravik.

All this was very moving and fell like dew on my heart, and yet perhaps the most touching thing of all was the relationship in which Jona and Siggi stood to their foster parents. Siggi was a couple of years younger than my cousin Björgvin. He was a hardy, noisy little chap whom Sister-in-Fagravik had more trouble to keep tidy than all the other children put together. No sooner was he outside the door than he was dirty, torn, blue and bloody. He was always smiling, showing two rows of shining white teeth, full of mischief and fun. It was said that he could not go through a door without bumping his head, could not see water without getting wet up to his waist. His hair was always cut very short and his head continually changed its shape according to the situation of his bumps.

From Breidale I was accustomed to open-handed hospitality, many kinds of cakes, much food. Nevertheless, our reception in Fagravik overwhelmed me. In the midst of our hide-and-seek I was called in. The table shone with damask, silver, white-and-gold porcelain, and at each place there were two cups and a cake plate and in the middle of the table many plates piled with cakes. First of all, we were served with chocolate, and when no one wanted more chocolate we were offered coffee. When I had eaten five kinds of cake and was obliged to stop, there were still seven other kinds that I had not sampled. When at last we had finished our coffee—which was rounded off by a schnapps that even I was allowed to taste—the table was cleared, but only to be laid again, this time for dinner.

I slipped quietly down from my chair, crept under the table between the legs of chairs and of people and got out of the room. At the table in another room I found the children and the servants collected around the rest of the chocolate, the coffee and the cakes. There we sat and thought up practical jokes, guessed riddles, and told tall stories—a gay pastime. The best story-tellers were Jona, my cousin Beta, and an old woman, Ragna, whom all my cousins loved and who loved them, a gray and colorless little creature, very silent when she was not telling stories. Hanna and Stina had their own method with stories. Gravely and convincingly they gave themselves up to the tale as one abandons oneself to a dream. Later on I came to like their stories best of all; for they could make even the simplest narrative glitter and shine like snow in sunshine, and just as, on a sunny winter's day, the traveler may be overcome by snow-blindness, so their inspired stories were able to shut off the outside world, and the listener would sit absorbed in a rare, poignant wonder.

When Sister-in-Fagravik had at last served up all her food— soup, roast, stew, salted and smoked meat, fresh salmon, dried fish, sharks' meat, halibut, sweet soup thick with almonds and raisins—we all went in a group to visit my mother's sister, Halla-in-Fagravikurfjara. I had eaten a big meal, but all the way down to the shore I felt extraordinarily empty, starving and unwell, plagued by suspense. I walked along holding my mother's hand and would not leave her, although the children laughed at me, turned somersaults, made jokes, asked me to run races. I walked with my eyes on the ground, clutching my mother's thin hand. I was certain that she understood me; otherwise I think I should have been forced to sit down and give in. I saw, in spite of the gaiety she assumed, a glimmer of tears in the corners of her eyes, and this comforted me and helped me.

If Fagravik stood open to all beholders and to all the winds of heaven, Fagravikurfjara was so concealed that one almost fell over it, as it were. Suddenly it stood there, just in front of our feet: a couple of green mounds in a field verdant and grassy— safely hidden, with small smiling windows. A deep healing calm suddenly relieved my tension—here surely no one could suffer need! A crowd of toddlers tumbling over one another in the yard like a litter of puppies suddenly rushed into the house, tripping over themselves and rolling and falling. We children began to laugh, but to my surprise only Bjarni laughed with us, and even he started at once to speak of other things.

We remained for a time in the yard waiting; but as no one came, my father knocked three times, in the usual way, on the outer door. After some delay a man with a broad, pale face came out, a short man with small eyes and a large mustache. He pretended to be surprised at our visit, greeted us all a little too loudly and wordily, and at the same time blocked the entrance.

"I can find my own way in," said my mother, and wanted to go in, but he moved between her and the door with small tripping steps and said, in a harsh voice:

"She's coming in a minute. Halla's coming in a minute."

His small eyes traveled up to my mother's face, and then suddenly he stepped aside and let her go in; and, hanging onto her skirt, I followed her through the dark, narrow, worn passages.

We found Halla in the living room. She was sitting on a trunk with the children round her and under her skirts, like a hen with her chickens. She looked broad as a hen, too, and she was very ugly. Her face was a cross between my mother's and Ketilbjörn's, but it lacked my mother's radiant vitality and Ketilbjörn's hard energy. It was flabby and dull, and her whole appearance was slack, supine and unhealthily fat. My mother stopped for a moment. They looked at each other, but neither of them said anything. Then they fell into each other's arms, and the memory of their tears still cuts me to the heart.

The windows that looked so happy and safe from the outside gave little light. The green-roofed house was very small inside and so damp that water was running down the walls. The floor and the paneling did not look clean, and smelled very bad. A cupboard fastened to the wall was full of cracked cups; the cakes lay in a heap in a bread-basket which had once been lacquered but was now rusty, warped and shabby, and all of them were of the same kind that we had just eaten at Fagravik. My cousin

Beta came in when my mother and Halla had had their cry out and had begun to talk a little. Out of a big basket which she had on her arm she took a cloth, cups and plates. It was heart-breaking to see Halla arrange these foreign things with trembling hands, but most sorrowful of all was the obvious joy which slowly spread a shimmer of childish pride over her face with its greasy, dirty skin. From behind boxes, from behind the clothes hanging on the wall, from behind the beds and even from under the beds, the unkempt, dirty, sniveling faces of children looked out with the frightened eyes of animals. The tender skin of their faces was marred by scabs and running sores. If any of the little ones were captured by my mother they allowed themselves to be petted with obvious pleasure, but at the first opportunity they slipped away and hid again. I saw Beta wink at them, saw a certain understanding on the faces with the open mouths and roaming eyes—then suddenly they ran away out of the living room.

"I think these cups are lovely," said Halla, and pointed out to my mother the gilded cups which Sister-in-Fagravik had brought. "Mama had a tea-service just like that, I remember. If you get it, one day I will come and drink coffee with you at Grims-stadir."

My mother answered with a little laugh that a lot of our things had been broken in moving, but that she still had a cup or two of her own if Halla would come some day and visit her, which she really must do soon. Couldn't she come home with her now?

Halla sighed deeply and shook her head.

"Who would look after the children?"

"I could do that," offered Beta, eagerly.

"No, you must bring the children with you—you must all come. I will find sleeping-places for you all," said my mother, gaily.

Halla sat down despondently.

"How in the world could we travel with all these children? No, dear sister; I am afraid we must wait. My Eiki is the only one who can go away from home. I will arrange with him to come and see you some Holy Day. Then he can tell you how we are. We others will come another day—next year."

Halla went off and made the coffee. She made my mother promise to sit still. We sat holding hands and avoiding each other's eyes. The others were called in and sat on boxes, bed-steads or on one another's knees. My father and Bjarni had been cheering up Eirikur, and he was now talking ceaselessly, noisily, with a queer, cold, surface gaiety. It seemed odd to me that he did not understand that my father and Bjarni spoke to him and treated him as if he were a child, or, rather, a moron. The women talked to each other in low voices, while the Fagravik children all had Fagravikurfjara children on their knees and whispered to them and caressed them. These small outcasts of humanity felt safe and at home with them, and the children from Fagravik saw to it that most of the cakes went the right way.

Halla kept on pressing us to have more. Her whole face beamed when my father, either innocently or thoughtlessly, praised her baking and said:

"Look here, Veiga, your cakes are not a patch on these; they were not nearly so crisp."

"I did not know that your teeth were so bad, Brother Greipur, or I would have tried to make mine crisper," answered Sister-in-Fagravik, sympathetically.

The coffee was bad, hopelessly bad, impossible to praise, and it was for this reason that most people drank three cups and some even four: no one wanted Halla to notice that it didn't please them and that they had already had enough.

After we had finished the coffee we children ran out. We went along the shore and collected mussels and shells. Each of the Fagravik children took one of the Fagravikurfjara children by the hand, and my big cousins were almost bent double with friendliness and solicitude. I succeeded in getting hold of a little girl of about two years, bow-legged and very wet behind, with the eyes and expression of a lamb.

"What is your name?" I asked her.

"Celia," she laughed, and looked up at me, showing small, damp teeth.

I stood quite still and looked down at her. So she had been named after my mother! I was so glad that she looked as she did. I found even her bow-legs quite pretty. . . .

The next year all these children died in a murderous epidemic. I saw my little cousin only this once and I was with her for perhaps an hour—perhaps two, perhaps three—but when I heard of her death I had a queer feeling that it was a mistake; that it was not true she was dead. Other people, on leaving this world, have changed color in my mind . . . I still sometimes expect this little cousin Celia to come from round a corner, from behind a bush—small, bow-legged, with a wet behind and the eyes of a lamb. . . .

My mother and Halla walked on together, sat down on stones by the seaside and talked or sat silent, looking out over the sea. Once they had played together at Knör, had baked little fish in half a frying pan, until they were called home by their mother and put to bed—two small, sleepy heads on the same pillow. Now they sat there, a pair of dark, heavy creatures against the green white-edged ocean.

I kept away from the line of seaweed, in which there were dried jellyfish and the remains of dead fish and other sea creatures. Little Celia talked without ceasing. I did not understand much she said, but it didn't matter—we were friends.

When we went we left Halla standing in the midst of her flock of children looking after us. She was one large smile, although the tears were running down her cheeks without ceasing, from her small eyes down over her fat cheeks. Eiki, who had become more and more loud-voiced, wanted to come with us. Never shall I forget Halla as she stood there, or Eiki, hovering round my father and Bjarni like a little yapping dog. I put my hand into my mother's—I was so tired.

Then we went back to Fagravik, the sea breezes wrapping us round.

The following day we rode home. Sister-in-Fagravik and

Bjarni accompanied us as far as the Stada River. When my mother said goodbye to Sister-in-Fagravik she whispered a few words of thanks and burst into tears, weeping heavily. And the rest of the way home she cried at intervals. My father was silent, chewing his tobacco. I sat and thought about Hildiridur. . . . I would give her a gray horse.

6

ONE day Stebbi arrived—Sophia's cousin, Stefan Arnason the carpenter. He came, with his plane, his saw, his chisel and his wooden hammer, to build our new house, a large house with two stories and an attic, eight rooms in all. Our horses dragged home timber, dragged it after them like tired, folded wings.

Stebbi carried a carpenter's rule also. He measured and he sawed. He had whole boxes full of strange-looking planes, such as had never been seen before, and with these he made our doors and windows. He was forever twirling round, jumping here and jumping there. All his things disappeared, seemed to hide themselves. He forgot everything he had been told, and was forever rushing after my father.

"Listen here, Greipur, what was it we decided?"

My father decided there were to be crosses on the doors. But which way were they to be turned?

Stebbi wanted to have the long arm downward as in church windows.

"That is like Our Saviour's cross," he said eagerly, and took a pinch of snuff. "That is how the crosses are in the churchyard."

"Well, yes," answered my father, shortly, "but this is not a churchyard, and we are not going to crucify anybody on our doors. It is usual to have them the other way."

"Both ways are usual," objected Stebbi. "I have seen them both ways. I cannot say how they have it abroad, but a cross is a cross. To put a cross upside down I should consider almost blasphemy."

Stebbi measured boards lengthwise and crosswise, measured planks, measured and measured, muttered numbers, wrote them down with a broad, blunt carpenter's pencil; was uncertain what he had said, measured again, wrote again. His head became quite round and very large with all these figures, and yet he often held his forehead, had no room for more, could not stuff it in. Sometimes he lay down all among the shavings and slept with his jacket over his head. He had thick legs and was short in the body, and how such short thick legs could have such supple knees was a constant riddle to me. Also he had a peculiar way of walking, heels first, "hack-hack" on the ground.

He worked in the shed, but moved out into the yard whenever the weather permitted. There was a strange muted music in all his work, the music of the plane gliding over the soft wood or rasping against the branches, the songs of the various types of saws, the wood breaking under the chisel, preceded by the heavy thud of the wooden hammer, the twitter of the gimlet, the violent struggle between hammer and nail, and the sharp scratching of the file.

My sisters and I liked to stay near him, and to play with the shavings, the sawdust and the bits of wood. We were not welcome, but he left us in peace—he very seldom answered our questions. He was certainly a little deaf, but it was a queer deafness, it came and went, I don't know how. He used to mumble to himself and speak to his tools, to his own limbs, to his materials or to unseen friends—always with a drawl, as if the words stuck to his mouth.

"I am coming tomorrow . . . today I have no time. . . . Silence, creature! I tell you I'm coming tomorrow. . . ."

So he would stand and talk to himself while he planed, or would say to a finger that he had scratched:

"All right. *All* right, I'll see to some ointment for you—only leave me in peace now! If blessed Frederick had been alive he would have put some new skin on you already. Sophia and Disa do not understand such things as the old man did. . . . Now then, you old knot, was it really necessary for you to spoil my plane? That scratch cannot be remedied for two kroner fifty, and you won't be any the better for it. If I turn you inside you will sit in the dark. If I turn you outside you will be painted over. Even dead things are full of evil and try to be annoying. The branches act as thorns in the flesh of the tree."

Stebbi was very childish. If anyone neglected him he went to bed and pulled the coverlet over his head—and I think he cried. Things that affected others did not touch him. Irritable or angry words did not trouble him, and he was not upset by nagging and mockery. He even laughed at such things, and they put him in a good temper. But if his after-dinner coffee were forgotten he would probably go to bed and refuse to get up before the next afternoon, and then he might turn deaf and dumb for several days and speak to no one.

But if a wagtail flew over his work and left droppings on some plank or other he would forget everything, stump right through the yard, take large doses of snuff and ask everybody to come and see the mess.

One day Hjorleifur, my enemy, came over from the other farm. I was not sure what he wanted or whether he meant to fight me, so I only stood and looked at him and remained at my post. Leifur did not say much to begin with. His brown oval face with the quick dark eyes attracted me very much. I thought it was a pity that we were enemies, but avoided showing it.

Leifur pulled a pretty painted sheep's horn out of his pocket and said:

"Here's a bellwether for you. If you would like him you may have him. He knows the neighborhood well, but you must keep him tied up for the first few days."

I accepted the gift and murmured my thanks, overwhelmed, remorseful and embarrassed.

"Doddi told me to tell you that if you would like some of his sheep and cattle he will sell them to you very cheaply."

I went off with Leifur to the West Farm, bargained with Doddi and we were all happy. Doddi and I agreed to build a dairy together and in the midst of our planning who should find us but my mother and Gudrun—my mother happy and playful, Gudrun no longer angry. My mother said that as we were all such good friends we must come back to the East Farm for chocolate and fresh-baked pancakes, and she insisted until Gudrun and even Toroddur agreed to come back with her.

Stebbi laid aside his plane and hammer, as happy as a child. All work was neglected. The house smelled of chocolate, cakes and coffee—there was great joy at Grimsstadir.

"Your children are really very well-behaved now," Gudrun said as she drank her third cup of chocolate.

My mother was just about to fill up the coffeepot; probably she did not hear—at any rate she did not answer.

Toroddur's eyes danced happily round the room, and his slow tongue struggled with the words like a giant with blocks of stone:

"With the late . . . Frederick . . . I was . . . good friends . . . I shall not quarrel . . . with you without reason . . . either."

My father laughed.

"There is no hurt in a little bickering between neighbors; it's always a change. But one must keep one's temper—must never be unforgiving."

Toroddur looked at him thoughtfully, a little uncertain how to take him.

This Toroddur was a worthy man in every way, and Gudrun was a good woman. She was rather petty and apt to be touchy about her children, but, although her manner and appearance were against her, she was in reality kind and sympathetic. We always got on very well with these neighbors of ours, and when, a few years later, they went to America, I continued for years to exchange letters with the boys. For some months every year we all had lessons together with a wandering schoolmaster, and at the examination in the spring, held in the presence of the parson, there was always a rivalry among Doddi, No-No and me. I kept the first place bravely for a few years; then, in spite of Doddi's conscientiousness, it was No-No who beat me. Gudrun smiled awkwardly at me every time I gained the first place—but when No-No won she was so glad that she could not restrain her tears. However, all this happened, of course, much later.

At this particular chocolate feast Sophia also was present. Sophia! . . .

I was fascinated by this mysterious woman with her dark, intelligent eyes, her aggressive smile, her talkative tongue and carefully-modulated laughter. For a time I was quite in love with her, as I had formerly been with Sigridur-in-the-Loft. I would sit and watch the play of her features during a conversation, allow myself to be rocked on the waves of her talk and her laughter, sit and devour her with my eyes. She sometimes noticed it, and I felt that I was not displeasing to her. But even when she smiled the most—and she was accustomed to making herself felt, enjoyed her power to dominate—there was something hectic, something unnatural, about it, like sunshine in winter. Her manner toward most people had in it a rather contemptuously teasing quality which amazed me with its mixture of openness and pretense. If she used this manner toward my mother, as she did now and again, I would seek out a solitary place and cry with anger and despair. My mother was quite capable of answering back, but, as the daughter of Ketilbjörn-from-Knör, she sometimes lost her temper a little, and that irritated me, for I thought that in this lay defeat.

Otherwise my mother and Sophia had been friends from girlhood and got on well together. But I do not think, although she never in my hearing said anything about it, that my mother liked Sophia's staying in bed so late every day and at night keeping everyone up beyond the usual bedtime. A certain unusual irritability in my mother, coupled with certain isolated remarks of hers, made me suspect this.

"Don't you think it would be a good thing for you to have a husband who could teach you to get up in the morning?" she said one day, jokingly—but it was a Ketilbjörnish joke.

To this Sophia smilingly answered:

"If I had a husband I should, for the first time, have a real reason for staying in bed."

Sophia was often gadding about, generally to town, but she also visited the sick here and there in the parish. She never had to be pressed to go on a journey, whatever time she was fetched, and if it was a case of nursing, which she both liked and had a talent for, she would sit night and day with the patient without taking off her clothes and with no more sleep than forty winks on a chair now and then. She had nursed many. They all wanted her again as soon as there was anything the matter, and she was always willing to go—and she was respected and loved by all her old patients. I realized nothing of all this to begin with. I saw her leading a desultory sort of life on the farm, an existence which both attracted and repelled me, chiefly the latter. She could never keep quiet for long at a time. If someone did not come and fetch her she would borrow a horse from my father and ride off to visit her friends in town. She often wanted to borrow my mother's gray, even if she did not say so in so many words, but my mother openly refused to understand her hints.

"What a lovely horse your gray is!" Sophia would burst out while she sat preparing herself for a visit to town.

To which my mother would answer heartily but shortly: "Yes," and then no more would be said on the subject.

Sophia always took a long time titivating herself, going about in her nightclothes, rich nightclothes, several skirts and dressing-jackets over her nightdress—going about with a comb in her mouth, with flashing glances and a joke on her lips, but always very much afraid of meeting a man.

She was mysterious to me, an unsolved riddle. She was always whispering and talking to Disa. If I came upon them they raised their voices and went on talking of things about which I could not imagine they ever needed to whisper.

They were certainly very fond of each other, but sometimes they quarreled. Sophia would be snappish, and Disa would snap back at her, and there would be much unpleasantness. Then they suddenly seemed to belong entirely to this old decaying farmstead where even the necessities of life were scarce and ineffectual, and where an acrid musty smell pervaded the place; where the desolation, so strangely akin to her, which at times spread itself over Sophia's face in a single hour, could take from it every vestige of youth and gaiety, and turn her great eyes into two dead glass marbles. . . .

How strange are human beings! How ruled by terror amid

the vast misunderstandings that engulf them! Deep are the
wells of their souls; rich the sources from which they draw endur-
ance; incomprehensible their capacities alike for short-lived joy
and endless disappointment—for hidden suffering, and the
roses that spring anew each day on life's blood-spattered battlefield. . . .

We called at Vegeirsstadir one day on our way back from
church, and were invited in. I cannot remember whether it was
the brother and sister, Valdor and Sigurborg, or Goldsmith Karl
and his wife Ingibjörg who asked us, for both couples were
present in the room where we were entertained with coffee,
chocolate and cakes.

And what did I do but fall violently in love with Anna, while
for minutes at a time I did not even look at Hildiridur?

Now that I found my feelings toward Hildiridur changing,
I felt there was a double necessity for becoming a parson. It
was a good thing that my father and mother had already begun
to discuss who should prepare me for the grammar school.

What was this Anna like? She was a cheerful arrogant girl,
sleek and big-limbed, with a good figure. She resembled most of
all a wet stone glistening in the sun, a large, well-formed stone,
fine and well-polished—almost a precious stone, or at any rate
a rare stone. Her heart was a stone too, at any rate toward me.
My infatuation for her was long and unhappy, the longest and
unhappiest in my life, the only alleviation being other infatua-
tions which occurred now and again, like lovely days in a year
of bad weather. How often are our hearts most faithful in
adversity! However, it was not always Anna who followed Hugleik the Reckless into war, or was saved by him and taken to wife;
sometimes it was Hildiridur. But the radiant Anna—who did
not always seek protection but who gave it, who was straight and
resolute, unbending and undismayed, cold in appearance and
cold of speech but with a warm, strong hand and a hidden glow
behind her ice-gray eyes—was created to be a Valkyrie, created
for vengeance, for war and for heavenly glamour.

Valdor and Sigurborg had another sister on the farm. She

had once been married but had lost her husband and was now insane. She cried continually or sat silent and remote. Everyone on the farm loved her, was sorry for her, cared for her, looked after her like a sick child. Her name, Arnbjörg, was the name also of one of Valdor's and Sigurborg's servants, apparently a sort of foster daughter, a queer girl and a clairvoyant. She spoke very seldom, and when she did it was in a strange, thin, bird-like voice, hoarse but penetrating. They had still another foster daughter, Sigrun, and the insane Arnbjörg also had a daughter, Sigurborg, a dark, quiet girl, with skin like ivory, a face that never smiled, sad eyes. I saw very little of her—she never played with the rest of us—but she would sit on a little mound or stand at the window, patiently watching us but without any apparent pleasure, and then suddenly she would disappear.

Goldsmith Karl was a man with irascible lines in his forehead, quick glances and movements, a silent man who attacked all outdoor tasks like a berserk, and did the work of two. But whenever he was free he sat indoors at his work-table, often with a yellow flame on a bluish root planted beside him, making gold rings, engraving names or decorating riding whips. He made silver filigree, brooches and narrow rings for cap tassels from silver leaf, or strung together coins for chains and bracelets, all with a tender, careful hand and with a glint of joy in his expressive gray eyes. A splendid man, silent yet full of life, early gray-haired, a lover of horses.

His wife Ingibjörg was a vigorous woman, worthy and well-dressed. On their house, themselves, and their pretty daughter there was the stamp of cleanness and well-being, happiness and comfortable living. They were excellent people, reserved, with hidden but strong feelings—good people, proud and honorable.

One day the lambs were separated from their dams and driven up into the mountains. It was wonderful to see them rushing off in a flock, scarcely reaching to the knees of the men who were shepherding them—yes, scarcely as big as our largest dog! Such a noise of anxious and plaintive bleating surrounded them that the barking of the dogs was almost drowned. And then suddenly all the sorrowful noise ceased, seemed to sink into the earth and disappear; just here and there a voice was heard. And then the whole flock of lambs burst out in full power again—*maa-a! maa-a!* Their voices showed how the hearts of the little lambs slowly tired and gave in. It was strange to watch how every mound and dip in the landscape they went through was outlined by the curly backs of the lambs.

The lambs had gone, the wool was washed and sold. Summer was coming, the haymaking was upon us. Wood for new rake-teeth, new scythe-handles, a summer place for the anvil—all was in order.

Then one day came Grandpa-from-Knör, Ketilbjörn Hrana-son-from-Knör.

"Celia, Celia! Have you quite deserted us?" he shouted, and jumped off his sweating horse. "Mama's tears washed me out of bed, and I almost fell and hurt myself. What have you been thinking of? The glass in my telescope is almost worn out, it has been so polished, so polished. And I, the old man, I have comforted her by saying, 'Celia has forgotten you—now you must forget her!' . . . Oh, I see! Now I understand! You want children, more children, always children. . . . At last I said to Mama: 'Now I am going off to fetch her—have my stick ready!' But of what use now are all our preparations? . . . Can you be ready in the autumn—visit us before the winter? . . . Good. There, I will shut down the telescope when I go back to Knör. . . . I know you, Maggi, you stick. Here, take my horse!"

Life and jollity and liver oil came to the farm with Ketil-björn—liver oil, cod-liver oil! In his broad, flapped breeches he stood there, legs wide apart, a flaming orange scarf round his neck.

When he saw Disa he laughed.

"Why, there's Disa! Good day, Disa—still childless?"

Disa stalked off on her chair-like legs, blushing right down into the depths of her wrinkles. Grandpa-from-Knör turned to Stebbi:

"Listen, you semi-giant. Why do you let your plane drag you along? Be a little lighter in your movements; don't be so heavy, so heavy."

"It is not the plane that drags me, but my hand that directs the plane, and my brain that directs my hand," Stebbi answered, laboriously. "The blessed Frederick always said, 'Stebbi is ruled by his soul.'"

"Does your soul live in your brain, you bit of wood-shaving?" replied Grandpa-from-Knör, in a vexed voice. "Never have I heard anything so absurd. 'Blessed Frederick,' did you say? He paid his rent, it's true, but look at the farm here! Look at the buildings! Just a rabbit-warren. His homeopathic soul has evidently ruled here, ruled here long enough."

"Blessed Frederick was a wise man," answered Stebbi, decidedly, but quite calmly.

"And you are a fool, a fool," laughed Ketilbjörn, patting him on the shoulder.

Grandpa-from-Knör grumbled discontentedly about my father's building plans.

"Is it a palace you're trying to build? Look at it! You will never get this house finished—not in this life, nor in the next. When you die you will chop the wood from it for your coffin, your coffin."

My father reddened.

"Do you people at Knör make your own coffins?"

"Nonsense! Splitting hairs!" said Grandpa-from-Knör. "If one shaves away the skin from one's own jaws, it's one's own affair—but think of your children, think of Celia."

"You mention children—I can give you greetings from your Halla," answered my father, and added innocently: "We were in Fagravikurfjara the other day."

Grandpa-from-Knör put his hands behind the flap of his breeches, walked up and down, was silent. . . .

Ketilbjörn hung about his daughter like a spoiled child about its mother.

"Celia! Celia! Where are you? Where have you hidden

yourself? . . . We miss you every morning and every evening at
Knör. Your mother's ewe lamb, your old father's fatted calf,
fatted calf! . . . No, no! We mustn't have all this caressing.
There, there, my dove . . . there, there, my dove!"

If my mother mentioned her sister Halla or Fagravikurfjara
he immediately changed the subject.

"About that matter enough has been said—more than enough.
Eirikur is a braggart—and that's enough. A boaster he is, a
boaster! Whatever made her go off and marry him? One child
would have been enough, one child, perhaps two, and then she
ought to have sent the wretch off! . . . Arranged to send him
away, to America, or under the ground—preferably under the
ground. I don't want to see him, don't want to meet him, don't
want to have anything to do with him. One wades about in his
chatter as in a bottomless morass. A ticket or a funeral . . . he
will never get anything else from me, never from me, never
from Ketilbjörn."

Grandpa had brought us children numbers of presents, all
sorts of sweets, handkerchiefs with pictures on them, a gold
watch with a gold chain.

"*Tick-tock, tick-tock,*" he laughed, and held it to my ear.
"Here are secrets for you. A watch in the pocket, look after the
time, get up early, four o'clock in summer, six o'clock in winter,
keep busy, keep a hand on the servants, cheat the merchants—
brisk in your dealings, a fox in commerce. These are Old Papa's
injunctions, Ketilbjörn's catechism."

How happy I was listening to all his talk! His incredible nose
hung down right into the iron-gray beard and, as it were, emphasized each sentence, put full stops everywhere. Now and
then he cheered it up with a pinch of snuff. Sparks of gaiety
radiated from his gray eyes, but all his liveliness was double-
edged—one had a suspicion all the time that there was something
dangerous behind it. The sparks were playful, but they emanated
from steel on stone.

"I've brought some barley-sugar, too," he laughed, and unpacked it with the hard generous hand of an old man. "Good

for the gums, good for the teeth, healthy for the throat, indifferent for the stomach. Do you want it all the same? Then take it, take it. I've got liver oil here, cod-liver oil. Excellent for red hair and other deficiencies. Good in porridge, sweet in soup. Like the kiss of a lover when the stomach is empty. Listen, Celia, my little girl, my darling. Teach your children to drink liver oil, cod-liver oil. They are turning up their snouts at it—flip them on their snouts. Where is the stick? The castigator? You haven't one! New times, new manners! Ridiculous customs! Come to Knör, children. There I will give you a whacking, a whacking by Ketilbjörn, Ketilbjörn-from-Knör, Ketilbjörn Hranason-from-Knör. Herrings too you shall have, excellent food, the food of Paradise!"

I followed him wherever he went or stood, slept with him at night, was treated to snuff and talk.

"Now don't you become a priest—you leave that alone," he advised me, shaking his head so that his fleshy nose waggled. "A melancholy profession, a meager living—unless one has the Devil for uncle and can pinch a bishop's daughter. The farmer has the best time of it to my mind, preferably one on a farm by the sea, or high up in the mountains where he can breathe, can move about. Every business man has someone over him, a superior to whom he must kowtow, wave his tail; but only God is over the farmer—and the law, God and the law. If you have a head for learning and no desire for manual work, then learn the law, get learned in the law, get wise. For anyone who knows the law well enough there is a way out, always a way of salvation. It is only the fool who gets caught in its meshes. The wise man presses his fins close to his body, keeps his tail stiff and slips through the meshes—Hm! Hm! Hm!—slips through."

I thought to myself that there could not be much satisfaction in such an occupation, and Grandpa seemed to read my thoughts, for he altered his tone, suddenly spoke more coldly but at the same time more earnestly.

"There are three things by which a man can live: the riches of the sea, the produce of the earth and the stupidity of his neighbor. . . . From the man who begins life with a pair of empty hands the sea and the earth demand work, moil and toil, sweat and watchfulness—and if you ever become rich you must still be watchful, you must be sly and alert; the first up, the last to bed, the last to bed! The stupidity of your neighbor is the easiest source of income, but also the most tiresome, dealing mostly with simpletons or foolish old women. The priest cuts himself a thin slice from it, the business man a thick one— therefore, be a business man. Cut the slice thick or take the whole loaf, the whole basket of bread."

My Grandpa-from-Knör was never petty or revengeful. I had heard a story about him. He had filed a lawsuit against a neighbor (he was always starting lawsuits about one thing or another). This neighbor bribed a poor wretch in Grandpa's employ to make a false oath—it happened at a court at Knör where the case was being tried—and Grandpa lost the suit through this oath. Just after it had been closed, Ketilbjörn found the man sobbing his heart out behind the farm. He feared his false oath would send his soul to Hell.

"Don't you bother about that," Grandpa-from-Knör comforted him. "God is sure to forgive you, you are so stupid, so stupid! . . ."

I tried to ask him about this story, but he cut me short.

"It is so long ago that I have forgotten it, forgotten it. Don't you believe all the stories you hear about old Grandpa, about Ketilbjörn-from-Knör."

But any occurrence in which there was something funny he was only too ready to talk about, even if the laugh was on him; and he never extolled himself nor excused himself in any way. He seemed to be quite indifferent how he appeared in any story he told. If his leg had been shrewdly pulled, he expressed, without annoyance, a great admiration for the rogue who had pulled it.

"I must admit that he thought that out well, the beast, the dirty dog."

He talked to Nonni a great deal, and from vague remarks I

at last gathered that he was trying to get Nonni away from my
father. This surprised and disquieted me. I knew well enough
that men of Nonni's caliber were sought after by everyone, but
within a family it was usual to talk over such matters openly with
the man's master. One day, as he stood talking to Nonni, my
mother came toward him, very determined, uncommonly pert
and Ketilbjörnish.

"I think, Old Papa, that Greipur would prefer it if you would
negotiate with any of his men you want, openly and with his
consent."

"Is Greipur the sort of man who can't stand up to a kick?"
asked Ketilbjörn teasingly. "Jon here is neither a tethered goat
nor a slave."

"Nonni can do what he thinks best," answered my mother,
calmly, "but as for you, Old Papa, I promise you I will never
walk the same grass at Knör with a man whom you have enticed
away from here without Greipur's consent."

"Now, look here, you fox, you monster!" laughed Grandpa-
from-Knör, good-naturedly admiring her and following her. . . .
"There, there, my dove . . . there, there, my dove."

An extraordinary man was this grandfather of mine. He
somehow seemed to carry his whole life about with him. The
past was finished with, the future did not worry him at all. He
had very strong feelings, and was vehement and unreserved, and
open opposition appealed to him. Victory or defeat were all
the same, but he demanded one or the other. He wasted words
in all colors, but he knew only one real term of abuse, and that
was: "You slacker."

Stebbi planed and planed.
"The sea is very big," he said to himself, "very big.". . .
I had built myself a little cottage with bits of wood and roofed
it with shavings. I sat inside it and felt unhappy because
Grandpa-from-Knör had gone, and there I sat, listening to
Stebbi's groanings and chatterings.

He was always groaning; mere bagatelles were a great burden to him.

"They say that in Arabia they have beautiful horses," he told the plank. "Likely enough . . ."

Probably it was bits of blessed Frederick's wisdom and reading that he remembered from time to time; everything floated about in his childish, feeble mind like tiny clouds in a blue sky.

"Mary, Mother of God," he said, and was silent for a long time before he went on. "He said She was wrapped in a sheet. That the elect should walk about in their grave-clothes is one thing, but that Mary, God's Mother, should, while living here below, have gone about with so little on Her—who could have believed it? She would have looked well in Icelandic dress. . . . A carpenter, well, well . . . with such a Wife and such a Son . . . every carpenter is not so fortunate. . . . Of course Paulina is a fine figure of a girl, taller than most. . . ."

I lay dreaming, surrounded by the sharp acid smell of carpentered wood. I sailed in the vault of heaven, and suddenly the Day of Judgment arrived—the sea congealed and my ship could not move. So I took Hildiridur by the hand and we stepped out onto the sea, our servants following us. "Where are we going, Hugleik?" Hildiridur asked. "We are going to God," I answered proudly. "This is the Last Day. Hugleik the Reckless Sailor must answer for his deeds and misdeeds." Round about us the stars ran after each other on the blue wavy surface like lost golden lambs. "Let us gather the stars together," I commanded, and we collected all the stars and drove them right up to Our Lord where He sat on His throne, dividing the elect from the condemned. "Here I find written," said God to me, "that you have often been disobedient to your mother, forgotten to say your prayers, sworn in an unchristian manner, and been a quarrelsome pup. Are you guilty of anything else?" "Yes," I answered with great frankness, "I am guilty of plunder and murder." "That does not improve matters," answered God, sternly. "But since you have brought me My stars—have you counted them, by the way? Angels, are they all there?—since you have brought me *all* My stars, I will prefer mercy to justice. Enter thou into My blessedness." "Lord God," I answered proudly, "isn't that my Grandpa-from-Knör I see among the condemned?" "Yes," answered God, "he has deserved nothing better." "But did he not have the *Psalms of the Passion* read from cover to cover every winter?" I asked further. "Yes," answered God, scratching Himself behind His ear, "but you should just hear all the other things he has done." "Indeed!" I said. "But without him I cannot accept my salvation." ... "Look at your mother standing over there and weeping. What your words cannot accomplish has been accomplished by her tears. Gabriel, call out Ketilbjörn!" ... I saw other members of my household among the condemned, but by those tears we were all saved. And who was it that Maggi was dragging along if not Torgrimur from Vidivellir, that old sinner, whom he has smuggled in among the saved? "Couldn't have been done any other way," Maggi excused himself. ...

"Not everybody can tell the difference in steel by its taste," Stebbi boasted to himself, entirely self-satisfied. "There he was coming toward me with two knives. 'Taste, Stefan Arnason,' he said. 'There must be a witness,' I answered, and then I tasted, letting the knife-blade glide over my tongue. 'Swedish steel; English steel.' I was right. I have the knives in my pocket."

"Give me one of them," I begged, crawling out of my house.

"Who is that crawling about?" asked Stebbi, surprised. "Is that you, Uggi? I didn't hear you. Were you sleeping? I would be very pleased to give you one of the knives if only you knew which was the better—because that's the one I want to keep myself.... Wait a little longer, and one day the point will surely be broken off one of them ... then you shall have the animal."

He said this so frankly and simply that it seemed to increase the value of the gift. As a matter of fact I never got the knife. The point was certainly broken one day, but he polished on a new one and could not bear to give it up.

You would forgive him everything. One day he came to me

with a ship roughly carved with an axe out of a piece of wood—clumsy as himself.

"Are we quits?"

"Yes."

"Good."

Old Begga, who could not reconcile herself to Grimsstadir or, for the matter of that, to Hamrafjördur, could not bear Stebbi.

"I cannot understand how Farmer Greipur lets him carry on as he does with that expensive wood. Everyone knows that he isn't right in the head. Sawing, chopping and planing—why, anyone can do all that—and the way he goes about measuring with his rule! Houses don't get built that way. What's he coming for now? What's upset him now? Perhaps another wagtail mess. Ah! What a master! What a carpenter!"

In the warmth of the summer evening Maria Mens sat on a little hill, weeping. Under the red evening sky came Nonni—even his walk was shadowy and unreal. Unreal was also the weeping of Maria Mens, far-away and unreal. Only the warm light of the evening was real—coming toward one like a shout in a foreign tongue.

7

My picture of the world at this time of my existence was something like this: I lived in the center of a globe, the bottom of which consisted of land interspersed with sea, the walls and roof being another sea called the sky. My "world," therefore, fulfilled the condition that it should be round, a ball. Above me was the Kingdom of Heaven, where God ruled over a bevy of angels who, singing loud praises, flew about like sea-swallows in the blue sky. Below me was Hell, where the Devil reigned supreme—rather a simple old gentleman. The sun was to me God's eye, the moon one of the Devil's odd little inventions— a sun-ghost to mislead human beings, to cause them to make mistakes and worship the master of the night instead of the master of the day. Where I had got hold of these fantastic notions, which I never divulged to anybody, I do not know. But the idea that there were secret countries under the sea, where happy people lived in lovely homesteads and cattle grazed in juicy meadows, had come from Old Begga; and from innumerable stories told me I knew all about the Little People who lived in stones and rocks.

All this seemed to me very simple and natural; it was only the stars that puzzled me. Were they tallow candles which the Mother of God lighted each evening on the angel's tables? Were they small, glimmering flames—tongues of light in the air—over every little angel's pillow? Were they precious stones lying on the bottom of the sky? Or were they birds with glittering eyes swimming about in the sea above us? I had even a name for these imaginary birds: I called them "the birds of God." But perhaps the stars were simply night-lanterns on the ships that sailed the sea of heaven. In my picture everything seemed to fall into place except these annoying spots of light which, when all was said and done, might simply be nails with golden heads that the angels had amused themselves by hammering into the floor of Heaven. Or, they might be holes made by a finger in that floor so human beings might have some conception of the glory of God.

Infinitely near to me was God at this time, a friendly old man, the best of grandfathers.

I considered the universe and its laws as nothing but a casual fancy of this, My God. He had created the world in the same way as I, any morning, might build myself a farmstead. I realized that He felt obliged to keep to the rules which He Himself had made for this world; but during the night, or when no one noticed it, He allowed all sorts of wonderful things to happen. The flower which I found one evening among the tussocks and which I talked to until it went to sleep, closing its eyes like a tired child, and which the next day I searched for in vain, had doubtless at God's command grown into a human being during the night and was now playing about as a little five-year-old child somewhere in the world. . . . Why five years old? Why so far away? Who could tell? I pictured her parents to myself, and it amused me much to think they never suspected that they had not had their little girl for five years; nor did their neighbors suspect it, nor the dog, nor the cat, nor the cow, nor the horses; for God had altered the memories of animals and of people. I hoped that one day I should meet the little girl, although probably it would not be for many years—and how I hoped that I would recognize her! But I should be sure to do that, for I remembered so well the look and the smile of the little flower. Then I would say to her: "Do you remember when we stood at home among the tussocks and you were only a little flower?" Next night I tried to dream her name—no name that I knew seemed to suit her. I developed these fantasies to such an extent that at length I was not quite sure whether I had actually sat one evening talking to a flower among the tussocks, or whether it was just something I had imagined.

God could allow many other wonderful things to happen if He was in the mood. After a week of cold rain and damp mist it might occur to Him to send us a Sunday with shining sun and a soft wind, as if He wanted to say: "Go to church now, My people, and rejoice and be glad." If the people then spread out their hay to dry in the fields instead of going to God's House, the following Sunday was sure to be one with rain beating against the pane, asking with each smack: "Aren't you going out to dry your hay?" . . . That was God—it did not pay to make a fool of Him. As a matter of fact, it was impossible. He understood all languages, and no one could invent one that He did not understand, for He read everyone's thoughts as easily and plainly as if they had been printed in large letters. If you even considered the possibility of clearing yourself with a lie, you would be sure to bite your tongue that very day. If, against orders, you took off your shoes and stockings to slip across the stream, Gaul, the monster, would immediately think of paddling across with one of your stockings, letting go of it in the middle of the stream, so that it would never be seen again. Only once—when, to my shame, I had fallen from a beam in the barn and had to choose between standing absolutely still on both legs, if anyone looked at me, or saving myself by trying to conceal a limp—did God come to my rescue; He arranged for Stebbi, blind with zeal and calculations, with his pencil in his mouth and both hands full, to knock me over, so that I could limp freely and openly and with good reason.

"Are you so blind and deaf that you can neither hear nor see when a grown man is coming toward you?" asked Stebbi, intensely. "Could you really not have got out of my way? . . . It is a different thing where I am concerned. Think of all that I have to keep in my head. I have to sleep half Sunday just to rest my brain; have to forsake church and the Word of God. Do you know what my Paulina says? She says: 'Give up all this building. Here you come, absolutely dazed, talking of nothing but figures and measurements. A minute ago you squeezed my waist as hard as if I had been a beam, and mumbled "It must be split in two"; I will not submit to it. And if I only touch you, you cry out: "Oh, my finger . . . oh, my big toe . . ." just as if I were an executioner who had been paid to torture you. No, I can bear it no longer . . .' All this and a great deal more my Paulina has been saying lately."

"Who is your Paulina?" I asked.

"Who is talking about a Paulina?" Stebbi suddenly became attentive and wide awake. "Blessed Frederick always said: 'Talk about the things that concern you and that you understand.' "

I thought to myself: "That Paulina, who can *she* be? And what is wrong with *her?*"

The grass was falling before the scythe. A moment ago it had stood there green and swaying in the wind, mixed with flowering herbs and seed-bearing stalks. But the harvester came. Stroke by stroke the scythe approached—*huit! huit!* Between the heaps of hay which my father and the men had raked together, the ground stood yellow and bare. Sharp as sunless air was the sound of the thin steel scythe against the sandstone. The ear responded to it like teeth to ice-cold water. Madame Anna toddled about on round, thick legs, happy and unsteady amid the hay. She fell down, got up, laughed, pulled the straws out of her nose and her mouth. Veiga and Beta built hay houses, crept in and out. No one seemed to mourn the grass; it fell, wondering, and lay where it fell. The wind blew through the fallen stems, but they no longer bent and nodded in the gayest of play. They were ill—they were fading.

I felt homeless in the midst of all the bustle that attended the haymaking. Only one servant remained behind at the farmstead—one week Old Begga, the next week Disa—and whoever stayed at home had not much time for talking. Even Stebbi was taken from his carpentering and put to the scythe during the busiest time, and Maggi was made shepherd—he went off with the sheep early in the mornings and did not return until late at night. My mother was the only one who had any time for me, but her face often showed me how tired she was, and that cut me to the heart, filled me with anxiety and concern.

Great peace always followed her wherever she went: a rare sweetness and felicity. Wherever she was, there to me was the nucleus of the day. Even the light that surrounded her was unlike any other light. Satisfaction, comfort, the night's rest, the meaning of everything, were centered in her. She was the answer to all riddles. She satisfied all hunger, all thirst. She brought with her all that was good. She drove away all that was bad. In her mouth the least important words attained to dignity. At her call a ripple passed through me like sunshine, like the song of birds, like the smell of flowers. But if she looked reproachfully at me, my heart contracted; I would sit on a stool with a spirit withered and fading, like new-cut grass. Sometimes she collected us children around her and gave us warm bannock and butter, sang songs to us or little nonsense rhymes, happy, with smiling eyes that grew suddenly damp and then, as suddenly, lighted up again.

On weekdays she wore a light-brown knitted handkerchief with a red border which fitted tightly round her shoulders and over her firm breasts. To me this kerchief had something secret about it. If I felt ill I would ask her to wrap it round me, and never did it fail to make me well again. I liked to take hold of it, stroke my cheek with it, dry my eyes on it when I had been crying. If I woke from a nightmare I crept out of bed, hunted for it, and stuck it in under my pillow. If my mother missed it any morning she always looked for it there. My sisters laughed at me, called it "Uggi's wife," but I did not care a rap.

On the whole, I cared very little for what people thought of my actions. One day I heard someone, probably Sophia, remark that Goldsmith Karl had said of me: "That boy looks to me both self-opinionated and obstinate."

This was a blow for me, for I had just decided on Goldsmith Karl as my father-in-law, but it never occurred to me to brood over what could have caused him to make such a remark. Dear me, I thought, "self-opinionated and obstinate"! Am I really? Well, if I am, I am. I suppose he knows.

I remember that in my mother's attitude to me at this time there was a protective quality which surprised me. When people were irritable with me, or snubbed me, or made me increase my friendliness toward them on the score that they were ill or in some difficulty, she used to catch me by the arm, take me aside and say: "You must not let yourself be bullied."

I did not understand her and would ask her what she meant.

She would not answer, but would be suddenly very kind to me, keep my hand in hers, tell me stories and let me help her in her work.

"Life will be very hard for you," she prophesied once. "One day perhaps you will learn to know human nature."

I understood only dimly what she meant, but from her tone I realized that it was not just an empty phrase. Something in her voice reminded me of hearing Grandpa-from-Knör say:

"It is easy enough to be sorry for a repentant sinner, but who wants to be bothered with the poor wretch?"

In such a statement as this I felt a sharp discord—and sensed a deep truth.

On the same occasion Ketilbjörn had said: "From a superficial point of view Our Lord seems to be very easily contented, easily contented."

I could not understand how contentment, which we children had been taught to regard as one of the chief virtues, could be used of Our Lord as a term of reproach. Utterances such as this, which I only half understood or definitely misunderstood, gave me a feeling of uncertainty toward older people and toward the world in general; but my doubts and anxieties were still only as light clouds in a sunlit sky.

So far, I had no great knowledge of human wickedness, that quagmire of apathy and stupidity. I did not yet really believe that people were "wicked" as I was told they were. I had, of course, seen them treat animals cruelly, and I had seen anger flare up in them and heard hatred alter their voices, and had noticed how it licked round me like burning tongues of flame from a horrible fat coal fire—but I imagined all these things to be the result of possession by the Evil One. It was the Devil, or one of his wicked spirits, who had obtained power over the defenseless soul of him who was angry or full of hatred. When the evil had burned itself out he would be himself again—I had seen that so often. I felt as if I knew these evil spirits; I even had names for them. "Stubbly-Tail" was the name of the spirit that entered people and made them thrash their dogs; I could see his features mirror themselves in the face of a man who madly attacked his hound. "Fire-Wind" was the name of the spirit that worked people up to wildness on horseback. "Skroggur"* was the spirit that incited people against each other. There were many of them.

My soul was encased in a shell of trustfulness and credulity. As, in my ignorance, I had enclosed myself within the visible and imagined worlds as in a protecting shell, so, in my inexperience, I created a suit of armor for my mind; and like my imaginary ships in the starry heavens, which, with the most fairy-like adventures, carried the riches of the world from land to land, so had I also, in the heaven of my heart, a number of ships that carried to mankind peace and happiness, goodness and generosity, purity and innocence of mind, all the jewels of the soul.

Little did I know the world; little did I know human beings; little did I know God. So little did I know the world that I did not even notice how rigid were its laws. So little did I know God that I believed that He went about personally supervising each entity like a farmer on his farm. So little did I know men that I thought them noble and sublime and took little notice of their consuming egotism, their innocent—one might almost be tempted to say, their pious—depravity; their pitiable vices, their vulgar though sometimes almost heroic self-deception— all their deep degradation and wretched blindness.

---

* A spirit mentioned in Icelandic folklore.

Take, for instance, Roadside-Simbi. Did he seem to me pitiable? Not at all. He struck a chord somewhere in my mind, and his eyes—which were cold and gray like river water in early summer—gave me a sharp feeling of discomfort. But his position as an outlaw, as one who was persecuted, gave him, in my eyes, a certain dignity. He was always a leader in my heavenly fleet. A few years later he moved to Teigur and became our neighbor, but my estimate of him still held, although people continued to despise him. . . . One day he was due at the Spring Fair in the town. They expected him early in the morning; he had undertaken to look after the cows of the neighborhood, and was to begin his work that day. Everybody was greatly amused that Simbi should have undertaken such work. It really seemed quite laughable. . . . I well remember that day, a cold, desolate day in early summer. Simbi did not come in the morning nor all day long. In the evening we found him in the Stada River below Teigur. From a cord around his throat hung a block of rusty iron. We found him in the shallow water, and icily, like the river water round my feet, ran in my mind the phrase: "Gray carries; gray tarries!" As Simbi lay there majestically motionless, he seemed to be lifted up, high above scorn, above pity. . . .

But I am anticipating.

Let me mention another example: Einar Bjarnason. People were sorry for him, crossed themselves, shook their heads. Once he had been a clever and promising young man. But was he really clever no longer? He made saddles and reins better than any other man in Hamrafjördur, probably better than anyone in the whole land. His leather-work filled me with a feeling of richness and well-being just as did Goldsmith Karl's laced engravings and ingenious silver filigree work. Besides, he was waiting for a letter with money—had treasure behind him, so to speak. People called him mad. Well, his beard was without rival. . . . Besides, once he had winked at me, bent down over me and whispered:

"Most people are mad—pretend you don't notice it! . . ."

I remember him especially on one visit he paid us. He walked up and down the living room, supple and sunburned. Outside the window the wet grass shone in the rapid sunny rain.

There was another so-called "poor wretch"—Jon Eyjolfsson, our district tramp. He seemed to rock from farm to farm on a pair of short, solid legs, with a striped sailcloth bag on his back. He was dressed in rags which, for the most part, were hidden by his most elegant rag of all, a flowing brown sack-cloth coat, so worn that the coarse threads were plainly visible through the weave. He was very quiet, quiet and shy. He would sit and make all sorts of movements with his body, apparently as a result of vermin. But was such a man really to be pitied? When others went to work he wandered on to different weather, different mountains, different valleys. I imagined his life as being infinitely rich. I trusted him to such an extent that many years later I gave him a love-letter to deliver for me.

These people, whom other folk pitied, awoke in me a sort of disquiet, but in no sense a feeling of pity. On the contrary, I was inclined to rank them higher than other people; ascribe to them superior qualities, and even envy them a little. Certainly I pitied the mad lady at Vegeirsstadir, for she cried so much. On the other hand, her grave and solitary daughter filled me with a tender admiration and dreams of a deep and serious happiness awaiting her. I always thought of happiness as something serious.

But even stupidity and ugliness interested me only superficially, leaving my heart untouched.

On a farm in our neighborhood there lived an oldish servant who was the stupidest and certainly one of the ugliest persons I have ever seen. She was called Sigurrose. She was very proud of her name, and was quite satisfied with her warty face, her reddish skin, her stupidly happy eyes, her yellow horse-like teeth. She waited endlessly for a lover; waited for him with longing and a rare kind of hot expectancy. It was certainly inexplicable to her that he never came, and the older she grew the more she felt it important to hold herself in training, and be well prepared. At any rate, every Holy Day she shut herself in the room where she kept her trunk, washed her hands and face, combed and plaited her thin, colorless hair, decked herself out with satin and silver tassels—doing all this in front of a spotty looking glass that she had hung on a beam. She was too stupid to realize that she could be seen through the window, and it did not occur to her that her talking to herself could be heard by others. She sat there smiling, blushing, casting down her eyes, waiting for a lover and ready to receive him. She held out her fat arms and braceleted wrists, her silk-covered and decorated bosom heaved under her rustling pinafore, her thick legs trembled in happy anticipation, and she rejoiced to herself as if she actually heard her lover's voice:

"Rose—Rosa—Sigurrose!"

It would be difficult to find a greater tragedy than this poor woman's—the hopeless craving of a healthy and exacting body, the single desire of an entirely uncultured and therefore restricted spirit. People laughed at her, and it was only her extreme innocence that protected her from seduction. I too laughed at this maiden, but in the bottom of my heart I felt a certain admiration for her.

"Rose—Rosa—Sigurrose!"

Like stupidity canonized, she stood at the window in front of her spotted looking glass, while the sun played on the curly hair of her warts. Godlike were her glowing desires, her golden dreams—deep and dead, like the charmed life of the looking glass.

This Rosa was supposed to be completely ignorant. She had never been able to learn to read; she said she could not distinguish one letter from another. Sira Björn had promised to confirm her when she was eighteen if only she could learn the Creed and the *Our Father* by heart. She could not manage it, but he confirmed her nevertheless.

"I confirm her on the responsibility of the Holy Ghost, giving her a part in the body and blood of Our Blessed Lord," he said. "Glory be to God."

Rosa was very proud of the ceremony and of the priest's words, and when later on she became one of our servants she reminded us of it on all possible occasions. A few years later she had something else to boast about. She was obliged to go to the hospital for an operation and the doctor said to her: "In one way you stand alone, Sigurrose; no one can equal you in stupidity."

How proud was Rose, Rosa, Sigurrose of this testimonial! The greatest gifts that life ever gave her were certainly the tributes of these two men. She never mentioned the doctor without' adding "dear" or even "beloved" to his name, and from the bottom of her simple heart she was convinced that he was one of the best and most lovable people in the world; otherwise he would not have spoken so kindly to such a poor creature as she. Besides, he must be extraordinarily clever and learned, to discover that there was anything in which she was unique.

And yet one might well ask which of the two was the simpler—Rosa or her learned doctor.

For clever, really clever, and rational people I had, even at that time, a certain pity. Those miserable beings who stand like sheep in a pen behind the high and steadily-growing fence of their own reason—no others are condemned to such life-slavery or such desolation of soul. Like a gigantic nightmare the so-called "reasonableness" of self-satisfied, rational people rests over the world . . . like a damp mist rising from humanity's most stagnant swamp, like the depth of darkness . . . the root of all evil. Fenced in by their own cowardice and the evil eyes of their neighbors, men live on moribund or condemned. Only he who is protected by a mother's love, by his own blind child-ishness and a kind destiny, can for a time nourish the delusion that the Hell into which mankind has turned this earth is a happy place; that good and evil are two separate things be-tween which the struggle is comparatively simple; that God lives outside His handiwork like a careful manager—in fact, that there are ships in the sky.

"My little flock," my mother often called us children, and these simple words and the voice in which she spoke them bound the four of us very closely together. How strange is the secret power of words! They dominate life and death. They can hasten final obliteration for, like a bird with a shot through its heart, a soul may fall in flight, hit by the word that kills. But a word can also give life eternal. When my mother, out of the depths of her loving and affectionate heart, called us children "her little flock," she bound us to one another with strong bands. Our slight disagreements were blown away; my little sisters became to me intensely living and near: the calm Veiga, the violent Beta and the decided Madame Anna.

Veiga was the best to play with because she was the most amenable and most persevering in pretending that a game was real. Beta was sometimes full of inventions and suggestions, and had often to be spoken to sternly or sent away for an hour from the society of reasonable people. Madame Anna found our farm very boring and had a mania for thinking things out for herself. She talked baby talk and was uncertain on her legs, and was in every way as "good as newborn." She often gave us a great deal of trouble and caused us much inconvenience, teaching us many lessons in patience and unselfishness. But she belonged, of course, to "my little flock," and was besides very sweet, round and plump. If she were too impatient we put her to play with my puppy, Gaul, and they tumbled over each other very happily, Gaul barking, Madame Anna prattling and laughing, both of them very young and irresistible.

The summer passed. The barns were filled with fragrant hay. Anyone returning to the farm after wandering along the banks of the stream would be met, as he drew near, by a damp, heavy perfume that filled him with a sense of calm and well-being. Maggi was very busy bringing the hay home from the meadows on the panting horses. He filled the home field with stacks of hay, which later on were spread out, turned over, raked together and carried into the barn. The drying-days were full of life, laughter, hurry. It was sometimes even possible to catch a glimpse of Maria Mens smiling through tears, sweat and hay, and to hear a sound like a tearful hiccough (her only way of laughing) deep down in her pretty, well-formed bosom.

A very good-looking girl was Maria Mens, if only she had not always been so red-eyed and tearful. When men looked at her—which they sometimes seemed to avoid doing—it was with a look quite different from that which they gave the other women on the farm. Mundi, who nourished a great and hopeless passion for Sophia, and who used to tell us that, when he was a farmhand working with her foster father, he would stand for a whole night with the horses outside the house in the town where she was visiting—even Mundi was often found in the neighborhood of Maria Mens, looking very melancholy.

The fair head, too small for his height, waggled about on his sloping shoulders. His bowed legs straddled uncertainly. He handled the scythe or the rake as if he meant, with every movement, to demonstrate his superiority; but all this innocent display sat as loosely on him as down on a dandelion. Suddenly he stood there, as it were, stripped, denuded.

Mundi gave his full name, Gudmundur Jonatansson, whenever the opportunity occurred, and emphasized it with a twist of his mustache. He was a good farmhand, devoted to duty, rather particular never to do either more or less than his share of the work, but otherwise ambitious and willing and very easygoing. He was extremely self-satisfied—extremely faint-hearted. The girls would not look at him except to laugh at him in secret and make him run their errands. Maria Mens would not even use his services; she had her Nonni.

This summer Nonni was generally silent and often unhappy. He was jealous of everyone and everything, even of Maria's rake, and of anything else that she took into her hands. His jealousy was entirely groundless, for he was one of those men who are either ignored or very much beloved. And although Maria did not look at him often she was never really happy unless he was somewhere within sight. Their love filled me with great joy and happiness. I was so fond of them both that

I seemed to be part of them. When Nonni was unkind to Maria
I used to press myself against her and cry with her; if at that
moment I happened to look at Nonni there was a coldness in
his eyes, a coldness toward me, which amazed me to such an extent that there was simply no room in my mind for unhappiness.

However, such a look was, of course, only passing. Nonni
was always very friendly to me, full of care and generosity.
He never came home from town without bringing me sweets
or some other present. If he had been to church, or been
sent on an errand, his kind eye always found something for
me along the road: a stone, a flower, a pretty branch, a bit of
wood, or a bone whitened by weather and wind which he would
get off his horse to pick up because he thought it would please
me. He used also to bring me back little things he found in
the meadows: an eggshell or a bird's nest. When I thanked
him he patted me awkwardly on the head and said in his quiet
voice: "My friend!"

Both of us had our difficulties with Old Begga. Men and
milk, grass and growth, butter and cheese, wind and weather,
fish and fowl—all had been better in Breidale.

"But people have lived here in Hamrafjörd before, and lived
well, dear Bergljot," said my mother, trying to reconcile her.

"I don't call it living," answered Old Begga, obstinately.
"Why, even in the churchyard it's tight quarters. The proud
have to shut off their graves with iron railings. It does not
matter to me, of course; I would as soon lie in the burial
ground of the poor as of the rich."

"But it is the custom of the neighborhood to put up those
railings round the graves," said my mother, with a little smile.

" 'Custom'! Yes, of course," answered Old Begga, kneading
the dough with such force that it oozed through her strong
fingers. "God has His customs, the Devil his. In life we can
boast and make a show with stones and crosses and names, and
flowers in tin and gold, but earth to earth it is, and will remain!
'Christ has rolled away the stone, He our cross has carried';
therefore let us sleep as children under our coverlet of turf

when the time of our wandering is finished. Our Lord will not allow us to throw dust into His eyes. He will read what is in our hearts, but will pay no attention to what is written on our gravestone. He has promised the crown of life to those who await the Last Day in patience and in the fear of God."

" 'In patience and the fear of God,' . . . yes," repeated my mother, thoughtfully.

Old Begga stood looking at her uncertainly out of her darkness. Between them lay the crooked rays of the sun like a golden ladder up to heaven. My mother hummed and spread large slices of pot-baked bread* with a firm hand. Old Begga kneaded and was silent.

"It is a great joy for a mother to have a son like your Nonni," said my mother, her tone closing over the words like a hand over a tool.

Old Begga looked at her uncertainly—was silent and went on kneading.

"A great gift from God," continued my mother, as if to herself. "A consolation for the heart and an honor for the soul—a noble shoot from a noble root."

Old Begga stood there looking straight in front of her; then she rubbed the dough off her hands thoughtfully. There were small withered tears in her old eyes. Then she began to work again with renewed energy, her floury arms and her doughy fingers kneading the dough as if she were kneading something quite different.

My mother was silent for a moment. Then she said: "One can die happily if one leaves good children behind one."

"A good boy my Nonni is, certainly, that is true," answered Old Begga, with calm conviction. "But his heart is greater than his understanding."

"Don't speak like that," said my mother, kindly reproachful. "Remember that the Evil One is clever, but God is wise. Maria Mens is a good girl, a blessed lamb."

---

* Bread baked on the cinders under a pot.

"Oh, yes—a blessed old hen," shouted Old Begga, "with her tears dripping like everlasting autumn rain."

"How are we off for coffee? Have we plenty roasted?" asked my mother. "When Maria Mens is happy with a home of her own, things will be different, you'll see."

Old Begga rubbed the dough off her hands. "We've got enough roasted for one pot. . . . I'll have this dough under the pot in a moment. . . . Can you grind the coffee, my pet? I'll have the fire going in a minute. . . . What was I saying? As far as Maria Mens is concerned, it seems to be touch and go. If only I knew whether it were God or the Devil who has taken a hand there."

Old Begga stumped off. My mother shook her head with a quiet smile.

I went on grinding. The coffee-grinder crushed the beans and growled: "Crosses and stones—bury my bones."

When it was Disa's week in the kitchen there was quite another atmosphere altogether. My mother would look at her in an odd way, but never carried on a personal conversation with her; both her words and her voice had a certain crispness about them. Disa, on her side, was very capricious. One day she was willing and friendly, and almost wheedling in tone and word; another day she hummed, was cross and very hard of hearing. When she was in a good mood she called my mother "dear mistress" or "dear heart" or "loved one" every other minute, and took great pains to find out how she wished things done. On her bad days, her tone was quite different: then she had "strained milk before," "seen a soup kettle," and was not afraid to let my mother know that she had baked bread to the satisfaction of blessed Frederick and blessed Maria, and they had, of course, "understood what was meant by bannock."

My mother's tone to Disa was always the same, whether her manner was friendly or disagreeable.

"Your moods, Disa, make you very difficult in a home."

Disa took it well. She was silent for a moment and then she said: "All have not been through what some have had to endure, good mistress."

Disa's behavior to me was about the same as to my mother. The only person with whom I never saw her cross was my father. One day she would tell me stories about blessed Frederick, hint at her own mystical experiences and visions or sing me rhymes,* of which she knew whole books by heart. The next day she would probably refuse to answer me when I spoke to her, pretend not to hear me and not to see me—only hum. Her stories attracted me. They had a more dangerous tang about them than Old Begga's, in the same way as her God was a different God. She always mentioned Him shyly and with obvious anxiety, as if she had an unpaid account with Him. Her Jesus, whom she generally called "God's Son," was He who should "come in the skies on the last day." The apostles and prophets were the only ones she spoke of warmly and without fear.

By degrees she became quite at home with me—so at home that, in her queer hidden way, she expressed criticism of my father's actions.

"Blessed Frederick always left the marsh meadows till late in the summer—to take them in hand as early as this may be better, of course!" Or:

"East of the river, where the cows are now put to graze, the pasture is undoubtedly very good—we can see that from the milk. Formerly, we used to save that pasture in the summer so as to have it for winter fodder."

At that time I did not doubt but Disa's unbalanced behavior, and the odd look in her shrinking, grayish-blue eyes, hid some tragic secret—an unhappy love affair, the death or desertion of a lover. Looking back, however, I am inclined to think that her unhappy manner had its roots in a bad tone in the old home. Nothing is so infectious as a bad or uncertain humor:

---

* A *Rima* usually has as its subject an old legend. Each stanza generally consists of four short alliterative lines.

where it rules in a household, it transforms in a short time the most fruitful mind to a desert, exposed to spiritual storms, a playground for evil spirits and the powers of darkness. Such an unhappy person becomes like a house with battered doors and windows: both mild and bitter winds pass through it; the wintry storms of the soul fill it with snow and ice—but the sun also has unhindered admission. How had Disa become like this? What sort of people had they been, this blessed Frederick and this blessed Maria? In any case Sophia had something of the same spirit. It was only that she was younger and better-looking, and, on the whole, had other cards in her hand.

I thought Sophia very pretty, and I enjoyed the excitement of her self-confident, teasing laughter. She always had the word "elegant" on her lips. To get up late, to have a white skin, to be dressed up on weekdays, to let others do the work, to have soft hands and polished nails, to take an hour brushing and plaiting one's hair, to pick at food, to turn it on the plate as if it were uneatable, to hold out one's little finger while drinking from a cup—all this was "elegant." This was how they behaved in citizen Sigfus's house in the town and, in fact, in all cultured houses.

Even her speech differed from that I was accustomed to. She knew everything about everybody, and as she had also a luxurious imagination and always talked in hints, she disquieted me and filled me with curiosity about almost any person she mentioned. Some of her usual expressions were: "But has he any right to judge?" and "I heard a little bird say about her . . ." Not even inanimate things escaped. She would say: "That cliff has seen something," or. "If all that happened behind this rock were known . . ."

The clouds scudded angrily across the sky. A pale sunbeam shone obliquely across the valley and lighted up the river with a single white gleam. Strong winds blew round the corners of the house. The dry grass on the roofs sighed mournfully.

My mother stood at the well rinsing tiny vests, long binders, linen and woolen squares, and dresses which were very long from the waist downward. Sophia sat on a mound beside her. She leaned her elbows on her knees, her chin against her clasped hands, and she tapped a little with one foot, which stuck out broad and solid under her full black skirt.

I stood looking down into the deep dark world of the well.

My mother and Sophia did not say much. It was the sudden gusts, the coarse grass, and a waterfall up in the cleft, which suddenly made itself heard in a faraway tone, that were talking.

"I wonder what awaits him here!" said my mother, very quietly. "The first and the last shirt a man wears are often wet with tears. . . . Oh, my God!"

Sophia was silent, tapping her foot. It was dark down there in the depths of the well, a deep underground world, with silent inhabitants; a world getting its cold meager light from a leaden sun which rose without glamour and sank without the glow of evening.

"Be good to him and help him onto his feet if he is alone. Let him have your healing hands to depend on," said my mother, shortly, as before. "Who knows, perhaps you will be mother to all of them—to all my little flock!"

"How you talk, woman!" exclaimed Sophia, with a laugh, sudden and short, like one of the homeless puffs of wind.

"No one can alter fate," said my mother, in a voice which was strangely cold. "What is to happen to us, happens."

"Do you think I am really suited to be mistress of a household?" Sophia asked sarcastically.

My mother wrung the water out of a couple of little garments and touched them with loving fingers. "That does not matter; the ability comes with the responsibility."

"If you really believed all this you would not talk about it so calmly," said Sophia, with a queer emphasis. Her foot continued to tap against the dry earth.

This time it was my mother's turn to laugh; and her laughter, too, was related to the capricious wind.

"It is God who searches the innermost being. Has the same power been given to Sophia Einarsdottir?"

This conversation seemed to me very strange; my heart became as dark as the depths of the well.

Later in the day my mother ironed the little garments, laid them with loving hands in a drawer. Her face was red, and red were her eyes from tears that welled now and again; and yet over her face lay a light that filled me with reverence and stillness.

Then she called Sophia and showed her where everything was put away. Then she pulled out another drawer where lay very smooth, stiff linen. They exchanged a look. The drawer was shut.

"Breidale was so far from the town that it was almost necessary to have a supply at hand," said my mother lightly.

Sophia went away. Her broad face was expressionless and full of shadows.

My mother opened the top drawer again, busied herself with something.

She said to me with a smile that reminded me of the meeting between the pale sunbeam and the stream: "And you, will you always be very good to your little brother? . . . Always be a good boy, won't you? . . . There, there, don't cry, Uggi child. It will be great fun when mother can ride to Knör next summer with her big boy. I will show you everything—even my mossy stones where you can rest your head as comfortably as on the softest down."

Heavy was my heart, darkened by angry clouds; infinitely far away seemed to me that journey—why speak about it now? I only half listened to my mother, who was describing our journey to Knör as she had done so many times before. Her words meant nothing to me, nothing. But her voice, the pauses she made, all that she left unsaid, found a painful echo in my mind.

Summer had returned, smiling, after a few weeks of rain

and dampness. White clouds delighted in the smiling blue of the sky. The heavens were again reconciled to the earth—there was peace and toleration everywhere. Cowberries begged to be eaten, but they were too sour, too sour. Along the sunny paths wandered the ptarmigan with her large brood—it was difficult to drive her back among the tussocks. It seemed impossible to make her realize that when horseback riders or stupid cows wanted to use the path they would trample her little ones to death.

On the whole, I thought, there is more trouble, more anxiety, in the world than one is led to believe. For instance, I could not find that piece of paper which I, with my heart's blood, had inscribed to Hildiridur Karlsdottir and signed with my full name and the addition of "future priest"! Such a paper must not be left about. Anyone might find it. Well, at any rate, I could not. But think if a squall of rain had washed it out of its hiding-place and somebody had found it! Think if Hildiridur had found it! Or, even worse, Anna. Hildiridur was very useful for saving from perils and difficulties, from a wicked stepmother and things like that; but if one wanted a queen to defend the kingdom while one was away fighting, or to stand by one's side in battle with a cold, impassive face, and yellow hair floating in the breeze, then undoubtedly Anna was a great deal better . . . Anna, who had fixed herself in my mind like a thorn leaving me no peace. I could not pull her out when I wished to build a solitary house and sit there alone in the twilight with Hildiridur on my knee. I would look round and find that the wall had fallen down, and that there was Anna in a cold light, smiling, overbearing, demanding.

When, therefore, on a happy, sunny day with white clouds overhead, I found Disa's medicine cupboard laid out to dry between the grassy roofs where I had found a solitary and secret hiding-place, my life was not so dear to me as to prevent me, with death before my eye, from calmly beginning to empty the bottles and taste their sweet contents. I poured the tiny, tiny pills into my hand, let them melt on my tongue. With yellow straws I fished up the tough, sweet mass from the tiny bottles which were as narrow as stalks, or emptied them, drop by drop, of their liquid contents.

"Before the white cloud over there reaches Fagravik mountain I shall be stiff and dead," I said to myself, looking closely at the label on each bottle, spelling it out and trying to make sense out of it. I nodded importantly to myself: it was Latin.

Both Hildiridur and Anna would probably follow me to the grave. Hildiridur would cry a great deal, and Anna would shed a tear in secret. Both would sing the hymn: *"As earth's gay blossoms . . ."*

I was by now walking behind my own coffin singing at the top of my voice while I thought over what I, the priest, would say at this poor boy's grave to comfort his poor parents; but before I reached the end of the first stanza my sisters came rushing over the roofs, stopped, sat down, and began to shriek.

"Are you drinking out of blessed Frederick's bottles? . . . We'll tell Mama. . . . Don't you know that you'll die? . . . Oh, Uggi, Uggi!"

I quieted them as best I could and looked for the cloud which had already got long past the thick Fagravik mountains.

"If you aren't quiet, I won't let you taste," I threatened in a whisper.

It worked. They stopped crying, and shut their mouths, to make no sound. Then, after a moment:

"Won't we die of it?" asked Veiga, perplexed.

"Do I look as if I'm dying?" I asked importantly, and Beta pulled a long nose at me and tried to grab the bottle at once.

"Are you mad?" I shouted, and snatched it away from her. "Can't you read what it says?"

"Can you?" asked Beta, crossly.

"These are very small letters, these are," I said thoughtfully. "Run in and get me a pair of Old Begga's spectacles."

Beta soon came back with the spectacles and—Madame Anna.

"I thought the little thing would like a lick too," she said.

I put on the glasses, looked closely at the little bottles, and then divided them up magnanimously.

"That is Latin—you can eat that. . . ."

Madame Anna threw herself upon me. "Me too Latin—Madame Anna Latin, too."

And Madame Anna had her Latin and we all had some Latin, and it tasted good, tasted splendid, and things went merrily with the pills, and the drops seemed to melt away; it was only with the tough mass which had to be fished up that we had trouble.

I read the words on each bottle in turn and authorized the eating of its contents. I lost time on this, and at last I cried impatiently: "Don't finish all the medicines before the doctor has a chance, you greedy things!"

"What is happening here?" asked Sophia, and arrived, climbing heavily over the roofs.

Then there was great sorrow and wailing, but we escaped punishment, as no one knew whether we would live the day through. Only Madame Anna was sick—whether it was the medicine or fright, or because Sophia poured so much milk into her and pushed her finger down her throat, I cannot say. I was spoken to very gravely again and again, but I always maintained: "I kept them away from death; I gave them only the Latin ones."

As a matter of fact, Veiga, Beta and I were very quiet for the rest of the day and waited for the pains to begin, for death to come—waited in vain. When the folk came back from the meadows we were still sitting there waiting. They all walked round us, gravely shaking their heads and saying nothing—all except Maggi, who said: "Well, it can't be denied that you are a shrewd lad. There you have in one day taken enough medicine to last you for your whole life—and *gratis* in the bargain. . . . In future you need not be afraid of illness. I suppose you managed to smuggle a few bottles away with you?"

I shook my head.

"What a fool you are after all!" burst out Maggi, crossly. "What's the good of being friends with you? Did you ever hear anything so stupid! He has eaten all the medicines himself. My goodness, what a dirty trick!"

Disa asked me next day, when we were alone: "Whatever made you eat all that expensive medicine?"

"I only wanted to taste a little pill," I answered, conscience-stricken.

To my great surprise Disa's thin body suddenly bent double with laughter and she grew very red in the face and hid it in her many-colored apron, as always when she laughed.

"We once had a calf who ate our sheets," she groaned, and her unaccustomed laughter ended with a cough and an attack of breathlessness. "Jesu, Son of Mary, forgive my sins!"

At this time I did not see much of my father except on Sundays. Then he chewed tobacco, spat, walked about with his hands in his pockets.

"With a grass-cutting machine we could cut the fields here in a day. It takes four men a week," he said crossly.

"Why don't you buy one then?" I asked innocently.

"It costs money," he answered. "Besides, nobody has invented one yet that will cut such tough grass. . . . It couldn't be done with all those tussocks, either."

He often spoke of strange and remarkable things such as grass-cutting machines, plows, wagons for which roads must be built. He suggested a bridge over the stream, a dam for the meadows, arrangements for watering—and I took the whole thing very seriously, was dreadfully impressed, and delighted in the thought of such an enterprising future. Not for a single moment did it strike me that all this was only my father's "ship."

I saw him managing the horses, managing our servants, always quiet and superior to them all. When he ordered a thing it was done. We were to have a big house with a cook-stove and a proper chimney going up through the house. Stebbi, after reluctantly taking part in the harvest, was back again at his original work. My father measured up the walls, planned passages, was extravagant with the space. On two sides of the house a wall of sods three feet thick was to be built.

"Don't you think it will be too high, Greipur?" asked Stebbi, scratching himself behind his ear.

"If you don't think that three feet is thick enough, make it four," said my father, measuring again.

"Will you ever get the sods to stand?" asked Stebbi.

"We'll support them until they have settled," answered my father, carelessly. "Sods too are subject to the law of gravity."

"Yes, to a large extent," answered Stebbi, looking at his drawings. "Cross-beam, window—cross-beam, window. What is all this nonsense? That'll never do—oh, all right, all right."

"The living-room windows there. Have you remembered to calculate the windows for the kitchen?" asked my father, suspiciously.

"Let me see, let me see," said Stebbi, bending over his greasy papers. "Extraordinary how everything has got mixed up here. I don't think even blessed Frederick could have put it straight. . . . Where is my snuffbox? Extraordinary how everything gets lost. Now there I have a double cross . . . what can I have meant by that? My head is going round and round. I think I will go in and lie down. Perhaps when I wake up I shall remember a number of things."

My father too lay down. In the evening they began again. . . . Maggi was very proud of his Dreyfus. He was forever exercising the dog.

"A strong bark puts fear into everybody," he instructed me. "Once there was a man who strengthened his voice by filling his mouth with pebbles and walking along the seashore, shouting louder than the waves. The stones I put in Dreyfus's mouth he spits out again, the ass—and if I tie up his jaws he cannot bark. The Devil knows what I am to do with the creature! What do you really think about his bark?"

"Oh, nothing special," I answered peaceably.

"Then you think, do you, that your Gaul's bark is stronger?"

"You yourself have a thin voice," I laughed, and there we were rolling about on the ground, the dogs rolling with us.

Just about this time I had a lot to do with Stebbi. Soft and warm like sheep's wool, his simplicity wrapped itself round one.

"Here have I been kept away from my tools for several weeks," he said to me vexedly, one day when I was turning the grinding-stone for him. "And it is the same with tools as it is with animals in autumn—they do not recognize you. The plane that used to follow my hand so willingly is now hard and stubborn. 'Keep away from me,' it says. The hammer makes itself heavy, and all the iron has become damp and rusty. All is misery and annoyance, my little one. It is the same with us people. I go to Paulina. 'You did not have that wart before,' says she. 'Good God, what are you talking about now? I clipped away the hairs from that wart for the first time at my confirmation.' Or else she says, my Paulina says: 'What thick fingers you have! . . .' Have I always had thick fingers? And if fingers are thick or thin, what does it matter? I ask her, in answer: 'When did I notice anything about you?' And believe me, she flares up: 'What is there to notice about me? Tell me that—just you tell me that, you faithless creature.' Thus we waste the short time with tears and complaints."

I took the opportunity of interrupting him. Of this Paulina I knew nothing except what he told me, but sometimes I could see details of her appearance rise up before me. Doubtless she had a little nose.

Stebbi told me many other things. We were very good friends, the two of us.

"My master, Lars Höjgaard," he used to say, knocking his plane and blowing away the dust from it, "my master Lars Höjgaard, on a stormy evening, found a dead whale drifting by the seashore and threw a rope round it. It was the longest whale I have ever heard tell of. My master Lars Höjgaard slung a rope round the head of the animal—his neighbor had tethered the tail—and tied it to the head of his bed and let the night go by. In the morning the whale still lay there, but there had been such a heavy sea that only one whole rib was left in the creature's body. A hundred and twenty-four tons and a quarter of oil did that record animal give."

"What about that rib?" I asked excitedly. "Could it possibly be what we use as a post for holding up the clotheslines?"

"Highly probable," answered Stebbi, taking a pinch of snuff. "Let us look closer at it some time. Blessed Frederick and Lars Höjgaard were friends; why should not the rib be here? That is how it hangs together, you can be sure of that."

When I asked my mother about this story she answered:

"This Lars Höjgaard was our neighbor for many years. Old Papa let out a part of Knör to him. When he could not think of a lie he told the truth, never otherwise! There are many stories I could tell you about him."

"But why have you never told me any?" I asked her, surprised.

"Because his adventures have never amused me particularly," she answered, and went on with her work.

Stebbi talked much to himself, and I used to enjoy listening to this chatter.

"God has created useful, useless and harmful birds—now why did He do that? He is not easy to understand, the good God. Well, in a house the posts which support it are hidden, and the nails disappear in the wood and are hidden by the painting. But an entirely useless little wagtail, or a weed— what kind of a post or a nail would a thing like that make? Here lie my bits of wood, my shavings, spread about all over the place, no good at all—well, they do for burning. God, who needs neither food nor warmth, has perhaps left His bits of wood and His shavings lying about to be blown into the world. While He is making an eider duck, perhaps a piece of wood falls down. *Pip, pip,* in the air, over Our Lord's head, sings a lark. Well, well, says God, light in the wing, that's right. But don't leave your droppings here on my tools! . . .

There you are, a bird is created. 'Listen now, Lord,' perhaps
St. Peter says. 'Is there room for all this rubbish on the earth?'
'That's Death's business; he must look after that,' answers Our
Lord, and takes a pinch of snuff. 'Plague, hard winters, fam-
ine, I have given him all these to help him when his scythe
is not enough. Haven't you room enough in Heaven, Peter?'
There stands St. Peter, abashed. 'Don't disturb Me,' says God,
'an idea has just flown through My head. Snow-white, with a
long neck—but now it seems as if things are turning round Me.
I think I must go and lie down for a moment.' When He wakes
He creates a swan."

Another day Stebbi said, while taking a pinch of snuff, re-
placing the snuffbox in his pocket, fishing it out again, knocking on the lid, taking another pinch:

"The summer is passing . . . sun and rain and tears and
all sorts of winds. . . . In the blue mountains the sheep wander
about, fattening themselves for the day of slaughter. May the
fox keep himself to the rich farmers' lambs! It is strange how
everything is ordered. A cold summer can give a good harvest.
On the other hand, a greedy merchant always gives bad prices. . . .
'Gently there, gently there,' said the Devil, as he was being
shod by Beelzebub. . . ."

The summer passed. I woke up one night surrounded by a
deep and heavy darkness. Far away in this darkness I could
hear my parents and my sisters sleeping; I could clearly distinguish one from the other by their different breathing. I
thought: "Where are they now? Is there a world for sleepers?
A world into which we enter when we fall asleep, and leave
when we awake? Do we know each other there? Are we the
same as here, father, mother, children? Or perhaps, in that
world we have other names, our ages are different? Am I
red-headed there? Perhaps in that world my mother is my
sister and we both have yellow hair and blue eyes. . . . And I
say to this sister of mine:

" 'Look here, Celia—come and sit down. . . . We will put

this label, with the lovely flowers, and the trees and the Chinese on it, between us on the floor. Shut your eyes. When you open them again we shall be sitting in the midst of real flowers, and there will be green trees around us, and the Chinese will be standing staring at us. . . . Did you know that this could happen? If we are frightened we have only to open our eyes and we shall be home again.' "

From far away out in the dark comes my father's sleepy voice. . . .

"What are you jabbering about, boy? Whom are you talking to?"

I did not answer, and breathed as quietly as I could. . . .

I was holding my mother's hand as we went through narrow clefts between large gray stones. Beneath our feet there was moss into which our footsteps sank. There was not a sound.

"What land is this?" I asked her anxiously.

"Sh! Sh! These stones are the houses of the Little People. Do not wake them," whispered my mother in my ear.

We walked and walked. . . . In one of the stones the door stood ajar. Through this door my mother suddenly disappeared. I tried to follow her but there was a door no longer. I ran round and round the stone. I hammered on it with my bare fists, but there was no door, no window—only a gray stone.

"Don't cry so," my mother comforted me, and laid her warm face close to mine. "How late you have slept today, child!"

We were alone in the living room. Outside, soft and homely, the rain was falling. It ran gaily down the windowpanes.

While I was dressing my mother sat over by the window mending one of my stockings.

"You are now in your eighth year," she said in a strange, confidential tone. "Next winter I suppose you must begin lessons. If you want to learn to read well you must be very industrious right from the start, and, especially develop your memory. The way of learning is long and dull; you are intelligent, but I wonder if you are persevering enough? It is a good thing, first of all, to make up your mind what you are aiming at. Tell me, is there anything you like better than anything else?"

I pressed close to her, hid my face on her shoulder.

"Yes, Mama—you."

My mother hugged me to her with a little laugh. Then she held me away from her, looking at me lovingly and teasingly, with damp, laughing eyes.

"Do you really mean to say you're fond of me? Well, I can tell you that it will not be easy for Mama to spare her big boy for the whole winter—but there are still some years before it will come to that, thank God. . . . But answer me properly. Except for playing games, what do you like doing best?"

"Reading," I answered quickly.

"Reading? That's right. But reading what?"

"Stories. . . ."

My mother laughed at the stocking in her hand; then she said:

"Businessman or priest—which do you think you would rather be?"

I pulled myself together.

"I think I'd rather be neither," I answered heavily.

My mother let her hands sink into her lap and looked at me gravely.

"What then? . . . A doctor perhaps?"

I thought of blessed Frederick and his bottles, and shook my head energetically.

As my mother still sat waiting for my answer, I braced myself and said as frankly as I could:

"I don't want to be anything."

"Now, what have you got in your red head now?" asked my mother, laughing gaily; and biting off the wool she handed me my stocking. It would be soft and warm against my foot where she had mended it.

My mother sat with her chin in her hands and looked out at the rain. Then she turned to me for a moment.

"Well, I expect you will have to be something," she said softly and gravely. "But you must be a good person—or else you will be unhappy."

I thought to myself, "What is a good person?" And suddenly I burst out:

"Is Grandpa-from-Knör a good person?"

My mother smiled.

"Old Papa? . . . Yes, Old Papa is good enough. He can do many things without their doing him any harm. But there is not a drop of priestly blood in his veins."

"Can I be like him then?" I asked.

"That depends," answered my mother, with a gay look in her eyes. "Would you not rather be like Grandpa-from-Fjall?"

"That depends," I mumbled.

My mother sat with a faraway look in her eyes.

"Listen to the rain," she said. "It is raining at Knör, too—on the stones along the seashore and on the gray water close by them. Perhaps Mama is standing in the doorway with her hands under her apron, sniffing at the rain like a cat and saying: 'What weather!' And Old Papa is going in and out in his shirtsleeves and bellowing: 'Always grumbling, always grumbling—you will grumble in Paradise!' Oh dear, just imagine: when I lived there you were not born, and your Mama was just a little girl."

"—And was called Celia," I said, and smiled to myself.

"That and nothing else," smiled my mother, and kissed me. "Call your sisters—I want to see all my little flock!"

8

THERE was a light in the living room when I suddenly woke up . . . an unexpected light that divided it off into a world of its own, unconnected with time or space . . . a bubble of light rising up through a sea of darkness. Nevertheless, I noticed there was movement—upward, upward—and I was eager to know how long it would be before this bubble of yellow lamplight, within which were hurrying shadows and pulsing, groaning life, would reach the edge of the darkness and burst against a gray, boundless day and we, whom it carried with it, would sink like shipwrecked mariners into the depths of the sea.

Somebody groaned.

Yes—somebody groaned. . . . It was my mother.

It was my mother. . . . I raised myself carefully on my elbow. On a chair by her pillow sat my father, bending over her. Sophia and Old Begga tiptoed noiselessly round the bed. They so obscured my view that I could not see my mother, and I could not recognize her voice in the heavy poignant groans, but I knew it must be she. Then I heard her whisper in a queer, thin, penetrating voice:

"Don't wake the children, for God's sake—don't wake the children. . . . O God, God, protect my little flock."

"Lie still, Uggi," breathed Veiga, imploringly, in my ear, and I saw now that both she and Beta were awake. They lay without moving, with big, apprehensive, listening eyes in a pair of expressionless faces—eyes that closed quickly as soon as anybody moved toward us or appeared to be looking our way. From Madame Anna's cradle came the sound of comfortable breathing, substantial and decided, like the whole of her little person.

I let myself slip back onto my pillow, and turned my head

to the wall. A stream of hot tears flowed from under my eye-lids and would not stop. A strange anxiety had taken pos-session of me. I realized that no one could help but God, and I prayed fervently: "Dear God, if my mother dies, let me die too. . . ." My heart beat heavily like a sledgehammer against my ribs. Each time my mother groaned I clenched my teeth and hugged myself. I had a dim idea that by doing so I would relieve her of some of the pain that was tearing her to pieces, and all the time I had a feeling that we were rising, rising—rushing with mad speed toward a merciless dawn, desolate as an autumn day, blind and deaf as the stones on the mountains where even moss will not grow.

"Shriek, dear Celia," I heard Sophia say in a cheerful voice. "Let yourself go. . . . We can take the children over to Old Begga's bedroom for the time being."

"Oh, no," whimpered my mother, with tears and entreaty in her voice, usually so brave. "Let them sleep. They will wake soon enough."

The stuffy, oppressive smell of steam and medicaments half choked me. I stopped crying, and my tears dried on my cheeks. Sophia and Old Begga moved round the lamp, from which came a buzzing noise, at times the loudest noise in the room. The shadows flitted quickly from floor to ceiling and then sank back into themselves again. I tried to read my mother's destiny in this shadow-play, but the threatening and favorable signs and figures alternated so rapidly I could make nothing of them. There was something sinister abroad—a mys-terious presentiment of some horror which so far was only a tiny, tiny black spot, scarcely visible, but which I felt might grow with the rapidity of a shadow and envelop us all in its scintillating darkness.

A shiver of surprise passed through me when my mother asked suddenly in her natural voice, in which was no pain or fear:

"What is there actually in the way, Sophia?"

"Nothing—so far as I can tell," answered Sophia. Was the

sincerity in her voice really to be depended on? If only one knew whether it was genuine or not!

"It's never been so bad before," whispered my mother, and groaned again. . . . "O God. . . . How you are torturing me, you little child! Be a little more careful—remember I'm your mother."

When the room was quiet again I opened my eyes carefully—and started violently. Against the gabled wall I saw a queer distorted picture of Sophia's round head. It was a picture in which all her features were grossly exaggerated, and yet essentially accurate and terrifyingly lifelike.

At that moment something happened within me: I do not know what, except that something happened. At that moment I definitely changed. Everybody knows these quick turns of the mind. It is like sailing with the wind so as not to upset. . . . Now we were no longer traveling through space; we were nailed tightly to the earth. The windows did not reflect the lamplight any longer, but were beginning to get faint and gray in the desolate dawn of the coming day. In the depths of my mind a cold destiny had been sealed and accepted.

"It will just have to take its time, dear mistress," muttered Old Begga, in a dead, despondent voice which seemed to come from far away. "How would a drop of fresh milk taste—fresh from old Skjalda?"

"Dear good Bergljot," answered my mother in her new voice, quickly and warmly. "You faithful old dear, give Skjalda my love—don't forget to give her her bran. . . . O God, who will supervise everything now? And here am I interrupting work in the middle of the precious harvest! . . . and we, who have so little hay. . . . The men and the girls—send them off as usual. . . . I expect you can go yourself—this afternoon—Greipur."

"Don't think of that," answered my father, gently.

Old Begga slipped quietly away toward the dark square of the trap-door opening and sank noiselessly, step by step, down into insubstantial depths.

Perhaps during the night something had happened to the stairs. Perhaps now they led right down into the center of the earth, and Old Begga was going farther and farther down, and could not understand where the floor had got to—till at last she would reach the trap door into Hell. "Come nearer," the Evil One would say. "One little jump and you will be here!" . . . But Old Begga would put her hand to her eyes and gaze at him hard and long. "I don't suppose I shall meet my blessed bishop Jon Vidalin down there?" she would ask. "Aha, you belong to that sheepfold!" the Devil would burst out. "What are you doing here then? Get away!"

It was very quiet in the living room now. My father was sitting there motionless. There was something quite hopeless about his powerful frame. Every little movement he made seemed to express his helpless perplexity. Even when at last he pulled himself together and whispered: "Hadn't we better send for the doctor?" there was something in his tone that made the suggestion sound hopeless and as if it were impossible to carry out.

Sophia, who was standing with one hand on her hip, holding her chin with the other and watching my mother, who had fallen asleep, answered quickly:

"It can do no harm. . . . I will go and wake Mundi."

On my mother's face, which seemed to me so young and fresh, there were beads of perspiration, as if she had been running and playing with us children. But I soon realized that the dew that covered her face was of a different kind.

Dew. The word seemed to stick in my excited and anxious brain: evening dew, morning dew, the dew of death. . . . No, there was nothing called that! I had not thought it! That word had never been in my mind! I wiped it out . . . but it was not so easy as that to escape from a word. In spite of my will my heart began to hammer it fast: the dew of death, the dew of death! . . . Then I tried to lead the conception away from my mother, but that wasn't quite successful—and with an icy coldness the idea fixed itself in my mind that I, with these unfortunate words, had pronounced a death-sentence. At the same time I remembered with shame and horror that several times lately I had amused myself by walking backward, although Old Begga had warned me that in this way I was walking my mother "down into her grave." Here lay my mother now, very ill. Death was asking Our Lord: "Shall I take her?" "Yes, take her," answered Our Lord, looking at me with an awful sternness in His glance. I cast aside all memories, all terror, and began to pray frenziedly. "Dear God," I prayed with my whole heart, "it is quite right for you to punish me—but if you do it in this way you will make Veiga, Beta, Madame Anna and the one who is not yet born, all motherless. Let mercy go before justice!"

The floor creaked faintly under Sophia's footsteps. The stairs complained—and I heard my mother's voice, wide awake, say: "I'd rather you woke Nonni—he will fetch the doctor."

In my deep anguish these words penetrated as a relief. I felt suddenly: There is still hope.

"Are you awake, beloved?" whispered my father, helplessly. My mother fumbled for his hand, found it, and over her face came a smile which in spite of her pain and agony moved me by its beauty and its radiant warmth.

I jumped out of bed with determination.

My mother started, put her hand to her heart, lifted her head. "What is it, Uggi child?"

"I am only going to hurry Nonni up," I answered, tripping across the floor toward the trap door. But now her smile included me, and her weak hand beckoned me. Sobbing, I threw myself on her.

As if by command Veiga and Beta began to cry heartrendingly, and Madame Anna sat up, rubbed her eyes in wonder and then decided to drown us all.

My mother raised herself on her elbow, smiled and waved to my sisters, hushed us.

"Now, then, children, don't cry like that. . . . Mother will

soon be well again, and you will have a little brother. . . . O
God," she groaned, biting her lips, sinking back against the
pillows. "O dear God . . . Greipur! Can no one help me?"

I dashed toward the trap door, past Sophia, who was rushing
up, tore myself free from Old Begga's bony arms and found
Nonni, who was almost dressed. But when I wished to help
him saddle the horse, he said in his friendly, patient voice:

"Don't hinder me, Uggi dear!"

There I stood, shivering, bewildered, no good to anybody.
I realized desolately that all that was happening just now
was outside me; and this realization stole my strength and robbed
me of my artificial courage.

Powerless, I dragged myself along the passages, up the stairs.
In front of my mother's bed, with both hands under the coverlet, knelt Sophia, and my mother was groaning, abandoning
herself to anguish and misery as never before. But what was
this? How could my father sit there and watch Sophia torturing
my mother? Or perhaps he hadn't noticed it. I gave a shriek
so as to draw his attention to it, and would have hurled myself
on Sophia had not Old Begga caught me and, in spite of my
floundering and kicking, carried me downstairs, not stopping
until I caught hold of a post in the passage and held myself
fast.

"She is torturing Mother!" I shouted in despair. "She is
torturing Mother!"

"Do you mean Sophia?" asked Old Begga, quietly. "Don't
be such a little silly—she is only trying to help her."

I could hear from Old Begga's tone that she was speaking
the truth, and ashamed of my mistake and uncontrolled fury,
I allowed myself to be carried away to the stairs leading to the
bedroom which Old Begga shared with Maria Mens.

"Your sisters are up there," said Old Begga, putting me
down on one of the steps. "Go and get into bed and be good
children. I must hurry back. Later on I will bring you something nice. When the child is born we shall all enjoy ourselves and be happy again. One must not disturb one's mother
when she is in childbed. . . ."

A deep despondency gripped me. There I had been behaving stupidly again—a good thing that Old Begga got
hold of me in time. . . . When she left me I went on up the
stairs. Up in the bedroom I heard Madame Anna's chatter, and
Veiga and Beta answering her with sober monosyllables.
Doubtless they would begin talking to me and asking me questions as soon as they saw me. . . . I turned back. In the outer
room I found the dogs curled up in a corner, and I crept down
among them. A little surprised, they made room for me on their
warm couch of sacks and snuggled close up to me. Dreyfus
went to sleep again, but Gaul began to lick one of my legs with
sleepy friendliness. By degrees he became more and more eager.
His warm, wet tongue reached farther every time, and he
licked eagerly and energetically, as if he wished to lick away
both my skin and flesh down to the bone. With a dog's in-
stinct he understood my misery and tried, in the only way he
knew, to lessen my unhappiness. Gradually the pressure on
my chest dissolved itself into tears and hopefulness. I leaned
down over him and he licked even my tears; and as I went on
crying he tenderly and carefully scratched at my arm with his
paw and gave one or two very soft little barks, his sweet, innocent dog's heart sympathizing with my despair. I hugged him
close to me. Dreyfus was patient with our restlessness, and
then in came Gryla from the yard, sniffing the raw morning
air, stretching her taut yellowish-white body, yawning and
shaking herself. She advanced in a dignified way to our little
group, glanced at us with her ears falling in attentive folds,
looked me straight in the face and waved her tail graciously
and indulgently—a rare gesture with her. Generally she kept
a tight hand on us children. At her dinner time she would insist
that we stay indoors and not play any noisy games. In the
mornings we must not play on the east side of the yard, and in
the afternoon not on the west, for that was where she wanted
to lie in peace and sun herself. In a word, we must mind our
p's and q's. But in this solitary morning hour she was in a
gentle mood, and she also seemed affected by a certain anxiety
and expectation. Now and again she listened tensely and with

an uneasy glint in her audacious light-brown eyes. Slowly her tail drooped and was still; then she wandered off aimlessly and lay down in a corner with her nose hidden and one eye on the door . . . my father must come *some* time.

Maria Mens found me among the dogs, and as she was crying as usual, only more so, she had no way to show her surprise and sympathy but by drying her eyes and ceasing to cry for a little while.

"What are you doing there, child!" she exclaimed. "Dear me, dear me, how upside down everything is today!"

As I definitely refused to allow myself to be dragged up to my sisters, she fetched my clothes and helped me to put them on. Then I followed her to the cowhouse where she was going to milk the cow.

In the cowhouse there was also anxiety and uncertainty. Old Skjalda was mooing, pulling at her halter; mooing again, listening.

"I believe she knows," whispered Maria Mens, with a little shiver. "But it would be strange if she didn't, seeing how that animal loves your mother. It is a comfort to know that in Paradise there is eternal summer and rich pastures; for you know, of course, that if an animal loves a human being it becomes blessed and is allowed to follow the person it loves to all eternity."

I had not heard this before, but I felt that it was right and as it should be. My mother would be followed by Skjalda and her gray, my father by Gryla, and I myself by Gaul. . . . I crept shyly into Skjalda's stall, began to stroke her smooth, taut side. She seemed to like it, but otherwise paid no attention to me, seemed scarcely to notice me. Her great ears twitched hither and thither, speaking a silent but expressive language. Her round eyes rolled and rolled, looking in all directions to catch a glimpse of someone whom they could not see. From the stall beside her was heard the dull rhythmical smack of the milk going into the pail, and Maria Mens' calm words to the cows that stamped, moved, would not stand still.

"Come here, Uggi, let me look at you," said Maria Mens, in a subdued voice.

I went over to her indifferently and stood by her side. She took my hand, laid it against her warm smooth cheek, pressed it—a good thing that Nonni was not there.

"Don't be so despairing," she comforted me, sending me a loving and sympathetic glance from her tear-sodden eyes. "When Madame Anna was born you children were kept out of the way—otherwise you would have been just as unhappy as today and to no purpose. A child may take a long time coming into the world, and it is very bad while it is going on, but when it is over the pain is forgotten."

These weak generalizations did not comfort me at all; on the contrary, they settled on my mind like a dead weight and depressed me still more. Then suddenly I remembered Maria's sister—Sigga Mens. One of the stories she had told me was about a child that was dragged out of its mother's womb limb by limb. Yes, even the head was separated from the rest of the body. Oddly enough, I felt a sort of comfort in thinking of this grim incident. Things like that didn't happen very often, I knew. Was it possible that it might happen now? . . . But in this way my tortured mind sought relief: There was no help for it, such things had happened; but that was in the olden time, they were no longer possible.

Maria Mens wanted to make me drink some milk, warm from the cow, but this reminded me how often I had sat beside my mother while she milked, and had enjoyed the fragrant drink drop by drop; and I could not get a mouthful down. But I could not bring myself to leave Maria Mens. I was so sorry for her because she could not comfort me. I must not let her know this. When the milking was over I followed her to the larder.

The other servants were up now. They crept about silent, with anxious looks. Seldom did any of them ask a question— more seldom still was any answer given. I came upon Disa just below the bedroom stair. She stood there with her lean arms

crossed over her flat bosom, and her silent listening made the
gray freckled face still sharper, the narrow head still narrower.

"N-n-n," she began to hum when she saw me, took a few
steps forward, looked at a knot in the staircase, fingered it with a
pair of thin gray fingers—but pulled herself together and said
in a distant but friendly voice, as she went away:

"Poor woman! . . . And what is the good of being born?"

It was very odd to see the trouble Old Begga and Disa took
to be friendly toward each other and do each other little services.
Disa hunted out all sorts of things for which Old Begga could
not possibly have any use, and gave them to her, and Old Begga
blessed her in a loud voice and in return did everything she
could for her, even to putting the salt into her porridge saucepan, and forgetting to tell her about it in time. But all the
servants, and even we children, except Madame Anna, ate
the salt porridge without a word of complaint. Then we were
all very thirsty and drank a lot of water, and this gave Maggi
the opportunity of sacrificing himself and carrying heavy water
pails to and fro crookedly.

Maggi amazed me. He didn't actually cry, but now and again
a little tear would steal from his left eye down his thin nose—
now and again one also from the right. Added to this he was
very silent, dead silent. And when he had not a pail to carry
he sat there absolutely immovable.

I knew that Maggi loved my mother. Ever since the time she
had boxed his ears for some prank or other he had hung about
her. He would sit and follow her with eyes in which there was
not the least gleam of mischief, and as he was not her own child
he was much more careful than we others to obey her and
avoid doing anything she did not like. From the time when
she treated him as one of us he was fond of her—but from the
day when he was given his share of punishment he loved her
from the bottom of his thin brave heart.

Now he sat there on the flat, rough lid of a box, with large
patches on the knees of his trousers, and his very thin legs

crossed, gazing straight in front of him, or looking covertly now and again at the pail of water to see if it needed replenishing.

"Maggi," I said, trying to get him to talk, "won't Nonni soon be here with the doctor? Oughtn't they to be here already? Dear Maggi, do answer me."

He did not hear me, sat there with his thoughts far away. Suddenly he broke out:

"If only I were a doctor I would go to Hell . . . !"

"Don't swear like that, child," Old Begga reproved him in a friendly tone. "It would be better if you brought in some more fresh water."

Maggi's little head above his thin neck sank down onto his chest—I had never seen him blush so before. His lips moved. I wondered whether he was crying or saying a prayer. I was so surprised that I almost forgot my own anxiety and sorrow.

"Can you tell me, you old bluestocking, why your mother has to suffer so much when she gives birth to her children?" asked Old Begga, turning toward me.

I looked expectantly at her, and she explained:

"The mother must suffer so because a child is God's most precious gift. God wants her to know that this life is not made up only of happiness and pleasure; sorrow and pain also have their places in our lives. But the fact that the child is so often a gift of sorrow is not God's fault, but the Devil's. That gentleman is always to the fore. He has his spies and henchmen everywhere. A child is to be born in Greipur Uggason's house. Ha, ha! thinks the Devil, no doubt that Maggi boy, that good friend of mine, will warn me, and he is quite right. Before the innocent child has been born into the world Maggi obediently calls on him and endeavors to be his faithful servant. If there were not a band of God's angels round the bed of our dear mistress we should have the Devil in command here, and perhaps a life lost and a human soul made desolate."

Maggi sat like a bird in the rain. It was impossible to catch his eye. I had never before seen him openly defenseless, and I was very sorry for him. Furthermore, I could not but think that Old Begga was exaggerating on purpose. Of course Our Lord had arranged in time to have His angels present.

"Pooh!—the Devil!" I said with forced courage. "Just let him come. I will deal with him."

"God forgive you, child," whispered Old Begga, crestfallen. "What do you mean?"

"I will bury him in the ground with psalms, and make the sign of the cross over him," I answered keeping up my courage.

"Well, you're a priest all right," tittered Old Begga. "It is a good thing that your mother didn't hear you, you little sparrow."

With a heavy heart I lounged out of the room. I had made a fool of myself again. Nothing but bad luck came my way. I had challenged the Devil to no purpose, and if he came now, which I fully believed he would, the angels would have so much to do that they would not be able to look after my mother properly, and then she would lie there tormented and dying, though perhaps it was not really Our Lord's idea that she should die just now. Perhaps He had meant only to give us all a useful fright. I roamed about miserably; I wanted to go outside, but when I heard the sound of Stebbi's plane out there I turned back and sought a dark and solitary corner, where I sat down and inhaled with a certain pleasure the smell of dry rot, damp and moldy. I sat there deserted, shivering in my misery, until I heard the sound of horse's hoofs outside and rushed out through the passages to see if it could be the doctor.

In the doorway I saw coming toward me "the little man" whom I remembered from the day when Madame Anna was born, our doctor from Breidale, and I was so surprised that I stepped backward—for, in such a short time, it would have been impossible for Nonni to get all the way to Breidale and back again.

"Don't be afraid of me," smiled the little man, pleasantly. In the middle of his small colorless face there was a sharp but curiously stubby nose, not fully developed, born too early, like the whole man, but in no way frightening.

A deep and refreshing confidence suddenly streamed through the whole of my being. I went to him and held out my hand as if I were grown up.

"Show me the way," he said, and gripped my fingers with a hand as soft as Sophia's or Madame Anna's. "I have helped your mother once before, my lad."

"I know that," I answered, and caught hold of his coat so that he should not lose his way in the dark passages, and dragged him after me.

"Oh, I see, you know," he said pleasantly. "Now look at that—an observant lad. Can you read? What are you reading now?"

"Oh, books and papers," I answered, and could not understand how he could talk about such things now. How strange grownups were! They seemed to stand outside events. Things happened and no one seemed to take any notice of them.

"I see. Newspapers too?" asked the little man, and he seemed to be impressed. "Do you also know *Synnöve Solbakken*—and *Arne?*"

"Yes, yes," I said, remembering the rhymes which my mother had sung to us before I could read, and which I had now read so many times and yet never tired of . . . the houses, the scenery, the weather, the people. I saw them all before me, so living and so warm. I did not know that none of it happened in Iceland and that it was all tradition had never occurred to me for a moment.

"Dear, dear, you know those books?" said the little man, interested. "That's a pity. What can I give you then? There is another book translated by the same man who wrote *Arne* and *Synnöve*—perhaps you would enjoy that. . . . I must try to remember to bring it for you."

We had now reached the stairs to our bedroom. The little man fumbled in his pocket and brought out a paper bag.

"Share this with your sisters, and keep out of the way and

be good children. You can't be much use in a confinement until
you are a doctor."

Comforted, I left this good man, found my sisters, whom
Maria Mens was now dressing, and divided out the sweets in
equal numbers to each of us. They were lovely sweets in many
colors, red and yellow and white, and tasted freshly acid. But
scarcely had I put one in my mouth before I remembered how
ill my mother was at this moment, remembered the groaning
which had reached me as I ran away with the bag—a groaning
which I pretended not to hear—and I spat out the sweet. I
thought of Maggi, found him still sitting on the trunk, pressed
my handful of sticky caramels into his mouth all at once:

"Here is something nice for you, dear Maggi."

I stood and looked on while he, without any pleasure, chewed
and chewed them between his teeth, made a face and then
sank back into apathy.

Before I knew where I was, I was again standing below the
bedroom door, listening. I heard footsteps up there, subdued
talk, otherwise nothing . . . yes, thank God, my mother was
moaning again. My heart freed itself as from a heavy grasp,
beat more freely. She was groaning, she was moaning. Thank
God! . . . For now it was silence that I feared.

People came and went. Sometimes they said something to
me, but nothing affected me; I took no notice. Nonni stood
for a time looking at me, then he went away. I listened and
listened. I held my breath during the pauses, breathed more
freely when the groaning started again, hopeless and heartrending.
And yet I was tortured, tortured. . . .

Disa stood in the half-darkness and spoke to me with her
hoarse, dusky voice. I understood at last that she was offering
me coffee, and as I suddenly felt ready to fall from fatigue and
at the same time smelled a strong aroma coming from her room,
I had a great desire for a cup and went with her. To my surprise
I found Old Begga there. They were talking about my mother.

"One gets fonder and fonder of her every day," said Disa,

as if excusing herself, and busied herself awkwardly with the coffeepot and coffee basins.

"A blessed woman," whispered Old Begga, near the breaking-point.

Then we were all three silent, gulping down our black coffee from our flowered basins.

"If blessed Frederick had been alive," began Disa—but then I could stand no more, got up, thanked them for the coffee, and went.

What was the good of this blessed Frederick to me—he and his wisdom, and his eternal medicine? He was a poet too. . . . Pooh!

I felt suffocated; I must get outside for a mouthful of fresh air. I met Gryla in the doorway. She whimpered questioningly and twisted her ears in the oddest way—perhaps she thought it was my father who was ill. I felt angry with her too, passed her coldly, did not answer her question, gave her no comfort.

The autumn weather, with its white driving clouds on the glorious blue sky and a stiff cold wind, swept round me with a queer harsh brotherliness. The grass paths were brown now, but the heather was gradually changing into red. These flames of color, newly-lighted and indefinite, would lick up the mountainside and in a few days the autumn tints would be lighting bog and mountain. Then my mother and I would wander among the whortleberry hummocks; my sisters too would be there. We would pick whole buckets full. Then we would build us a fireplace in some convenient place, collect dry branches and warm our milk.

I found Stebbi in an outbuilding. In spite of the good weather he kept indoors today. He was planing hard—very quiet. I sat down on a heap of wood shavings. Then he suddenly woke up.

"Why have you dumped yourself down just there?" he asked crossly. "I have collected only fine clean white shavings in that heap. . . . You always make trouble."

"What are you going to use them for, dear Stebbi?" I asked, and moved.

"That's nothing to do with you; you ask about everything. Don't you know that it is ill-bred to be so inquisitive? A child should hold its tongue and listen. . . . Blessed Frederick gave his foster children a good upbringing."

I was silent and listened. It was not Stebbi I was listening to but the plane, for it is from dead things, otherwise silent, that we can learn our destiny—they are in league with the hidden powers. But today I could learn nothing from the plane. One moment it shouted jubilantly, "Silence—redeemed!" In the next it threatened, "Affliction—death!"

Stebbi had forgotten me and was talking to himself.

"I said to my cousin Sophia, 'Haven't you a pair of old rings?' Yes, she had—but I was not to touch the names. Blessed Frederick's and blessed Maria's names must not be obliterated by human hands. Well, well, let that be. But Paulina rebelled and said, 'How can I marry a man called Stefan and wear a ring with the name of Frederick? If I did, all the Fredericks in the land would be welcome.' 'No, no, Paulina,' I said, 'I will go to Goldsmith Karl.' 'Whatever goldsmith you go to makes no difference to me,' shouted Paulina. She was so vehement, so uncontrolled. 'Don't you love me?' I asked. 'Love you?' she shouted. 'I must know your name first. I see, your name is Frederick. Darling Freddie, beloved Freddie . . . of course I love you.' Women—ha, ha!"

Stebbi shook his head, put his plane aside and calmly took a pinch of snuff.

"What a scene there would be with Sophia if she were ever to know! Alas, alas, the world is a vale of mourning. Here I am going off and getting married. Freddie. Ha, ha! 'Call me by my own name,' I counseled her. 'Don't play with fire.' Then she kissed her Freddie, caressed her Freddie—and what can I do? Is it me, or is it her Freddie she kisses? Well, well, it will right itself in the end. Good sense will come with the children. Paulina is, after all, a sensible girl."

Stebbi sighed, and left his Paulina for the present.

"In foreign countries I expect they use oak coffins," he mumbled, "and for kings, silver and gold and marble. But whether they lay wood shavings in the bottom, that I don't know."

Quite silently and unnoticed I stole away. The glorious smell of hay surrounding the farm, the black-breasted ptarmigans preparing for flight, the shrill notes of the stream which we always heard when the wind was in the east—all these things that usually gave me pleasure and uplifted me lay now like a heavy comfortless burden on my mind and increased its pain. I realized it suddenly. As my mother was too ill for me to have my cry out in her arms, there was nowhere for me to go for comfort—nowhere—not even to God.

And what if she should die? But why should she die? A mother does not die every time a child is born, and everybody in the world has been born in the same way as that boy in there is just about to be born. That Sigberg who is to become a priest—Sira Sigbergur. Happily there would now be no need for me to become a priest, and I did not wish to become one in any circumstance. I wanted to wander through the world, to visit Heaven and earth, sea and desert islands. I longed to see it all and to know it all. Now and again I would return to my mother and father, stay with them for a time, see my sisters' husbands, and listen to my brother Sira Sigbergur, who would intone those services from the altar which I had rejected, and keep, as it were, a good relationship between the family and God. . . .

Toward afternoon my brother was born, and a little later we children were allowed to visit my mother. We stood holding one another's hands beside her bed, well-washed and quiet. We looked at the little one sleeping with his head on her arm, and enjoyed the warmth of her tired smile and radiant eyes.

"Now I have two red-headed boys," she said, smiling at me. "Here is a little brother for you to look after, Uggi child."

I swallowed the tears in my throat, and tried to blink away

the tears in my eyes. I was not able either to answer or to smile back at her.

"Me look after little brother," shouted Madame Anna, and toddled forward to take him over at once. "Madame Anna look after little brother. . . . Uggi silly boy."

In the midst of the laughter and noise at Madame Anna's expense, little brother woke up and began to cry. Madame Anna stood still a moment as if turned to stone, with her fat arms outstretched. Then she turned away, ran hastily off to the stairs and began to crawl down them.

"Uggi have little brother," she shouted at me.

As my mother was now to rest, we children were sent away. With a heart infinitely light, but feeling very tired, I walked about but could not calm myself. Was it possible that it was all over? Or had I been dreaming—had the whole thing been a bad dream?

Everybody on the farm was now in the highest spirits. Only Maria Mens cried, and no one took any notice of her, not even Nonni. There was a smell of coffee and of fresh-baked pancakes everywhere. In Sophia's room, which had been made available in honor of the great occasion, sat our doctor, Björn Jonsson, and drank coffee with my father. There was also a third cup on the table. It was meant for Sophia, who went backward and forward with sparkling eyes and a brilliant smile.

"Do you know, Doctor Björn," she said, and sat up straight, picking up a cake and eating it fastidiously, "you have an excellent pair of midwife's hands."

"Ha, ha!" said the doctor, leaning back in the chair, swinging his short legs and making the thumbs of his "excellent midwife's hands" (which were clasped at the moment) turn round each other at a tremendous speed. "You would not have managed without me this time, Miss Sophia!"

"No, I'm afraid not," she agreed, with her briskest laugh, and suddenly grew serious. "Where God is present, there is seldom any real danger."

"Tja!" answered the doctor, and laid his face into pious folds, seeking for something on which to fix his eyes. "You are right."

My father sat looking from one to the other. His eyes lingered, not unwillingly, on Sophia.

"That gray of yours, Greipur, is a good horse, a matchless animal," said the doctor, waking up, as it were, from a dream. "Is it for sale?"

"No, that it certainly is not," answered Sophia, using her eyes. "I'm not even allowed to borrow it to go to town."

My father blushed a little; then he cleared his throat.

"A pity," said Dr. Björn, looking round. "A pity!"

I lay long that night listening to my mother's labored breath and to the quick breathing of my new brother. I would be really kind to this little boy, never run away from him, never be impatient with him. Then God would forgive me for all the stupid things I had done and thought during the day. Time and again I had imperiled my mother's life, but now I would try to improve. Never would I walk backward, never again be violent, swear, or creep away to give the dogs the food I did not like. When my sisters annoyed me, I would stay with them and not hide myself in gullies or between tussocks. Never again would I irritate Maggi, and some time or other I would ask Disa to forgive me for having taken so much of blessed Frederick's medicine.

I said to Maggi the next day:

"Shall we two organize a society for giving up swearing?"

"All warriors swear," declared Maggi, in a superior tone of voice. "Generals worst of all. I'm not going to give it up for anybody. I have even taught Dreyfus to bark, 'Hell, hell.' More I can't make him do, the silly ass. Go off to Old Begga. You will get all the old women on your side, all the mollusks, all the sanctimonious fools. You thought you were helping me yesterday when Old Begga suddenly began to talk. Didn't you understand, you nincompoop, that I had the best of you all?"

Young as I was, I understood very well that Maggi was now ashamed of the emotion he had shown the day before, and I endeavored to sound surprised and pretended to believe him.

I was sorrier for him today than I had been yesterday, for, as often, my mother's words sounded in my ears: "A good boy, that Maggi . . ." I knew she was right, even though Maggi behaved so rudely and appeared so rough and ill-bred. . . . Decency is found even in the dirt, though it may disguise itself. The most wonderful flowers can be found behind the prison walls of sin and depravity that human beings, in their ignorance and misery, often build up around their souls. No wonder things go wrong in a world where each can boast of his bad qualities, while he tries eagerly to hide his goodness, so he may not run the risk of being laughed at, imposed on, persecuted. . . .

It was very funny to see Disa and Old Begga. They did not seem to be able to find the right attitude to each other today. Each avoided the other carefully, and if they happened to meet, they passed with downcast eyes and in the greatest haste.

I had seen only a glimpse of my father early that morning. He was out in the field cutting the grass. Toward afternoon Sophia sent for him. Then someone went for the doctor. He came, but he did not bring a book for me; no doubt he had forgotten it. Everyone was full of confidence that my mother had only a slight fever.

It was difficult to get through the next few days. It did not occur to me to be frightened for my mother now that my brother was actually born, but I missed her more every day, sat for long hours at a stretch on the chair leading to the living room, and felt inwardly depressed. We were not allowed to go in to her for fear of disturbing her. The fact that the doctor came every day I thought good and reassuring. But I could not get the days to pass. I had not the patience to look out for ships in the sky. My talent for dreams and fantasies seemed to have forsaken me. I could not read; it wearied me, and I did not want to listen to the stories with which Old Begga tried to shorten the hours. Was there a sinister suspicion in some dark corner of my consciousness? Was it accidental that all the clouds I saw were immediately transformed into monsters looking down into the stream, frightening me and sending cold shivers down my spine, that the wind was able to make my mind quiver and vibrate like a clothesline; that every night, and sometimes several times in the night, I woke crying from bad dreams, and that, as never before, I feared solitariness, was suddenly able to feel the silence around me and would fly full of terror? I do not know. But I remember well the day on which the doctor brought me a thin book wrapped in brown paper. That day I remember more clearly than any other in my life.

There was nothing extraordinary about that day, nor did anything happen. I was not even conscious of my anxiety. But the pale sunshine; the light-blue hazy autumn sky; the mild but treacherously cold east wind; the shadows that lightened and darkened, and then lightened again, the desolate rhythm of the landscape, slender in tone and far away, but so frostily clear, so starry; the faint blue of the mountains which hid itself here and there in clefts and under promontories—all this penetrated into my blood, stamped itself on my soul. Under the sky of *that* day was my life lived out.

The book was called *The Wedding March,* and I tried to read it at once but could not get through it. It wearied me and it still wearies me. That I did not like it gave me, for some reason or other, a bad conscience—and oddly enough still does.

In the evening they told me that, so as not to disturb my mother, I was to sleep in Old Begga's bed. I took this alteration calmly, or was it that I just did not dare to be afraid? That I cannot decide. I only know that within me everything had become very quiet—very quiet.

I was allowed to go up and say goodnight to my mother, but I was told to be "a good boy" and not upset her in any way.

I went up. . . . I stood for long, without moving, beside her bed, and did not know if I dared touch her. She herself lay quite still, just looking at me—just looking at me. . . . Suddenly her eyes filled with tears.

"Good night, my boy," she whispered with trembling lips, so low that I could scarcely hear her, and I understood that I was to kiss her, understood too that she was not able to lift her arms.

I leaned against the bed, lifted myself up, and bent down and kissed her carefully. With an uncertain hand I carefully and shamefacedly wiped away the tears which, against my will, dripped down onto her hot cheeks.

She shut her eyes—and I thought she meant me to go, and I went. . . . There must have been others in the room, but if there were, and who they were, I did not know.

As soon as I lay between the sheets in Old Begga's bed I fell asleep. I slept like a log.

When I woke next morning I saw, through the west window, that the sun shone happily from a cloudless sky. I was alone. . . . There is always a great stillness in real sunshine, but in this sunshine there was a peculiar stillness. There was not a sound to be heard. I listened toward the yard in case I might hear some-one in the passages, or at least catch the sound of conversation. But I listened in vain. Was it so silent because the door was shut? Scarcely, scarcely just because of that. But the haymakers must have gone off to their work. Probably only my mother, Old Begga, Sophia and my sisters were at home. I thought I heard Nonni's penetrating voice, but that was impossible, quite impossible. There was no hay to be dried at home. . . . That was Gryla's barking . . . but why wasn't Gryla in the fields with my father?

I tried to go to sleep again. Impossible.

The trap door in the floor, the closed trap door, drew my eyes toward it. It was obvious that it was not often shut, except at night, for it was not half as worn as the floor around it. There was something safe about that trap door; I could easily live here all my life. Time would pass and I should just lie here. Why should one live among people? Why should one travel? If God would make this room invisible and immovable, I could lie here till Doomsday, doing nothing but look at the sunshine. All human beings who are alive now would die, and others would be born and die, and I would just lie here. People might come as far as my trap door but no farther—that would be a pact between God and me. In return I would never move, never wish for anything, never be impatient . . . just wait. . . .

I recognized Old Begga's footsteps as she came along the dark, narrow passages toward the stairs. She came up them slowly, as if she were carrying something heavy, and in spite of the pact I had just made with God the trap door was lifted and her gray head appeared.

Today she was altogether gray: her hair, her face, her eyes. Why was she looking at me like that?

"Dear God," I prayed feverishly, and shut my eyes so she might think I was not yet awake—"Dear God, she has not said anything yet. I don't know anything yet. Hurry up and change things round. Hurry up and let my mother wake again. No one need know it was a miracle. Let them think that she only seemed to go away. . . . God! God! God!"

My heart beat wildly. The words of prayer stormed wildly through me. I hammered out the words against the God who hears all and sees all . . . and, as usual, He answered nothing.

Old Begga had been sitting for some time, stroking my hair with her stiff fingers, allowing her wrinkled hand to glide carefully over my cheek. She knew I was awake. She knew more. Suddenly our eyes met. I could hear the tiny sound of a tear— evidently from the tip of her nose—falling onto her starched apron. No doubt she partly understood me. Yet she did not understand how unwilling I was that she should say something, for she began to murmur pityingly:

"Poor motherless lamb—poor motherless lamb!"

And so it was said. I opened my eyes and asked with a hoarse voice quite foreign to myself:

"Why doesn't Father come?"

I did not listen to Old Begga's explanation. Something snapped in my heart. Now I was alone in the world.

It was long before Old Begga's awkward caresses and mild words thawed my frozen tears, but when they came they were short and useless. Nothing was gained by them.

A great apathy came over me.

My head ached so badly, I went about feeling as if I had a bad abscess, which was about to burst, just at the top of my backbone.

When my mother was to be "sung away," when I for the first time was to see what remained of that which, but yesterday, had been my mother, my heart began to stammer wildly. But as soon as I saw her body stretched on the bier that Stebbi had knocked together, saw her lying there with a strange and quite unapproachable expression on a face I scarcely recognized, my heart grew calm, and remained calm.

My father sat on one of the beds with his face hidden in his brown hands. There was something strange about him too. When he took the hymn book which was pushed into his hand, and I saw his face, distorted with grief, while he tried to sing the hymn, I realized I did not know this man. I looked round at the others. Not one of them did I know. Even Maggi and Nonni had, as it were, glided away from my consciousness. My sisters: I realized suddenly how undeveloped they were—only in bud, just children. Emotions chased across their faces leaving no trace, like swift breezes over quiet lakes. With a silent and agonized heart I hid myself behind Old Begga. All this singing, all this crying, all this sobbing . . . what was the good of it all? My mother was dead, was dead.

My mother was laid, on her bier, in Sophia's room, and she lay there with sheets hung in front of the window, and the days passed. Thin and exhausted she lay beneath her white linen, with crossed arms and an open psalm book on her breast. My father went in to her, and Old Begga and Sophia. They did not encourage us children to go in, but once I saw a glimpse of her uncovered face. She seemed to be staring with closed eyes at something she could not cease to look at. The smell that emanated from her, and that made me sick in soul and in body, was like a lost cry, a despairing cry for mercy, mercy! But there was no mercy. All was inevitable. All must take its course.

Sophia had taken charge of the new-born child, fed him in a

motherly way, cared for him ceaselessly, carried him in her arms during the day and looked after him at night. There was something in all this that did not appeal to me.

"I suppose I can use some of the planks which were meant for the floor?" Stebbi asked my father in a subdued, sorrowful tone—and took a pinch of snuff.

My father nodded. . . .

Stebbi went on planing the boards.

Why did this hurt me so? After all, boards were just boards, and no one had stepped on them yet. But they had been intended for the floor.

I tried to talk to the autumn flowers, but either they did not hear me or they were vexed with me—for they only looked at me. Nor had the birds anything to say to me; they only flew past me with anxious wing-beats. But I did not want to do them any harm. And my ships? . . . There were no ships.

"I never see you nowadays," said Stebbi, in a friendly voice, Stebbi who had never really seen me except that time when I sat on his wood shavings. "Come and sit down over here."

I did not move.

"I suppose it is only a lie that the world is round?" I asked him.

"A lie?" repeated Stebbi, gazing at me with his childish eyes, and cleaning his plane by blowing through it. "Blessed Frederick thought it so at any rate—and why should it not be round just like all the other stars?"

I went away.

Well, then, the earth was a star. I remembered that I had already been given this explanation, but had either not believed it or not paid any attention to it. At any rate the earth must be a very lonely star. Here it lay all by itself, while the others were part of a whole collection.

"If only I were grown up," I said to Old Begga.

She looked at me with eyes that were swollen with weeping and kitchen smoke, tried to say something, gave it up, and pushed a piece of candy into my mouth. It tasted of sailcloth and the warmth of bed, but Gaul ate it up with enjoyment.

Of all the people on the farm, I was sorriest for Maggi. I never saw him crying, but I often saw that he had cried. He picked heather for the little crosses and wreaths that Old Begga and Sophia each made. He looked for all the different sorts of heather it was possible to find, and took a great deal of trouble with it. . . . I noticed that there was something he wanted to say to me.

"Come with me," he said one day.

He took me up into the gully where the sandstone was, carefully cleared away some gravel, and the following words came into view: "To my mistress Cecilia. Rest in Peace. Magnus Jonsson Bachmann."

I read it through; we were both silent. An indescribable sorrow filled me. She was only his mistress, but she was my mother.

"Do you think it matters, leaving it there?" he asked me softly.

I shook my head. He carefully covered over the writing.

From various kinds of heather, leaves and straw I had made a little bird with speckled wings, a red breast, a green tail and a little bundle of yellow straw sticking up on top of its head. I could not bring myself to show this bird to Maggi; I felt rather conscience-stricken about it, but I just could not.

I was allowed to follow my mother to her grave. I had not brought my bird with me.

My mother's coffin, which Stebbi had covered with several layers of lampblack, swung on two planks fastened between her gray and old Brunka. The gray walked in front, proud as always and very determined in her gait. Did she know whom she was carrying?

Bjarni-from-Fagravik, Parish Constable Toroddur, our neighbors Valdor and Goldsmith Karl from Vegeirsstadir, Grimur-from-Ulfsstadir, Nonni and Maggi were the pall bearers. Nonni and Maggi—I heard that my mother had arranged this herself.

They had both shaved that morning, Maggi for the first time. He bled from several cuts, and I saw him scratching the wounds as soon as they began to dry so that they should not heal.

Ketilbjörn-from-Knör was the eighth bearer. He had come the previous evening, silent, and with only one horse. He had scarcely spoken to anybody, had immediately gone into the room where my mother lay in her coffin. I crept in with him. Softly he lifted the cloth from my mother's face, stood there a moment, laid his forehead against hers, put the cloth back again, went out, did not answer when he was offered a meal, said with no life in his voice, which was generally so vibrant:

"Where shall I sleep?—sleep?"

Then he went to bed and slept, perhaps.

Today he was silent; not a glimpse of a smile enlivened his grotesque old face. His nose hung dejectedly over his mouth. If anything got in his way he was lightly impatient. The leadership had passed imperceptibly into his hands.

"Here I bring you my child, my child," he said to Sira Björn, who, in his black cassock, stood in the darkening door of the church. "Have you any room for her?"

Sira Björn reddened and cleared his throat, greeted us all in a dignified and sympathetic manner. He went before us into the church.

"Well, well, I suppose we must follow him," muttered Ketilbjörn.

No one seemed to hear him. All showed him great respect and were ready to do his least bidding.

Sister-from-Fagravik took my hand, but there was no comfort in that. Didn't she understand nothing could be done? There in her black coffin lay my mother.

A shiny silver cross had been nailed on the lid, and on it Goldsmith Karl had engraved her name and the dates of her birth and of her death. This cross glistened in the sun. There were flies around the coffin, church-flies.

Psalms were sung, and Sira Björn spoke. There stood Eiki. Halla was not there. She had not been able to leave home. At the thought of her, I noticed that my eyes smarted as if from tears, but there were no tears.

We came out to the grave. In the earth which had been thrown up I saw glimpses of bones and something odd—gray and matted. I poked it with my foot; it was yellowish inside. Suddenly I realized that it was woman's hair. . . .

When the coffin was about to be lowered into the grave, Grandpa-from-Knör took out his knife and tried to loosen the silver cross, but in this my father stopped him.

"I thought you would like to have it on your wall—your wall!" Ketilbjörn excused himself sulkily.

I pulled Sister-from-Fagravik's head down to mine and whispered in her ear:

"Is this west of the church?"

Sister-from-Fagravik looked at me, nodded without understanding, rather uncomfortable.

Still I could not cry. There were plenty of tears among all the others. "It is because they are good people," I thought, dispirited.

I was so distressed because I could not cry. I held my free hand in front of my eyes and tried to force the tears out. Here was my mother being buried, and I stood with dry eyes. I was tortured by shame and remorse. In my distress I smeared my eyes and cheeks with spittle so as to be able to show a wet face like all the others.

Ketilbjörn had stuck both his hands down behind his trouser flaps, and stood looking at the filled grave.

"Sleep well," he mumbled shortly and went away. There was something liberated about him, as if he had slipped a burden from his bowed shoulders.

We mounted our horses. . . . Now we had not even the coffin.

Again we rode along the marshy bog path, toward Grimsstadir—as on that day. . . . Again we rode at a snail's pace up over the ridge. Again we passed the little tarn. But today the breath of autumn came to meet us instead of the scent of spring. The tarn was desolate and without birds, and in our ears sounded withered winds. There was the summit. We should never get there now, my mother and I. A bog lay between, my father had said, a bog between. . . .

And there was Grimsstadir.

I rode beside Grandpa-from-Knör.

"Everybody here misunderstands God, cringes to Him. Nor do I understand Him. Here He has taken my Celia, has made you children motherless—should one thank Him for that, thank Him for that? He is angry with *me*, I am angry with *Him*—that makes us equal. He has given . . . let Him take away! . . .

"Everybody has his own thoughts of God—stupid thoughts. God, you see, is like a mountain path. One toils on, follows it or takes a sidepath, follows it to the top. There it winds down the other side of the mountain, divides into several paths, and each one of these paths leads to strange districts, to faraway mountains—winds away, away. No one can follow all the paths. No one can attain to God."

My Grandpa-from-Knör was silent.

I suddenly remembered a small book in a worn cloth binding—the *Psalms of the Passion*—on the flyleaf of which was written: "Cecilia Ketilbjörnsdottir of Knör." It was in copybook writing . . . the name of a young girl.

Home from the church rode Sophia on my mother's gray.

217